by

Dedication

To every girl who ever cheered
when Princess Leia shouted,
"Somebody has to save our skins!"
and then proceeded to do it herself

CHAPTER ONE

"You have got to be kidding me."

"I beg your pardon, ma'am?"

Fuss.

I hadn't meant to say that out loud. I shook my head and did my best to fake a smile.

"Oh, nothing," I lied. "Sorry."

"Yes ma'am."

The little yeoman gave a quick nod before turning again to face forward. He continued ahead without so much as a break in his stride. It was his job to lead me to the airfield, and he appeared inclined to do so with the eagerness of someone who'd been told this mission was special.

It was not his job to quell my unease at the particulars of this very special mission. Even if he had been briefed on the details of today's embarkation, my woes were well above his pay grade. It wouldn't do either one of us any good to make my unease his problem.

I put on my calmest, most diplomatic face lest he turn to look at me again.

What in all seven Feirin hells had I gotten myself into?

There was a flaw in a seam on the little yeoman's collar. I fixed my gaze on that in an attempt to stay focused and keep pace. But it was a challenge. It was all I could do not to stare at the airship tethered to the spire above me.

If there'd been any doubt left in my mind that not only was this mission a trap, but everyone involved — from the top down — knew it was a trap, those doubts vanished the instant I set eyes on our intended conveyance.

Not only was it an airship — an outdated and out-moded vehicle that ought not be flying at all in this day and age — but it was the absolute least airworthy hunk of metal I'd ever seen in my life.

The ship was decrepit looking: a pre-war design with apparent combat damage and a number of obvious slapdash refits. I recognized the airframe from a textbook I'd had at the Academy. It was the old semi-rigid Mangan design, dating the airship as at least fifty years old. A long, angular gondola hung beneath a bloated-looking lifter canopy, neither of which appeared to be in good repair. Slide mounts for sail-style stabilizers protruded from the gondola's underside. A pair of thrust nacelles stuck out inelegantly from the airframe, and mismatched smokestacks came off the hull at odd angles. The rudder and skeg were rust-colored and covered in blisters, especially around the bolts that fastened them to the greater hull.

The whole thing was a hodgepodge of chipped paint, bare metal, and rust. It was a wonder anyone had gotten her off the ground.

She looked like a death trap.

"That's really our ship?" I asked my escort. "That one? Up there?" Part of me was hoping he'd turn and smile, make some sort of *gotcha* joke at my expense, and we'd share a hearty laugh on the way to our real aircraft's hangar.

But that's not what happened.

"Yes, ma'am, Lieutenant," he replied, turning his head again to smile at me, "that's her, the *AFS Dawn*." He seemed pleased with the state of things — proud, even.

My stomach turned a flip.

"Why aren't we in a fixed-wing?" I surprised myself with how calm I sounded. I didn't want to unload on this kid, but holy damn, this was even worse than I'd expected — and that was saying a lot.

The little yeoman shrugged.

"From what I understand, ma'am, the Alliance doesn't have a fixed-wing asset that can get you where you're going."

"But you don't know where that is?"

He shook his head.

"No, ma'am."

I thought not.

"Well, that's just fantastic," I muttered.

"Ma'am?"

"Never mind, Yeoman Basel," I said, finally getting a proper glimpse of the name tape on his uniform. Giving this kid grief wasn't going to do anything to improve my circumstances. And the ship assignment wasn't his fault. Looking up at the thing as it loomed above the airfield, I resolved to find out just whose fault it was. I'd be giving that person a piece of my mind when I got home — provided I made it back alive.

What in the name of Queen and Country was I getting myself into?

It would be unbecoming of me as Officer of the Diplomatic Service to simply refuse to board this hulk, but that didn't stop me from considering the prospect. Would the ensuing Courts Martial be worth it?

I had not, even for one minute, been excited about this mission. But I'd been assured it was critical for the future of the Alliance. The longer I looked at the rusting jalopy hovering above me, the more I was convinced that had all been a line of malarkey.

Our former enemies claimed to want to open diplomatic relations with the Alliance. But they'd given no reason for their unexpected overtures. If their sudden and unprecipitated desire to initiate peaceful discourse had been in good faith, why weren't they the ones coming to us? Why were we the ones tasked with intercontinental travel into once-hostile airspace?

To my mind it didn't make any sense.

The war had been over for thirty years. It had ended with the Alliance handing a sound defeat to the Xy Federation, and no one from our side had been in any sort of contact with anyone from their side since the Accords were signed.

I liked it just fine that way, but those who ostensibly outranked me thought differently.

Or maybe they didn't.

Maybe our government was only going for the *appearance* of diplomacy. Sending a ship that would likely founder before it reached its destination would give the Alliance plenty of cover; they could seem to be interested in opening relations all the while not having to do any actual relating.

As I looked up again to watch the *Dawn* as she swayed on her tether, I couldn't help the feeling this mission was wholly, and intentionally, expendable.

And I would know — I'd been expendable for most of my life. *Expendable* was practically my middle name.

I followed Yeoman Basel around the corner of the

City Airfield's central terminal and was surprised to find the grounds had been set up for a formal departure ceremony. From all the cloak-and-dagger I'd been subject to in the lead up to this morning, I'd half expected the expedition to steal away under cover of darkness.

The full Royal rigamarole was an even bigger surprise than the busted-up airship.

It was also equally unwelcome.

A small brass band penned in with bunting and an honor guard flying the colors of all five Alliance member states flanked a small, raised dais that had been erected on the tarmac for the occasion. A few dozen Air Service personnel, mostly Mangan and Gammran as best I could tell at a distance, stood at attention in tight formation facing the whole production. Two rows of diplomatic personnel of all nationalities were behind them, also at attention. I wondered how long they'd been standing like that: stiff-backed and severe in their wool dress blues, baking in the late morning sun, awaiting the Royal Arrival.

I hoped they hadn't been waiting too long.

It made me a little nervous to think of *Dawn* hovering above our heads unmanned. The thing looked as likely as not to burst into flames and fall out of the sky right there at City Airfield. Then again, if the ship were to crash and burn here and now with no one aboard, that might be the best possible outcome of this whole ordeal.

I was finding it difficult to imagine any of the ship's crew could be much more pleased with being assigned to *Dawn* than I was. And I wondered how long they'd had to train for this. Most of them looked far too young to ever have crewed an airship before; with few exceptions, all current Air Service vehicles were either fixed-wing or whirligigs.

I wasn't sure whether I felt more pity for them or for myself.

Focused on maintaining a neutral expression, I let Yeoman Basel lead me up the stairs to a position on the stage. If the rank-and-file could handle this, so could I.

I'd barely made it to my mark on the dais when a flurry of activity behind me caught my attention. I turned my head just in time to see a man I didn't recognize tripping over the hem of his ceremonial robes on his way up the stairs to join us. The strange man righted himself, lifted his tunic above his ankles, and proceeded to mount the dais with what little dignity he had left.

The man was tall, even by Feirin standards, and appeared taller still thanks to his stiff-backed posture. His long hair and close-clipped goatee were an obviously wyndera-dyed shade of red, a sure sign he hoped to be mistaken for a member of the Nobility. To my eye he wasn't fooling anyone. He was also wearing formal Prayer Whites. His robes were shantung and linen, tied at the waist with metallic cords signifying which Ordeals of Devotion he'd successfully endured, and topped with a stole of gold satin piped in crimson.

I'd never been sure which I found more distasteful: the fact the Feirin faith had nested within it such things as Ordeals of Devotion, or the fact that men like this one wore their Endurance Cords as an expression of superiority.

His clothing marked him as a religious, his hair color as an ambitious member of the petit bourgeoise, and his bearing as a man who'd had the privilege to spend his life praying and hobnobbing in the name of good politics.

This had to be Ambassador Berholtz.

It had been roughly twenty years since any member of the Feirin Diplomatic Corps had needed to do much more than smile at parties. In the immediate aftermath of the war, as the terms of the peacetime Alliance Government were being hammered out, there had been plenty of work for those who were skilled in the art of diplomacy. But as the five nations of The Alliance had more and more melded into a single government, diplomatic relations between the member nations had evolved into little more than handshakes and party toasts.

My years serving in the Diplomatic Corps had taught me there were very few genuine diplomats left. And a man in Prayer Whites hardly struck me as one with the necessary deportment.

I wasn't sure who had decided Berholtz was the one person in all The Alliance with adequate skill to open relations with the Xy Federation, but then again, I couldn't be sure this whole thing wasn't a trap. If the only selection criteria had been an Ambassadorial credential and a willingness to die for your country, that would go a long way toward explaining both his assignment and my own.

"Lieutenant Merteuil," Berholtz greeted me with a pompous condescension that told me precisely which brand of false nobility I was dealing with. I managed not to roll my eyes.

"Ambassador," I replied with the slight nod of deference that was expected under the circumstances. The man was wearing *robes* for Feirin's sake. There was no way he wouldn't expect me, his ostensible subordinate, to stand on ceremony. I could tell he was about to launch into some rehearsed remarks about my place on this mission when the dozen bugles at the margins of the brass band sounded.

"Attention!" called a booming baritone voice from somewhere behind me.

The color guard snapped-to and presented their flags, a signal to all assembled The Royal Arrival was commencing.

Annoyance, relief, and bone-level terror were fighting amongst themselves to be my dominant emotion. I supposed I'd have plenty of time to suss myself out during the impending unpleasantness.

A Feirin Departure Ceremony was no small thing. We'd be standing on the tarmac paying homage to the Queen for at least the next hour — longer if Her Majesty felt like pontificating. There would be prayers and blessings and a very long invocation. And through it all I would be expected to comport myself like a proper officer of the Alliance Diplomatic Corps. I was anxious to get it over with, save for the fact Her Majesty's pomp and ceremony were all that stood between me and having to board that steaming heap in the sky.

Berholtz placed his hands over his heart, as did a few identifiable Feirin in the ranks on the tarmac. The Gammran officers saluted. The Mangan and the T'wesh dipped a shallow bow. All assembled turned their heads toward the presented colors adjacent the dais, waiting for the Queen to make her appearance.

Her Majesty, Queen Salian Siobhan Feirin Lohengrin, had ascended the throne not long before the war, and had been party to the formation of The Alliance. It was a credit to her reign that she led her nation out of its isolationist past and into the modern era. She was a stern ruler, firm but fair, and had made no secret of her expectations of deference from all Alliance citizens — not only those who were Feirin subjects.

Feirin subjects, though, held her in particular esteem. Her Majesty, by right of birth, was not only the nation's sovereign ruler, but its chief deity as well.

I did my best to appear impressed as Her Majesty approached, standing at attention and hoping my demeanor would pass for something like reverence — or at least for respectful engagement. There was no getting out of this; the best I was going to be able to do was to get *through* it.

That was going to be a chore.

Neither the Queen's nobility nor her divinity was of particular interest to me. She was far too familiar to be impressive.

To my fellow Feirin subjects Her Majesty was both ruler and god. In their eyes, she was a paragon to be revered, venerated, and adored. But I was no ordinary Feirin subject.

I was her second born daughter.

CHAPTER TWO

I'd never been much of a Princess.

I lacked both the talent and the desire to be anything more than ordinary. My lack of interest in all things royal and sacred might have risen to the level of sacrilege had I been anybody else; perhaps the only right of my birth from which I stood to directly benefit.

The older I got, the happier I was to be lacking in the magical talents endemic to the royal line. That particular deficiency, although an endless source of frustration to my mother and my tutors, had continued to be a relief to me every time it proved itself to still be true. It was the ultimate provenance of my mundane cover story.

A Royal without magic is no god; and what is a Royal if not a god? Having no interest at all in ascending to the level of a deity myself, I found my lack of magic to be very affirming. My mother and sister could keep the powers and the accolades; I'd been happy enough to be left out of all of it.

I also considered it good fortune that my hair was deep auburn — far darker than the golden red of the rest of the Royal family of Feirin. I was ginger-haired enough I could have looked the part had I cared to make the effort. Even if my hair wouldn't pass royal muster on its own, there were ways to "improve" on nature. Pretenders and hangers-on had been reddening their hair with wyndera root for as long as anyone could remember.

I was neither pretender nor hanger-on. The Royal family was my family, but I had no desire to remake myself in my mother's image. In fact, most of my life's effort had been to escape the shadow of throne and crown. Fortunately for everyone involved, I was the spare, not the first born. Royal fervor wasn't a requirement. Neither lauded nor paraded, it was my job to sit quietly and cause no stir while my sister was grandly and publicly groomed to someday ascend the throne of Feirin.

I'd done the best job I could at that.

And if this was my reward — a one-way trip on a doomed ship to perdition — I supposed it was a just one. I could at least be glad I'd been granted the dignity of boarding that ship under my chosen name and wearing the uniform I'd earned, rather than a set of robes bestowed upon me by right of birth.

Absently, I fingered the fabric of the pocket where I'd secreted my royal insignia.

When I'd first been tapped for this mission, I'd been sure it was because of my royal bona fides. The Xy Federation might think twice about shooting down the expedition knowing a member of the royal family of

Feirin was among its members. When I subsequently received orders from the Palace that this undertaking was to be executed under my assumed name, and not my Royal ipseity, I'd gone right back to the first impression I'd had of this mission: this was a trap.

Not only was this a trap, but the Palace knew it was a trap. Alliance Parliament probably also knew it was a trap. In fact, I couldn't imagine anyone attached to this mission who didn't, on some level, know it was a trap.

But my mother hadn't wanted to discuss it. And what the Queen does not want to discuss is not discussed — full stop. And so it was.

And now, here we were.

Not being acknowledged as a royal had its advantages. I knew that well. I greatly preferred the freedom my made-up identity allowed me over the constraints of palace life. The Alliance Lieutenant about to board this airship of the damned was the person I'd chosen to be. This uniform and this rank liberated me from the stifling expectations of having been born a Royal Highness.

As good as that freedom felt, it hadn't escaped me that exposing my royal lineage could prove useful down the line. There was always the chance a Princess would be able to help in ways a Lieutenant of the Diplomatic Corps couldn't. I was happy to hide my royal signets for the duration, but I wasn't about to leave them behind.

Not where we were headed.

Berholtz turned his attention to the honor guard behind the dais. Taking my cues from him seemed as good a policy as any; I turned my head toward the avenue of flags in time to see a somber looking man make his entrance from behind the closest hangar. He paraded solo through the gauntlet, his hands clasped at his waist and his eyes cast downward in front of him.

His Highness: my father.

My father was here. That was unexpected.

He was wearing an ivory velvet tabard over his usual silk suit, a garment I hadn't seen him pull out in years, and one that spoke volumes as to his feelings about this morning. As he climbed the stairs at the rear of the dais, I caught his gaze just long enough to confirm by his expression that he didn't like this any more than I did.

Not that I'd had any question. His presence alone said enough. The Prince Consort had no role in matters of international import; there was no official reason for him to attend this send-off.

I was pretty sure he'd come only because of me.

My father was the nurturer in the family — the parent. His concern had always been for his children above his country. He'd never seen us as a pair of gods, or future rulers, or an heir and a spare. Unlike my mother, he'd always shown me the same care as he did my sister. And he knew — I could tell from the look on his face he knew — there was a chance I wouldn't make it home.

He'd come here today to tell me goodbye in the only way he could — wearing a fancy velvet tabard and an expression only I could read.

I could barely stand to look at him.

I was tempted to give myself away right then and there. The impulse to run up and hug my father and whisper in his ear that I was scared was almost overpowering. I struggled with whether it would be worth it.

But before I could make a decision, he turned away. He knew as well as I did our feelings on the subject didn't matter. The Queen of Feirin had set this mission on its course in accordance with the wishes of The Alliance Parliament, and there was no force on the planet that could change it now.

I was going to Xyland and that was that.

The bugles sounded again. It was a fanfare I hadn't heard in years, even then only in rehearsals. "Entrance of The Queen with Gravity" was the name of the piece, and as best I knew it hadn't been played publicly in my lifetime. It was my understanding that fanfare hadn't been played publicly since the war.

Just another indication I was headed into a trap. And my mother knew it.

It was all I could do to keep calm and pretend everything was okay. Because everything was most certainly *not* okay. I set my jaw and turned my attention once again to the rear of the dais.

Her Majesty made her entrance with a grace and ease that made Berholtz's feigned nobility appear all the more pathetic by comparison. She was flanked on both sides by an honor guard of six soldiers dressed impeccably in Alliance blue uniforms with the distinct Feirin Red piping signaling their service in the Royal Detail. As I watched their approach, I could see that none of these men were from Her regular retinue. She'd purposely brought guards who wouldn't recognize me. I wasn't sure whether I should take that as a slight or a kindness. But I was glad to have the cover. The fewer people here who might give me away, the better.

Her Majesty barely made it onto the dais before Berholtz prostrated himself at her feet. Any other person would have likely stumbled over him, but my mother was accustomed to such displays. Not tripping over procumbent peasants was a skill she'd perfected over the years. I expected her to dismiss him with a flick of her wrist — the same tiny gesture with which I'd seen her acknowledge similar demonstrations my entire life. Instead, she waited for him to finish the soft-spoken prayer he was offering before she inclined her head to him and spoke.

"You may rise, Ambassador," she said in a tone so magnanimous I almost didn't recognize it. Berholtz was trembling as he came to his feet. He kept his eyes downcast, very obviously trying to keep from making eye contact with Her Majesty but failing sorely thanks to their disparate heights. "Feirin thanks you for your service," she added.

I managed to keep myself together as I watched Berholtz struggle to stay upright on his wobbly knees. The fact I wasn't doubled over with laughter was the best proof I could have asked for of my own diplomatic skill.

I supposed I ought to give the guy a break — it wasn't every day a person got to meet the deity they'd worshiped all their life. But I found his obsequiousness mightily off-putting, and it was all I could do not to let it show on my face.

Berholtz managed to shuffle his way out from in front of my mother and looked up again — this time at me. In a flash, his expression went from amazed to admonishing and I felt a sudden urge to fish my Royal signet from my jacket. He was about to give me an order, and I wasn't going to like it.

"Lieutenant," he snapped. "Come to. You are at liberty to pay tribute to the Sovereign."

"Sir," I replied curtly. It was a rote response to an order I didn't appreciate — drilled into me during my years at the Air Academy. He wanted me to kneel before The Queen. He wanted me to bow to her the same way he had bowed to her. In his mind, the only reason I hadn't done so already was because I was waiting for permission from my superior officer.

My mouth went dry. I had not expected this.

Either I had to out myself as royalty here and now, or I had to kneel before my mother in a feigned show of reverence.

In the space of a breath, I decided it wasn't worth exposing myself. I'd seen less-religious Feirin subjects greet my mother in the past; surely I could come up with some minor display of respect that wouldn't try my dignity too badly. I squared my jaw and managed a nod at Ambassador Berholtz.

I could do this. For the purposes of my cover, I could do this.

I took two steps forward, toward Berholtz, before turning to face where my parents were standing. I dared to catch my mother's eye for an instant before casting my gaze reverently downward. No Feirin citizen was to look the Queen in the eye without invitation; an instant longer and I'd have had to reveal my royal identity or else be subject to arrest.

I was sure nobody else in attendance caught the twitch in Queen Salian's lip that said she hadn't thought this part through. It was cold comfort to know she hadn't considered the possibility of this little ignominy when tapping me for today's assignment. My father's expression, although likely still unreadable to most, was all the apology I was likely to get.

As I crossed to stand before them, I became acutely aware of the size of the crowd that stood between the dais and the spire. The airship's entire complement was about to bear witness to this moment. Bile was rising in my gut, my stomach was full of buzzybugs, and my ears thrummed with my ever-rising blood pressure. This was a shade more humiliation than I'd been prepared for.

At least my sister wasn't here to witness this.

The Crown Princess Acca Schulte Feirin Lohengrin was being kept in the dark on purpose. She would know nothing about the diplomatic mission to the Xy Federation until after the initial contact had been successfully made. That way, if it went as sideways as I guessed it was going to, she would have all the deniability in the world. If opening relations with our former enemies blew up in Feirin's face, my mother could safely abdicate in favor of a properly groomed successor who would *never* have approved of such a thing. Royal machinations were always a calculated risk, never more so than when the future of the entire Alliance might be at stake.

I had to admit to myself that being part of a governmental function so secret as to preclude my sister's participation had been a big part of my having accepted this assignment without complaint. It felt nice being the one in the know for once. It did *not* feel nice being forced to venerate my own mother on a dais in front of an audience of a hundred or more.

My head stayed down, but I kept my eyes on my father's face for as long as I could as I crossed to stand before Her Majesty. I didn't dare meet my mother's gaze again. I had no interest in her opinion of this moment, but more than that, I didn't care to risk being caught by my obviously very religious 'superior officer' failing to respect the Sovereign. That would not end well for one of us.

I balled my right hand into a fist and brought it to my heart as I dipped into a genuflecting posture for just long enough to take a breath. Fortunately, my mother found a shred of compassion in that moment. She flicked her wrist to indicate I could stand almost as soon as my knee hit the deck. I stood up quickly and returned to my assigned spot on the dais.

Suddenly that dilapidated old airship started looking pretty good. At the very least, it would take me away from here.

CHAPTER THREE

It wasn't long before the prayers began. I hadn't noticed the Royal Chaplain in the crowd, but his presence didn't surprise me. As a youngster, I'd developed quite the skill at tuning him out, a skill I found equally useful this morning. The monotonous droning of his voice was enough to put a person to sleep on a good day, and today was very much *not* a good day. I supposed his tone was soothing to some, but as far as I was concerned it was tiresome and unpleasant.

I seethed through the invocation, distracting myself by trying to recall everything I'd ever been taught about airships.

The band started up again — this time led by drums that must have been hiding amongst the brass the whole time. The music was a Hymn of Adoration — common enough on occasions over which Her Majesty presided. This particular one was called "How Majestic," and I'd always found it an insufferable earworm of a song. It wasn't the most obnoxious of these hymns, not by a long shot, but I was sure it would be stuck in my head for the next several hours ... if not days.

Berholtz, of course, sang out at the top of his lungs. His voice was grating and off key and suddenly I was longing for the smooth baritone of the Chaplain; at least he could carry a tune. I halfheartedly mouthed the words as I scanned the crowd on the airfield for who was also singing along.

There weren't a great many Feirin among the crew, and of those only a handful seemed to be singing. It was expected that only the very religious would know the words to these hymns by heart. Had it not been for the possibility of being upbraided by Berholtz later on, I would have kept my lips still as well. The Feirin crew members who were demonstrably less religious deserved to know I wasn't going to hold that against them. But I also didn't want to do anything to incite the ire of my CO. As it was, I figured a halfhearted display was the best way to hedge my bets.

I was absently mumbling my way through the second verse when I spotted a familiar face in the back row of personnel lined up on the tarmac. And not just any familiar face.

A face that changed everything.

My ... favorite face.

Raline Khatri worked as the Chief Administrator for the T'wesh Embassy in Feirin City. While not a diplomat herself, she was a highly skilled facilitator and a master of interagency and international coordination. Her understanding of the ways and means of compromise and cooperation along with her almost-encyclopedic knowledge of customs and protocols made her an excellent addition to this mission to be sure.

The fact she was quite possibly the most beautiful human I'd ever had the privilege of meeting made my delight at having her aboard a little more complicated.

I'd had a crush on Raline for years but had mostly given up on anything ever coming of it. For one thing, I was pretty sure she wasn't into women at all; her only romantic relationship I was aware of had been with a man. But that hadn't stopped the two of us from flirting whenever we'd found ourselves in the same room. At least, I thought it was flirting ...? And it surely hadn't stopped the buzzybugs from invading my stomach every time I looked at her.

It was all I could do not to stare at her from up on the dais.

When the hymn was over, the band segued into a tune I didn't recognize. Not that it mattered, but familiar music might have soothed my nerves. And I was double nervous now. Not only was I about to fly directly into enemy territory aboard the most decrepit craft I'd ever had the displeasure of beholding, I now knew I would be doing so in the company of a person whose mere presence could turn me into a stammering puddle of goo.

A Protocol Officer stepped forward from his place beside the Honor Guard and moved to indicate the first row of personnel were to approach the dais. The time had come for Tributes and Blessings. Luckily, I'd paid all the tribute I'd be expected to pay already. All I needed to do now was bear witness to my mother's whispered blessings over the assembled crowd, possibly receive a short blessing myself, and be on with my life.

The officers came first. The skipper, I think, led the way. She was a Mangan woman well into her sixties as best I could tell, with the bars of a Captain on her collar and a broad gold stripe at her cuff signaling her status as a combat veteran. Behind her came a stream of officers and enlisted personnel filing toward the dais in order by rank. One by one, they were blessed, glittering swirls of tactile magic dripping from my mother's fingers with each gesture of benediction.

She'd told me once, back when there was still a chance my own arcane talent might develop, that the blessings and the magic weren't actually related. There was no active magic to a blessing; it was merely a word spoken by a Queen that had the belief of a subject behind it. But generations ago it had been decided that a touch of visual magic — a tiny glamour of sparkle, mist, or light — helped to reinforce the belief in the Queen-as-deity, and so it had been done this way ever since.

I'd always found the practice dishonest.

But I had learned over the years to bite my tongue about such things.

And this morning, I was paying far more attention to the blessed than to the blessings, anyway.

The crew was mostly Mangan, with a smattering of Gammran and T'wesh and very few Feirin among them. I wondered if that was intentional or merely an accident of qualification. It could have been either. The last thing I needed this morning was to start looking for conspiracies, so I presumed this was the best crew the Alliance could muster for an airship this age on a mission this fraught and not that the Royal House of Feirin had arranged for the vast majority of those sure to die aboard said ship to hail from outside its borders.

It was an orderly matter, these men and women filing toward the dais to be blessed. I'd often wondered what it must be like for non-Feirin to have to put up with our protracted rituals. None of my soon-to-be crewmates seemed to mind. They approached the dais and accepted their blessings with grace before proceeding onto the lift to return to their ship.

I tried not to stare at Raline as she waited her turn for a blessing. But I did steal a glance every now and again. I'd never seen her in uniform before; in fact, I'd always presumed her, and her position, to be civilian. She wore the dress blue frock coat of an officer, but with cording and insignia I didn't recognize. My guess was she likely had a rank in the T'wesh Diplomatic Service that wasn't universally recognized within the greater Alliance military. Those kinds of things were rare these days, but not unheard of.

And it wasn't like I was going to ask her.

She looked good in blue. Or maybe it was just that she looked good in everything.

I couldn't help looking as Raline approached the dais. I'd been watching the rest of the crew receive their sparkly blessings — it wasn't like I was doing anything wrong or unexpected by watching her as she came forward. But unlike the dozens of crew members who'd come before her, Raline caught me looking.

She smiled at me when she was second in line.

My face felt hot, and I did my best to smile back without looking like a complete and irreverent fool. It wasn't like she was *smiling* smiling at me. She was probably just being polite.

Right?

I tried not to think too hard about Raline and her smile and how good she looked in her dress blues as I watched her and the rest of the back row move through the ritual of blessing, back across the field, and onto the lift up to the ship.

The airship dock's original hand-cranked elevator

system had long ago been retrofitted with a steam powered gear driver; more people could get up to the boarding plank at one time with the added power of a mechanical lift. I'd managed to keep a pretty good eye on the activity at the base of the spire while the blessings had gone on. It was almost directly in my line of sight and had been far more interesting to watch than my mother's bestowing magical glitter upon the airship's crew. The last of the luggage had been loaded by airfield personnel, including my own flight bags. Seeing the condition of our ship and its obviously questionable flight capabilities, I was starting to wish I'd packed lighter. But my clothing choices and the heft of my luggage were the least of my worries.

Berholtz and I were the last ones brought forward to be blessed. The Protocol Officer led us down the back stairs from the dais and around to the same spot on the tarmac where the others had stood to receive their blessings. It was easier to keep from looking at my mother this time, now that she stood on an elevated platform and I on the ground before her. But it was still a challenge to pretend I believed in the holiness of her words and gestures. I had to actively fight the urge to run my fingers through the sparkling mist of the glamour — the way I'd done as a child while my sister was learning. But I got through it.

I didn't even frown. I was pretty proud of myself for that.

As we departed the dais for the spire, Berholtz was practically glowing. Parts of him were *literally* glowing — a residual effect of the magic my mother had set upon him. I probably had some shine left on me as well; I tried not to think about it as I followed my temporary superior toward the spire and onto the waiting lift.

We were the only ones aboard the apparatus — the

last of the ship's crew having already alighted onto the boarding platform while we were being blessed. The ride up was smoother than I'd expected from the appearance of the gears, and I did my best not to stare as Berholtz twisted his still-shining hands around in front of his eyes. What might it have done to him to know the truth about this magic he revered so much?

The lift came to a stop at the boarding platform. I had bigger things to worry about than my counterpart's religious fervor. I was about to spend days — weeks maybe — aboard an airship that looked even worse up close than it had from a distance, and our destination was likely an ambush. And I was about to spend those days cooped up in this rattletrap with Raline Khatri. What did I care if Berholtz spent his time praying to my mother — provided I wasn't expected to participate?

I bit my lip as I followed Ambassador Berholtz out of the lift and onto the boarding platform. The platform was empty when we arrived, save for one man standing at the foot of the gangplank. I was momentarily disappointed that Raline hadn't waited for me, but that disappointment soon turned to relief. Better not to see her until I had myself a little more under control.

As it was, I could give my full attention to the gentleman who waited for us on the platform. He was a tall, broad-shouldered Gammran, as handsome as any man I'd ever seen, with slate-dark skin and a thoroughly disarming smile. His presence seemed to pull Berholtz out of his religious reverie instantly.

"Sergeant Major Gowon," Berholtz addressed the other man with the clear cadence of someone reading rank bars and a name tape as he went, "I am Ambassador Edvard Berholtz. I am the commander of this mission and as such ..."

"Captain Taiko is the commander of this mission," Gowon interrupted.

I saw a tiny twitch in Berholtz's jaw; a tell if ever there was one. He was chagrined at having been corrected thusly, but he didn't want our greeter to know it.

"At least that's the case as long as we're aboard this bucket," Gowon amended. "And you wouldn't want it any other way. I sure don't want to be in charge of an eighty-year-old, rusted-out former warship that's supposed to get us to the other side of the planet. But what I think you're trying to say," he continued, "is that you're the lead ambassador on this mission — which I already knew."

I liked Gowon immediately.

"You're our liaison, then?" I asked him as Berholtz worked to appear nonplussed by Gowon's lack of deference.

"Yes ma'am," he answered. "Sergeant Major Ayan Gowon, Alliance Intelligence. Ambassador Berholtz, Lieutenant Ambassador Merteuil: I'll be briefing you both on our mission specifics once we're over open water." He turned to face the open hatchway. "I'll show you both to quarters in the meantime."

Berholtz fell into step behind Gowon, and I followed close behind. Gowon led us through a labyrinthine series of corridors, down one ladder, up two more. The ceiling was low, the passageways all narrow and cramped. That was to be expected on an old Mangan ship like this one; I could tell the airship's provenance not only by the style of its construction, but by the Mangan words painted over some of the hatches.

Pre-Alliance languages were a dead giveaway. Of a lot of things.

Berholtz ducked and cowered his way along, tiptoeing his velvet slippers across the grimy deck plates as he held the hem of his prim white robes up around his ankles. I didn't mind the deck so much. My boots had been high shined for the occasion, but even if they were to get scuffed, I'd have plenty of time to buff them back into compliance before I needed to impress anyone. If the deck was good enough for the ship's crew, it was good enough for me. And the low overhead didn't bother me either. Unlike the much taller Berholtz (and the taller still Sgt. Maj. Gowon), I barely needed to duck to get through tight hatches; the average ceiling height cleared the top of my head with inches to spare. The one thing I found irksome was the apparent inability of the light fixtures to maintain a steady glow. That flicker was going to give me a headache, the only question was how soon.

There was plenty to complain about aboard airship *Dawn*, but the low overhead and the dirt on the floor didn't qualify.

The ship jolted. The rumbling of ill-tuned engines and the clanking of tether chains sounded far louder than I thought was appropriate for where we were in the ship. Either something was misconfigured on this boat, or the insulation wasn't what it ought to be for an overseas voyage. Whichever it was, it wasn't good.

My suspicion was it was probably both.

"Sorry 'bout that," Gowon offered as he led us around a sharp corner and down a short ladder with wooden treads. "She's no luxury liner; probably not what you're used to. Your quarters are in a quieter part of the ship, but I can't make any promises as to comfort. You've both got workspace, too, but I think you'll want to get changed before going up there, or, quite frankly, doing anything else." He turned and regarded Berholtz. "I know you Feirin are all religious and such, and you're going to need to say your prayers and what-not, but those fancy clothes won't last long with all the jagged metal we have around here. And that's not to mention the fact that you're both going to get real cold real fast once we reach altitude. You'll want to change into a flight suit. And warm socks. Soon."

Gowon led us down another long ladder, through a foul-smelling area low in the ship's belly, and then up a twisting series of narrow steps before turning sharply into a corridor that almost seemed to belong to a different ship. The deck plates were cleaner here, and damp as though they'd been recently swabbed. And to my surprise and delight, the lights were burning bright and steady. The doors were clearly labeled in block Feirin characters, and the whole place smelled of fresh paint. It was easy to guess we'd reached the Diplomatic deck.

My supposition was borne out when Sgt. Maj. Gowon stopped us in front of the second door from the corner. He pulled the lever on the narrow door, then pushed hard to slide it open. The panel took more effort to move than it looked like it should. Likely the crew sent to polish this deck for consular use hadn't made much beyond cosmetic improvements.

"Ambassador," Gowon addressed Berholtz, stepping out of the way of the open hatch, "your stateroom."

"Excellent," Berholtz declared as he swept past Gowon and through the open door. "I trust my luggage has already been delivered and ..." He came to an abrupt halt the moment he was inside.

I watched as Gowon suppressed a chuckle.

"I warned you, Ambassador," he said. "She's no luxury liner."

"This is unacceptable!" Berholtz declared, letting his robes down and stomping his foot as he crossed his arms over his chest. "I demand to be moved to better quarters!" I looked past Gowon into Berholtz's cabin. It was a spare room, all orange-painted metal, and as cramped as the rest of the ship. The thing that made it unbearably cramped, though, was the way the Ambassador's copious luggage seemed to have been piled onto every available surface. And I thought I'd overpacked ....

"No can do, Ambassador," Gowon replied. "This is the best we've got. It's either this or a hammock strung between bulkheads. Like I said: *Dawn*'s an old warship. The Alliance doesn't have any comfortable accommodations that could get us to Xyland. We're all having to make the best of what they gave us. Fact is, we're lucky to have her. *Dawn*'s the last in her class that the engineers could get aloft. Found her in a junkyard when we got word that Xyland wanted to meet."

Berholtz sneered and shook his head.

"That, I believe," he groaned.

"I'm sorry we couldn't do any better," Gowon said. He sounded disingenuous, but it wasn't for me to point it out. "I'll leave you to get settled. I'll be back in a while to show you to your office. Chief Khatri has already set things up for you. She'll be handling the logistics, both while we're aloft and once we arrive."

I felt a jolt of nerves at the sound of Raline's name. But at least I knew what she was doing here. I don't know why it hadn't occurred to me we'd be working together on this mission. It made sense the most adept logistics officer among the five Alliance member nations would be tapped to facilitate our first talks with the Xy Federation since the war. That didn't make me any less likely to make a fool of myself, though.

"I have prayers first," Berholtz sneered, visibly offended by the contention he'd be doing anything other than seeing to his religious obligations any time soon.

"I know that," Gowon replied, smiling as he gave Berholtz the most patronizing nod I had ever seen one human give another. "I know you Feirin are all about getting your prayers in and having your things set up just so. We've got time," he said. "We've got at least a week airborne. I'll brief you when you're ready."

Berholtz gave an authoritative nod and reached for the lever to shut the door.

"Good day," he dismissed us, tugging on the door, which didn't budge.

I followed Major Gowon's lead and pretended not to notice. But I couldn't help a chuckle as we headed farther down the hallway.

"I wouldn't laugh too hard, Lieutenant," Gowon said. "Your room's just the same."

"I don't mind."

Gowon looked dubious.

"You don't?" he asked.

I chuckled again.

"Don't let the Diplomatic epaulets fool you," I said. "I went to The Air Academy. I can't imagine anything this ship has to offer could be worse than the room they stuck me in my plebe year." Gowon narrowed his eyes at me but smiled.

"I'm pretty sure they had me sleeping in a closet my plebe year," he answered, stopping in front of another closed door, and pushing it open. "With three other guys — all of whom were bigger than me."

I laughed at the mental picture, but he probably wasn't far off. Rough living conditions were a rite of passage for first year cadets — it was one of those universal school experiences that bonded Academy graduates together. It wasn't a real surprise to hear an Intelligence Officer was also a graduate of the Air Academy; the thing that surprised me was how comforted I felt hearing that.

I grimaced. This revelation was ... less comforting.

"This one's mine?" I asked. But I already knew the

answer.

"Yes ma'am, Lieutenant," he said. There was odd stress on my rank when he said it. It set me to wonder if he knew things no one on this ship was supposed to know.

"That other room was bad," I said. "This ... is also bad." My room was easier to take stock of than the Ambassador's had been — owing to the fact it wasn't filled to brimming with sacks and cases. Both rooms were painted orange, and much of mine wore a thin sheen of black-brown grime that looked as though it had outlasted a thorough scrubbing and was there for the long haul. A small writing desk was attached to the left-hand wall and a built-in stool jutted out from beneath. On the right-hand wall was a basin and spigot, and the ill-padded bunk spanned the entire width of the far end of the room. Nothing about this cabin had been built for comfort. But it wasn't anything I couldn't handle.

"I warned you ...."

"I'm not complaining," I assured him. "I'll be fine."

"All right," Gowon said. "Go on and get settled. I'll be back after your prayers."

"I'm not religious," I replied.

Gowon nodded, but not in the way he'd nodded at Berholtz. The knowing look on his face made me want to ask him what was up, but I thought better of it. Best not to call out an Intelligence officer within ten minutes of meeting him. And if it was what I thought it was, I didn't want it said out loud anyway.

"All right," he said. "If you need anything, there's an intercom here on the wall. You can use it to call me any time." I looked at the spot he'd indicated. The intercom unit hanging beside the door looked like the bastard child of an over-the-air radio receiver and a toddler's toy horn. Gowon was clearly pointing out a CALL button at the base of the thing. I grinned as I looked back at him.

"You didn't show this to Berholtz," I said. Gowon shrugged.

"The one in his room doesn't work."

Yes. I definitely liked this guy.

"I suppose that was intentional?"

"It was," Gowon admitted with a shrug, "but maybe not in the way you think. We know he's not going to have a lot to do with the rest of the crew. He's going to stay in his cabin and then in his office, and he's going to pray a lot and he's going to consecrate some spaces so that he can feel like he's doing his best work. And what he's not going to do is a whole lot of anything else for himself. From what I was given to read about senior Feirin diplomats in general, and this Mr. Berholtz in particular, he's likely to have you and Chief Khatri doing most of his running around for him. So it made sense for you to be the ones who had a way to talk to the rest of the crew."

He had just used my name and Raline's in the same sentence. Even knowing the two of us would be working together hadn't prepared me for the way that made me feel. I tried to keep my face neutral as I worked to digest the idea of her and me working together. I had no idea why that hadn't occurred to me when I'd first spotted her on the tarmac. It should have been obvious. She was, after all, diplomatic support personnel — and here I was a diplomat.

Just another example of how my brain tended to shut itself down almost completely when in Raline's presence. I was going to have to work on that; I'd need to be able to be around her with some of my wits still about me if we ever made it to land in the Xy Federation.

"It absolutely does make sense," I agreed. "That's a

thing I've noticed about the Gammran: it seems like everything you do makes sense." That sounded awkward. My eloquence was clearly suffering from proximity to my crush. I was going to have to work on that, too.

The Gammran, culturally, were tactical thinkers. They were pragmatic, practical, and never unnaturally polite. A person always knew where she stood with a Gammran. Most foreigners, Feirin and T'wesh especially, often found their bluntness abrasive and unpleasant. But to me it had been a welcome break from the fake smiles and false courtesy of life at the Royal Court. It made sense to me that the Alliance had put their military operational arm under the leadership of the Gammran.

"We do try," Gowon said, not obviously offended by my awkward ethnic stereotyping.

"I'll let you know when I've settled in," I told him. "But it'll probably be a while before Berholtz is ready for a briefing."

"I'm your liaison officer, too, Lieutenant," he said. "So if you need anything — even before we brief — if you want to have a look around the ship — maybe if you get stir crazy waiting for your boss to finish his prayers ... no offense."

"None taken," I assured him. "I can appreciate other cultures' frustrations with the very religious."

Gowon smiled again.

"Just let me know if you want out of your quarters. For any reason."

"Will do," I said, turning to step further into my so-called stateroom, "That is," I corrected, "I will want out of my quarters, and I will let you know before I leave."

"Got it. I'll be waiting for your call."

"Thank you," I said as he was turning to go. I resisted the temptation to ask which cabin was

Raline's. If I was going to make a fool of myself, it wasn't going to be by knocking on her door at some odd hour with a flimsy excuse for coming by.

"My pleasure, Lieutenant," he replied.

There was that knowing tone again. I almost stopped and asked him about it. We were alone; it should have been safe. But I decided against it. Gowon seemed perfectly pleasant and completely competent to boot. He was the first thing about this whole undertaking that didn't smack of a possible suicide mission. And if he knew things about me no one aboard was supposed to know, I was sure it would come out in time. Meanwhile, if he *didn't* know those things, best not to stir anything up so early into our association.

When I tugged on the door to my quarters, it shut easily behind me. Maybe my cabin was better than my superior's after all. I took in a deep breath of the diesel-tinged recycled air and began to make a plan for unpacking. Major Gowon had said we'd be a week airborne; that was too long for me to reasonably live out of my flight bag.

I was going to have to do my best to make myself at home aboard the *AFS Dawn*.

She wasn't a luxury liner; Gowon was right about that. I just hoped she wouldn't turn out to be a tomb.

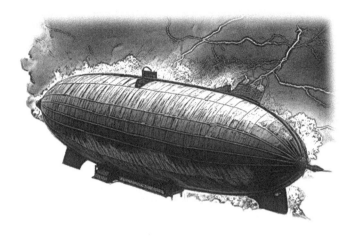

CHAPTER FOUR

A gear-fed chrono hung on the wall of my cabin. It was small, but its face was freshly painted. I could easily read it while lying in my bunk. And so I was vaguely aware of the passage of time during those first two and a half days we were airborne.

Two and a half of the most miserable days of my life.

I hadn't been in my flight suit for half an hour and was barely beginning to get my quarters squared away, when the first volley of sky sickness hit me. I hadn't been expecting it; I'd never been prone to sky sickness before. But all my previous air travel had been aboard fixed-wing aircraft (save one very brief and memorable ride in a whirligig that had left me giggling, but not at all puny). Apparently, airship travel worked on the constitution differently.

Although I hadn't been expecting the nausea, it was clear my Mangan hosts had seen it coming. On the side of my basin, reachable from the fetal position on my bunk, someone had thought to leave a tin of quick-dissolve zingiber tabs. By holding one under my tongue, I could stave off the worst of it. But zingiber tabs made me drowsy, so all they really did was keep my stomach still long enough for me to fall asleep.

A predictable cycle developed. The nausea would awaken me. I'd spend a few minutes heaving over my basin, decide the worst was over, and lie back down on the bunk with a tab beneath my tongue, hoping it would do its job. The tab would take effect, I would feel well and functional for approximately fifteen minutes, or just long enough to wash my face and brush my hair, and then I'd have to crawl back into my bunk for more sleep.

It was frustrating and unpleasant.

At least I had a basin in my stateroom with a working graywater tap. I don't know what I'd have done if I'd needed to make it down the hall to the head every time I felt ill.

It was a tiny blessing, but I was grateful for it.

When I woke in the middle of that third day with a slightly less nauseated feeling, I hoped the worst was over. Even the most sickness-prone people usually get their air legs after a day or so. I was slow and deliberate as I pulled myself up to sit on the edge of my bunk, and when the spasms failed to materialize, I dared swing my feet beneath the ledge, fishing out my tanker boots from under the bunk with my toes. Carefully, I bent at the waist to pick them up, then set them down beside me on the mattress. I held very still for a moment, taking a deep breath before making any further movements. When no sickness overtook me, I set to unbuckling my boots, lifting my feet one at a time to gingerly slide them on. Fastening the buckles came next, and then a slow-and-steady rise to standing.

Yes. The sky sickness had officially passed. I stepped over to the basin and examined my reflection in the polished metal sheet hung above it. I looked a mess and felt the same. I knew from my Academy training that after two days of powerful sky sickness I wasn't going to feel much better than I did right now without getting some food and water into my system. The small canteen of potable water I'd found on the far side of the basin from the zingiber tabs had been emptied two bouts of illness ago.

I considered calling someone to bring up a replacement. Surely this ship had a steward aboard — someone had to have put that water here in the first place. But what I could really use were some calories. I needed some juice, maybe a handful of berries, and a protein lozenge if I could get my hands on one.

And to get any of that, I was going to have to leave my cabin. Even if there were a steward aboard, this ship didn't strike me as the kind that would offer room service.

Seeing as there was no guarantee I was completely recovered, getting some food into my system might prove easier said than done. But it was the logical next step. I ran my fingers through my mussed and tangled hair, looping it into a loose knot on the top of my head before tucking it into the flight cap I'd hung on a hook just inside my door. I checked the fastenings on my flight suit and patted the breast pocket where I'd secreted my rank and royal insignia; nothing missing, nothing out of place.

I moved slowly across my cabin until I was able to reach the call button on the intercom box. Leaning against the wall with my eyes closed, I pressed it, hoping not to use up what little energy I had just to make a call. I'd need something left in my tank to get to ship's mess.

"Sergeant Major Gowon," I called into the speaker. "This is Lieutenant Merteuil." My voice was weak and raspy from two solid days of chundering. I sounded even worse than I felt.

When no answer had come after a moment, I stood up straight and tried again, this time with my eyes open. Maybe there was another step — something that would become apparent if I gave my full attention to what I was doing. I cleared my throat and pressed the button.

"Lieutenant Merteuil to Sergeant Major Gowon," I said, making sure I was holding the button all the way down. "Gowon, Gowon. Merteuil."

Not only was there no answer, there was no activity at all: no lights, no static, not even that diffuse buzzing sound that often accompanies aging electronics. I was pretty sure the box wasn't working.

And I wasn't going to spend the next hour talking into a dead contraption like a fool. I had rank and clearance; there was nothing keeping me from going about the ship on my own. I'd have to find the mess myself. I knew Gowon had said I was to get in touch with him when I wanted to leave my cabin, but I *had* tried my best. I figured this was one of those occasions where I was going to have to settle for asking forgiveness rather than permission.

I flipped the lever to unlock the door and went to pull it open.

It didn't budge.

Supposing it was my comeuppance for thinking it so hilarious Berholtz hadn't been able to get his door closed, I tried again. Still nothing. I let out a curse, and then another as I tried repeatedly to pull open the offending portal.

It was either somehow locked, or I was a whole lot weaker than I'd figured.

"Um ..." I heard a voice from out in the hall, "Lieutenant Ambassador?"

"Yes," I answered. "Hi. I think the door is stuck!"

"Um ... no," the voice called back. "It isn't. Not really. It's magnetic. Or ... well ... it used to be. They don't work right anymore. The magnets get all out of whack — something about the electricity. Try putting one hand on the opposite wall while sliding the lever with the other one."

It sounded preposterous, but I had nothing to lose by trying. I did as he said: placing my right hand against the far wall of the cabin, I tugged the lever with my left. Sure enough, the door came open as easily as it had slid shut. A man on the other side of the door was smiling.

He was obviously Feirin, and apparently very young. I'd have just as easily referred to him as a boy than as a man. He was slight of build, with golden hair and blue eyes and a flight suit that looked as though it hadn't seen much wear. His rank was pinned to his collar, but the garment was so new his name tape and other insignia had yet to be sewn on. If a person could be an opposite of a place, this officer was the antithesis of the ship on which he served.

I could tell from the look on his face he agreed with my earlier assessment of my appearance — not that there was anything I could do about it. I hadn't brought along much by way of cosmetic implements, and even if I had, I was possessed of neither the desire nor the energy to paint my face.

"Thanks," I said, trying to sound as well and pleasant as I could manage. "I would never have figured that out."

"No problem," he replied. "I don't really understand

it. It's something to do with the electricity and completing a circuit ... somebody explained it to me once, but all I know for sure is that it happens to this whole side of the ship when the engines are running."

I shook my head.

"Wow," was all the answer I could manage.

"Yeah," the young man, an Ensign according to his insignia, said. "*Dawn*'s got a lot of quirks."

"That's one way to put it. But I'm glad you happened to be here. Who knows how long I'd have been stuck in there trying to get the door open. I tried the intercom, but it doesn't seem to be working," I told him. "Major Gowon said to use it, but when I tried to call him just now ..."

"Yeah," the Ensign said. "Even the stuff that's technically working isn't really working," he explained. "But if you're looking for Major Gowon, I was just up in the mess. He was coming in right as I was leaving; he should still be there. I can take you up if you'd like."

"Yes, please," I replied, stepping the rest of the way out of my cabin. "That's where I was hoping to go, anyway."

"Just getting over the sky sickness?" he asked.

I couldn't help but chuckle.

"How did you guess?"

"You and everybody else who came aboard in Feirin City," he replied. "Actually, you're one of the first to emerge. *Dawn* seems to have a nauseating effect on people," he added. "It took me six days the first time — if that makes you feel any better."

"It might," I replied, laughing a little more. On the one hand I was glad it wasn't only me, but on the other, it was another tick in the column of this whole mission being a trap. Surely a mission designed to succeed wouldn't have been billeted aboard a ship prone to making all aboard her violently ill. If we were truly expected to perform as diplomats, I would think they'd want us well rested and feeling our best.

"Yvan Declan," the young Ensign introduced himself with the offer of his hand. His handshake was firmer than I'd have guessed from the look of him.

"Maran Merteuil."

"This way," he said, gesturing for me to follow him as he turned to head down the corridor.

I pulled the door only most of the way shut.

Ship's mess was three decks up from where my quarters were situated, and down a corridor with an even lower overhead than any I'd seen on the way to my cabin. The hall was bigger than I expected based on what I'd seen of the rest of the ship. Its higher ceiling and a diffuse smell of sanitizer seemed to be conspiring to try and make us all forget the rest of *Dawn* was a fetid and filthy deathtrap. It was a longish room, with evenly spaced portholes along the right-hand wall and a counter stretched across the far end. The shelves behind the counter appeared to be well-stocked; an appointment I found as welcome as it was surprising.

Round tables peppered the tile-planked floor, with varying numbers of chairs pulled up beneath them. At the table nearest the door sat a collection of Feirin officers, all of them dressed in flight suits as new and as untested as Ensign Declan's. Major Gowon was at a large table near the back of the room, alone save for a diminutive Mangan man in stained coveralls sitting two places to his left. Declan waved when he spotted them, gesturing to me with a tilt of his head.

Gowon stood up and beckoned us over. I followed Ensign Declan to the table.

"Lieutenant Merteuil," Gowon greeted as I took a seat. "I wasn't expecting to see you here."

"I tried that intercom you showed me," I said, "but ...."

"They told me they'd gotten that fixed," Gowon interrupted me.

"We did get it fixed," the other man at the table insisted. He was a stocky fellow, short even by Mangan standards, and yet his voice was deep and resonant, as though it belonged to a much larger man. From a distance his uniform had looked tattered, but now that I was closer, I could see it was as new as Declan's, only covered in a fresh coat of grease and grime and with a rip in the sleeve that hadn't even begun to fray. His insignia identified him as a Sergeant, his deportment as a mechanic.

"You did?" Gowon asked.

If the other man heard, he pretended not to.

"Wyn Eiji," he introduced himself, extending his hand in my direction. "Ship's engineer."

"Nice to meet you, Sergeant Eiji," I answered as Major Gowon took his seat, his attention fixed on an open pot of purpolate on the table in front of him.

"Ugh," Eiji said, turning his head toward Gowon and his nose up to the sky, "How can you eat that stuff?"

"I eat it because it's delicious," Gowon answered, scooping a giant spoonful into his mouth.

"I don't think I'd go that far," I said, "but it's food."

"You hungry?" Gowon asked me. "I can get you one."

I took a moment to consider his offer. Would putting something as rich as purpolate in my stomach make me feel better or worse? I knew I *needed* to eat, but I wasn't sure I was ready to. Maybe I needed to sit still for a moment first.

"No thanks," I finally answered.

"Still feeling a little sky sick?" Gowon asked. I shrugged — loathe to admit I was an Air Academy Graduate who couldn't hold myself together on an airship.

"Yeah, sorry 'bout that," Eiji said. "That's part of why the intercom's back offline. That system's got so many corroded wires that every time someone went to use it, somebody in another part of the ship got an electric shock. I'll get to it eventually, but right now our priority has got to be getting the port stabilizer to deploy."

Suddenly my sky sickness made a lot of sense.

"We've been flying for how many days without a port stabilizer?" I asked.

"All of them," Eiji answered me with a frown. "And we've been flying without *any* stabilizers," he corrected. "When we tried flying with only the starboard rig locked in place, we were listing really bad, and the pilot couldn't compensate. So ...."

I tried not to look as panicked as I felt.

"So we're flying a sensitive diplomatic mission over open water, and we're having trouble ... *steering*?" I asked, fully aware that I sounded more incredulous than I'd intended.

"I'm working on it!" Eiji insisted.

"No offense."

"None taken."

"But that explains why I've felt so rotten," I offered, glad at least to know this was an extraordinary circumstance — albeit a dangerous one — and not an unforeseen weakening of my constitution.

"Even the Captain's been sky sick," Gowon said. "None of us are feeling right. And we haven't heard a peep out of your boss, either."

"If he's even the slightest bit woozy, he's going to stay in his cabin and pray until it stops," I shared.

"I swear, we're working on it," Eiji said.

I allowed myself a chuckle.

"This may be the first time in recorded history a Feirin's prayer gets answered in a real, quantifiable way," I told him, still chuckling. The group of Feirin at the next table grumbled under their breath. I'd have bet my bars they'd been praying too.

"I should dye my hair red and say I'm a deity," Eiji joked back. "No offense."

"None taken," I replied, laughing harder still. I decided right then Sergeant Eiji was someone I could be friends with.

Gowon, who hadn't paused in his conquest of the purpolate in his hand, stood up.

"I think I'll have another," he said. "You sure you don't want one? It might make you feel better."

"Might as well." I did need to put some food in my stomach, and something as familiar as a pot of purpolate was probably the best I was going to do. Of course, what I'd wanted to say was 'a pair of working stabilizers is what might make me feel better,' but I managed to refrain.

Eiji was shaking his head again.

"You're having a second one?" he asked, his nose wrinkling in clear disgust.

"I've never seen this much purpolate in one place before," Gowon answered as he pulled two pots down from a fully laden cabinet above the galley sink. "And I intend to eat as much of it as I can."

"Well, if it doesn't agree with me, you can finish mine, too," I offered.

"You've got a deal there, Lieutenant," he replied.

"Just keep it away from me," Eiji insisted.

"How is it you don't love this stuff?" Gowon asked as he returned to the table.

"Ugh," Eiji replied, "I can't even stand the smell of it. My parents grow it," he explained. "The plants in the field aren't so bad, but when the fruit ripens it really stinks. And there's a cannery not too far from where I grew up. When they're processing the fruit, the smell is sickening; it hangs in the air for days if the wind isn't blowing. And it gets into everything. It's disgusting."

"Sounds to me like someplace I'd want to build a summer home," Gowon said as he took his seat again and passed an open pot and a spoon in my direction.

"I could see where smelling it all the time might get old," I said. "But we definitely eat it a lot. Maybe that's why I don't get so excited about it."

"Yeah, it's all over the place in Feirin," Gowon agreed. "Every time I go, I try and load up as much as I can to bring back."

"Maybe we can set up some kind of import/export thing when we get home," I said. "I'll send you purpolate from Feirin and you can sell it at the Gammran markup."

"Sell, my tailfeathers," Gowon replied, popping a generous spoonful of the purple gel into his mouth, "I'd eat all of it."

"I appreciate your optimism," Eiji said. "And by that, I mean: the presumption that we're all coming back from this."

"I'm faking," I admitted. Gowon laughed, but I could tell he wasn't altogether amused.

"Yeah, well," Eiji said, rising from his seat with a shake of his head, "I'm going to head back and see what I can do about at least getting us where we're going."

"Don't take this the wrong way, Sergeant," I said, "but could you use any more help with that stabilizer?"

"Don't take this the wrong way," he said back. "But you're a diplomat."

"Don't let the fancy uniform fool you," a familiar voice sounded beside me. "Maran went to the Academy. If she says she can help, she probably can."

I will never know whether it was the rumble of the ship, the fact I was distracted by conversation, or her unusually delicate footfalls that were to blame, but somehow, I had managed to let Raline Khatri sneak up behind me. I had all but forgotten she was aboard the *Dawn*, thanks to the days spent barely able to do anything but retch into my basin. I suddenly regretted not taking a moment to tend to my appearance.

If I'd had any hope of her ever being attracted to me, having her see me with busted capillaries around my eyes and hair that hadn't been properly brushed in three days was enough to extinguish the last of it. I had a mouth full of purpolate and had to fight a sudden bout of shakiness in order to swallow it.

"Chief Khatri," Major Gowon greeted, "we were just talking about your boss."

"He is still locked in his room the best I can tell," Raline replied. "I've eaten the whole jar of porra nuts from my desk waiting for him to come to the office. I'm getting a lot of work done," she added. "But I figured I should come and refill the supply while I was between tasks."

"Do you want to have a seat?" I turned around and asked her before I had a moment to think about it. I immediately regretted the invitation. I felt like hell, looked even worse, and was doing fuss-all to my blood sugar by choosing processed fruit gel as the first food to pass my lips in three days. And that was before considering the massive burst of adrenaline I'd gotten at the unexpected sound of Raline's voice behind me.

Asking my crush to join us at the table was not likely to end well.

"I wish I could," she replied, stepping around the table to face me. "Another time?"

"Of course," I replied, hoping the flush in my cheeks was enough to counteract the wan-ness left by my three-day illness.

Raline smiled back at me, and once again I was glad I was sitting down. Damn, she was pretty. I shoved another bite of purpolate into my mouth to keep from saying so out loud.

"It's good to see you," she said. "I like that we're getting this chance to serve together. And I mean it," she added as she turned to head toward the stores behind the counter. "Lunch soon."

My mouth was full, so all I could do was nod.

I hoped Major Gowon and Sgt. Eiji hadn't noticed how flustered I got talking to her. I took another bite in hopes of getting ahold of myself before I needed to speak again. But Major Gowon caught my gaze, and I knew right then he had my number.

I shrugged.

"I won't say a thing," he said softly.

"Thank you," I replied, as quietly as I could.

Raline had already taken a large tin of nuts from a shelf and was on her way back out of the mess. She waved as she approached, smiling at me again in that way that made me completely melt. I smiled, too, waving back as she passed by. I took a deep breath and let it out as slowly as I could. The last thing my exhausted body needed right now was the adrenaline crash I could already feel was coming.

"Not a word," Gowon said, stifling a chuckle.

"Not a word," I grumbled in reply.

"She seems really nice," Eiji said.

"Not a word," I repeated.

"All right," he agreed with a little shrug, "but she really does seem nice."

"She is nice," I agreed, "and she's also right."

"Huh?"

"About letting me help with the stabilizer," I reminded him of where the conversation had been before Raline had surprised me. "I am an Academy Graduate — this rank I wear isn't honorary. I'm good with my hands and I can follow instructions. And I have absolutely nothing to do as long as Berholtz remains in confinement."

"Yeah," Eiji said with a nod, "sure. I've barely got enough crew to keep the ship going as it is. You want to come help us with banging that stabilizer into submission? I'm not going to tell you no. Get Gowon or Declan to show you to the Mechanical Deck. I'll get you set up with the crew."

"Excellent," I said, taking another timid bite of purple gel. "I'll see you shortly." As Eiji turned to go, I cast a glance sideways at Major Gowon. "I hope that was all right," I said. "I don't mean to overstep, but I'm liable to be bored to tears with nothing to do. And I really do think I can help."

"I've got no problem with it," he answered. "If you want to spend the rest of this trip down in the guts of this jalopy, be my guest. But don't expect me to come down there to give you your briefing when the time comes."

I took another bite of purpolate and sighed.

"About that," I said, "I know you're supposed to get with Berholtz first. But seeing as he's locked himself in his room for what might be the entire trip, I'd really appreciate anything you'd be willing to tell me."

"Yeah," Gowon said, "I hear you." He stood up again and looked pointedly at the table full of young Feirin officers by the windows. One of them caught his gaze and nodded. She got the attention of the rest, and the lot of them quickly stood up and filed out.

"Wow," I said quietly as the last of the group passed through the door, "you sure know how to clear a room."

"A major outranks a corpsman any day of the week," he said. "And they all know I'm the intel guy and you're a diplomat. They know better than to even give the impression they're eavesdropping on a conversation between the two of us. And anyway, they don't want to hear what I'm about to tell you."

"I'm not entirely sure *I* want to hear it," I admitted.

"Yeah," he allowed. "But you asked."

"That I did," I replied with a shrug. "So does that mean you're about to tell me all your secrets? Or at least why the hell somebody thought it was a good idea to send a busted old airship mostly full of green young officers and a pompous ass of a Chief Diplomat to the damn Xy Federation?"

Gowon shook his head and took another heaping spoonful of purple gel.

"First off," he told me after a pause, "we're not headed to the Xy Federation."

I frowned at him over my pot of purpolate.

"Come again?"

"Let me be more precise," he said. "The invitation to open up diplomatic relations did not come from the Xy Federation. It came from Xyland — full stop."

"Just ... from Xyland?" I was having a hard time wrapping my head around that idea. Xyland and Xylanth were two halves of the same continent. Their people were ethnically and culturally almost indistinguishable from one another — at least they were from an outsider's perspective. When they'd formed an army and moved to attack the nations that would eventually make up the Alliance, they had done so as a unified Federation. Hearing that Federation may be fractured was both shocking and concerning.

"Just from Xyland," Gowon confirmed. "There's no indication the Xylanthians have any knowledge at all of the Xylans having reached out to us."

"How is that even possible?" I asked. "Everything we know — everything we've *ever known* about the Xy Federation has been the two nations acting as one. They're completely interconnected. How in the wild skies can Xyland make contact with the Alliance without Xylanth knowing?"

"It isn't like they rang us up on an official wire," Gowon answered, scraping up the last bits out of his pot of purpolate.

"Wait, what?" I asked. The impression I'd been given was that they had done precisely that. What the fuss was going on here?

"They didn't use official correspondence," Gowon replied. "What they did was to put a little message traffic across an old channel — one they hadn't used since the war."

"And they did that because?"

"It's a channel they know is compromised," he answered firmly. "They stopped using it halfway through the war because they knew the Sluudi had tapped into it. They've known for years the Alliance could hear everything coming across that channel, so they opened it up again."

"To invite us to Xyland?"

"Not exactly."

"Please tell me they invited us," I implored him. Not that I thought an express invitation was any assurance we weren't flying squarely into an ambush, but the idea we might be heading into enemy territory *without* an invitation was definitely worse. I couldn't imagine our showing up unannounced and uninvited would be met with anything other than open aggression. And even though, at the close of the war, the Xy Federation had been left with little (if any) ability to make war, a lot can happen in thirty years. There was a chance we could be shot clean out of the sky. No one would blame the Xy for failing to see we were coming in peace.

At least, I wouldn't.

"Invited is a strong word," Gowon said.

This did not inspire confidence.

"Go on."

"The Sluudi were alarmed when traffic started coming across a channel that hadn't been active in thirty-five years. What they were able to translate told us there are internal troubles in the Xy Federation. It's mostly the kind of squabbling over resources that caused them to start a war with the rest of us in the first place."

"But now they know better, right?" I asked. "They started a war with us once and it didn't end well for them. So they wouldn't do that again. Tell me they wouldn't do that again."

"We don't think they're about to do that again."

"'Think' isn't the word I was hoping to hear," I said, "but I suppose I'll take it."

"The message traffic doesn't hint toward aggression toward the Alliance," Gowon shared. "Actually, quite the opposite. What we're hearing on this resurrected channel — that we're pretty sure the Xylans started using precisely so we would overhear this stuff — is that the Xylans are concerned about aggression from the Xylanthians, and they'd be open to contacting the Alliance for assistance."

"Open?" I asked, setting my full spoon back down into my pot of purpolate, "But not, 'hey Alliance, if you're listening, we'd love to have you over for tea and cakes'?".

"I'm afraid not. Nothing that explicit."

"Great."

"But experts from all five member nations have agreed there is enough evidence in the transmissions to believe they are asking us to make contact."

"Well, all right then," I said, polishing off my pot of purpolate. "I guess I'm going to have to trust the experts." I rolled my eyes for emphasis as I stood from the table to deposit my empty canister and dirty spoon into the scourecycler. It occurred to me halfway through the gesture how inappropriate it was for a Lieutenant to be rolling her eyes at a Major, but I was pretty well convinced Gowon wasn't about to call me on it. "We're either invited, in which case we very well may be flying into a trap — or we're *not* invited, and therefore headed into enemy territory unannounced aboard a ship that is barely airworthy and has absolutely zero chance of surviving even the most rudimentary of assaults. Good times."

"I think that was the point of sending *Dawn*," Gowon said, following me toward the scourecycler. "If we were to come at them, invited or not, aboard some shiny new fixed-wing equipped with the latest and greatest in tactical gear, that could give the wrong impression."

"So we show up defenseless to help make the point to them that we come in peace?"

"Or so I understand."

"This information does not fill me with joy," I said as I turned back around to face him.

"Yeah, I bet not," he replied, "and I don't think your boss is going to be too thrilled about it, either."

I tried to stifle my laugh at that but couldn't quite contain the sound. A tiny guffaw escaped my lips in spite of myself.

"Yeah, I don't guess," I said. "Pretty please send someone to let me know when he's been briefed. He may have work for me in light of this information. Probably not," I qualified. "He'll probably want to go back to his room and pray about it. But there's a chance he'll insist I be there for that. So until then, I'm going to go bang on a stabilizer."

"Feeling better then?"

I shrugged. Mostly I was feeling the double dose of adrenaline from seeing Raline and learning about our mission. Experience told me the best thing to do was to find a way to burn it off. Fighting with a stuck stabilizer sounded like just the thing.

"I'll feel better when we're done with this whole mess and I'm back in Feirin snacking on jimblebeans and cussing at paperwork. But I think the sky sickness is over. And if I can help get the stabilizers deployed, all of us will be a little less miserable. Plus, pounding on things is my preferred method of stress management."

"All right," he said, smiling. "I'll come find you when there's news."

CHAPTER FIVE

The Mechanical Deck, as it turned out, was a misnomer. Rather than a single deck, the term referred to a series of half-decks, cavities, and access tubes that snaked and webbed their way through and across the entire ship. It was an uncomfortably warm quagmire of dark iron and dim gaslight, but it smelled of coal and oil and engine grease in a way that made me feel instantly comfortable.

The place Major Gowon described as the best spot in which to rendezvous with Sergeant Eiji was the main engine room. Firebox boilers nearly as tall as *Dawn* herself sat dormant in the background as a newly installed petrol engine grumbled in its retrofitted cavity. Its exhaust pipes coiled skyward, putting its most noxious output into the clouds rather than the lungs of the men and women who tended it. I had never seen a setup like this one: most fixed-wing aircraft had their engines on the *outside* — one for each propeller usually. I supposed having an inboard engine made things easier if the need arose for an in-flight repair. Not having to strap on wing-walking gear probably made this setup appealing to technicians. But the thought of possibly flooding the ship with deadly gases in the event of a pipe-fitting failure mitigated my personal appreciation of it.

I found Sgt. Eiji to one side of the rumbling petrol engine.

"Follow me," he said as soon as I was in earshot. He pointed out a well-worn but not-immediately-visible path around the ship's engine and started down it as soon as he was sure I understood. I traversed the slick metal deck carefully and met him on the far side. He was a lot nimbler on this floor than I was. I was trying not to think too hard about the cause of the slipperiness; if the engine was spraying fluids, I presumed Sgt. Eiji was well aware and would keep the fluid levels within tolerances. He had plenty to handle without my registering a complaint as to the condition of the flooring.

Eiji turned around to smile at me before heading into a long spit of narrow corridor. The bulkheads here were polished metal, and pipes of varying gauges ran along the walls from the floor to waist level. The overhead lights burned with the bluish light of a carbon monoxide flame, leaving me to wonder if engine exhaust was being diverted to use for light. That would account for the heat in here — carbon monoxide burns a lot hotter than the methane or hydrogen these lights were probably designed for. I was surprised they hadn't been updated to incandescent electric filaments, but then again, *Dawn* wasn't exactly bursting with upgraded hardware.

She seemed to be the kind of ship where nothing that wasn't broken was going to get fixed — doubly so considering how much of her *was* broken.

After a minute or so the tunnel began to open up a little, and Eiji called out something in Mangan. Before I had the chance to ask him what he'd said, the room had gotten wide enough to let me see who he'd been speaking to. A pair of Mangan officers were dealing with what I assumed was the troublesome stabilizer. The man, a Private, was kneeling on the deck plate, using a hammer and pick against a patch of corrosion beside him. A female PFC stood nearby, daubing the same spot with solvent from a tub.

"Lieutenant Merteuil," Eiji addressed me. "This is Private Phamm and PFC Ioato."

I inclined my head toward them and managed to stumble through a greeting in Mangan; years in the Diplomatic Corps had to account for something. Ioato smiled at me and asked what I recognized as a question as to my understanding of their language. I winced.

"That was the extent of it, I'm afraid," I replied. "I'm fluent in Gammran," I added, "and I'm learning T'wesh." My cheeks got warm at the mention of my language studies. I had been studying T'wesh in secret for months now, in hopes of impressing Raline. This was the first time I'd mentioned it to anyone.

"Is all right," PFC Ioato said. "We speak Feirin."

I nodded and tried to smile. I knew that.

At the end of the war, as the Alliance member nations were formalizing the new, united government, Feirin had been chosen as the language of commerce. Owing to the fact Feirin had been a net exporter for generations, our language was already the most widely spoken and understood. In the years since, the Feirin people had earned a reputation of being ethnocentric snobs over that decision. The "we don't need to learn your language because you're required to know ours" mentality hadn't been good for relations between the Alliance member states. And I wanted these Mangan officers to know I wasn't one of the Feirin who thought their language beneath learning.

"So, this is the stabilizer that's been giving us trouble?" I asked Eiji, hoping to change the subject from the awkward matter of who spoke whose language and why.

"That's the one," Eiji said. "You can see what the problem is. While *Dawn* was mothballed, moisture and ... who-knows-what seeped in and corroded the whole mechanism. We need to get through the crud, take a look at the fin to make sure it's serviceable, clean out the gunk from all the moving parts, and then put it all back together before we can even try and get it to work."

I took a deep breath and shook my head. Cursing this flying junkheap and all its shortcomings wasn't going to help anything. I could tell Sgt. Eiji was already fed up with the ship, too. Any comments I made weren't going to tell him anything he didn't already know. And cursing my mother for sending me aboard this damnable vessel would tell everyone more than I was ready to share.

As Sgt. Eiji bid us adieu and good luck, I sat down to work on the problem in front of me.

Sitting there, on the ick-dotted deck plate of a spit off the maintenance deck of this busted old airship, I felt more like myself than I had in years. This assignment was refreshingly simple in comparison to diplomatic work. There was a well-defined problem, an agreed-upon solution, and a way to use my hands and my know-how to get through to it. There was no guesswork to a corroded stabilizer. Clear it. Clean it.

Reassemble it. It was this kind of concrete thinking I missed most from my days in the Air Corps.

Neither charm nor finesse would make any difference to an aircraft. The thing either worked or it didn't. I'd always appreciated things like that, but never more than after years in the Diplomatic Service — where almost nothing was so straightforward.

It took the rest of that day and half of the next before Phamm, Ioato, and I were able to clear enough of the rust and crud to begin to jimmy apart the mechanism of the stabilizer. It was another day still before it really started to come apart. I liked my cohorts; Phamm and Ioato were a genial pair, and they were more than happy to have a third pair of hands to help. The heat didn't do much to alleviate the nausea we were all still feeling, but the ability to concentrate on the work sometimes did.

We had finally freed the fin from its prison of corrosion and had begun the tedious process of disassembling the rest of its mechanism when I was sent back to the engine room in search of a second pail of solvent.

I knew something had to be up when I found Major Gowon there, and in conference with Sgt. Eiji from the looks of it. I did my best not to frown. Gowon wouldn't be down here for no reason. He'd made it clear he wasn't a fan of the Mechanical Deck; this couldn't possibly be a social call. Chances were that Berholtz had finally emerged from his cloister, and I was about to be needed for matters much less rewarding than stabilizer repair.

Even the thought of seeing Raline wasn't enough to make me ready to stop what I was doing. It wasn't just that I'd always enjoyed mechanical work far more than diplomatic work. I'd been at this project for three days already. I wanted to see it through to completion — and we were so close!

Gowon and Eiji looked to be engaged in an intense conversation; I wondered if I could sneak around behind their backs. Or, better yet, I considered retreating down the maintenance tube and sending one of my colleagues out for solvent. But before I was able to fully consider my options, I knew I'd been spotted.

"Lieutenant Merteuil," Gowon called to me from across the room. I saluted him weakly as I emerged from the maintenance tube into the rotunda that housed the *Dawn*'s inboard engine.

"Nice to see you again, Major," I replied as I crossed the fume-filled engine room. It wasn't entirely a lie. I liked Gowon. He was as honest and forthright a person as I could have imagined in the Intelligence Service. And I had enjoyed his company up until now. What I held back was how much I didn't enjoy running into him here and now.

"How's it coming with the stabilizer?" Sgt. Eiji asked. I shrugged.

"It's a stubborn little pewtypot," I replied, "but we're getting there."

"Good," Gowon affirmed, nodding at me before exchanging a look with Sgt. Eiji that made me a little bit nervous. "We're going to need that stabilizer," he said. "And then some. But for the moment," he added, turning his gaze back to me, "you're going to have to come with me."

"Right," I answered. "Let me guess: Berholtz finally came out from under his prayer blanket?"

"Quite the opposite," the Major replied. "He's still in cloister. We've got a serious matter on our hands, and the Captain would like a diplomatic officer to weigh in. Since Chief Khatri is technically a civilian and Ambassador Berholtz doesn't want to be disturbed, that leaves you as our only option."

"Great," I groaned, wiping my dirty hands against the thighs of my still-dirtier flight suit. "A meeting. My favorite. Do I get to change clothes first?"

"Don't worry about your uniform," Eiji said, gesturing toward Major Gowon and the hatch to the general corridor. "Just sit by me and you'll look clean by comparison."

I let myself laugh at that. Eiji had a point. None of us who'd been spending our time in the maintenance decks had taken too much care of the appearance of our uniforms. I'd been doing the best I could to spot-treat the worst of the grime while I showered every evening, but there was no stopping the solvent stains or the tiny scuffs from propagating. Not that I cared overmuch. I'd be back in dress blues before doing any official business — and before I had the chance to run into Raline again — or so I'd thought, anyway.

I could at least hope to avoid running into her between here and wherever I was going.

I followed Gowon and Eiji through a series of corridors and stairways that seemed to get cleaner, better maintained, and more clearly labeled as we went. By the time we reached our destination, I was giggling under my breath at what Queen Salian would think of her daughter attending a meeting with the highest-ranking members of the expedition in a grimy flight suit with smudges on her face and her hair in tangles.

"Lieutenant Merteuil," I was greeted as I came through the door. I took note of the fact the two gentlemen alongside me were not. The woman who'd spoken was tall for a Mangan, pale, and wore her hair tied back in a knot so severe I wondered if it was affecting her expression. Still, she looked serene and in control as she stood at the far end of the conference table the others were seated around.

This had to be Captain Taiko. I'd seen her from a

distance when she'd received my mother's blessing at the departure ceremony, but this was the first chance I'd had to see her up close. She looked younger than I remembered, and somehow even tidier and more put together in her flight suit than she had in her dress blues.

"Ma'am," I answered with a nod. My branch of the service wasn't expected to salute, but as a former member of the Air Service, I still felt weird about it. The Captain gestured for me to have a seat, which I did. Gowon and Eiji also found seats at the table as Captain Taiko continued speaking.

"I think you know most everyone," she said, "but I should introduce my Executive Officer." She gestured to her left, to a T'wesh man half a head shorter than she. He wore a Major's bars on his collar and an expression that said he didn't want to be here. He was the only one in the room dressed in a Class-A uniform instead of a flight suit. There were several medals pinned to his chest, and his hair was as close-cropped as any I'd ever seen. Everything about him smacked of a man who was trying too hard. "Major Malli," she introduced, "Lieutenant Merteuil."

"Sir," I greeted him. His reply was a curt nod and a sneer.

Lovely.

The last thing I needed was some insecure snollygoster of a second-in-command asserting his entitlement all over whatever meeting was about to take place. I wondered if his issue was a racial one, or a sexist one, if he had a personal beef with Captain Taiko, or if perhaps he was just a generally unpleasant person. I had a feeling I'd be spending the rest of the mission hoping not to deal with him again.

Using all the diplomatic skill I could muster, I kept my disdain for Malli's apparent imperiousness and condescension in check as I scooted my chair closer to the conference table. The tabletop wobbled when I leaned against it, nearly spilling a well of ink onto the lap of a very attractive T'wesh officer sitting across from me.

"Apologies," I offered, trying to sound like I wasn't slightly agog at her beauty.

She looked way too much like Raline for me not to feel flustered. It wasn't just her tawny skin and coal-black hair, either — the curve of her lip and the angle of her cheekbones all bore uncanny resemblance to my crush. Of course, I couldn't tell her that, even as a compliment. Saying she reminded me of someone would almost certainly come off in that terrible 'all T'wesh women look alike' way the Feirin were notorious for.

"It's all right," she said, straightening the ink well and the pages before her as she gave me a smile. "Lieutenant Commander Jira Paar," she introduced herself, reaching across the table for a handshake. "Chief of Navigation."

I was glad I was able to reach her hand without standing. Her smile had me a bit weak-kneed.

She really did look quite a lot like Raline.

"Maran Merteuil," I introduced myself in turn as Lieutenant Commander Paar shook my hand and settled back into her seat.

"I know," she said, still smiling. "My cousin Raline speaks highly of you."

Now there were buzzybugs in my stomach. Raline's cousin: that would explain the resemblance. Luckily, I'd spent my life cultivating a royal demeanor and a diplomatic fooler face — otherwise I'd have turned into a bumbling fool right there and then. As it was, I was saved from myself when the Captain took control of the room.

"I regret this interruption," she said, allowing herself a deep sigh as she settled her posture into what was commonly known among the military branches as Parade Rest. "I understand you all have duties elsewhere. I will do my best to make this brief." She looked each one of us in the eye as she spoke. I could tell that whatever we'd been called here to discuss wasn't going to be pleasant. "We're headed into some bad weather," the Captain said. "Possibly the worst weather into which any of us has ever flown. And I think it's worth a conversation as to what we're going to do about it."

Suddenly, the buzzybugs in my stomach all turned to boulders. This floating wreck of a ship was no match for even the mildest of storm systems.

This … was bad.

"In ordinary circumstances," Captain Taiko said, "we could add lift to manage the situation." She looked down across the table at Sergeant Eiji.

"Let me guess," he said, in a tone much more casual than I'd have used to address the Captain. "It's one of those vertical supercell storms and the clouds extend higher into the atmosphere than we're capable of lifting?"

"Indeed," Captain Taiko answered with a deferential nod. "Even if we were to push our lift capabilities to the limits of what's theoretically possible, *Dawn* isn't properly pressurized for such an altitude."

"Which leaves us a few options," Commander Paar interjected. "None of them particularly appealing."

I sat up straighter. I still had no idea what I was doing in this meeting, but if my job for the moment was to listen to Raline's cousin talk about lousy navigational options, I could do that.

"There's an uninhabited island, the Sluudi call it Akachon, half a day's flight to the southwest," she said.

"We could get there and tie down until the storm has passed over."

If there was one thing a Royal upbringing and a decade of diplomatic service had taught me, it was how to read a person. And what Commander Paar *wasn't* saying in that moment was coming through loud and clear. She didn't like that idea, and I wanted to know how come.

"What are you not telling us?" I asked, taking my cue from Sergeant Eiji as to whether it was proper to speak out of turn. I'd be shushed soon enough if it turned out to be inappropriate, and the question would still be on the table. "Why does that sound like a great idea — except when you say it, it sounds like a bad idea?"

"It's fuel," Sgt. Eiji piped up.

"Pardon?" I asked.

"Fuel," Sgt. Eiji repeated. "The fuel we burn to get to Akachon island, the fuel we burn to keep the lights on while we're grounded, and the fuel it takes to fill the lift bags back up may be more than our surplus," he explained. "We'd make it to our destination, but unless they're willing to top off our fuel supply, we could risk running out halfway home — or wind up there indefinitely."

"Willing?" It was Maj. Gowon who chimed in this time. "We don't even know if they're able. They could be willing to do anything we want, but if the Xylans don't have the fuel to give us, that doesn't mean a hill of tubers."

I snapped my head sideways to look up at Major Gowon. Suddenly this meeting made more sense. With the exception of the still-cloistered Ambassador Berholtz, and possibly our civilian assistant, the people in this room were the totality of those who knew where we were going. This meeting was to discuss in plain terms what any weather delays might mean for our mission as a whole.

"Indeed," Captain Taiko said. "The worst-case scenario is that we find ourselves stranded in Xyland."

"Captain, if I may," Gowon injected, "the worst-case scenario is that we're stranded in Xyland *and* they're not happy to see us. We're still not sure they know we're coming. Going in without any way of getting out seems inadvisable."

"What are our other options?" I asked the room, proud of myself for not bringing up what I figured to be the *actual* worst-case scenario: the one where the Xylans aren't expecting us at all, shoot us down, and use our incursion into their airspace as an excuse to start another decades-long war.

"I'd like to tell you to fly straight through it," Eiji said. "And on any other ship, I probably would. Turbulence doesn't bother airships like it does other kinds of flying machines. And *Dawn*'s from a class built to withstand lightning strikes. If I'd had more time to get her airworthy ..." his voice trailed off and he shrugged. "I just don't think she can take it, Captain," he said after a pause. "If we fly into that storm, I can't promise she'll hold together. And I'd argue breaking up over open water would be an even worse outcome than getting stranded in Xyland."

"So where does that leave us?" I asked.

Commander Paar turned to me and inclined her head.

"I've plotted us two possible alternate courses," she said, sliding a map from in front of her into the center of the table. "If we want to stay over open water, we can adjust our heading forty degrees to port and skirt the westward edge of the storm until we're past it, then double back to land on the northern coast of Xyland."

Captain Taiko crossed her arms over her chest and

shook her head.

"Sergeant Eiji?" she said.

"I don't know," Eiji replied. "If the going's as smooth as we hope, we'd theoretically have enough fuel to get back to Alliance airspace after our visit — although not enough to get us into port."

"Under this plan there's still a very good chance we have to ditch in the ocean," Major Malli said. It was his first contribution to the meeting. "Correct? But at least it's likely we'll have to ditch close to home instead of in Xy Federation territorial waters?"

I couldn't tell whether his disdain was for the plan or for Commander Paar, but either way, his disapproval was more than apparent.

"Yes, sir," Paar answered. There was a tremor in her voice that warned me of possible escalation on Malli's part.

"You said two routes?" I asked her, hoping to assuage her unease by getting her to talk more about the plans she'd made.

All in all, skirting the edge of the storm at the expense of maybe not having enough fuel to get us all the way back to port didn't sound like that terrible of an idea to me. A tow back to safe port, or even a controlled evacuation of a foundering airship over friendly waters didn't sound so bad, considering. Even if we did wind up having to ditch near home, as long as we did so within reasonable proximity to land and using proper communications protocol, there was every chance rescue vessels would beat the *Dawn* to her final coordinates. It wasn't like the Alliance would be losing much of an asset in that case, either. It was the most noble end I could think of for the AFS *Dawn* — a dignified retirement as an artificial reef. Those were points I'd gladly make in Paar's defense if that was the better of the two plans she'd made for us. I was curious to hear the second one.

"There is another option," Paar answered me. "It will save fuel, but it's risky."

"Riskier even than the possibility of having to abandon ship over open water?" Malli challenged.

"Differently so," was Commander Paar's answer. She looked up at me then back down at the map. "We could instead adjust course twenty degrees to starboard. That doesn't take us out of the storm entirely, but it puts us rather quickly over land. The farther inland we are, the weaker the storm system should be. We travel the remaining days over land, readjusting course as we go, and land on schedule at our intended coordinates."

Gowon crossed his arms over his chest as he leaned back in his seat.

"Am I reading that map right?" he asked, inclining his head toward Commander Paar. "That was a rhetorical question," he added, in response to her confused expression. "I know I'm reading that map right. And in case anyone else here isn't reading the map right, or isn't looking at the map, or for some reason doesn't understand what is printed on the map, I feel I need to point out that the land mass over which it's just been suggested we might fly is Xylanth."

"Xylanth?" I repeated. My eyes were wide and the rocks in my stomach were turning back into buzzybugs.

"Uh-huh," Maj. Gowon answered me. "As in 'the half of the Xy Federation that absolutely has no idea we're coming'."

"But what would that matter," Captain Taiko posed, "if we keep to the frontier? We're not looking to set down in Xylanth. There's a very good chance they would never know they've been overflown. Correct, Major Gowon?"

"In theory," he allowed. "We have nothing concrete on the current state of Xy air defenses. We might be spotted, we might not. Probably not. But I'm not sure 'probably' is good enough under the circumstances."

"Plus we're still talking about flying through the storm," I said, "not around it. So there's a chance we are talking about having to put down in Xylanth."

"If that's the case," Captain Taiko said, "we are confident the Xy lack the assets to travel by air in inclement weather. They may have no flight capabilities at all. If we were to have to effect an emergency landing in Xylanth, we would surely be able to lift off again and be clear of their airspace long before they would be able to engage us."

"Provided *Dawn* came through any emergency landing unscathed," Eiji qualified. "Airships of her class were designed to anchor on spires, not go to ground. If there's a chance we have to tie down because of inclement weather, we need to account for possible hull damage, no matter where we're talking about doing it."

"And that's before we consider the mountain range in the way," Major Gowon added. "We crash into the side of a mountain and 'hull damage' is about the best we can hope for."

"I can steer the ship," Paar snapped. "I won't crash her into a mountain."

"If there was a chance of that, we'd just land, right?" I asked. I wasn't sure why I was so fiercely on Paar's side in all this. But I was. Maybe it was because she was Raline's cousin, or maybe it was that I knew what it felt like to have my competencies questioned by people who didn't always know what they were talking about.

"Correct," she replied.

"And if we have to put down in Xylanth, so as to not get blown sideways into a mountain," Gowon asked, "we're sure we could get back up again?"

"I think so," Sgt. Eiji replied. "Unless the lift bags take serious damage, I don't see why we couldn't lift back off. But there are no guarantees."

"That's the same concern we'd face if we went to put down on Akachon," Paar reminded him. "Sure, the island is more sparsely wooded than the Xy frontier, but anyplace we tie down could cause problems for our ability to become airborne again."

"You're saying if we fly over Xylanth, there's a chance we won't have to put down at all?" Captain Taiko asked.

"Yes ma'am," Paar answered.

"It would be easier on our fuel supply, too," Eiji offered. "It's nowhere near as far out of the way as Akachon Island. In fact, it's a shorter route than the one we'd originally plotted. We fly over Xylanth, we'll still be in good shape to make the return trip."

"Very well then," the Captain said. "Unless I hear a strong objection, I will be instructing Commander Paar to set course for the overland route." She looked at Major Malli, her expression enough to say she expected no contrary words out of him.

"This is the most likely plan to result in the ship still being in one piece when all is said and done?" Major Gowon asked the room. "And the one that's most likely to get us home with fuel still in the tank?"

Both Captain Taiko and Commander Paar nodded in agreement.

I looked over at Gowon, who met my eyes with a nod.

"I support the overland plan, Captain," Sgt. Eiji said.

"As do I," Major Gown added.

"Me too," I chimed in, not sure whether my opinion mattered in the slightest, but wanting to show Captain Taiko and Commander Paar my support all the same.

"Then we are in agreement," she said, turning her attention back to the lot of us. "Commander Paar, plot the overland course and lay it in as soon as possible.

And those of you who pray," she added, clasping her hands at her waist, "I would ask that you please do so now."

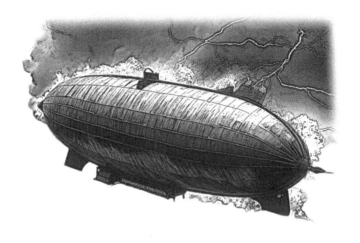

CHAPTER SIX

The meeting adjourned without much more discussion, save Major Malli making sure to repeatedly express his displeasure with the overland plan. I wasn't sure why he was being so contrary. There wasn't any official record being taken of this meeting, so there was nothing substantive to be gained from his grousing.

I'd dealt with men like him before — both in the Service and in Royal employ — self-important neddies who couldn't stand the thought of anyone else getting the last word. I'd always hated people like him.

Even if I hadn't wanted to escape Malli's griping, I'd have been in a hurry to get out of that meeting. We were about to head into bad weather. It was more critical than ever to get the stabilizers online and deployed.

I was halfway to the ladder, and a clean getaway, when I felt a hand on my arm. My jaw tensed reflexively; The last thing I wanted to do was discuss this situation further. When I turned around and saw Commander Paar, some measure of my annoyance released, replaced in a moment by the awkward tension I only ever felt in the presence of a particularly beautiful woman.

I tried to say, 'hello' but no sound escaped my throat.

"Did I embarrass you back there?" she asked.

I frowned. What had she done that I might possibly find embarrassing?

"Uh ... no," I managed to say.

"Raline would probably be embarrassed," she said. "But she really is fond of you. She is also quite shy and would likely never say so herself."

"Raline Khatri is your cousin," I said. It was obvious, and I felt like a fool as soon as I'd said it, but the family resemblance seemed to extend to a common ability to rob me of my eloquence.

Paar laughed, nodding her head knowingly.

"You knew that," she said.

My cheeks got suddenly warm. I could only hope the lighting in here was dim enough to hide what I was sure was an obvious flush.

"I wondered," I replied. "And then you said, and ..."

"People say we look alike."

"There's a definite resemblance," I agreed.

Paar laughed again.

"Don't tell her I told you," she said. "But she was excited when she learned you would be working together. I think you should ask her out when we get back."

My stomach's resident buzzybugs returned with a flourish.

"I ..." my tongue got all tied and my palms out in sweat. "I wasn't sure she was *arunish*," I confided. My romantic senses had never been particularly well honed; being able to tell whether someone I was crushing on was attracted to me, or to women *at all* had never been a skill I'd developed.

Probably why I'd been celibate for so long.

"She's *egalit*," Paar replied. "She was engaged to a man several years back. But she likes you. I know she does. If you ask her out, she'll say yes. Just don't tell her I said anything."

"No," I agreed. "I won't. But I'm glad you told me. Otherwise, I might never ..."

"You two would be good together," she interrupted.

"That's provided we make it home," I qualified.

"Indeed," Paar answered. "I promise to set the safest course."

"The safest course would have been turning this whole mess around and heading home."

"I will admit I was surprised no one suggested that."

"*I* will admit I would have if I thought anyone might consider it."

"The success of this mission is of critical importance to the Alliance," she said.

I crossed my arms over my chest and frowned. I wondered what she might know that I didn't. No one had come to me with any indication this was some sort of vital undertaking. And if the Alliance was, for some reason, counting on successful contact with the Xylans, why in the seven hells had they sent us aboard such an irksome craft?

As far as I was concerned, this was still a trap, and I doubted there was anything that might convince me otherwise.

I still wanted to know why she'd said that.

I clenched my hands into fists and tried my best to

smile. Even if Paar had answers I wanted, now was not the time to try and get them out of her. We were headed into an ugly storm system, and it was on her to plot our way around the worst of it. And it was up to me to help get our decrepit stabilizers back online before we reached the outer bands.

Quizzing Paar on what she might know about the mission itself was going to have to wait.

"Well," I said, hoping to disentangle myself from this line of conversation, "the stabilizers are of critical importance to the *Dawn*'s ability to fly straight. If you'll excuse me."

I didn't wait for her parting words.

We'd made reasonable progress on the stabilizer already, and I was anxious to get the work finished and the ship fully operational.

Sgt. Eiji was already on the Mechanical Deck when I arrived, and he was in the process of gathering the staff for an impromptu briefing on the storm and the state of the ship. I was glad to hear he had a plan, but I wasn't thrilled by the rest of what he had to say.

The ship's retrofitted engine, it turned out, had never been tested in the rain. There was every chance enough moisture would get in through the air intake to shut the whole thing down. The lift bags should stay inflated — as they were the newer, static variety and not the old positive-pressure kind — but that was little reassurance in the face of being possibly adrift in foul weather.

I wondered why this hadn't been brought up in the meeting. It was bad enough to be headed into a storm over enemy territory in a ship without stabilizers, but it was even worse to be going that way in a ship that might just ... stop running.

I couldn't ask Eiji — not then. I was sure most of the others on the mechanical crew had no idea where we were going. I wasn't about to spill classified information to the enlisted personnel, even if I did think it was kind of a rotten deal they'd gotten: being assigned to this ship and not knowing why.

Maybe I'd ask Eiji about it later, but probably not. He was likely to have his hands full. And I also had a job to do.

For a moment, as I headed back into the bowels of the ship to bang on the stabilizer some more, I entertained the notion of popping in on Berholtz. He'd likely appreciate being told we were about to deviate from our planned course. And there was also the very real possibility his prayers had taken this long because they'd been held up for a few days thanks to nausea.

If that was the case, he'd also probably appreciate my warning him of the weather we were about to encounter. Flying through even the edge of a storm the likes of which Captain Taiko had described was likely to exacerbate any sky sickness he might already be feeling.

If Berholtz wanted to stock up on zingiber tabs, now was the time.

But I didn't care, at least not enough to make the effort. Helping my purported superior get through the bad weather wasn't nearly as important as getting the ship in its best possible state to face the storm.

Maybe after I got the stabilizer online, I'd go warn Raline. I might even offer to share my dwindling supply of zingiber with her. It would give me an excuse to seek her out, and I kind of liked the idea of having an opportunity to show her I cared. I wasn't sure how much she knew about where we were going and what we were up to. There was a chance she was as yet unaware of our intended destination even though she was going to be tasked with setting up diplomatic logistics once we arrived.

If I were to tell her more than she was authorized to know, I could wind up in a heap of trouble. Not that I cared overmuch. She deserved to know what was going on. It was also very likely she could keep a secret. If all went well, she'd know about our mission soon enough. We were only a few days from Xyland, and our Commanders would have to tell her sooner or later who she'd be dealing with once we arrived.

Also, telling Raline under the guise of making sure Berholtz was prepared seemed like reasonable cover. I really did want to see her. I couldn't get Paar's voice out of my mind: *She likes you. You should ask her out. She will say yes. She really is fond of you.*

Plus, I didn't like the idea of her having to go through the foul weather without warning. I, for one, couldn't imagine being aboard this clattering junk heap in the sky in a terrible storm without having had at least some forewarning.

I'd probably poult out when the time came, but I planned to talk with Raline as soon as the stabilizer was back in its place and doing its job.

I moved more quickly than usual back to where Phamm and Ioato were still working.

The welding and patch work was onerous, but at least it was straightforward. That was a world better than meetings in my opinion. A troublesome stabilizer had no ego and required no special handling.

Get it unstuck, get it where it can do some good, get it to stay put.

Then go and talk to Raline.

The three of us who'd been working with the corroded stabilizer, with the blessing of Sgt. Eiji, had decided from the get-go we'd be welding the thing in its deployed position once we were able to force it into place. Knowing what I did about our possible need to put down, I now understood the risk we were taking in doing that. But when I asked Sgt. Eiji if he thought we should reconsider, he said no. He was still on board with our plan to permanently install the stabilizer. Having it break off later was a chance we were going to have to take. It was his hope, as well as mine, that having the thing in working order might help us keep from having to tie down in the first place.

This hulk wasn't designed to go to ground, and I'd rather not have to test its mettle inside enemy territory.

Though Phamm and Ioato had been hard at work in my absence, there was still much to be done before the stabilizer would be functional.

The weather was already getting bad by the time we started on the welding. And I daresay we didn't leave a moment to spare. No sooner had we gotten the weld in place than I started praying to all those Feirin gods I never believed in for it to hold. The ship was already bucking and rolling enough we had a hell of a time getting out of the access tunnel without taking a tumble or losing hold of our gear.

I supposed the idea of warning Raline of impending rough weather had expired. Maybe I could still find her later with an offer of antiemetics. But maybe I was about to be too sky sick to function again myself.

My experience with storms up to this point was entirely land-based. The Air Service would ground us cadets for anything more threatening than a low cloud ceiling, and the Royal Yacht only sailed in truly fair skies. The thing I knew best about skyfaring vessels and bad weather was that they shouldn't mix. The impression I'd gotten in the meeting was that airships often stayed aloft in rough conditions, that SOP was go high or try and skirt the system, and that ships the size and class of this one could possibly fly through even a severe storm when in proper trim.

Nothing about *Dawn* was in proper trim.

"It's in!" Private Phamm called out to Sgt. Eiji as we clambered the last few meters from the access tube into the main space of the Mechanical Deck. I was sweaty, and a little shaky with nerves, but I could already feel the difference in the way the ship was handling with the stabilizer in place.

It felt good to have *done something*. Over a decade in the diplomatic corps had left me feeling mostly useless, and this posting — junior to a pompous charlatan on a ship almost surely destined to founder — hadn't helped. Putting in a few days' work on a project that would appreciably help the operation of the ship had been a nice change of pace.

"Thank you," Eiji said to the three of us as we approached.

"What's next?" I asked. This was a good feeling, and I wanted more of it. As much as I'd been thinking about trying to see Raline, keeping the ship aloft and running had to take priority.

"I'm glad you asked, Lt. Merteuil," Eiji replied. "I wasn't sure whether you'd want to stay with us."

"If you'll have me," I said, trying to let my hopeful face show through the fatigue and the adrenaline. "I feel like I'm doing good down here. And unless the Captain says she needs me someplace else, I'd be glad to stay down here for the duration."

"You're hired," Eiji half-joked.

I smiled back at him. I would rather ride out this storm down in the belly of the ship trying to keep her aloft than in my room fighting another bout of sky sickness or trying to come up with something intelligible to say to Raline.

The weather was already starting to get ugly, and I was sure it was about to get a whole lot worse.

But if *Dawn* was going down, I wasn't going to let her go without a fight.

CHAPTER SEVEN

I had guessed, when looking up at the *AFS Dawn* tethered to her departure spire back in Feirin City, that life aboard the airship was going to be uncomfortable.

I had no idea.

In my years as an Air Service Cadet, I'd seen some weather. I'd seen tropical cyclones, clusters of waterspouts, wind that blew the ost and zabbov trees over fully sideways. I'd seen flooding and firestorms and lightning so big and furious it lit the night sky bright as morning. And in all those times, under all those circumstances, the attitude of the Air Service had remained constant: don't take off.

Easy enough for a fleet of fixed-wing and whirligig in a peacetime flying corps — but impossible for an old airship already several days underway. I appreciated the argument against putting down and waiting out the storm; I didn't fancy the idea of being without adequate fuel to return to friendly airspace any more than the next person. But by the time I was ordered to my bunk late that first night, I wasn't sure my mind hadn't changed.

I'd understood it would be rough, but the way the ship was bucking and rolling was beyond even the worst my imagination had prepared me for. The idea of being someplace still and calm — even still and calm and out of fuel on a deserted island — was sounding better and better. There was no way I was going to be able to sleep, possibly not even with a generous application of zingiber tabs; I doubted anyone would. I had half a mind try and find Raline, to maybe check on her.

But I'd been ordered to my cabin to try and rest so I'd be fresh for duty in the morning. So I stayed in my bunk and did my best to keep my eyes closed.

We'd done everything we could to shore up the Mechanical Deck for the rough ride to come — including putting some time in protecting the engine from possible water intrusion. The overnight crew was getting started on a sort of makeshift bilge pump in case our efforts weren't enough.

But the overnight crew was less than half a dozen people, and it was likely to take all their time and energy just to keep the engine running. The modifications Sgt. Eiji had made to the fuel system would hopefully keep the diesel from sloshing so badly the engine would stall, but that was no guarantee. Between keeping pressure in the fuel line, ensuring as little water as possible got into the system, and staying on top of the damage the ship's kicking and rattling would surely cause, the graveyard shift was going to have its hands full.

The day shift, with me now all but officially assigned to it, needed to get whatever rest we could while things were holding together. The intercom wasn't really back up and running, but Sgt. Eiji had made sure the emergency klaxon was functional. If things on the Mechanical Deck went too far downhill before it was time for the rest of us to return, tones would sound, and we'd all come running.

As much as I wanted to sleep, I decided against taking a zingiber tab. It would surely have knocked me out, and maybe even kept any sky sickness from materializing, but it wasn't worth the risk of being under the influence were I to be needed on the Mechanical Deck.

Lack of sleep felt like the lesser evil in this case.

After all, working through the haze of sleep deprivation was a skill I'd honed finely during my time at the Air Academy. One night's missed rest wouldn't be too much of a hinderance if push came to shove. Two or three and I'd probably be a mess, and were this crisis to last longer than that, I'd be so exhausted I'd pass out whether I wanted to or not.

Fuss. I hoped it didn't last that long.

I kicked myself for not thinking to ask what the crew knew about the size of the storm or how long they figured we'd be in the middle of it. But, then again, maybe it was better not to know. Not counting days and hours might do a better job of keeping me in the moment; I sometimes had a lousy habit of borrowing trouble. Maybe it was better not to know how much trouble was in this particular bank.

I was surprised when the klaxon woke me up — less so that the alarm had sounded than the fact I'd managed to fall asleep in the first place. I scrambled to my feet and pulled on my flight suit over my night clothes, silently thanking my past self for setting things up so it would be possible to get dressed in the dark. I slipped my boots onto my feet and tugged at the straps just enough to get the buckles to catch. It only mattered that they wouldn't fall off my feet between my cabin and the Mechanical Deck. I'd deal with getting a proper fit later.

Or not.

As I palmed the control to open the door, remembering the trick Declan had taught me on my first trip out of my quarters, I took a glance at the chrono on the opposite wall. It had been almost five hours since I'd gone off shift. I wondered how far into the storm we'd gotten in the meantime. The ship lurched, knocking me off my feet and through the hatch into the corridor. I landed hard on my knees.

It took me a moment to catch my breath and start to haul my sore and groggy body up off the deck. The ship was bucking like an angry bronc, cabin doors rattling in their frames, emergency lights flickering all around. It took me a couple of tries before I was able to get my feet under me.

This was going to be rough.

As I got back on my feet, I patted the pocket where I'd stashed my Royal and Rank insignia when I'd first come aboard. Everything was in its place. I wasn't sure when having those pips and bars secreted on my person had become such a reassurance, but it was. And it was kind of nice to see my habit of not bothering to empty my pockets before bed was serving me well. Score one for laziness, I guess.

I dashed across the bounding decks as best I could, zipping my flight suit up as I went. I raced up ladders and down ramps, ducking through tiny hatches and wrestling sticky doors out of my way until I finally made it to the Mechanical Deck. Over half the day crew, in various stages of dress, was already there when I arrived. Others straggled in behind me.

"Maran," Sgt. Eiji called as I ducked down to finally fasten up my boots. Wearing them loose had gotten me here a moment sooner than I otherwise would have arrived, but I wasn't sure it was worth the number of blisters that had formed between my cabin and the Mechanical Deck.

"Yes?" I replied. I was surprised to have been addressed by my first name, but not enough to comment on it. There was surely a crisis going on or else we wouldn't have been summoned. Having never been one to stand on rank to begin with, I didn't mind the familiarity — especially under the circumstances.

Sgt. Eiji jogged through the crowd of newcomers to meet me where I was crouched.

"There's something I need you to do," he said. "Immediately. Now. As soon as possible."

"Okay," I said, finishing the buckle on my right boot and standing up as quickly as I was able. "Whatever you need."

"I wish I had time to explain to you the finer points of airship control rigging," he said. "But you'll forgive me that I don't."

I only nodded.

"This class of airship was built with dual helm control," he said. "But *Dawn's* rudder was unusable when we pulled her out of mothballs, and when we replaced it, we didn't have the time to put everything together to factory spec. One of the places whoever was in charge decided to cut corners was in the steerage. I thought it was a bad idea, but nobody wanted to listen to me. Anyway — they only had us rig up the one wheel — which might have been fine had the weather held. But as we are all painfully aware, the weather has *not* held, and now our pilot is having a hell of a time keeping control without someone on that other wheel."

"And what do you need me to do?" I asked. I had to admit I was amused by his choosing to give me a history lesson even though he'd said that wasn't on his agenda. But mostly I wanted him to get to the point and give me my orders so I could get to work.

"I need you to go up to the bridge and hook the rudder cables up to the second helm."

All of a sudden, there were rocks in my gut.

"You want me to ..."

"I'm going to give you the tools," Eiji interrupted me. "When you get up to the bridge, the second steering column will be obvious. It's sitting on a metal footplate — a platform, sort of. You'll take off the bolts and pull off the plate. In the meantime, I've already gotten the cables attached at the rudder end and I've got someone in the access tube right now running them up to where they need to be for you to connect them. You'll see what I'm talking about when you get there — there'll be two half-inch metal cables sticking out into the cavity. Just grab hold, thread them through the pulleys and attach them to the steering column. The repair itself is basically a pair of glorified saddle clamps. You'll be able to do it no problem."

"Okay," I said. "Yeah ..." I couldn't keep the trepidation out of my voice. "But are you sure I'm the right person to do this?" It wasn't that I didn't want to try, but I'd never made this type of repair before — unless a classroom simulation counted — which, in my opinion, it did not. I had zero confidence I'd be capable of doing it for real, especially not with the way the ship was jolting and shaking. Something as important as the ability to *steer the ship* didn't seem to be the kind of thing that ought to be left in the hands of a rookie.

"Listen," Eiji said, taking me by the elbow and walking the two of us closer to the door — away from where the others were working. "I'm counting on you."

He shook his head and looked me in the eye. "I would do it myself, but there's so much going wrong down here. I don't think it's a good idea for me to be head down in a critical repair, especially not one all the way at the other end of the ship. I need to be down here putting out fires and solving problems as they come. Which means you're the only person who can even attempt to do this."

I shook my head.

"Why me?" I asked. "You have two whole shifts of people down here who I'm sure know better how to do this than I do. What am I missing?"

"Maran," Eiji said, his voice with a sudden edge I hadn't heard from him before now. "You're the only one with clearance to be on the bridge."

I let myself inhale slowly as the thought sank in.

The mission was Top Secret. I'd been in that meeting. The Captain and First Officer, the Chief Navigator, the Chief Engineer, Major Gowon, and the Diplomats. We were the only people who knew where we were going — and we were the only people allowed on the bridge. That made sense, I guess. Although, had I been in charge of the expedition, I'd have waived that rule in favor of getting the very most qualified person for the job up there to make it possible to *steer the ship*.

But I was not in charge of the expedition.

What I was in charge of was a toolkit and a critical repair.

Sgt. Eiji sent me off with what he promised were the right tools for the job and let me know the bridge was adjacent to the conference room where we'd first met to discuss the storm. I was pretty confident I could get there.

That is to say: I was pretty confident I would remember the way. Physically getting there was another matter altogether.

The entrance to the Mechanical Deck was just aft of midships, deep in the belly of the hull; the bridge was forward on the ship's uppermost deck. Moving from one to the other was the longest journey a person could take without leaving the ship. That was a lot of distance to cover with a heavy tool bag. More than once the lights shut off for long enough my eyes had begun to adjust before they came back on.

The ship pitched and rolled with ever-increasing intensity as I got closer to where I was going. Just as I was passing through the hatchway onto the bridge, we lurched so hard to starboard I didn't make it through on my feet. My hip found a junction in the deck plates and my elbow caught the lip of the door hatch.

"Dammit!" I cried. That hurt.

"Lieutenant?" Major Malli addressed me as though he was thoroughly offended by my outburst. I didn't give a damn, but he was the ship's XO and I had work to do.

"Sorry, sir," I lied, still lying on the floor as I tried to figure out where my tool bag had ended up. I found it several feet to the left of where I'd landed. I rolled over, trying to reach the bag with my left hand as I flexed my right hand in and out of a fist. I'd banged my elbow hard, and the numbness needed to go the hell away before I set to working on the airship's steerage.

"I do not know your familiarity with airship operations, Lieutenant Ambassador," Malli said, putting odd stress on my diplomatic title. "But whatever business you have on the bridge can surely wait."

What in the seven hells ...?

"Sir?" was all I could say as I clambered to my feet, trying not to frown too hard in the XO's direction. Did he really think I'd come up here to discuss some diplomatic matter? In the middle of the night while the ship was barely holding together? I must have misunderstood.

"Not now, Lieutenant!" he yelled.

I suddenly didn't mind how profoundly I was frowning. The look on my face was the absolute least of my concerns. This follypang could complain to my superiors later if he wanted to, but he wasn't about to shoo me away from making a major repair to the ship that both our lives depended on.

I turned to face Major Malli where he sat. He was in the Captain's Chair, holding on white-knuckled to the ends of the arm rests as the ship bounded and yawed beneath him. He was sweating profusely, his uniform blouse was damp in places, and what little hair he had on his head was soaked through. I had to guess that Captain Taiko had gone off shift around the time the engineering staff did and that, unlike the amiable and collegial Sgt. Eiji, Malli hadn't cared to admit he was in over his head.

I took two steps across the wobbling deck and held my tool bag out in front of me.

"I'm here to hook up the cables to restore your full helm control," I said, not giving one tenth of a damn how rude I sounded. I would be lying if I said I didn't enjoy the look on his face when those words sank in.

I didn't give him a chance to say anything else before turning my back on him and getting to work.

Sgt. Eiji had been right when he said things would be obvious. The bridge was smaller than I had pictured it. The forward bulkhead was inlaid with a twelve-foot-wide windscreen from waist-height to the ceiling. There was a growing crack in it near the upper starboard corner; carbon scoring at its edge hinted at a lightning strike. No wonder the lights hadn't been reliable. The ship's whole electrical system, already held together by SturdyTape and good intentions, was probably well and truly fried.

Something told me we'd be spending the next few days converting the electric lighting back to use the old gas lines like in the engineering corridor. But first we had to get through this storm.

In the center of the bridge sat the high-backed Captain's Chair with a low, angled map table before it. Just forward of the table, on either side, stood the twin helm positions. The two wheels, wrapped in cracked and aging leather, stood on tiny platforms. I hadn't understood the layout when Sgt. Eiji had described it to me but seeing it in person his words made sense. The small step up allowed for a minor change in perspective; it would have put the average Mangan at eye level with the very center of the windscreen.

Commander Paar stood at the starboard helm, grasping the wheel with what looked like all her might as she divided her attention between the view of the storm out the windscreen and the compass built into the steering column in front of her. Her throttle lever looked to be set to wide open, and the lift control was locked into steady state. Her face was resolute, her stance was firm, and yet something about her seemed oddly relaxed.

"I see you're pulling double duty, too," I said as I approached the port helm and went to set down my tools. I sat down beside the platform and pulled open the latch on the top of my bag.

"I know where we should be," she answered without looking away from her task. "But we keep getting blown off course. Since I'm the one who plotted that course, I'm the best person to keep us going generally in the right direction."

The ship rolled again, listing hard a-starboard as the windscreen rattled in its frame. I managed to catch the starboard helmsman's platform with the sole of my boot, keeping myself from sliding more than a few inches. Paar held tight to the wheel in her hands, tugging it furiously back to port using all of her body weight. I took a deep breath and scooted back in front of the port platform.

"Let me see about getting you a second pair of hands," I said as I pulled the ratchet out of the tool bag and set to work loosening the port platform panel from its base. It would have been a pain in the tail even if the ship hadn't been jerking in all directions. The panel was probably original to the ship, and although it had gotten a fresh coat of paint in anticipation of *Dawn*'s relaunch, I could tell no one had bothered to do anything about the corrosion underneath. The bolts were stuck fast, but I wasn't about to give up.

Leaving the ratchet perched over the bolt and hoping its snug fit was enough to keep it from flying off as the ship bumped, swayed, and shook, I lay on the deck and braced myself sideways against the starboard helmsman's platform. Trying to ignore the discomfort from the still-growing bruise on my right hip, I placed both my heels against the end of the ratchet, backed my feet off a few inches, and kicked with all my might.

It budged. I was sure it had. But when I sat back up and tried to turn it with my hands, it still felt stuck tight. I did it again. Laying on my side, I threw both heels at the end of the ratchet handle. This time it moved an inch, maybe more. Instead of sitting up, I braced my heels against the ratchet handle and gave it a mighty shove with both feet. My legs were shaking as I pressed against it; my stomach muscles clenched so tight I could barely breathe.

When I thought I couldn't stand another second, I gave it one more concerted burst of energy. If this didn't work, I was going to have to go back to Sgt. Eiji and ask for a cutting torch. And even if there was one to spare, I didn't want to waste the time unless I was absolutely certain there was no other way to get this done.

It gave.

There was a quiet cracking sound as the corrosion broke apart. The bolt came loose, and the ratchet handle spun almost a quarter turn. I scrambled up to sit again and had no problem completing the removal, sliding the bolt into the pocket opposite my Royal Insignia as I turned my attention to the next one.

There were three more of those things, each of them just as stuck in place and corroded as the last. And I didn't have a whole lot of time to coax them into coming undone.

I set to work on the remaining bolts, forcing them to open through whatever means I could, kicking, pulling, scraping, banging, and cussing — and silently wishing, maybe for the first time in my life, that I'd been gifted with the magic endemic in the Feirin Royal line.

I couldn't help but hear my mother's voice in my head as I fought with the bolts on the platform. *Let your sister do it, Maran. Acca has power — you don't. She could handle this easily if you'd just get out of her way.*

But I was the one who was here. My sister couldn't do a damn thing in this situation. If a member of the Royal Family of Feirin was going to save this expedition, it wasn't going to be the Heir Presumptive. I channeled all the rage those intrusive thoughts had dredged up into freeing the final bolt. Even as the ship quaked and eddied, I felt a rare surge of satisfaction as I tucked that last piece of hardware into my pocket and pulled the panel away from the platform.

The inner workings of rudder control were far simpler than I'd imagined. The wheel above turned a gear in the steering column, which turned a rod connected to another gear at the column's base. That gear moved a metal drum which pulled on a pair of cables threaded through pulleys on either side. I could only presume these cables connected somewhere aft of the bridge to the cables from the starboard helm and eventually to the ship's rudder.

I was there to run these cables through the pulleys and attach them to the drum.

Sgt. Eiji hadn't been exaggerating when he told me the job would be obvious. And he was right to presume it would be within my skillset. The cables were the same gauge and variety used for fixed-wing rigging. I'd run meters upon meters of the stuff back at the Air Academy. First year cadets had been historically tasked with the grunt-level maintenance of the aging fleet of trainer biplanes. It had never been my strongest skill, but none of this looked unfamiliar, and that was a plus.

The port and starboard rudder control cables had been clearly labeled — a step for which I was intensely grateful as I set to work threading the port cable through its intended pulley and around its place in the drum. The labels not only saved me time in trying to determine which one to put where, it also reassured me they had been run from the rudder properly. Whether the labels had been affixed as instruction to the cable's installers or as a message to me *from* them, they were helpful, and I was glad to have the guidance.

Getting the port cable threaded was a straightforward enough process, although the continued movement of the ship made it more difficult than I'd have liked. I ran the length of cable around the wheel of the pulley and through the slot in the drum. Still holding the doubled-up end of cable in one hand, I grabbed the saddle from the inner pocket of my tool bag with the other, slipped it on, and hand-tightened it. I grabbed hold of the saddle, sliding it forward until it was snug on the drum before taking out the small ratchet and tightening it down.

I knew I'd gotten it properly attached when the wheel above my head started to move. I looked over at Commander Paar and back at the port steering column. My wheel was moving perfectly in tandem with her wheel. That was good.

Or, rather, it was until it came time to connect the second cable.

The wind was off our port beam, blowing us hard to starboard and requiring Paar to keep the wheel hard to port in order to not be blown even farther off our intended course. I wasn't sure whether we were over enemy land already, but I knew the farther off course we went in that direction, the farther we were from friendly skies. The wheel's being hard over with the port side cable already locked down meant I was having a hell of a time getting the second cable threaded through it.

For a moment I considered undoing the work I'd just done. If I took off the port side cable, I'd be able to connect the starboard side no problem and reconnect the port cable with the drum slack from starboard. But that theory presumed we'd be hard a-port for long enough for it to matter. And Paar was already letting up on the tension a little.

It wasn't worth the time I'd lose undoing the work I'd already done. I tugged on the starboard steering cable and Commander Paar grunted. Damn. I hadn't thought through the fact I was hooking in a complementary system with the primary system already engaged. Every move I made had an effect on her ability to keep the ship right.

"Sorry!" I yelled.

"That was you?" she called back.

"Yeah," I replied. "Yeah. The systems connect

farther down, and I can't get to that juncture to disconnect them from each other while I hook this up."

"Okay," she said.

"It'll only be a minute, though," I assured her, still working on getting the starboard control cable threaded through its place in the drum. "If there's any way you could let up some more on the wheel, that'd be a big help."

"For every degree of heading we lose, that's fuel and time we also lose trying to get where we're going and home again," she said.

I understood. I had no idea what calculations had been made to account for getting blown off course — but Commander Paar did. And if she was concerned, I was concerned. I'd spent enough time in the Air Service to know the best policy was always to trust the person who knew more than you did.

"I'll do my best not to pull against you," I said, finishing a loose loop with the cable. I was barely able to hold it together as I reached out with my far hand to snag the saddle from its place in the bag. "But I have to get this thing attached. Once I do this, you'll have double the steering force. So if you're willing to lose a couple of degrees in service of getting it done, we should be able to make it up."

"Okay," Paar said. "Let me know when you're ready to pull it tight. As soon as there's even a tiny lull, I'll put her back to dead ahead and hold until you tell me it's done. As soon as I say I'm turning, get that cable on!"

"As quick as I can!" I answered her. I slid the saddle over the loop and twisted the bolts on loosely, the same as I'd done on with the port cable. I held it in place as best I could on a trembling ship, clasping the cable with both hands while the small ratchet tool I would need to tighten it down was held in my teeth. It was hard to keep hold. So when Paar shouted,

"Turning! Now!"

I dove face first toward the steering column. With my left hand, I slid the saddle up until it was snug, while with my right, I took the tool out from between my teeth and put it over top of the first of the two tiny bolts. I tightened one, and then the other, and the other again, and so on, until the loop was closed and the saddle as tight as I could make it.

"All yours!" I yelled back to Paar.

"Mine," she affirmed.

Good. That hadn't taken long. Or at least it didn't feel like it had. I watched the mechanism shift back to port as Paar steered the *Dawn* back toward her proper course.

"This tension is me," I warned her as I put my hands on the wheel and turned it slightly to starboard. Paar let up enough to let me see it work before she pulled the wheel back to steer to port. When I pulled the wheel to port, she followed suit, teaming up the two wheels in one and finally showing me how much that mechanical advantage gained us in terms of rudder control.

"Thank you," she said as I gathered the tool bag and prepared to slide the cover back onto the platform.

Just then the ship lurched. It wasn't a buck or a roll like had been happening all along, this was something else altogether. The bridge leapt beneath me, then settled back at a steep upward angle.

"Helm!" Major Malli shouted, not even bothering to call Commander Paar by her name.

"That wasn't me!" Paar shouted back. Her eyes were darting back and forth between the windscreen and the navigational equipment built into the steering column. "I think it was lift," she said.

I could hear a tremor in her voice that hadn't been there before. Whatever was happening, it was bad.

Major Malli scooted to the edge of the Captain's

Chair and slammed his foot down on the lift pedal. The bridge lurched again, and the angle only got more pronounced.

"Somebody find out what's happening!" Malli bellowed, pounding his foot against the lift pedal, which had now stopped responding altogether.

Just then an alarm sounded. It wasn't the klaxon I'd heard earlier. That had sounded like a too-loud morning alarm coming over the ship's intercom. This one sounded more like the scramble sirens used at airfields to tell everyone to get off the ground as quickly as possible.

This sounded like it might mean *Abandon Ship*. And that was an even bigger problem than it ought to have been.

Because we couldn't.

CHAPTER EIGHT

Major Malli sprang from his chair and stumbled downhill to the aft of the bridge.

The sound we were hearing was the ship's General Alarm, which meant things had gotten as serious as they could possibly get. It didn't necessarily mean we needed to abandon ship right away, but it damn sure told everyone to get up and get their boots on.

"Report!" Malli yelled, slamming his palm into the intercom button. "Report!"

The speaker crackled, but nothing came through. The siren was still sounding — piercing and terrible — almost loud enough to drown out the groans and creaks of the metal hull being tugged and battered by the weather and whatever had happened to make us pitch so badly.

"We're losing altitude," Commander Paar said. Her lower lip was trembling, and her volume told me that maybe I wasn't supposed to have heard her.

I got to my feet and took hold of the port steering column, trying to feel what the ship was doing. And there it was. We *were* losing altitude.

"Mechanical!" Major Malli yelled into the still-crackling intercom. "Mechanical, this is the bridge. Report!"

"Malli!" Captain Taiko's voice called from the aft access door. She was in her nightgown. Her hair hung down her back in a loose braid that was badly mussed at the temples, and the laces of her flight boots hung loose on both sides. She was mildly out of breath — likely from the effort of climbing uphill to get here.

"Captain," Malli replied, his tone somewhere between disbelief and frustration.

"Status report," she ordered, making her way from the door to where Malli was standing.

"We're losing altitude!" Paar was the one to answer, this time repeating her earlier assertion loudly enough for all to hear.

Captain Taiko moved into the space in front of the intercom, forcing Malli to step aside in a power move I had to admit I would have enjoyed watching had it not happened in the middle of a genuine emergency. She pressed the call button on the intercom with gentle but firm intention.

"Mechanical, this is the Captain," she said. "Sgt. Eiji, come in." Her voice projected, but it was only her volume that was out of the ordinary. Her cool, calm, determined essence seemed wholly unaffected by the ongoing crisis.

Every interaction I'd had with her had called into question my theory of this mission having been designed for failure. You wouldn't send someone this capable on a deliberate suicide mission — at least I wouldn't.

"Captain!" I didn't recognize the voice that answered her, but I did see the look on Major Malli's face when the answer came. "This is Corporal Preeti in mechanical. Sergeant Eiji is unavailable. Ma'am," there was an audible gulp from Preeti, and I braced myself for what they were about to say. "The aft bag is losing gas," they said. "There's been a breach in the cocoon and the aft most bag is somehow compromised. We're already rerouting gas pressure to the other three bags in hopes of staying aloft. Sergeant Eiji and Private Phamm have gone up to see what they can do about the cocoon."

"Do you know what any of those words mean?" I asked Commander Paar as I bent down to try and wrestle the steering platform back into its place.

"When you look at *Dawn*'s lift bags," she answered, "you would think what you're seeing is one large chamber. But what you're actually seeing is the protective shell over four separate silk gas bladders. The silks themselves are treated with a compound to keep the gases from leaking through the fibers, but they're still very fragile. The cocoon is there to protect the silks from sun damage and to keep them in line in their proper positions so the ship lifts and lowers evenly bow-to-stern."

"And the cocoon is broken?" I said, reiterating what I thought I'd heard via the intercom.

"That's not the problem," Paar replied, turning the wheel in her hand hard to port.

I stood up and grabbed the second wheel, pulling it in turn.

"Thanks," she said.

"No problem," I replied. "You want me here?"

"Yes," she answered. "Whether or not we're going to

be able to stay aloft, steering is about to get harder."

"Whether or not?" I asked. I decided not to bother with the platform cover. I stood on the platform's frame ledges, balancing as best I could with both hands on the port steering wheel, and tried to make sense of what Commander Paar was saying.

"The cocoon is helpful," she said, "but it's not strictly necessary." She looked down at her compass and moved her hands in preparation to steer the ship farther to port. "We can go as long as we need to with damage to the cocoon — it's risky to fly without one; all the silks are vulnerable if they're exposed, but we can fly. But if that aft bag is losing gas and can't be repaired ...." For the first time since I'd come onto the bridge, Commander Paar turned her head away from her task and looked me in the eye. "We can't fly with only three bags in the air," she said then. "If they can't stop the leak or put in a replacement, the ship is going down."

It took a second for that to sink in.

"You're sure?"

"She can't stay aloft with only three bags," Paar replied, her attention back on the compass in front of her. "Most airships carry a spare — sometimes just a half-size — just enough to keep the ship in the air until it can reach a safe port. Maybe we have one aboard, but maybe not. And even if we do, and even if it's the kind that's designed to be deployed while underway, I can't imagine Sergeant Eiji being able to get a new bag installed and filled in this weather."

"So you think we're gonna crash?" I asked. I hadn't meant to put I so bluntly, but I lacked the capacity for tact at the moment, as I was trying very hard not to panic.

"No," Paar answered. She shook her head and pursed her lips. "Maybe," she corrected. "Your ship!" she said, letting go of the starboard wheel and darting off the platform to look at the map installed in the backlit table on the floor in front of the Captain's Chair.

My whole body tensed up. I had not intended to be given the helm of the ship. I'd never trained in airship operation and other than the five minutes education I'd gotten reconnecting the port helm control just now, I had absolutely no idea how it worked.

"My ship," I answered. I was terrified, but not so much as to leave Commander Paar wondering if she'd properly handed off helm control.

"Ease off," she said.

"Aye," I said back. I did what she said, silently relieved that she wasn't counting on me to figure out *where* to steer the ship at the same time I was trying to learn *how* to steer the ship. I had no idea where we were nor where we were headed.

"If the three bags stay inflated," she explained, moving around behind me. Her breath was almost heaving; I had to guess she was having a hell of a time keeping herself upright on the listing and quavering ship. "We'll be mostly able to control our descent. But with breakage in the cocoon, there's a chance the other silks could take damage, and if that happens, we go down hard."

"So what do we do?" I asked.

"We change course." It was Captain Taiko's voice that answered me. I turned my head long enough to see she'd come forward from the intercom station and was standing just behind the Captain's Chair, holding onto it for stability.

"Yes ma'am," Commander Paar answered her. "We're already so far off course that if we change our heading just here–"I could only guess she was pointing out features of the map to Captain Taiko. I could barely even hear them over the still-sounding siren of the

General Alarm. Part of me wanted to turn around and be part of the conversation.

But I had to steer the ship.

"How old is the information on this map?" the Captain asked. "How sure can we be of its accuracy?"

"Honestly, ma'am," Paar replied, "I don't know. I know it's the latest we have, but it may be as old as wartime."

"We got new maps at the end of the war!" I called out. Then I caught myself.

I probably shouldn't have said that.

Those maps were technically a State secret. I only knew they existed because my sister knew — and she'd always done her best to pass Royal knowledge on to me. My mother may have found me a thoroughly useless disappointment of a princess, but my sister had never let that color our relationship. Everything Royal my mother had kept from me, my sister had been sure to share. She'd long said when her time to reign came, she planned to appoint me an official advisor.

But that was before I'd possibly revealed the existence of something I wasn't even supposed to know about. Maybe Acca would do well to stop letting me in on Royal secrets.

But this was neither the time nor the place nor the situation for me to care that I might have just outed myself as a Royal to the other people on this bridge. And in this moment, I honestly didn't give a fuss that I may have spilled classified information. If what I knew might help, it was probably worth whatever price I'd pay when this whole thing was over.

I decided to keep talking and hope whatever came out of my mouth was believable as the kind of thing an officer of the Diplomatic Corps would know.

"It was part of the peace accord," I went on. "In order to enforce the cease fire, the Xy Federation was required to allow Feirin cartographers full access to their territory to perform a complete cartological survey. It took eight years," I recalled. "But the Alliance got all new maps."

"That would still mean our information is more than twenty years old," Captain Taiko said.

"I can work with that," Commander Paar responded. "Maybe the cities are larger, or the tree lines have changed," she said. "But a course toward a city, or away from one, won't have changed in twenty years. And a mountain range never moves."

"Right," the Captain agreed.

"I'm looking at this area here," Paar said. Once again, I was sure she was pointing at something on the map I didn't dare turn around to see. "It's leeward by a good bit, so the fuel cost won't be too high. Everything I know about the region is that it's remote and uninhabited. If we have to put down, this is going to be our best bet."

"You think it's safe to set down over here?" Captain Taiko's voice asked.

"Safety is relative, Captain," Paar replied. "This course seems the safest we can reasonably hope to take."

"You're not concerned about flying low so close to the mountains?"

"I'm not," Paar replied. "They'll be windward," she explained, "so the danger is minimal. And if we get the aft bag reinflated, or if we get really lucky and stay aloft anyway, we'll tack back to port, cross the mountains with as much altitude as we can manage, and be over friendlier territory."

"Across the mountains is Xyland," the Captain presumed.

"Yes ma'am."

"Then that's the decision," Captain Taiko said. "We

make for those valleys. For the time being that's all we can do."

Commander Paar spent the next few minutes running back and forth between the compass on the starboard steering column and the map table, with a facility I wouldn't have imagined possible on a pitching and kicking deck that was listing more and more aft as the time went on. I did my best to hold the ship steady on the course she'd given me and to make adjustments when either she or Captain Taiko said to.

After a while, Commander Paar came to stand in front of me. Bracing herself against the steering column, she looked up at me and shook her head.

"Is there any place else you're supposed to be right now?" she asked. "Or can you stay?"

"I'm good," I answered. In truth, I *wasn't* good — far from it. But I didn't have anywhere else to be. "Ambassador Berholtz hasn't given me any assignments and I can't imagine Sergeant Eiji having anything more important for me to do than keeping the ship on course."

"Good," Paar said. Using the two steering columns for balance, she climbed back up on the starboard platform. There were tiny papers in her left hand; she grabbed hold of the wheel with her right. "Just do what I say," she said. "All right?"

"Yes, ma'am," I replied, the answer that had been ingrained into me at the Air Academy somehow being the only thing I could manage to say.

"Now," Paar said, taking one more look at the papers in her hand before shoving them into her tunic pocket. "She's going to fight us," she explained. "And not like she's fighting us now. Right now, we've got the wind coming at us from the port forward quarter. We try to steer to port, into that wind, and the helm pushes back. Well, now we are about to make a turn to starboard. We'll have the wind straight abeam or slightly abaft, and she's going to want to turn farther than we ought to let her. And I think it's going to take both of us to keep her on course."

"All right," I said. I could do that. I was sure I could. If all Commander Paar needed from me was to have me as a second pair of hands to help ensure the rudder stayed where she wanted it to, I had no problem agreeing to do the job.

"Keep tension on the helm," Paar said as she began pulling the starboard wheel back to center. The General Alarm was still sounding, and Paar was facing forward; it was hard to hear her over the siren's wail and the rattling of the metal ship.

But I heard her well enough. And I did as I was asked. I held the wheel tightly, serving as a counterweight while Paar carefully took us off the port tack and headed us on our new course. I tried not to think too hard about the fuel we'd already spent fighting the storm, or the fact there was every chance we were going to have to make an unscheduled landing. I especially didn't want to think about what a landing — unscheduled or otherwise — was going to do to the stabilizer I'd worked for days to get cleaned up and welded into place.

And that was all without even considering there was a very good chance an emergency landing could very well put us on the ground in Xylanth. Grounding a ship like *Dawn* was a scary enough prospect under any circumstances, but putting her down in secret on enemy land in the midst of a gusting maelstrom was downright terrifying.

It was all I could do to stop myself from trying to picture whatever might be going on up in the lift cocoon. I'd once seen a master mechanic change out a broken tire on an open-cockpit fixed wing while in flight. That had been an incredible, albeit thoroughly frightening, thing to witness. And it gave me enough of a mental framework for what midair repairs looked like that I had all sorts of distracting mental pictures fighting their way to the surface.

"Good," Paar called out. "Good."

The ship lurched again, increasing our listing angle enough that I had to hold tight to the steering wheel in order not to fall backward off the platform. Captain Taiko let out a cry, but I dared not turn around to see whether she was okay.

I was pretty sure she wasn't.

I'd only thought I could feel it earlier when Commander Paar had said we were losing altitude; now it was unmistakable. We were descending steadily, at a pace that felt like being aboard a gear lift with a too-small counterweight. We weren't hurtling toward the ground, but we weren't going to be aloft for much longer, either. I could only hope Paar's assertion that we should be able to control our descent would prove true.

We'd be finding out soon enough.

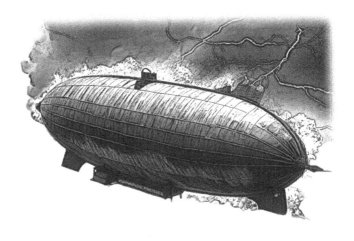

CHAPTER NINE

"I'm going to need all the speed you can give us," Captain Taiko shouted into the intercom. "And then I'm going to need a hard reverse on my mark."

"Captain," Corporal Preeti's voice came back.

Improvements had been made to the intercom since the Captain's last call. The static was gone; the Corporal's voice was coming through clearly — with no skips or crackles — and loud enough for me to hear and understand.

"I'm not sure the engine can take that," Preeti said. "And Sergeant Eiji isn't here to ...."

"Never mind what you think the engine can take," Captain Taiko interrupted her. That was the harshest I'd ever heard her speak. "We're going down, Corporal. If we can't control our approach," she said, "if we can't control where we touch down, it won't matter what the engine can do."

"Right," Preeti replied. "Yes ma'am."

"And be prepared to bleed gas from the forward bag," the Captain added.

"Yes ma'am," Preeti answered again.

"On my order."

"Yes ma'am."

I swallowed hard. I understood, in theory, that bleeding gas from the forward-most bag would drop the bow, level off the ship, and allow us to once again see something other than the sky above through the windscreen. But the idea of letting gas out of a perfectly good gas bag when we were already losing altitude due to another bag's failure was a hard concept to wrap my mind around.

We were going down, that much was certain. Captain Taiko had gone as far as to say so out loud. All she could do now was to give us the best chance of being able to take off again.

Another alarm sounded, a shrill and frightening wail that cut through the other klaxons and rattles and attendant noises so thoroughly it managed to startle me.

"What's that?" I asked, hoping someone would be willing to give me an answer, and hoping double that answer would be somewhat less terrifying than all the theories swimming in my head.

"Proximity alarm!" Paar shouted the answer.

Nope. No less terrifying.

"It's time, Captain," Paar declared.

"You're sure?"

"We're flying so low," Commander Paar said, her voice as shaky as I'd ever heard anyone's. "And we're so near the mountains. We're already close enough to something that the alarm is sounding. I don't think we can wait any longer; I need a visual. I need to see where we're going."

"Just tell me you're sure, Commander Paar," Captain Taiko implored. "With only two bags inflated, we'll more than double our rate of descent. Tell me you're sure we're close enough to a safe landing field."

"As best I can tell, ma'am," Paar answered. "But that's just based on the calculations I've been able to make. And I ... I can't know for sure. But what I do know for sure is that the lower we fly, and the closer we get to the mountains, the more dangerous it is that I can't see what's in front of us. I need to see!"

"All right," the Captain replied. "Major Malli, give the order. Bleed the forward bag."

"Aye, Captain." Major Malli, who'd been thankfully silent since the Captain had shown up on the bridge, pressed the switch to call back to the Mechanical Deck. "Initiate gas release from the forward bag."

"Aye, sir," a voice called back. I didn't recognize who had replaced Corporal Preeti on the comm. I wondered where they had gone. And I wondered what Sergeant Eiji was up to, and if he and Private Phamm were still up in the cocoon.

"How fast are we going to fall?" I asked Paar, bracing myself as best I could and wishing, not for the first time, that I'd taken the extra five minutes to put the cover back on the steering platform when I'd had the chance. Standing on the 2-inch lip hadn't felt like too much of a challenge when I'd first agreed to it. It was an emergency, and we didn't have the time to spare to put things back together. But more than two hours into this exercise I was regretting not asking for the chance. My feet were aching, my knees were wobbling, and I was sure I would be waking up tomorrow with soreness in muscles I didn't even know I had.

"I have no idea," Paar admitted. She was braced,

too, holding tight to the wheel in front of her as she turned her gaze toward the growing crack in the windscreen.

It didn't take us long to find out.

The ship pitched forward, then back, then forward and back again as the buffeting wind blew across the falling edifice. I braced my feet against the insides of the platform edges and gripped the wheel at its spokes to keep from falling. Eventually we settled. We weren't *still* by any means — the ship still pitched and bucked and shuddered from the force of the storm outside, but the deck was closer to flat now, with only a few degrees of incline from front to back.

Major Malli had instructed the mechanical team to only bleed the bag by two-thirds. If that hadn't been enough to allow for a reasonable degree of visibility, the Captain could have ordered more. The idea had been to lose as little lift gas as possible while leveling the ship enough to give Commander Paar a view the terrain below.

It was one thing to fly by instruments and calculations two thousand feet up and over the open ocean, but it was another thing altogether to try and do so over land, with a mountain range only a few miles windward, and while rapidly losing altitude.

"Hard to starboard!" Paar yelled.

I did as I was told, although I had no idea why she'd given the order. Visibility was terrible, and I couldn't make out much beyond the edge of the cloud we were flying through.

Paar turned her wheel with authority and with speed. She'd warned me when we'd first made the turn eastward that the rudder would want to go over farther starboard than we wanted it to. And now she was practically throwing the wheel in that same direction. My wheel slipped through my hands, its leather wrapping rubbing contact burns on my palm as it spun faster than I was able to keep up with.

I wanted to ask what the hell was going on, but that was an inclination my time in the Air Academy had mostly worn out of me. The last thing Commander Paar or Captain Taiko needed was to have me distracting them with my questions.

It wasn't long before I understood why we were turning. As the ship flew lower and lower, we cleared the cloud, and there it was. Or, rather, there *they* were: the mountains known locally as The Four Seasons — four near-identical peaks in a diamond formation, each with one face angled perfectly toward one of the four cardinal directions. They rose from the center of the mountain range separating Xyland from Xylanth and were far bigger than any mountains I had ever seen before.

And they were almost dead ahead of us.

"What the hell?" I whispered. I was having a very hard time believing my eyes.

This ... couldn't be right. How were we this far inland already? And how, after all the calculations Commander Paar had made, could we be this close to crashing headlong into the continent's biggest natural phenomena?

"It's not an exact science," Commander Paar said. I hadn't meant for her to hear me, or to try to explain. "Our knot meter isn't reliable in this kind of weather, and with the wind abaft, it's increased our speed over ground and ..."

"I don't care about the wind or the science!" Major Malli's voice boomed from the rear of the bridge. "I care only that we do not crash into a mountain."

Major Malli was a self-important ass, but he had a point.

"We need to vent gas now," Captain Taiko said. Her

voice was loud and commanding, but somehow still calm and under control. "I'd rather come down hard and take down a few trees than risk staying aloft and getting blown into those mountains. No offense, Commander Paar."

"None taken!" Paar said. "The wind is more powerful than our engine right now, and I, too, would prefer to avoid being blown into a mountainside."

"Tell the Mechanical Deck to vent gases," Captain Taiko ordered.

"Aye," Malli replied, working the switch to the intercom.

"And reverse the engines!" Paar yelled back to him. "We've turned so far that the wind is right behind us. Gusts off the storm have been pushing us eastward, but there's no telling what effect the mountains are going to have on the wind. We just need to be ready to slow down."

I did my best to remember everything I'd been taught about wind and weather when I was learning how to fly. I knew the winds at altitude were faster, but more consistent, and that the friction of air against the features on the ground meant that even though the air moved more slowly lower down, its unpredictability could mean it was far more dangerous.

And at altitude, there was rarely anything you could crash into.

"The sooner we can put down, the better state we'll be in to try and get back up later," Captain Taiko said.

Major Malli gave the orders to the Mechanical Deck.

The ship shuddered and the lights cut out.

"Keep her hard over," Commander Paar said, her voice suddenly calm and sure, as though nothing out of the ordinary was going on. "Just another moment. Get ready to bring the rudder to straight ahead."

I nodded, although I was pretty sure she wasn't looking. The bridge was eerily dark, with only the dim light of the overcast twilight coming through the windscreen to see by.

"Okaaaaaay," Paar started, with the cadence of a flight leader walking a demo squadron through a dry run, "turn!" she shouted. "Turn turn turn turn, hold!"

I realized as we turned the wheels in tandem that the rumble of the engine was missing. We were coasting. And that meant we'd likely lose steerage any minute now. Add to that we were on the lee side of four enormous mountains and the possibility of getting caught in a downdraft was growing with every moment. But something about the familiar and authoritative way Commander Paar was handling the moment gave me confidence in our ability to set the ship down.

We were losing altitude fast; I couldn't imagine this was a speed at which gas was vented when it wasn't an emergency. We were dropping at such a rate I could feel my stomach the same as I had the first time I'd experienced an intentional dive in a fixed-wing.

I wanted to ask why the engine had quit, but I suspected no one within earshot knew any better than I did.

Just then the ship jerked to starboard, the ground-level winds grabbing the lift cocoon and tossing it sideways, taking the whole ship over onto its side.

"Steer to port!" Commander Paar called out, but I was already doing it. I didn't know much about helming an airship, but I knew we'd just been blown into treetops. The clearing we'd been aiming for was now well to our port side, and although I wasn't having much trouble turning the wheel back toward it, the ship gave no indication of having been steered at all.

The ship jumped skyward, lifted on a gale at a speed that made my feet feel heavy and the flesh of my cheeks pull downward on my lower eyelids. She spun wildly in the wind — fully onto her side again and around — in a motion I could only imagine was like a child swinging a bucket overhead while trying to keep its contents from spilling. We were whirled around nearly a full rotation, ripping down trees with the hull then coming about, head-on to the mountains.

A downdraft caught us full force, hurling us toward the ground, fully out of control and at a speed that took my feet out from under me. Even if we could have reinflated the gas bags right away, we didn't have enough altitude to weather this and recover.

The ship was going to crash. Imminently.

"Brace! Brace! Brace!" Captain Taiko shouted.

"Brace for Impact!" Major Malli hollered into the intercom.

I closed my eyes and did as I was told.

CHAPTER TEN

I came to in a world of smoke and chaos.

People were screaming, I could hear them loud and clear, but there was no one in my line of sight. The lights were out, save one amber-hued emergency beacon flashing above my head. At first, I thought the orange flicker was the glowing of a flame, but I was able to identify the light bulb in time to quell my panic. The bridge wasn't on fire, but from the volume of smoke in the air around me, I was sure something was.

The ship had crashed, things were on fire, I'd been knocked out, and I had no idea for how long.

Everything hurt. Trying to move made everything hurt more. But I had to get out of there. I was in a wrecked ship with a diesel engine, a half-full fuel tank, and a fire somewhere onboard. I forced myself to sit up, fighting back the wave of nausea that hit me as I did.

As best I could tell, I'd hit my head on the starboard steering platform. I had a knot on the back of my head that hurt like hell; I reached around to check for bleeding but found none. That was good news.

As I looked up to try and get my bearings, I spotted Captain Taiko slumped over in the Captain's chair. I got to my feet as fast as I could and crossed toward her.

"Captain!" I called. The act of making my voice sound made me nauseated again, but I managed not to heave. I reached the Captain's side and put my hand on her shoulder. "Captain!" I cried, louder this time as I shook her gently. She wasn't responding. I picked up her hand to check her pulse at her wrist then remembered I didn't know how to do that. Her hand was warm; she was alive as best I could tell.

I bent down to try and pick her up, but quickly realized I wouldn't likely be able to lift her, much less carry her to safety. And I didn't even know where safety *was*. The best thing I could do for the Captain was to go and find help.

I thought for a moment about escape hatches and life kites and all the things a person might make use of to leave an airship in an emergency. And I didn't know where a single damn one of them was on this bucket. A safety briefing hadn't been on my agenda, and now I was regretting it heartily.

If I manage to live through this, I thought to myself as I began to strategize, I'm never traveling aboard another ship of any kind until I know where all the exits are.

The bridge only had the one door, which meant I had only one way out. But that's where the smoke was coming from. Whatever was on fire, it was out there, and I didn't love the idea of trying to find some nebulous exit someplace beyond while breathing in noxious gases.

There had to be another way out.

Right?

It only made sense the command crew of an airship would have a way out in an emergency. Surely there was a hatch hidden somewhere. A minute or so of searching the ceiling and forward bulkhead revealed no sign of an exit. I was frustrated, confused, and beginning to come to terms with the fact I was going to have to take my chances with the smoke-filled corridor beyond.

This was a Mangan ship — a Mangan *war*ship at that. Of course the bridge wouldn't have an escape hatch. A Mangan command crew under battle conditions would absolutely be expected to go down with the ship. If they couldn't get out any regular way, they wouldn't get out at all. They would willingly and stubbornly die at their posts.

Well, I wasn't a Mangan, and this wasn't wartime, and I had no intention of dying on the bridge of a derelict airship I never wanted to be aboard in the first place.

Some of the smoke coming in from the hallway was escaping through a hole in the windscreen. The opening didn't look large enough for a person to fit through, but it still might be a way out. Directly through that pane of busted glass was the outside. I just needed to bust it up a little more.

I looked around for the tool bag I'd brought with me to the bridge. The big ratchet handle could possibly help me break a large enough hole to crawl through. The bag was nowhere I could find, but while I was looking, I came across the loose plate from the port steering platform. It was a big, solid, heavy piece of steel.

This thing could definitely break glass.

Picking it up wasn't easy, but I got it into my grip and carried it to just in front of the windscreen before setting it down and considering my plan of attack. If I could swing it hard enough to hit the already-shattered glass right alongside the existing hole, it should only take a few blows to knock enough glass away to allow me to get out. I turned my head and took one more look at Captain Taiko, still slumped over in her chair, before picking up the heavy plate and taking a swing.

I hurled the plate toward the windscreen with all my might. Just as it was about to make contact, it slipped from my hands and flew into the glass, breaking off a generous chunk before continuing out through the hole and onto the hull of the ship outside.

"Fuss!" I yelled. For a moment I felt self-conscious, but then I had to laugh at myself. Who the hell was even here to hear me using that kind of language? And even if someone did overhear, I had to imagine that being trapped in a smoking shipwreck probably qualified as justification for using a swear word or two.

The closer I looked at where the panel had smashed through, the less I felt like swearing. The steel plate had hit the glass broadside and left a two-foot hole a few inches from the larger hole sustained in the crash. And both of those were along the axis of the crack that had been there since I'd arrived on the bridge. The glass between them had to be weakened. It was worth a try to break it on my own.

I stepped forward and reached my leg out slowly to gauge the distance, doing everything I could to remember the little martial arts training I'd had at the Air Academy. The dancing lessons I'd had as a child also came in handy as I plotted how to kick a tiny section of glass just above my hip height. I was dizzy, my hip was sore from when I'd hit the deck on my way into the bridge, and my head was splitting. Keeping my balance was proving to be more of a challenge than anything else.

But I was determined.

Concentrating on the space between the two holes, I took a deep breath and kicked as hard as I could.

I could see I'd done some damage; the glass was breaking. The cracks had combined into a spiderweb, and the spot was beginning to deform around the middle. I paused for a moment, caught my breath again and repeated the action. The glass cracked and distended, but it stood its ground.

Once more.

Then again.

The fourth time was the charm. The glass gave out adjacent to the lower hole, leaving a strip between the two openings that I was able to force out with my toe. I pulled my sleeve down over my right hand and tried to peel away the next section, banging at the loosening shards with the butt of my hand until I was sure I could pull them free.

It was slow going, but it worked. By the time I had opened the two holes up into one hole large enough I could duck through it, the bridge was almost completely filled with smoke. When I turned my head, I could barely see Captain Taiko in her chair.

I had to hurry. The chances of me getting to someone who could get the Captain out in time were getting slimmer and slimmer by the moment. The opening was snug, but I squeezed my way through it. The wind was still blowing outside, but the sky was oddly bright. I emerged from the bridge easily thirty feet above ground level; I didn't want to think about what that meant in terms of how many decks on the underside had been smashed flat in the crash.

The wind made the climb down rough, as did the

pain in my head, hip, and elbow. But the number of uneven hull plates and popped rivets made it easier to find a footing or a handhold than I expected. It was a harrowing experience, and I doubt I ever felt happier to have my feet on the ground than I did as I hopped the last yard and a half or so into the underbrush.

I followed the sound of voices just beyond the tree line and was relieved to see so many people gathered. Maybe as much as a third of the ship's complement stood together beneath the remains of the lift bag cocoon as it hung in the forest canopy. Turning back toward the ship, I could see how they'd managed to escape: a series of chain-link ladders and climbing nets extended from open hatches at several places along the hull.

I couldn't help myself but to look for Raline. I searched the faces of the assembled crowd, and it only took me a moment to realize she wasn't among them. My eyes were stinging with tears when I finally recognized a familiar face among the crowd.

"Ensign Declan!" I called.

"Lieutenant Merteuil!" he exclaimed. Yvan Declan lurched forward and took me by my upper arms, but before he had the chance to fully embrace me, I turned and pointed to the column of smoke coming from the hole I'd escaped through.

"Captain Taiko is still on the bridge," I told him. "She's alive but unconscious. I couldn't get her out on my own." My voice caught in my throat. I was talking about the Captain, but I was thinking about Raline. Was she still alive? Was she trapped somewhere in the wreckage? Was she someplace accessible but unconscious, the same as Captain Taiko?

"We have to go back and get her," Declan declared.

I nodded, glad I wasn't alone in that thinking. Several others had gathered around us at the mention of the Captain's name.

"I'll go," a young Mangan wearing pajamas and jump boots volunteered almost before Declan had finished his thought.

"Me too," said the T'wesh corporal whose hand the Mangan boy was holding.

"No!" Major Malli's voice boomed, echoing off the metal of our makeshift roof. "You will do no such thing."

"Didn't you hear me?" I asked him. "The Captain is in there!"

"And she can't be the only one," the T'wesh corporal said. "We ought to go back for all of them."

Yes. Yes!

"No," Malli said again, this time with no follow-up.

"You can't be serious," I said, becoming aware in that moment that I was the only person present who dared challenge his authority.

"I am in command of this detachment, Lieutenant," he barked. "And I will not allow any member of this crew to step one foot back aboard the ship. Do you understand?"

That hit like a punch in the gut. I understood him completely. Major Malli had always had an air about him that said he felt as though he, and not Captain Taiko, ought to have been in command of the vessel and the voyage. As of right now the Captain was lost in the shipwreck and he wasn't about to let anybody try and change that.

And there was absolutely no way I was going to let him get away with it.

I'd been around men like Malli all my life. He was the kind of bully that proliferated in politics and tended to shove their way into Royal circles.

There was nothing I hated worse than a bully.

I was about to take this one down a notch.

I reached into my breast pocket, but paused when my fingers found its contents. This wasn't the time to out myself as Royalty. And to be honest, I had no interest in taking command of this expedition. All I was after was a modicum of authority. I fished around in my pocket until my fingers found the proper insignia. I was looking our XO in the eye as I withdrew the pins and fastened them to my collar.

Sergeant Major — the same rank Malli held. That ought to be enough.

"You are not in command of this detachment, Major," I said, emphasizing the rank that now we both wore. "Captain Taiko is. And until we have made every effort to free her from the wreckage, I will not accept your usurpation of her authority." To the rest of the assembled crew, I said: "No one has ever been taken to Court Martial for attempting to save a crewmate's life." I wasn't entirely sure I was telling the truth about that, but it sounded good enough — and I knew I had even more power than I was admitting to. If they got into trouble in the long run, I could almost surely get them out of it. "Still, this isn't an order," I said. "This is a request. There are survivors aboard *Dawn*: Captain Taiko likely among them. And I'm asking — please — if those of you who are able bodied could please return to the ship and help bring them out of there."

"Sergeant Major?" Declan asked, addressing me by my new rank with an irrepressible smile as he did.

"Yes, Ensign?"

"I don't mean to be morbid or anything," he said. "But ... but what do we do when we find folks who ... um ... who *aren't* survivors?"

My stomach seized. That wasn't a question I was prepared to answer. I thought of Raline again. What if she hadn't survived? What would she want in that case? What would I want if it was me who hadn't made it?

I shook my head and squeezed my eyes shut for a moment. There were so many different death and funerary rites to be respected. The crew came from four separate and very distinct cultural backgrounds, only one of which I could say I fully understood. How the hells to even wrap my mind around this ...?

There was only one right answer.

"I want to tell you so many things," I replied, letting my emotion in this moment make its way into my voice. "But the answer is nothing at all. Not right now. We don't know how bad the smoke is or how far the fire has spread. We can't take time for the deceased — we have to concentrate on finding the survivors. Maybe tomorrow, or whenever the fire burns out, provided the damn thing doesn't blow the hell up, maybe then we can see about tending to the dead. But for right now, we've just got to do what we can for the living."

"Aye, ma'am," Declan said. Then, "Come on!" to the two boys who'd already volunteered. "Let's go."

The three of them took off at a flat run, followed by at least a dozen others. They shouted back and forth to each other — agreeing on which ladder each would take and in which direction they were intending to head. If any of them could hear Major Malli's protestations or his repeated insistence that they stop, none of them acted like it.

"What is this?!?" Malli snarled in my direction, turning to me once he was fully certain none of the volunteers was going to turn back at his orders. He looked up and down at my newly donned rank insignia as he fumed, nearly quaking with anger. "This is mutiny!" he bellowed.

I looked him square in the eye as I answered. "Not if I can help it, it's not."

He stormed off without saying another word. I was sure the fight wasn't over between us, but I'd won this round and hopefully saved a few lives in the process.

I looked back at the veritable throng of young men climbing nets and chains to get back aboard our burning ship. I wanted to go with them. But I knew I wouldn't be much help. My whole body ached, and my head was still swimming. I didn't know the layout of the ship nearly as well as they did, and I'd already proven to myself I couldn't lift an unconscious person, even someone as slight as Captain Taiko. It was better for everyone that I stay behind.

It felt like hours before the first of the rescuers returned. By the time there was a steady trickle of survivors being helped down escape ladders the sun had almost fully set, and the night air was getting a nip to it. By my count, the dozen or more people had come back with nine additional survivors; a few of them would need medical attention, but many had just been trapped behind bulkheads or lost in the labyrinth of distorted corridors. Sadly, Captain Taiko was not among them. I don't know if she'd been dead already when I left her or whether she'd passed on in the time it took me to get out and get help.

Commander Paar, Ambassador Berholtz, Sergeant Eiji, Private Phamm, and the others from the Mechanical Deck were also unaccounted for. I was beginning to lose hope of seeing any of my few acquaintances again when I spotted Major Gowon moving through the crowd toward me. I smiled and waved, my relief at seeing him clear across my face.

He was grinning as he saluted me, pointing with his other hand at his own rank bars with one eyebrow raised. It hadn't occurred to me to consider how he might react to my abrupt and unexpected elevation in rank. He shook his head, laughed a little, and turned to head in Major Malli's direction.

I gave the two of them a minute before I joined

them. The sun was almost down, we were shipwrecked in enemy territory, and most of our fellow survivors had no idea where we were or what we were up against. The three of us were wearing equivalent rank now, and as far as I was concerned, Gowon was the person in command. He was the lead Intelligence officer on the mission, and he'd been the one to express the sentiment that Captain Taiko was in charge of things for as long as we were flying aboard the *Dawn*. Since we were neither flying, nor aboard the *Dawn*, it seemed only appropriate that he be the arbiter of the information I wanted to share.

"Major Gowon," I said, hoping I wasn't interrupting anything too critical. "I think we need to tell them."

"Tell them what?" Malli snapped. "That you are a usurper and trying to undermine my authority in this crisis situation?"

I frowned at him, rolled my eyes, then addressed my answer to his question toward Major Gowon.

"I think they should know where we came down."

"Do you know where we came down?" he asked, "Because I honestly have no idea."

"Oh." I hadn't thought of that. I took a moment to look back at the ship, still smoking as a slow but steady stream of survivors were being helped to the ground. Where even to begin? "I do," I replied. "We ...." My breath caught in my throat; I almost couldn't believe my eyes. "Excuse me." I said. My conversation was going to have to wait. Without hesitation, I pushed past major Gowon and stumbled across the clearing.

I was waiting at the bottom the ladder when Raline stepped off of it.

There were tears in my eyes and I didn't even care.

"Hi," I managed to whimper.

"Hello," she said with a smile that made my already-weak knees nearly give way altogether. She had a cut on her eyebrow and the left arm of her flight suit was badly singed, but she was alive and smiling and standing in front of me and I was sure I hadn't seen anything more beautiful in the whole of my life.

I had never wanted to grab someone and hold them tight so badly.

"You're hurt," was all I could come up with to say.

"A little," she replied. "Are you okay?"

"Yeah. I hit my head, but ..."

"Major Merteuil!" Major Gowon was calling to me. Whether he'd been saying my name this whole time or if this was the first time he'd shouted, I honestly had no idea. I turned my head in time to see him coming up behind me with Major Malli in tow.

"Major?" Raline asked.

"Long story," I said. "Tell you later?"

"Promise?"

I nodded.

"Yeah," I said. "Get your arm looked at. I'm gonna ...."

"Okay."

I thought for a moment she was going to kiss me. I would have liked that. Instead, she smiled again before turning to head toward the makeshift medical station that had been set up against a downed tree alongside the wreck. I only had a moment before Gowon and Malli caught up to me to hope she'd realized my telling her to get her arm seen to was a suggestion born of personal concern and not an order from a superior officer. I turned around to face them as they closed the last few feet.

"Sorry," I said. I wasn't. But they didn't need to know that. "She was working for Berholtz," I said, somehow able to come up with relevant information to cover for the real reason I'd abandoned the mission's commanders mid-sentence and taken off across the clearing to meet Raline at the foot of the escape ladder.

"I understand," Major Gowon said. He probably did. He'd seen me make a fool of myself in front of Raline in the mess. "But you were about to tell me something I think I need to know."

"Right," I said. I had left in the middle of a critical situation, hadn't I? And now that the shock and relief of seeing Raline and knowing she was all right had passed I was ready to convince Gowon and Malli we should tell the crew where we were standing. "I was on the bridge, when we crashed," I told him. "Sergeant Eiji sent me to help repair the steering. I was at the helm with Commander Paar when …."

My voice caught in my throat at the mention of Commander Paar. She'd been so pretty, so smart, and so capable. And she was Raline's cousin. I wasn't looking forward to breaking the news to Raline of how she'd died. The wind had all but stopped by this point, and it wasn't lost on me how close she'd come to getting the *Dawn* out of dangerous weather and into calm skies. If it hadn't been for the break in the cocoon, she'd have done it; that part I wouldn't mind telling.

I swallowed hard and looked Commander Gowon in the eye.

"We're in Xylanth," I said softly. "These mountains are the border to Xyland. We're maybe six, could be as many as eight miles inland. We're probably a good day's travel from the nearest major city, and obviously the woods are a helpful barrier against anyone reaching our position. But we are in Xylanth," I emphasized. "And there's every chance they know we're here. I think it's only fair that we all know we're here, too."

"You make a good point, Major Merteuil," Gowon replied, an air of bemusement seeping into his voice as he spoke my elevated rank. "And I agree. You want to do it, or should I?"

"I'll do it," I said. Turning to the rest of the survivors where they milled about beneath our makeshift canopy, I called out, "Everyone! Gather 'round please. There are some things you need to know."

CHAPTER ELEVEN

The crew took the news better than I thought they would. There were a few tears, some concerned grumbles, and one instance of money changing hands between a couple of young corpsmen — one of whom had sworn he could see the Four Seasons and the other who was absolutely certain there was no way we were in the vicinity.

I explained everything to them — probably more than I should have. But I wore the same rank as the mission's commanders at this point; I had the authority, and the best course of action was to use it. I wanted the crew who had, for the most part, taken off on a mission to parts unknown that had ended in a fiery crash to be as informed as the officers were. They deserved to know the truth, and so I gave it to them.

I told them about the nebulous message traffic, the possible division between the member nations of the Xy Federation, our secret mission to Xyland alone, and the fact there was no way to know whether they even knew we were coming. I left out the part where we hadn't even begun to consider what we were supposed to do next, that we had no idea how in the hell we were going to get out of this alive, and that we currently had no possible means of communication, much less escape.

They were probably able to figure those things out on their own.

When I was done talking, I went to find Raline. She was sitting braced against a fallen tree while an older Mangan woman with a caduceus patch on her flight suit tended to her arm. The woman's name read "Mieko" and her rank as First Lieutenant. A doctor, probably — or head nurse. I figured Raline was in capable hands.

Her sleeve had been cut away and some sort of medicine was being dabbed onto what looked from where I was standing to be a pretty nasty burn. Raline's eyes were closed, and her face was scrunched up in a pained expression.

Without a second thought, I plopped down to sit in the moss next to her and took hold of her opposite hand. She turned her head and half-opened her eyes, smiling a little when she saw me there.

"This okay?" I asked.

"Mm-hmm." She nodded, squeezing my hand as she closed her eyes again to cope with the sting of whatever salve was being applied to her burns.

I don't know how long we sat there, but even when Lt. Mieko had moved on, Raline didn't let go of my hand. And I wasn't about to be the one to let go first. I scooted around and made myself as comfortable as possible leaning against the fallen tree beside her.

My head was still throbbing, and the dizziness didn't seem to have gotten much better. I don't know why it didn't occur to me to ask Lt. Mieko for a Sceritzene while she was still around.

In the time since I'd sent the search crews back into the ship to look for survivors, I'd let myself wonder a few times what this new rank was going to mean in terms of what might be expected of me. So it was a relief when a few of the young officers and several of the enlisted personnel took it upon themselves to create a watch system on their own. They divided themselves into three parties and synchronized three chronometers between them.

A couple of the boys who'd gone back into the wreck to look for survivors had also brought out emergency lanterns. Since I was the first ranking crew member they came across, they consulted with me as to where to put them. We agreed only one should be lit at a time, seeing as we had no idea as to the age or condition of the batteries, nor how many nights we might require their use. Since our preference was not to be left in complete darkness, that seemed like the sensible thing to all of us.

The fire in the ship seemed to have almost burned out, but the heat radiating off the hull was enough to keep us from getting too chilly. At least we didn't have to worry about anyone freezing to death.

I was sure that wouldn't be my last executive decision of the predicament. I lay my head against Raline's shoulder and tried to think my way through the next day or so. My head still felt strange, and it was a little hard to focus. I knew I had to be missing things, but keeping my mind in problem solving mode was the only thing staving off the panic at our overall situation.

We were going to need a campfire, but maybe not

tonight. And as soon as the wreck cooled, we'd need a plan to go back inside to look for food and medical supplies. A single first aid kit seemed to be all the few people tending to injuries had between them; there was no way that was going to be enough. I needed a Sceritzene myself, Raline's arm would need proper burn care, and I was sure there were more injuries than I knew about. Plus: all of us had just survived an airship crash, which meant every last person was going to be sore in the morning.

Every now and then, I'd look up at the wreck to try and suss out how many of her decks had been flattened in the crash, but my brain didn't seem to want to let me reach any conclusion. The mess hall was pretty high up as best I could recall, so the chance of finding foodstuffs was pretty decent, but I had no idea whether *Dawn* even had a sickbay, much less where it might be or whether it had been properly supplied.

I was making lists in my head and trying to decide what we ought to be doing and in what order when Ensign Declan's voice called from the woods.

"Major Gowon!" he yelled. "Major Merteuil!"

I squeezed Raline's hand before I let it go, standing up faster than I should have, a move that left my head swimming and my knees wobbly beneath me. Major Gowon must have noticed my unsteadiness; he darted to my side and took me by my elbow. I had mostly caught my balance, but Gowon still had a hold of me when Declan caught up to us.

"There's somebody coming," he said, breathless.

I was sure I couldn't have heard that right.

"Come again?" I asked. I was pretty sure I was slurring my speech.

"There's …" Declan paused, his breath heaving in his chest as Major Malli stalked over to where the three of us were standing.

"It's all right, Declan," Major Gowon said. "Take your time."

Declan nodded, took a few deep breaths, and tried again. "There's someone," he said, "coming this way. I could see movement and I could hear them talking, but I couldn't understand anything they were saying."

"It's all right, Declan," I said. "No one expects you to understand Xy."

"Yes, ma'am," Declan replied.

"And you're sure it's people?" Major Gowon asked. "It's not some wild animals?"

"Yes, sir," Declan replied. "Pretty sure it's people."

"Major Merteuil," Gowon said, any hint of bemusement at my new rank now gone from his voice. "I thought you said we're a day or more from the nearest city."

"Yes, sir," I replied. "That's where we are. The map's on the bridge if you care to look. Those are the Four Seasons," I added, pointing to the mountains behind him. "And even though our map's a couple of decades old, cities don't expand that far that quickly. Wherever these people are coming from, it's not the city."

"Sure," Gowon allowed. "Could be an un-mapped settlement, or a group of weekend hikers."

"The good news," I said, "is that it's probably not the cavalry. It's probably not a fighting force."

"What should we do?" Declan asked, his bewilderment clear in his voice.

"If it's not a fighting force," Major Malli answered him, "we stand our ground. The Xylanthians are still our enemies, and we will be well within our rights under the armistice to take them out."

"What the hell are you talking about, man?" Gowon said. "We have just invaded their sovereign airspace and landed within their borders, albeit unintentionally. You're trying to act like this is the first wave of an invasion instead of a goddamn accident. And even if we *were* trying to start another war, there is no provision in the armistice, nor in any rules of engagement I've ever heard of, for shooting civilians because they happen upon your shipwreck. I'd damn well like to think anybody who escaped that ship with a weapon on them would know that, too."

"And besides all that," I added. "We shoot a bunch of civilians out on an adventure weekend and sooner or later someone back in civilization is going to realize they're overdue to return. The next thing we know there's a jollyfussing search party out here looking for them. And you know they'll be armed even if these people aren't."

"What do you propose we do, then?" Malli asked me in a tone suggesting I'd have no idea.

But I did have an idea.

"I think we hide," I answered with a shrug.

"We hide?" Gowon asked.

"Yeah," I said. "I think we hide. I think there aren't that many of us, the woods are thick, and *Dawn*'s a big ship. I think we scatter, take cover, and hope that anyone who comes upon the ship presumes there were no survivors."

"I will not cower in fear!" Malli declared.

"No one's asking you to," Major Gowon told him. "But Major Merteuil has a point. I think she's got a solid idea. Ensign Declan, can you spread the word?"

"Yes, sir," Declan replied.

"It's not an order," I clarified. "If anyone's too tired or sore or injured and they'd rather sit tight and take their chances right where they are, that's understandable. But they're not to fire unless fired upon first."

"Yes, ma'am." He nodded once and dashed away toward the spot in the clearing where the majority of the survivors were milling.

"And Declan," I called after him. I waited until he turned around before I finished. "Tell them to lay low and stay low until we sound an all clear."

"Yes, ma'am."

Major Malli stormed off in a huff. I wasn't sure whether he was intending to try and hide or whether he was planning to sit here in the open and hope the incoming Xylanthians would be content with a fist fight. I shook my head in his direction before looking back up at Major Gowon.

"I'll see ya when I see ya?" I said.

"You sure you're okay?" he asked.

"No," I answered honestly. "I got a little banged up. My head's still pretty off. But I'll deal with that when I can deal with it. I'm already making plans to search the ship for Sceritzene come morning."

"You take care, Major," he said. "And I'll see you when I see you."

I nodded and patted him on his arm as he turned to go.

"C'mon," I said to Raline, reaching out my hand to help her up. She took hold of it and moved to stand but gave up halfway to her feet.

"Ah!" she cried in pain as she flopped back down, "I can't."

"Okay," I said. I could tell she was in more pain than I'd probably ever experienced. If she said she couldn't get up, I believed her. But there was no way I was going to leave her here alone. "I'll stay with you," I told her.

"No," she said, "You have to go. Get away."

"I'm not leaving you!"

"Maran," she said sternly. "I am a wounded civilian in the uniform of an enlisted person. You are an able-bodied officer — and a high-ranking one at that. If they find me — whoever they are — they will not see a threat. You, on the other hand ....”

I knew what she meant. I didn't like it, but she was right.

“You're safer if I'm not with you,” I said.

“For now, yes.” She squeezed my hand before letting it go. “Go now,” she said. “And be sure you come back.”

“Okay,” I said as she let go of my hand. It was all I could do not to fall to my knees and kiss her. But I wasn't sure how she'd take that, so I refrained.

“Go,” she urged.

I nodded as I turned away, hoping to hide the tears I was fighting.

I did not want to leave Raline alone and injured with the enemy approaching, so I wasn't going far. I slipped into the woods just beyond where she was sitting and headed toward the bow of the wreck until I was sure I was well enough hidden. Declan had put our light out already, and the cloud cover was heavy enough there was scarcely any moonlight to see by. I kept my gaze in Raline's direction, just in case.

I wanted to be sure she stayed safe. And almost as badly, I wanted to see whoever was coming.

I wanted to see these people up close. I wanted to be sure our guess was correct: that they were some random civilians and not a search party dispatched for the express purpose of locating this wreck. *Dawn* was still smoking in places, a fact I was sure was helping draw these strangers toward our position.

I wanted to see them when they saw the wreck, and with it so dark, I had to stay close if I was going to do that.

I heard them coming sooner than I thought I would. They were dead ahead of me and closing fast.

I may have made a grave miscalculation.

Heading into an unfamiliar wilderness in the pitch darkness to get a read on a bunch of approaching enemy strangers while dealing with a concussion and other sundry injuries was perhaps not the best idea I'd ever had. But it was too late to back out. If I made too much ruckus, I was likely to betray my position. The best I could do was duck behind a large tree and hope for the best.

The approaching group had flashlights, their beams piercing the darkness and showing me how lucky I was to have made it to my current position without having tripped over a bramble and fallen face first into the underbrush. There was a crackle, like from a two-way radio, and I could hear parts and pieces of a conversation that my scrambled brain kept trying to parse into Feirin. I tried not to listen too closely.

I'd had a habit most of my life of trying to make any language I heard into one I understood. And it had gotten worse the more languages I'd learned. I'd been having a hell of a time trying to learn T'wesh in hopes of someday asking Raline out because I kept applying the rules of Mangan grammar and Gammran pronunciation and making a mess of myself in the process. There was no way these strangers were speaking Feirin. Trying to force whatever phonemes I was overhearing into a framework I understood was only going to make my headache worse.

Instead, I did what I could to focus on the sounds of movement. There were a lot of them. Maybe as many as fifteen or twenty. Had I been wrong about what kind of intelligence the Xylanthians might have had? Could they have known we were close enough to their airspace to send a squad out in advance? Did they have some surveillance technology we didn't know about?

There were too many of them to be a group of casual mountaineers out for a hike.

I balled my hands into fists and tried to keep my breathing in check. Surely there were reasons for a group this size to be in the mountain wilderness in the middle of the night. Right? There had to be. A paid mountaineering expedition with leaders and tenders, maybe. A bunch of kidscouts or a school group out for an adventure.

It was either one of those or we were about to be in some serious trouble.

Any kind of group could have seen the smoke from the wreck and decided to detour from their intended course and investigate. Numbers didn't mean anything.

But proximity did.

They were getting closer. Too close. Terrifyingly close. Flashlight beams hit the brush just in front of me and I did the best I could to be still. I tried to appear as small as possible without actually moving my body.

A beam of light fell on the forest floor just in front of my boots. It was all I could do to move my eyes and not my head to try and see what direction it was coming from. Unable to be sure, I held my breath and closed my eyes, trying to keep calm and quiet as they passed me.

And then I felt it.

A beam of light fell onto my closed eyes, turning the inside of my eyelids bright red to my sight. My whole body was trembling. I wasn't sure whether I'd ever been so frightened in my life — and I'd just watched through the windscreen as the airship I was on fell out of the sky.

I was trying not to think too hard about what might happen next when I heard the unmistakable sound of a human voice say,

"Maran?"

CHAPTER TWELVE

I swallowed hard and cracked open my eyes, shutting them again immediately in response to the bright light still shining directly into my face. I could not have heard that correctly.

But then there it was again.

"Maran?" the voice asked. "Is that you?"

I tried again to open my eyes. This time the light was lower, but barely. The stranger had stepped closer to me, and I did what I could to make out their face in what light was available. My eyes, still accustomed to the darkness, were having a hard time resolving facial features into anything that made sense. Or maybe my concussion was behind that issue.

Because I couldn't possibly be seeing what I thought I was seeing. Before me appeared to be the very handsome, very familiar face of a Feirin man.

"Bryte?" I said his name, but I knew it couldn't be him.

"Yeah," he replied in an instant. "Maran, it's me."

If I hadn't been leaning on the trunk of a substantial tree, I would certainly have fallen over. Bryte Sonneman had been a childhood friend of mine. His father was my mother's third cousin, and his family had been in and out of the royal retinue throughout the history of the Lohengrin dynasty. How in hells he was standing in front of me right now was not a puzzle I was prepared to solve.

"What ...?" I began, trying to gather my thoughts as best I could.

"What the hell are you doing in Xylanth?" Bryte asked me. I frowned at him.

"We're going to have to circle back around to that because you just interrupted me asking you the same question."

"I'm stationed here," he replied. "We have a base here in the mountains. We saw the crash — weren't sure what the ship was, but it looked Mangan as best we could tell, so we came out to see."

"You're stationed here?" I asked. On the one hand, that made no sense. How was there an Alliance base in Xylanth? And how was it I didn't know about it? And why weren't they the ones making first diplomatic contact? But on the other hand, it was the only logical explanation for the fact the young Baron von Sonneman was standing in front of me in the Xylanthian wilderness. "There's a base?"

"Yeah," he replied. "A Feirin base, right here in the Four Seasons."

I frowned at him. There was no such thing as a Feirin base. There were only Alliance Bases. But I wasn't about to argue semantics with an old friend in the middle of the woods in the middle of the night. Especially not when a moment ago I had been afraid for all our lives.

The relief I felt was enough to keep me from giving him any sort of hard time.

"Wow." That was about all I could manage to say.

"Now it's your turn," he said.

"Okay, sure," I agreed. I figured there wasn't much harm in telling someone stationed in a top-secret base inside Xy Federation territory about a top-secret mission to one of its member states. "I'll tell you the whole ridiculous story. I'll even let you aboard the wreck if you want to look. But it'll cost you the use of your flashlight to get back to our muster point."

"Yeah, okay, I can accept those terms." Bryte chuckled and handed over the flashlight. "So," he asked as I shone the light's beam into the brush and started back toward the wreck. "Sergeant Major. Is that ...?"

"It's what you're going to call me in front of all the other survivors," I replied to him, turning a stern face in his direction that I was sure he couldn't see in the dark.

"Yes ma'am," he answered.

I couldn't tell whether his tone came from humor or surprise, but I didn't care as long as he was with the program.

"C'mon," I encouraged as I started back toward the wreck. My first order of business was to check on Raline, but I didn't need to tell Bryte Sonneman that. I kept the beam of the flashlight on the ground in front of us, hoping to keep Raline from seeing it until we were in sure earshot. If I could keep her from any additional fear, I was going to do that.

"Raline!" I called as soon as I was sure she would hear. "You're not going to believe this, but everything's okay."

My stomach jumped into my throat when she didn't answer. I quickened my pace, allowing the flashlight beam to extend farther out in front of me. When I spotted Raline, she was leaning heavily against the downed tree with her head back and her eyes closed. Either she was passed out from the pain or deep in meditation. And I needed to know which.

I ran to her, crouching down until my face was even with hers, and placed my hand against her cheek.

"Hey," I said quietly, "you all right?"

Her eyes came open as she nodded.

"What's going on?" she asked.

I couldn't help but chuckle as I shook my head.

"You're not going to believe this," I said, "but the people who were closing on our position are our people."

"Our?"

"Alliance," I assured her. "Apparently there's some sort of secret base nearby."

"Wow."

"My sentiments exactly." I turned my head to look up at Bryte. "Stay here," I told him. "I'll be right back."

"Yeah," he said, "okay."

I took Bryte's flashlight with me into the clearing, where I turned on our camp light before coming back to where he and Raline were waiting for me.

"Hey," he said, taking hold of my arm as I approached. "She doesn't look so good. Have you got more wounded?"

"Yeah," I nodded. "Bumps and bruises mostly as best I can tell, but *Dawn* came down hard, and there were a lot of fires, so ...."

"I've got first aid supplies," he told me as I handed back his flashlight. He used it to check a compass he had attached to the belt of his fatigues. Then he unsnapped a leather pouch beside it. From the pouch he produced an ovular microphone, shining silver with a large red button on the back. He pressed the button and brought it to his face.

"Feirin Feirin," he called. "This is red leader. Request medical." He proceeded to call out some compass data that made no sense to me.

"Does that broadcast aloud to all of your people?" I asked quietly when I thought he was done.

"Yeah," he replied, letting go of the button. "Why?"

"Can you tell them all to turn it up as loud as they can?" I asked.

"I can," he said. "Are you going to tell me why?"

"You'll see." I marveled at how quickly we'd fallen into the pattern of banter we'd enjoyed as children. It had easily been fifteen years since I'd seen Bryte, and probably more like twenty since we'd been together with the freedom of conversation only afforded to children in the Royal household. "Just do it."

He did.

"Feirin Feirin," he addressed them again, "broadcast to ten. I repeat: open channel broadcast to ten." He turned to me and shrugged. "Okay," he said, "I did it. Now what?"

I took the microphone from his hand. Stepping closer to him so as not to overextend the cord, I pressed the red button and spoke into the silver metal. Realizing what I was about to do, Bryte reached up to the speaker he wore buckled to his epaulet and flipped a switch to shut it off.

"Survivors of the Airship *Dawn*," I began, "this is Lieu … Major Merteuil." I frowned at myself for nearly forgetting my recent elevation in rank, but that was hardly the most important thing I was planning to say. "Personnel approaching the crash site are friendly. I repeat. Personnel approaching the crash site are friendly." I looked down at the pistol snapped onto

Bryte's belt alongside the case for the microphone. "But they are also armed," I added. "Approach them with caution, but please approach. Make yourselves known as Alliance personnel and return to the crash site as soon as possible."

I handed back the microphone and looked down at Raline.

"Help is on the way," I said. "Will you be all right here while I see to the others?"

"Yes," she replied. "Go."

I motioned to Bryte to follow me into the clearing.

"How many are there?" Bryte asked as he flipped his shoulder speaker back on and began the process of coiling the wire to put away his microphone.

"Thirty or so. I think. Everyone kept moving around," I explained. "I wasn't able to get a proper count."

"Then how will you know when you've got everyone back here?"

I shrugged.

"Ensign Declan will probably know," I replied. "And they were all sort of hanging out in groups. So I'm pretty sure it will be easy enough for them to notice whether anyone is missing."

"Okay," Bryte allowed. "And who's your CO?"

"Haha, funny story," I said, pointing to the insignia on my lapel.

"You're in charge?" he asked, clearly dubious. Bryte knew me and my history well enough to know it was highly unlikely that I'd been tasked with captaining an airship over enemy waters.

"It's complicated," I said. "But the short answer is no. Our Captain was killed in the crash. Ship's XO is a bully with a chip on his shoulder who fought the idea of trying to save her — or anyone. So I put on enough rank bars to make it to where he no longer outranked me and suggested strongly that anyone with an able-enough body go back into the wreck and look for survivors."

"But he's still technically in charge?"

"Maybe," I replied. "Technically. But the Lead Intelligence Officer for this mission is also a Sergeant Major: Ayan Gowon. He's a decent guy with a right good head on his shoulders. I'd defer to his authority over Major Malli's. If you want to address the person in charge, I'd say he's your person."

"Even though you're ..."

"I'm *Major Merteuil*," I said, cutting him off. I pointed to the area on my flight suit's lapel where I would wear my Royal Insignia if I so chose. "And I defer to Major Gowon."

"Gotcha," Bryte said as we watched the first of his detachment make their way into the clearing.

I directed the first person I saw carrying a first aid kit toward Raline. It wasn't selfish. Her burns were bad; she needed the attention. Or maybe it was selfish, but even so it wasn't wrong. I kept my eye out for other wounded survivors so I could send them over there as well. A central gathering place where our wounded could be cared for made all the sense in the world.

As the rest of *Dawn*'s survivors and the remainder of Bryte's personnel trickled out of the woods and into the clearing, I did my best to quickly fill Bryte in on everything that led to our being here. I told him about the nebulous message traffic out of Xyland, the possible fracture within the Xy Federation, the secret trip, the hope of diplomatic relations, and how the storm had literally blown the whole thing out of the sky. I asked him what he knew about relations between the two Xy Federation member states.

"You're right here," I said. "Have you heard anything? Seen any stirrings? Do you have any idea what might cause Xyland to want to open a dialog with the Alliance without inviting Xylanth into the discussions?"

"I wish I did," Bryte answered me. "But we're pretty cut off out here. We're mostly here to watch and listen for military activity, of which there's been none that we've detected."

"Did anyone tell you we were coming?" I asked, curious as to whether the Alliance's in-the-know would have warned the garrison of their secret mountain base that a friendly ship was approaching and not to mistake an Alliance asset for Xy Federation military activity.

"Well," Bryte replied, "no one told *me*. And while that doesn't necessarily mean my CO doesn't know about it, I'm going to guess that no one told any of us."

"I suppose that figures," I replied. "We weren't supposed to turn shoreward until we were well into Xylan territory. We shouldn't ever have overflown this region, so there was no real reason to warn you we were coming." I left out the part where they'd kept this mission from Acca, too. Neither my sister, the heir presumptive, nor those stationed in the secret base in the neighboring mountain range had been made aware of our mission.

I tried to let those things make me feel important — in the know. But mostly they made me feel disposable. I shook my head and frowned. This was neither the time nor the place to get caught up in my feelings about my mother and my mission. There were a few dozen airship survivors who were at least partly my responsibility; it would serve us all better if I concentrated more on them.

"How far a walk is it?" I asked him as the first of the groups were filing in.

"Walk to where?" he asked, as though he had no idea what I was talking about.

"To the base," I said. "Should we try and get moving right away, do we wait for daylight? I'm just trying to figure out what the next few hours are going to look like."

Bryte looked at me and shook his head.

"Ayan Gowon," he said. "That's a Gammran name?"

"Yes."

"Maran," he said, quietly enough to be sure no one would overhear his use of my given name, but with enough gravity in his voice that I was instantly on edge. "I don't think you understand. I can't bring all these people back to base with us."

"What?"

"Look," he said. "You can come back with me. Use our gear to reach out to the Sluudi, let your family know you're okay and get your position to the folks who could mount a rescue, but ...."

"No," I challenged him. "No. I'm not leaving my crew here in the middle of the enemy wilderness with no food and no supplies."

"We can send a team back with supplies," he interrupted me.

"Bryte!" I stopped him before he went any farther. "What the hells?"

"Maran," he said. "I can't expose a secret Feirin base to ..."

"There is no such thing as a Feirin base!" I asserted. "It's an *Alliance* base. Even if it's staffed entirely by Feirin subjects, it's still an Alliance base. And these are Alliance personnel, and we're not leaving them out here."

"Maran, we have to," he said. "I take everyone back with me and the next thing I know I'm being tried for treason. I know you don't want to run the risk of leaving the crew out in the woods, but I don't want to run the risk of being shot at dawn."

"We don't execute people for treason, Bryte," I reminded him. "We don't execute people for anything — haven't in twenty years."

"Maybe not civilians," he said. "But we have some pretty different rules out here."

"The law is the law."

"Maran, I can't."

I shook my head and leaned in closer to him.

"I think you're forgetting that I could *order* you to take us all back to the base."

"No," he said. "I'm not forgetting. I'm practically begging you to."

"You ...?"

"I mean it, Your Highness," he said, putting extra emphasis on the title. "I don't like the idea of leaving everyone out here any more than you do, but I can't be the person to take all these people back to base. You, by yourself? Sure, no problem. Maybe an adjutant with you, if they're also a Feirin subject. Maybe. But the rest of them? Especially the ones who aren't Feirin subjects? I can't."

"Unless I say you have to."

"Yeah," he affirmed. "A Royal Order — even one coming from you — trumps any say I have in the matter. If you assert your Royal authority, there's nothing I can do to stop you."

I tried not to take 'even coming from you' personally. I knew what he meant. I wasn't the Queen, nor the heir presumptive. He'd have said the same thing regarding my father.

"So you're willing and able to save all these people," I said. "But only if ...."

"You have to give the order."

"Does it have to be a Royal order?" I asked then. "Can't I just outrank you?"

"No," Bryte told me. "Our detachment exists outside

regular Alliance command structure. You could be the Secretary General Themself and it wouldn't be enough."

"But you know who I am," I argued. "As long as you know whose order you're following, do I really need to make it an official Royal Order?"

"Yeah," he answered. "You do. I have a detachment with me out here; and every last one of those people would fight me were I to acquiesce to an order from someone outside our chain of command. Every one of them. If you want to bring these survivors to the base, you have to be the Princess. It's the only way."

Was there even a choice here? If there was a chance, and there had to be, of the Xylanthians knowing about the crash and sending a team to investigate it, there was a chance anyone left at the wreck site would be dead at their hands within a day or so. And even if the Xylanthians weren't on the way, there were likely all manner of unknown dangers awaiting anyone who stayed too long in this forest. The surviving crew could just as easily be killed by wild animals or extreme weather.

It was up to me to save them all and I knew it. So what if I didn't want to reveal my identity? If ever there was a time to out myself, if ever there was a good reason to stop being the person I'd chosen to be and return to being the person I'd chosen not to be, this was it.

I reached into my pocket and pulled out the rest of my insignia.

I turned toward the wreck, trying to get a look at what was going on with Raline. I could only imagine how she was going to react to this development. But what choice did I have? Come out and tell her I'd been lying about my identity all this time or risk letting her die in the enemy woods.

The answer was more than obvious. I would have to hope she'd give me the chance to explain myself someday. I frowned at Bryte as I began fastening the pins and bars to my uniform. Ever so delicately, and sure to line the pins up one to the other, I gradually increased my rank from Sergeant Major, through all the ranks of General, and finally to Field Marshal: a rank that could only be achieved via Royal Decree. I then fastened the Royal Signets in their places above and beside the ordinary rank insignia.

I stood there for a moment, still, pensive, getting used to the weight of this much hardware hung on my chest and collar — getting used to being acknowledged Royalty. I'd never been good at it. I'd never been good at *noblesse oblige* and at courtly manners and issuing fiat. I'd never been good at receiving adulation or at abiding automatic deference. Those were all the domain of my mother and sister.

I had been running from that life for as long as I'd been able.

Queen and Country forgive me if anyone expected to see magic. I'd never been good at that, either. There was every chance I lacked the talent entirely. I could only hope Bryte's detachment and those we would meet at the mountain base would take my insignia and the word of the young Baron Von Sonneman as provenance of my identity.

"So," I asked, trying not to shrink under the emotional weight I'd just pinned on myself. "Do we try and leave now? Do we wait and hike out in the morning? What's the next step?"

"In the morning," Bryte said. "I'll handle the logistics. We've got some additional supplies staged not too far from here. I'll send some of my people back to fetch them. But Maran," he clipped his flashlight to his belt before covering my hands with his. "I need you to give the order. Formally. Please."

Right.

"Okay," I said back. "Baron Von Sonneman, Lieutenant General Sonneman," I added, covering all possible bases by using both his Noble and military ranks. "I hereby order you to allow myself and my fellow survivors of the wreck of the Airship *Dawn* to accompany you back to the base from which you departed earlier today. Is that enough?"

"Yes, Your Highness."

"Ugh," I replied. "And I also order you not to call me that unless there's someone listening who cares about such things. And for the record, I am not one of those people."

"Okay, Maran," he agreed. "I can do that."

CHAPTER THIRTEEN

Almost as quickly as I'd given the order, I removed my patents of rank and of Royalty. I wanted to have one final sleep as Major Merteuil, and I needed to give myself a few more hours to figure out how I was going to explain all this to Raline. Bryte wasn't so amenable to the idea at first, but when I pointed out how poorly his troops were likely to sleep knowing there was a princess among them, he relented. He ordered his people back to their staging grounds, where he said there were walkontainers and tread bikes filled with foodstuffs and more emergency medical supplies.

Hearing those things had come with them on a trip as short as Bryte had made it sound was giving me pause. Maybe his Commandant *did* know there was an Alliance mission in the area. Or maybe I was borrowing trouble again. Maybe it was SOP to send every expedition into the wilderness adequately equipped for several days — just in case. Trying to guess why they were so well supplied wasn't going to do me any good.

Whatever the reason, all involved were grateful for the rations, the blankets, the portable heaters, and the bandages. Raline was able to get her burns more properly tended to and some reasonably potent pain relief. I was even able to get a couple of Sceritzene for my headache.

Bryte's people required little convincing to stay with us overnight. According to them, these woods were home to a number of terrifying nocturnal predators, some of which were large enough to eat a person whole and others so tiny they could easily kill you without your ever having seen them. From their descriptions I could see why Bryte's decision to stay put until daylight had come so quickly. Whatever we might have suffered spending the night in the clearing, we more than made up for in avoiding things that were likely to kill us in the night in the woods.

I checked in with Major Gowon as the last of the survivors were settling in to try and sleep. But I didn't bother to talk with Major Malli. I'd have to explain myself to both of them in the morning, but there was someone else I needed to talk to first. I snagged a pair of emergency blankets from the dwindling pile near the camp light and headed back toward the wreck.

Raline was still where I'd left her earlier, reclining against the fallen tree with her eyes closed.

"Hey," I said softly as I approached. "I brought you a blanket." Raline waved, but she didn't open her eyes. I wondered how potent a pain killer she'd been given. As soon as I was near enough, I unfurled one of the blankets and draped it over her, careful not to jostle her arm, which was now bandaged and in a sling. "Can we talk for a minute?" I asked, lowering myself to sit beside her. "You don't have to say anything," I added. "But there's something I need to tell you."

Raline nodded and turned her head to face me, but she didn't open her eyes.

My stomach was full of buzzybugs, and my mouth was suddenly dry. I knew it was now or never, but that didn't make me any more eager to say what I was about to say.

"Raline, um ..." my voice caught in my throat, and I paused for a moment. I wrung my hands in the blanket in my lap and tried to figure out how to start. "I think you know that I think the world of you. Jira even said that maybe we could ... you know — that maybe .... And I may be about to spoil all that, but the whole mission is going to find this out in the morning and I just ...." I took a deep breath and blew it out slowly. "I just don't want you to hear this for the first time with everyone else. Raline," I said, "I'm not who you think I am."

I spilled my entire guts then. I told her about my mother and my sister, about running away to the Air Academy, getting kicked out on the eve of graduation, and taking the assignment in the Diplomatic Corps. I told her about accepting this mission and how I'd thought it was a trap and how happy I'd been to spot her on the tarmac back in Feirin City. I told her everything about everything and when I was finished, I reached for her hand.

I couldn't tell whether she was out cold or sound asleep.

Either way, there was no way to know how much she'd heard. I'd just have to see in the morning. I settled in to sleep, leaning against the tree right beside her, making sure my blanket overlapped with hers as much as possible.

Morning broke crisp and damp in the Xylanthian

wilderness. By the time I was awake and moving, two of Bryte's people were passing out ration bars from a small tin crate. Raline was still sound asleep beside me when I woke. She likely needed rest more than food or water. I covered her fully with my blanket before getting up to snag some breakfast for myself.

I pocketed an extra bar for Raline if she wanted one later and went to check in with Bryte and Major Gowon. The sooner we could get everyone moving, the better.

As the last of the dew burned off the grass and everyone who cared to had eaten their fill of ration bars, I knew I could no longer postpone the inevitable. My time as Major Merteuil was coming to a close.

Raline was once again being seen to by a member of the medical complement, as were a few other of the wounded survivors who'd been led back to the area where they'd been treated the night before. The sooner we could get those people indoors, the better.

And there was only one way to make that happen.

I found a spot at the edge of the clearing and fished the lot of adornments out of my breast pocket. I pinned them neatly into place, taking care not to let the process be visible to anyone else in the clearing.

When that was done, I turned around to face the group and found my way to stand on an empty crate that had brought water cans into our makeshift encampment overnight. Then I changed my mind.

"Bryte," I called out before I could catch myself. This was an official thing. I should address him accordingly. "General Sonneman," I corrected.

He probably heard me both times. Bryte jogged over from where he was apparently getting an earful of something from Major Malli.

"Thanks for the rescue," he said softly once he was close enough to be sure he wouldn't be overheard.

"I told you about him," I said. "What was he on about this time?"

"Mostly he's mad that I don't fall under his command," Bryte replied.

"I think he may be mad he isn't the Secretary General," I joked.

"You may be onto something there," he chuckled. "And I see," he said, switching gears as he pointed to the regalia on my uniform, "you seem to be all set to get things moving."

"I'm as ready as I'll ever be," I said back. "But I think you need to be the one to make the announcement."

"You wanna tell me why?"

"Because," I said, shrugging as I looked over the group, hoping Bryte was standing in the right spot to block me from the view of the others. "What we need is for your people to understand they're being ordered to take my people back to the base with them. And I think they'll take the order a little better from their CO than from a member of the Royal family they've never heard of."

"You may have a point," he said. He took a tiny step back and frowned at me. "You're sure you're ready?" he asked.

"No," I admitted. I glanced over at where Raline was sitting, still wondering how much she remembered of what I'd told her last night. "But we need to do this. The longer we're out here, the closer a Xylanthian expedition could be getting to us. And I can imagine the only thing worse than the Xylanthians finding us out here would be those same Xylanthians finding us approaching your base. You didn't even want *us* to know where it is."

"Yeah, you have a point," he said, stepping up onto the crate I'd recently vacated. I was barely able to pay attention to what he was saying as he revealed my identity and explained the morning's plan to everyone. Instead, I watched the faces of his personnel as he gave the order to move out. I could tell they were displeased, and possibly about to challenge him. Rather than let that come to a head and have to explain the broader situation to a cadre of disgruntled GIs, I put my hand on Bryte's sleeve and gestured for him to alight from the makeshift platform and allow me to step up.

Before I could even begin to speak, it happened. Row by row, group by group, as though a conductor was giving the cues, the Royal homages began. The Feirin fell to one knee, the Mangan bent over to hold a shallow bow, the T'wesh clasped their hands before their faces, and the Gammran brought their left fists to their right shoulders.

"Everyone, please," I implored. "As you were."

I waited for a moment while the assembled people reversed the postures of reverence. But I couldn't help but notice few among them returned to their previous stances. The Feirin all stood at full attention, the others mostly at parade rest. It was precisely the manner of Royal treatment I'd eschewed all my life. I tried to get a glance of what Raline was doing, but she was still around a corner from the clearing.

"Thank you," I began again, trying my best to think of what my sister might say in this situation. "Many of you have known me for the past week as Lieutenant Merteuil," I said, "and then as Major Merteuil. But in truth my name is Maran Merteuil von Feirin Lohengrin; I am the second-born daughter of Her Royal Majesty, Queen Salian. My identity was to be kept secret for the purposes of opening diplomatic relations with one or both of the member states of the Xy Federation. I have commanded Lieutenant General von Sonneman and his detachment to take the surviving personnel from our expedition to the base from whence they departed yesterday. General Sonneman has agreed to do this under duress, and only because a member of the Royal Household has commanded. By accompanying them back to their installation, we will be compromising the secrecy of the base itself and possibly its operation as well. I do not know what that means for any of us going forward.

"What I do know is that I have not given this order lightly, but rather with consideration for the life, health, and safety of all my present subjects and their fellow Alliance citizens. And with that same spirit of consideration," I added, "I ask you please show me no more displays of Royal deference. I understand such gestures are appropriate to my station, but I would argue they are not at all appropriate to the circumstances. Although I will use my authority when necessary, I ask that you continue to treat me no differently moving forward than you have prior to this morning. I intend to defer to Major Gowon, General Sonneman, and the Commandant of the local outpost whenever possible. I may be Royal born, but I spent the past week aboard the same ship you did. I ate the same food, suffered the same malfunctions, and survived the same shipwreck. We are, for the purposes of the trek we are about to embark upon, literally in this together. And I would appreciate your behaving as such. Now please," I added, turning to look at Bryte where he still stood beside me. "Let's get moving."

Bryte squeezed my arm as he stepped back onto the box and started giving the orders to break camp. It couldn't have been more than fifteen minutes before we were walking away from the hulk of the *Dawn* and toward the vehicles staged in the woods nearby.

I made a point to bring up the rear, wanting to be sure no one would be left behind. The woods were thick, the underbrush was gnarly, and the folks who knew where we were going were young and fit and moved with alacrity. Meanwhile, I wasn't sure how many injuries we had among the survivors, and I didn't want to run the risk of a slow mover getting somehow lost along the way.

Mostly, I wanted to be sure that Raline, who hadn't been so much as capable of standing last night, was being adequately tended to. Once I spotted her, being led into the woods by a pair of young men from Bryte's complement along with several other of our visibly wounded crewmates, I let myself relax a little.

I made one final inspection of our campsite once everyone had cleared. After walking concentric circles checking for forgotten personnel or equipment, of which I found none, I upped my pace to try and catch up with the others. When I reached the edge of the clearing, I turned back to take one last look at *Dawn* where she'd come to rest. It was the first time I'd seen the wreck from any distance. In daylight, I had to admit, it was terrifying; a hulk of twisted metal, smashed from beneath into the shape of a baguette, with the flattened cocoon and its attendant silk bags still attached fore and aft and hanging from broken tree branches. The whole thing looked like a chewed-up piece of chicle gum wadded back up in its tin wrapper and waiting to be thrown away.

I shuddered to think how close we'd all come to perishing aboard it. As I walked away, I gave a silent prayer for those who we were forced to leave behind. I'd never been a religious person, I didn't even *like* religion as a concept, but still it felt like the right thing to do.

CHAPTER FOURTEEN

Even at the slow pace our injured comrades demanded, it was less than an hour's walk to the place where Bryte's team had left their vehicles waiting. The locals made quick work of loading the supplies back onto the walkontainers and the drivers of the tread bikes eagerly put on their gear and got ready to roll.

"We need to decide who walks and who rides," Bryte said. "Each of the tread bikes has room for one passenger."

"I count nine," I said.

"That's right."

"The bikes are going to need to keep pace with the walkers," I said. "And we want to get to where we're going as soon as possible. So I think it only makes sense for us to have our fastest people on foot and our slowest on the tread bikes."

"Agreed." Bryte looked around the assembled troops, obviously trying to determine who the slowest among us were going to be.

"So we start with the most injured," I suggested, knowing Raline would be among them. "And then go from there."

"But you first," he said.

"No," I countered immediately. "No, I'm walking."

"My troops are going to have a problem with that."

"Let 'em." I knew the rule in Feirin: no one sits while Royalty stands. But these were extraordinary circumstances. And if I could use my Royal prerogative to get this mission moving, I could use it to force the tread bike drivers to carry the wounded and to let me walk.

"Yes, Your Hi —"

I put up a hand to stop Bryte from what he was about to say.

"Maran," he corrected mid-syllable, finishing his sentence with the name he best knew me by.

"That's more like it," I replied, wrinkling my nose at him as a reminder that he'd agreed we would keep things casual between us whenever possible.

"So, who do you think ...?"

"Ensign Declan!" I called out, interrupting Bryte once again.

Declan came running, nearly as fast this time as he had when he'd come to warn me there were troops approaching the night before.

"Yes, Your Highness?" he asked, only a little breathless when he arrived. He dipped his head in reverence, but caught himself almost right away, so I chose not to make anything of it. It was hard enough for me to be treated like Royalty, I couldn't imagine what it had to be like for the Feirin subjects — who'd had the mandate to show deference to Queen Salian and to all with whom she was connected drilled into them since infancy — to suddenly be ordered *not* to do that.

"First," I said, "I'd like to ask you not to call me that. You knew me mostly as Lieutenant Merteuil, which was who I had chosen to be for this mission. You may continue to address me as Lieutenant Merteuil. Or Major Merteuil if that makes you more comfortable. Honestly, I'd be fine with your calling me Maran, although I'm pretty sure you wouldn't do that."

"If you insist, ma'am," he said, struggling to maintain eye contact, but doing a better job than I'd have guessed he would. "I can try. But I'm pretty sure I couldn't call you that. No."

"I understand," I said back. And I did. This was all new and strange and I wasn't trying to make him uncomfortable. But I'd pretty much already decided to elevate Declan to my personal adjutant for as long as we were all stuck in Xylanth and we needed to find a form of address that didn't make *me* uncomfortable, either. "My official military rank is Field Marshal," I said. "Do you think you could address me that way?"

"Yes, ma'am," Declan replied after barely a moment's thought. "I can do that. I'd be happy to do that."

"Good. Now, I have a task for you."

"Yes ma'am," he replied. "What can I do for you, Field Marshal Merteuil von Feirin Lohengrin?"

"Marshal Merteuil is fine," I said. "Let's not spend half the day listing all my regal surnames. Please."

"Yes ma'am" he said. "Marshal Merteuil. What do you need?"

"How many injuries do we have among our crew?" I asked. "And I mean real injuries — I know we've all got bumps and bruises — I'm talking about people who're going to have a hard time walking all the way to the mountains."

"Five," he said. "Three of them are worse than the other two. But we've got five who aren't in the best shape for walking."

"And does that include Chief Khatri?" Not that I wanted to be seen as showing Raline any favoritism, but if her injury didn't qualify in his eyes as making it hard to walk, I wanted to know right now.

"Yes, ma'am," Declan said. "That includes Chief Khatri and Sergeant Chan, both of them have arm and shoulder injuries that are pretty bad. There are some other people with those kinds of things that I didn't count because they're not as bad. And there are a couple of head wounds that might make things worse down the line."

"Good," I replied. "Good. Thank you. Ensign Declan, would you please approach each of those five severely injured people and show them to one of the tread bikes?"

"Yes, Field Marshal," he replied before turning to dash off and do as he was asked.

"All right," I said to Bryte, "that's five. We should put the head wounds on bikes too — he said a couple, but I think I've seen three, so that's eight. And, rather than try and figure out who best qualifies for that last seat, what if we offer it to Major Malli?"

"I thought you hated him. Why do you want him to be more comfortable?"

"Oh, it's not that," I replied. "And you're right: I hate him. But he's the oldest person here, maybe by a decade or more, and as best I can tell, he's spent his career aboard airships. He's got to be in the worst shape of anyone here save those with serious injuries. If anyone's likely to slow us down ...."

"Yeah, all right," Bryte conceded. "You have a point."

"Declan will get our wounded sorted. You go tell Malli he has a seat," I insisted. "Make it feel like an honor, though, and not a concession. If he has so much as an inkling we're giving him a ride because we think he'd be a liability without it, he's likely to insist on walking just to be an ass."

Bryte suppressed his chuckle as he turned and went to do as I'd asked.

It wasn't long until things were all set, including Major Malli, who perched imperiously atop not just any tread bike, but the *lead* tread bike. That had been a bit of cleverness on Bryte's part, and it had worked like a charm. As suspected, Malli behaved as though he had been seated at a place of honor and that seemed to be enough to soothe his ego.

Raline had been seated on the rearmost tread bike. Part of me wanted to walk with her, to ask her how she was feeling — both regarding her injuries and the news I'd broken this morning. I wanted to ask whether she remembered that I'd tried to tell her ahead of time.

And I sort of *didn't* want to ask her how she was feeling about me — about the fact we'd been dancing around maybe finding feelings for each other for however long and yet it had taken a crisis of almost unimaginable scale for me to admit to her my true identity.

I think it was that fact that kept me from getting close enough to start a conversation.

We traveled in a loose arrangement with three of the tread bikes up front, clearing paths as best they could. Our slower-moving comrades came next, followed by the rest of the bikes, then finally the fastest walkers among us brought up the rear. I was sure they were frustrated at our overall slowness, but it was for the best they not set the pace and get away from the group.

According to Bryte, it was likely to take hours to

reach the base at this rate, but there wasn't much to be done about that. We discussed briefly trying to double up the passengers on the tread bikes but agreed they wouldn't be able to function as well with the added weight; it was unlikely to gain us much speed and could risk leaving one or more of the tread bikes dead in the woods.

So we walked.

Slowly but steadily, we made our way through the wilderness, only stopping one time to refill water jerricans from a stream so densely populated by waterfowl I had to be reassured the water would be safe for drinking.

I declined anyway.

Just as we were getting moving again after our pause, Major Gowon found his way through the crowd to walk beside me. He made a point of checking out the insignia I wore before speaking.

"How's the headache, Your Highness?" he asked. He said that title the way he'd always spoken my rank — with a tinge of amusement and a hint of a secret behind his tone.

"It's better," I replied.

"Good."

"You knew, didn't you?" I asked, pointing to the pins on my chest in case there was any question as to what I was referencing.

"I didn't," he replied. "But I suspected."

"Yeah?"

"I know Merteuil is a heraldic surname on your father's side," he explained.

"And you look like your father," a familiar voice joined the conversation.

My eyes got wide. How had I not noticed Raline was in earshot? Curse this damn concussion; the tread bike on which she rode was scarcely two meters in front of us.

"Do I?" I asked, quickening my pace to get closer to her. I wasn't sure I wanted to have this conversation at all, but I definitely didn't want to shout it.

"Yes," she replied. "And you have the same nose as your sister."

"I guess," I said. I'd never thought Acca and I looked alike in the slightest. I'd have to pay more attention to her nose when we saw each other again.

That is, *if* we ever saw each other again.

"Yeah," Gowon added, "I see it."

"So ... wait," I began. "You suspected," I said to Gowon, "but, Raline, are you saying you suspected, too?"

"I had my suspicions," she replied. "Yes."

"Anybody willing to tell me how come?" I asked. "I mean ... other than my nose. I feel like I tried really hard to keep this secret and clearly, I wasn't doing a fantastic job of it." I honestly did want to know what had tipped the two of them off. But mostly I wanted the chance to figure out how Raline felt about it all.

She was smiling, pleasant, and there was no discernable anger in her voice. She seemed to be taking the news of my identity — of my *lies* — far better than I'd feared, and I wanted to know more.

"I suppose," Major Gowon piped up, "I ought to admit I also knew there was a Royal daughter serving begrudgingly in the Diplomatic Corps, which may have given me an unfair heads-up."

"Wait," I said. "You knew that?" I had been under the impression *nobody at all* knew that. In fact, I had been promised when I agreed to the posting that my identity would be kept completely secret.

"Remember I'm in Intelligence," he said. "Once upon a time I pushed some papers related to your inauspicious exit from the Air Academy."

"Oh ...." That made sense. There had to be a record somewhere of my time at the Academy and of what had become of me afterward. And having those documents safely inside the Alliance Intelligence Service seemed the likely best choice.

"That was a hell of a prank you pulled," he said.

"A prank?" Raline asked. Her face was a combination of surprise and amusement and that smile that had always made me weak-kneed. "I must hear about this."

"It wasn't a prank!" I defended, shaking my head. "We'd fulfilled all of our requirements for graduation; we were perfectly qualified to fly anything with fixed wings. But then the Academy got a delivery of a dozen absolutely gorgeous, brand new, mono-prop fixed wing fighters and they weren't going to let us fly them — because they were *training* aircraft, and we were technically done with our training. There were a bunch of us who didn't like that, so we took it upon ourselves to log some extra flight hours."

"A bunch of you?" Major Gowon asked. "All decided together?"

"There were six of us," I replied.

"So it wasn't your idea?"

"It wasn't *not* my idea."

"But you took the rap — all by yourself."

"That part was my idea," I admitted. "Princess claims responsibility, all Air Cadets are allowed to graduate and enter the Air Service with good standing on the condition Princess — whose parents are only now finding out she's been in Gammran attending the Air Academy for the past three years — agrees to forego a career as a flyer and instead ride a diplomatic desk for the rest of her life." I shrugged my shoulders as I looked back and forth between the two of them. "It seemed like the best deal I could get at the time — for everyone."

"That was very noble of you," Raline said. She was smiling at me still, and I couldn't help myself but to smile back.

"It was the right thing to do."

"It was the Royal thing to do," Major Gowon corrected me.

"It was?" I was pretty sure I'd never had anyone refer to me as 'Royal' in quite that way before.

"Yeah," he said back, "It's what Chief Khatri said. You did a Noble thing, taking responsibility for what happened and making sure the others, who I'm guessing didn't have the possibility of a Royal bail-out looming in their futures, got to go on with life and do what they'd set out to do. That's real leadership. I'd be proud to be one of your subjects."

"As would I," Raline added.

My knees went a little weak. I was proud of myself for remaining upright. And miffed by what they were saying.

"Huh," was the only reply I was able to manage. I'd never thought about it that way before. Noblesse Oblige had been a thing I'd only ever heard in reference to my mother and sister; I'd never seen myself as capable of such a thing. "Thank you," I added after a moment, realizing a grunt wasn't at all a proper response. "But that's never going to happen."

"Oh?" Raline commented. There was every chance she was flirting, but I had no idea how to tell. So I shrugged my shoulders and answered like it had been a real question.

"First off, you're T'wesh, and you're Gammran," I said referring to Raline and Major Gowon accordingly. "And therefore, Feirin Royalty have absolutely no dominion over you. And even if you wanted to swear fealty to the von Feirin Lohengrin dynasty, no one is ever going to be my subject. My mother is the Queen, and my sister is the Heir Presumptive, and I am the extra princess who was born in case my sister didn't survive childhood, which she did, so I will forever have no official position of sovereignty nor of deity. And, quite honestly, that suits me just fine."

"You're so sure," Gowon said. "But you're still in line to the throne."

"I am," I allowed. "And if somehow my mother and sister were to both wind up dead before my sister has a daughter of her own to stand between me and the throne, I could conceivably find myself subject to coronation."

"So, it's possible," Raline said.

"If that happened, which it *won't*," I added for emphasis, "because both my mother and my sister live in a palace that's also a fortress and neither illness nor injury has ever touched either one of them. But, hypothetically, if that were to happen, I'd dissolve the Royal mandate and create a parliamentary republic — using the Alliance constitution as the basis."

"Really?" Major Gowon asked.

"Feirin will, I'm sure, never willingly be without a Queen. The monarchy is too tightly woven into culture and religion that trying to remove it entirely wouldn't work. Not only would it cause massive civil upheaval, it also wouldn't reflect the will of the people — thereby negating the purpose of creating a republic to begin with. But moving power out of the palace and into the citizenry? I think that's an idea that's long overdue."

"Something tells me you never said this to your mother or your sister," he said.

"Honestly," I said back, "I don't think I've ever told this to anyone. But you've apparently known all my secrets for years and never blabbed, so here: have another one." I looked over at Raline and shrugged, hoping the helmeted driver of the tread bike on which she rode hadn't overheard that part. This whole undertaking was going to be hard enough without the garrison of the host base knowing their visiting Royal was ready to end the monarchy as they knew it.

Major Gowon laughed. Which was good — I'd meant that last comment to be lighthearted. But everything I'd said was true. Until just now I hadn't known anyone outside the palace knew about my time at the Academy nor about what happened that landed me in the Diplomatic Corps. I found it bizarre that I felt this way, but it was kind of nice to know there was someone else who knew the story all along — like there was someone in the world who knew *me*.

And now he knew me a little better.

And so did Raline.

The way she was looking at me could have kept me warm in a snowstorm. As best I could tell it was something between genuine fondness and admiration, and I couldn't keep her gaze for long without my cheeks beginning to flush. I wasn't sure where this thing between us was headed, but I felt like we'd taken a giant step toward wherever that may be.

CHAPTER FIFTEEN

We didn't talk much for the rest of the trip, but it was honestly nice to just exist in companionable silence. Eventually the flat, brambly floor of the forest began to give way to the pebbled terrain of the foothills. The tread bike drivers debarked their vehicles for a time, allowing their passengers to remain seated as they pushed the bikes around sharp corners and through narrow passageways between boulders the size of the ship we'd left.

The sun was high in the sky when Bryte stopped us in front of a craggy outcropping.

"Everybody on your feet," he called. The tread bike drivers signaled to their passengers it was time to get off. Major Gowon helped Raline to stand; I was grateful for that, as I was once again wobbly-headed and would not have been a good person to lean on.

I had to guess we were getting close. Why else would Bryte have insisted the wounded go the rest of the distance under their own power?

"The tread bikes need to go in the other way," Bryte called to everyone. "The drivers know what they're doing. But the rest of you, follow me."

The route he took was not a groomed walking trail. In fact, it was quite the opposite. Over stones and pebbles, small boulders and slippery sand, he led us a good dozen meters up the mountain — the local garrison at the back and the *Dawn* survivors at the front. I stayed with Raline and Major Gowon, near the front of the group, close enough to Bryte I'd be able to hear him if he needed me. When I looked back, I could see Bryte's people checking behind them. And suddenly I understood why we'd come this way.

They wanted to make sure we didn't leave footprints.

They wanted to be sure, in case any Xylanthians ever happened this way, there was no trace of anyone ever having trod upon this mountainside. It wasn't a level of security to which I was accustomed, but I understood why it might be deemed necessary under the circumstances.

Bryte sped up his gait, practically jogging up the jagged rock pile and looking quite ridiculous, as he was running toward a solid rock face. Several of his men followed suit, weaving their way through the crowd of survivors and sprinting uphill toward the rock.

And then they vanished.

I was dumbstruck. They were there and then they weren't, and I had no idea how that could be possible. Was there some Royal magic afoot Bryte hadn't thought to tell me about? And if so, who had cast it, who was sustaining it, and what the hell was I supposed to do now?

"I'm gonna ..." I said, gesturing toward the spot where the men had vanished.

"Yeah," Major Gowon said. "Go, and ...."

"We'll be all right," Raline added, as though she understood how badly I needed to hear that.

"Okay," I replied. I reached over and squeezed her forearm for a moment before turning to follow Bryte's people — wherever they had gone.

I scrambled up the hillside to get a closer look at the spot where I'd seen my old friend vanish. It was a tough go up the near-vertical section of mountainside — I could see why Bryte and the others had done it at speed. Some momentum likely would have served me well. It was a struggle those last several feet, but I made it to the spot where Bryte had been standing just before he'd disappeared. It was a decently flat place to stand, and when I looked around, I was able to figure out the truth of his disappearance.

It wasn't magic at all — just a trick of the eyes. The rock face straight ahead of me wasn't solid. In fact, as I got closer, I could see it was actually two rock faces. The slab to the left overlapped the mountainside straight ahead of me in such a way they appeared to be a single surface at a distance. In reality, there was a two-foot-wide gap between them.

I couldn't see from outside what lay beyond, so I turned the corner and stepped between the two rocks. It was dark in there; what little sunlight might have come in from outside was all but blocked out by my shadow. My eyes did not want to adjust, so I placed my hands on the sidewalls and started carefully down the stone corridor. This had to be where Bryte and the others had gone, and the fact I could neither see nor hear any of them hinted at someplace beyond.

Soon, my right hand ran out of rock to touch. With

my eyes still not accustomed to the darkness, I carefully turned to face the void. Placing both hands out in front of me to ensure I wasn't about to walk headlong into the mountainside, I stepped in the direction of the nothingness. Six steps later, with my hands carefully scanning the area before and around me, I found another corner. This time the void was to my left, the solid stone to my right. Once again, I turned blindly, inching my way forward until I no longer could.

Not more than ten steps later, my hands happened upon what felt like a doorframe — a metal doorframe. It was smooth and even, and slightly cooler than the rocks around it. I could hear footsteps coming up behind me and I wondered who had followed me in here.

"It gets darker!" I called out to whomever it was. "Be careful not to run into anything. And that includes me!"

"All right."

"Yes ma'am."

There were two of them. Major Gowon and Ensign Declan likely had different, but not unrelated, reasoning behind their decisions to follow me into a maze of rocks inside a mountain, but I was kind of glad I wasn't alone.

I was annoyed Major Gowon had left Raline, but I had come to know him well enough to trust he wouldn't have done so unless he was sure she was taken care of. There was also every chance she'd wanted him to come after me. I figured it wasn't worth bringing up.

Best to focus on the here and now — and what in Her Majesty's Name had happened to Bryte.

My footfalls had started to sound different, and I was frustrated at being unable to see the ground when I looked down. The walls here felt different, too — not the same as the metallic-feeling doorframe, but like stone too smooth to be naturally occurring.

"Sorry about that," Bryte's voice called out as light suddenly spilled into the cavern from up ahead.

My eyes hadn't properly adjusted to the darkness, but they reflexively shut at the unexpected brightness anyway. When I was able to look again, I could see Bryte walking toward me. Behind him stood an open door leading to a well-lit room I couldn't quite see into.

"What's going on?" I asked him. I was still moving forward, but becoming concerned the stone corridor wouldn't be wide enough to let us stand two abreast.

"There's an alarm in there," he said, gesturing behind him to the room I was only beginning to see into. "And it's on the far side of the room. If you open the door from the outside and don't immediately run over to shut it off, a whole bunch of stuff happens that I promise you don't want to see. So I ran ahead to deal with it before everyone else got up here. Go on in," he encouraged me. "I'm going to head down and lead the others up here. Just be sure the door doesn't close. I opened it back up from the inside, so as long as it stays standing open, we can get everyone in no problem. We'll figure the rest out after everyone is inside."

"Sure," I said. "Okay." It was all making sense now. The idea of hiding an alarm far from the door by which it was tripped wasn't a new one. A good third of the doors in the official wing of the Palace in Feirin City had a similar setup.

It was a tight squeeze as Bryte and I each turned sideways to get past each other. I didn't want to think about how snug it was going to be when he tried to get past Major Gowon.

The room beyond the door was at the same time strange and familiar. Smooth rock walls were covered in places by sheets of polished metal, nozzles and spigots stuck out in places, and dark-iron wire conduits ran along the baseboards and the oddly low ceiling. The floor alternated between metal grating and solid stone. A series of mesh-wrapped wall sconces installed at intervals near the ceiling filled the room with garish blue-white light. I'd seen these features in use before — in the Palace, in the Royal aircraft hangar, and at a few pre-war military installations on the borders of Feirin — but I'd never seen anything like this in aggregate.

I could not, for the life of me, figure out what purpose this room might serve. My best guess was that maybe it had been useful while the base was being built, but even that didn't make sense. If it had been merely a staging ground for construction work, I doubt the metal finishes would have been so tidy and pristine. And stranger still, the room was completely empty. The thought of carving a chamber this big out of a mountain only to leave it empty and seemingly useless boggled my mind in ways I was sure I couldn't ascribe to my concussion.

I made a mental note to ask Bryte about it later.

It wasn't long until the others from the crew of the *Dawn* began to join me inside. Ensign Declan and Major Gowon had apparently been turned back in the corridor as Bryte was making his way out, as they were among the last of the crew through the door. I was relieved to see Raline being led inside by the woman who'd first tended to her burns after the accident. It mattered to me more than I cared to admit that she was being taken care of.

I wondered for a moment where the others who had first come in with Bryte had disappeared to; there was no apparent exit other than the one we'd come in through.

I'd have to ask about that, too.

But the thing I most wanted to know was what to do next.

Bryte had mentioned using this station's gear to put

out a message to the Sluudi. I figured I ought to make that a priority, but there was also the issue of what to do with the rest of the survivors in the meantime. I doubted this base had facilities to host three dozen visitors comfortably, and even if they somehow did, I was pretty sure I'd be in for a fight to make those accommodations available to my fellow crash survivors.

If there was any chance at all of that, I was going to have to take command of the group. I'd need to wholly and fully claim leadership and ownership over them in hopes the issuance of Royal fiat would be enough to see them properly looked after.

I ... did not want to do that.

But I couldn't see much of a choice. Bryte had made the point very clear that no one from outside of Feirin was going to be welcome in this place. And even if that hadn't been the case, leaving Major Malli to negotiate for their care wouldn't have put the survivors in the best position. He was currently walking the perimeter of the room, surveying it the way a person might assess a ship they were about to board, or a gallery they were planning to install art inside. I hoped he would find the walls and floors, nozzles and knobs fascinating enough to keep him occupied while I went to find Bryte and started in on whatever was to come next.

When I spotted my old friend, he was working to close, lock, and possibly further secure the door we'd come through.

"This room is bizarre," I told him by way of greeting. "And I don't like it. I'm especially concerned that I am unable to identify an exit save this door right here, and that's doubly troubling seeing as you were accompanied in here to begin with by a handful of your fellows — no longer in evidence."

"Don't worry about them," Bryte said back to me. "There's a real exit and they used it. They're upstairs already, filling in our CO what's going on down here."

"Probably a good idea."

"I ordered them to do it, so I didn't have to," he replied. "Privilege of rank."

"You think she'll be mad?"

"Furious." He finished bolting and barring the door and turned to walk away, gesturing for me to follow.

"Is she going to hate my guts?" I asked.

"Probably not."

"Really?" I was dubious. After all, I was the one who had given the order that could wind up compromising her super-secret base. If I was her, I'd probably hate my guts.

"She's not going to be happy you made me bring everybody back," he admitted, leading me through the center of the room toward a series of polished chrome panels on the far wall. "But she'll probably be glad it's you and not your mother or sister."

"Because I don't have any actual power?" I asked.

Bryte stopped his walking and turned to face me. He frowned as he shook his head.

"Yes," he said. "But no."

"Sure," I said, half in jest. "That totally makes sense."

Bryte rolled his eyes and smirked.

"I mean ..." He shoved his hands into his pockets and paused for a second. "It's not because you don't have power. You do. Of course you do. If you didn't, we wouldn't all be here right now — you and I would be here, and the rest of these people would still be back at the crash site waiting for me to send another squad out with more supplies. But the difference between you and them is that you don't care about your power. You don't throw around Royal fiat for the sport of it. It's not what defines you — at least it never used to be. Hell, Maran, from what I remember from when we were kids, it didn't even *interest* you." He took his hands out of his pockets and gave a proper shrug. "So I'm pretty sure you're not about to go upstairs and start giving orders just to prove you're in charge — which is something your sister always did, and forgive me, I'm guessing she learned that from Her Majesty. You are, as best I can tell, going to let her keep command of her own base and her own personnel."

"Unless or until I see a reason to do otherwise," I qualified. "Same as I let you keep command of your troops, except when I didn't."

"Right," Bryte said. "And it's not like she won't recognize your authority. It's just … it's just that I think she'll appreciate your not feeling the need to assert it all over the place."

"That's fair." I made a gesture asking whether we were going to start walking again. Bryte nodded and began in the same direction as before. "Is that where we're going right now?" I asked. "To talk to your CO?"

"In a minute," he replied. "But you and I need to have a conversation first."

CHAPTER SIXTEEN

"There is no such thing!" I wasn't sure how many times I had repeated myself, and I wasn't sure how many times I was going to have to *keep* repeating myself.

"Maran, you don't understand!"

"No, Bryte; no *Lieutenant General Sonneman*, YOU don't understand. There is no such thing as a Feirin base. There's no such thing as a Feirin Army base, or a Feirin Intelligence base, or a Feirin Naval Base, or a Feirin Air base. And there hasn't been in thirty years. Not in Gammran, not in Mang, not in Wesh, not inside the borders of Feirin herself, and certainly not in the middle of a Xylanthian mountain range. The only place where a Feirin base exists in actual reality is on the national field of zaftiball — and even that returns to neutral between matches. Everything — every space, every field, every building, every linear foot of shoreline — all things that were ever, at any time Feirin bases are Alliance bases now and that's just the truth and it's also the *law* and there is nothing you're going to say to me while you have me stuck in a hand-cranked lift that's going to convince me otherwise!"

Bryte shook his head and shrugged.

He'd talked me into the lift with him only to crank it a dozen feet or so before deploying the brake. He'd spent every moment from that one to this doing his best to try and convince me I was standing inside a Feirin military installation. Never mind that Feirin hadn't had its own military, much less its own military installations, since the Alliance was founded at the end of the war. All of Feirin's military and overseas assets had been folded into the Alliance before either of us was ever born.

I didn't care what Bryte thought he knew, and I didn't care what he thought he was telling me. I knew the facts. I also knew the substance of the treaty that had formed the Alliance at the outset: including the provision making any military or intelligence-gathering apparatus by any individual Nation State without the approval and cooperation of the Alliance at large expressly illegal.

Whatever my old friend thought he had inside this mountain, it wasn't a Feirin base.

"Okay," he said, shaking his head as he took hold of the crank and started us upward again.

It didn't sound like agreement.

Bryte had mentioned the base being around thirty years old; built during the cartological survey the Xy Federation had agreed to at the end of the war. But so far, every bit of tech I'd seen was at least fifty years out of date. The hand-cranked lift gears were no exception. The lift itself had been hidden behind one of the metal panels built into the walls of the huge room we'd first come into. Bryte had turned a knob I'd guessed belonged to an adjacent water spigot, and the panel had popped out of place on one side and opened just enough to allow us to step through. Beyond it was a tiny alcove into which the hand-operated lift had been installed.

So that made two things about this place that seemed to make no sense. Why would you build a big, empty room into the base of a mountain, and why would you hide the lift that was, apparently, the only way to reach the rest of the installation? Also: whose bright idea was it for the lift to be manual? That one in particular felt like a nonsensical decision.

I had a lot of questions. Maybe I would be able to get a few answers.

But maybe not.

It was a curious place, this secret mountain redoubt, and I still didn't know what function the room we'd just left was supposed to serve. For now, it was serving as an anteroom and holding area for the survivors of the *Dawn,* as Bryte insisted the two of us go up and meet with his commanding officer on our own. I'd agreed to that on the condition he immediately send some hot food and a person with medical training to see to the others ASAP.

He'd seemed concerned at the prospect, which didn't sit well with me, but had agreed when I'd stood fast. I understood, of course, that there would always be limits to the hospitality offered by secret installations, and that just having everyone inside this mountain was likely considered a breach, but that didn't mean I wasn't going to insist my crew be made as comfortable as possible under the circumstances.

That was one of the many things I hoped to discuss with the Commandant.

"How far up are we going?" I asked as Bryte continued to work the crank.

"All the way to the top," he replied. "As far as this lift will take us, anyway."

That wasn't a surprise. If the only ways in were at the bottom (and I still had no idea where the tread bike crew and their attendant walkontainers had gone) then it only made sense for the people in power to keep themselves as far from there as possible. It was a very Feirin architectural concept.

So we were headed to the Commandant's sanctum. I wasn't looking forward to it.

It wasn't like I didn't understand her position. I did. She was the commander of a top-secret base: a place probably full of top-secret things. She wouldn't have wanted anyone, even a member of the Feirin Royal family, to know the base's location — much less to see the inside, learn the layout, and get a glimpse at whatever fascinating and classified technology was likely hiding all over the place.

But these were extraordinary circumstances.

By bringing my people back here, I was very likely saving their lives. Most of them had been willing to sign on to the reconditioning of an out-of-trim airship for a mission to someplace they might never be told. As far as I was concerned, every last one of them had earned whatever clearance level was necessary to be aboard this base. And if they were not to be fully at liberty, I was going to do my level best to at least assure they'd be decently accommodated.

I had no idea when, or even if, we'd be able to arrange to get everyone home again, and I wanted my people as comfortable as possible while we were stuck here.

"Anything I ought to know?" I asked as we continued our journey upward. The longer we were at this, the more I thought the manual lift had been an absolutely ridiculous construction choice.

"Only what I've been trying to tell you," he said. He stopped cranking. He frowned at me and shook his head as he hit the brake, locking the lift in place before toggling the lever and sliding open the door.

As soon as it did, I understood what Bryte had been saying.

What he'd been trying to tell me.

Because I wasn't standing inside an Alliance base. I was, indeed, standing inside a Feirin base.

As impossible and illegal and as many shades of wrong as that was, it was the truth.

I almost didn't trust my eyes. I had a concussion; I could very well be seeing things. But as I looked into the room through the open door of the lift, my gut told me all of this was real. I wasn't hallucinating. This was, in every way, a Feirin base.

The consoles, computing towers, even the chairs and the rugs were all of distinctly Feirin design, but those things are easily explained by eccentricities of the construction process. And of course, the signage was written in Feirin; ours had been declared the language of commerce before the war had ended. Those things were Feirin, but they were ordinary.

But the other things ....

Beads of sweat broke out around my hairline as I stepped from the lift. On the wall to my left hung the pre-Alliance flag of Feirin. The original hand-sewn iteration of that flag hung outside Her Majesty's private chambers in the Palace; I'd walked past it every day of my childhood. That flag had no place in the modern Alliance save for in a museum, and yet there it was. Hanging from a pair of brass fasteners, one of them carved with the dynastic crest of the House of von Feirin Lohengrin and the other the seal of Queen Salian herself.

Prayer clocks atop intricately carved posts stood at regular intervals down the length of the hallway, their chimes polished and ready — not in the decorative and decommissioned trim I was accustomed to. And the room's staff was, to the last person, dressed not in Alliance blue, but in Feirin red.

I couldn't be seeing this. And yet I was.

"Your Highness," a woman called from somewhere I couldn't see. Her voice had a gasping, breathless quality to it and I couldn't help but wonder if she was having the same reaction to the impossibility of this moment as I was.

"Atten-HUT!" a man across the room called.

All present sprang from their chairs. At comm stations, listening posts, and writing desks, men and women snapped to an antediluvian iteration of attention I thought long forgotten. It was one of many old Feirin customs that had supposedly been relegated to the history books when the Feirin military had been absorbed into the various Alliance corps. But here it was by the roomful.

And then, like a chorus on the downbeat of a musical number, they fell to their knees in unison. Even Bryte was genuflecting.

That was weird.

I took a few steps farther into the room, trying my best to ascertain its size and that of its complement. I saw maybe a dozen people in red Class-A uniforms and three young men who, like Bryte, were still in their gray-black BDUs. All of them wore on one knee with their fists to their hearts and their eyes cast downward.

It was ... too much.

"As you were," I said as quickly as I could call the words up from my memory. Save this morning's brief episode in the woods, it had been a long time since anyone had knelt like this for my sake. I wasn't used to it, I wasn't comfortable with it, and I was trying very hard not to let that show as the soldiers came to their feet.

And snapped immediately back to attention.

Which was not at all what I'd meant for them to do. Although, to be fair, I'd said 'as you were,' and standing at attention was, indeed, how they were immediately prior to the kneeling. Still, I wanted them to not be doing that, either.

"At ease," I said. "Please. All the way at ease. Go back to whatever you were doing before I got here. This isn't a State visit and I'm not here to make an inspection. I understand it's an extraordinary circumstance. Let's all try and get through this while losing as little of our focus as possible."

That seemed to have done the trick. One by one, slowly but surely, they returned to their seats and, ostensibly, their duties. I could only imagine what kind of work went on up here — on the penthouse level of a place that didn't officially exist — but I was pretty sure it was important enough that kneeling for visiting Royalty wouldn't be considered time well spent.

I could feel Bryte looming over my shoulder, so I shifted my weight backwards and turned my head just so.

"Where's your CO?" I asked quietly. It wasn't that I was looking forward to meeting the commandant. But I had questions, and I was sure she would, too. Trying to facilitate communication via adjutants and go-betweens was only going to cause confusion and delay; best to have a face-to-face with her as soon as possible.

I was also counting on the tiny advantage a member of the royal family gained when asking for favors in person. We had business to conduct, and this would be the fastest way to get it done. The sooner I could see the commandant, the sooner I could get back down to my crewmates.

I also really, really wanted to check on Raline.

"C'mon," Bryte said, gesturing for me to follow as he brushed past me and started down the hall.

I made a point not to turn my head as we made our way along the length of the room, although my eyes were darting wildly in all directions. I was trying to take in this utterly impossible place while simultaneously attempting to appear royal and nonchalant. I put on my very best Princess impersonation and kept in step with Bryte.

I'd had a front-row seat to the Royal goings-on for most of my life, but I was years out of practice at conducting myself as the proper Princess Maran. With Bryte, it didn't matter. He knew me; he'd known me since I was a kid, and there was no need for regal pretense with him. But with whomever held dominion over this place, I was going to need to perform Royalty to the best of my ability if I was going get what I wanted for my crew.

The three men still dressed in BDUs scurried past us and through a door at the far end of the room. They saluted as they went by, a gesture I greatly preferred to the kneeling. I wondered where they were headed in such a hurry.

"Everything okay, there?" I asked Bryte as they got past us.

"Yeah," he replied. "They're just out of uniform."

"What?" As far as I knew BDUs were still considered uniforms.

"Class-A's or better on the Command Level," he replied. "They only came up here without getting changed from the field because I ordered them to. I'm sure they got a stern talking to from someone. I'll probably get one, too. But I figured this was close enough to an emergency it wasn't a good idea to waste time changing clothes."

I shook my head.

It wasn't as though I didn't understand what he was saying. I just didn't like it. I'd been in plenty of places with onerously strict dress codes. Parts of the palace were like that.

In my experience, places with strict dress codes were never particularly pleasant places to spend time.

Bryte led me all the way to the far end of the room, then through a brushed chrome door set into the left-hand wall. I hadn't realized how brightly lit the base in general was until we were on the other side of it. The hallway beyond was dim, giving it a somehow more formal, more dignified air. The corridor had a polished stone floor, and brushed chrome wainscoting capped at waist level with a polished bronze accent rail. The walls above were a smooth battleship gray, peppered with the cut glass and steel sconces that provided the pleasant, amber light.

That hallway led to what I could only guess was the Commandant's outer office. The gray walls opened up on all sides into a room with beautifully vaulted ceilings trimmed in the same bronze as the accent rail. A little desk stood beside a grand natural wood door. The diminutive Corporal seated behind the desk hopped to attention as we approached.

"As you were." I got the order out just as he'd taken a knee. I'd need to speak faster if I hoped to avoid that reaction in the future.

"Corporal Byron," Bryte addressed the man as he came to his feet. "Please let the Commandant know we're here."

"Yes, sir," Byron replied, scurrying out from behind his desk. He cracked the heavy door and poked his head inside. If he said anything while in that posture, I wasn't able to hear, but it was only a beat before he turned his head back to us. "Go on in."

I tried to let Bryte take the lead, but he pushed open the still-cracked door and gestured for me to precede him. Right. As long as I was here, I would not be holding doors for myself.

The Commandant was in the process of standing when I entered. She hurried to get to attention before lowering her eyes and descending to genuflect.

"Please," I said, trying not to take my annoyance out on her. "Stand. Or sit back down at your desk. I could sit, too," I offered, pointing at the red leather high-backed chairs between me and her impressive brass-and-glass desk.

The Commandant nodded. Using her desk for leverage, she came to her feet. She fidgeted a moment before addressing me.

"My apologies for any awkwardness, Your Highness," she said. "I'm afraid I'm still a bit addled by the news of the crash and all that's gone on since."

"Yeah," I said, trying to sound as amiable as possible. I wanted this woman on my side. She'd probably follow any order I gave, but I was hoping to avoid resorting to orders. Cooperation beat subservience any day of the week. "I'll admit I'm a bit addled myself. And I mean it," I added. "Please: we should sit."

"Of course." She indicated the chairs I'd pointed out. "I'm sorry, Your Highness."

"No need to apologize," I assured her. "This is an unusual and, I will hazard to guess, unprecedented situation for all of us."

"Indeed," she replied. "Please," she implored after a moment, "have a seat."

"Thank you," I said, taking a seat in the chair to my right as Bryte came to join us in the seat on my left. The

Commandant took her seat as well, giving me a moment to examine her rank insignia and the golden embroidery on the black field of her name tape. "Colonel Gertrune," I addressed her properly once she was fully seated. "I can only imagine how bizarre and unfamiliar this all is to you based on how bizarre and unfamiliar this all is to me. Here you sit in a base that shouldn't exist and suddenly here I come — refugee from a ship that should never have been flying and doubly so should never have been flying *where* it was flying. Our ship came down. Your people inadvertently came to our rescue. And now we're in this mess together whether we like it or not."

"Yes, Your Highness," she said. "That seems to be the situation exactly."

"We're going to have to solve a lot of problems together," I said. "Some of them more complicated than others. In the immediate term I'm mostly concerned about the injured crash survivors. I'd like to have them seen to by a medical officer as quickly as possible."

Colonel Gertrune sighed as she folded her hands on the desk in front of her.

"I'm afraid even that is more complicated than perhaps you understand, Your Highness," she said.

On the one hand, I was glad she was willing to level with me. Even with the Royal epithet on the end of her sentence, she wasn't going to just acquiesce to my request. That told me something about her character, and I liked that. But on the other hand, I did not like it that she considered getting medical attention to wounded people to be a complicated matter.

When I didn't respond immediately, Colonel Gertrune shifted uncomfortably in her seat. The light from her desk lamp glinted off the gold braid on her sleeve, and suddenly it clicked into place.

The uniforms.

"Your medical staff wears red," I surmised. "You don't want the people in the blue uniforms to see the people in the red uniforms."

Colonel Gertrune nodded, her expression at the same time contrite and defiant.

"Yes, Your Highness," she answered me. Her voice was soft, but firm, and I could see how badly she wanted to protect the secrets of this place.

I wasn't at all convinced those were secrets worth keeping, but I had more pressing needs than the international implications of this particular act of treason.

"Can you put them in BDU's?" I asked. "Or scrubs? Do they have civilian clothes? Hells," I added, "tell them to wear their pajamas. Or ... what did they wear to get here? I'm sure they didn't just board whatever transport brought them out of Feirin in red wool greatcoats. Can you just tell them to change their clothes and then go tend to my people? Please?"

I was trying not to let my anger, confusion, or frustration come through in my tone, but I wasn't doing a terribly good job. Colonel Gertrune was looking at me like I'd suggested the most unreal thing she'd ever heard of, but still she sat up straighter and nodded her head.

"Yes, Your Highness," she replied, sounding thoroughly surprised, yet relieved. "Corporal Byron," she called as she pressed a button on the side of a speaker box on her desk beside the lamp.

"Yes, ma'am?" Byron's voice came through the speaker accompanied by only the tiniest hint of static. The difference between this system and the intercom aboard the *Dawn* made me bristle at how poorly our expedition had been equipped in comparison to this treasonous place.

"Corporal," Gertrune said, once again depressing the

button. "Please request that the medical staff change into sterile scrubs then proceed to the Emergency Deck to see to the survivors from the airship. If they have questions or concerns, those are to be addressed to General Sonneman or myself." She made eye contact with Bryte as she spoke that last part. He nodded his agreement, or maybe just his acknowledgement. Whichever it was, he was on board, and that was good.

"Yes, ma'am. Right away," Byron's voice answered.

"Thank you," I said. "I appreciate your moving on that quickly. The ship came down hard. And as far as I'm aware, only one member of our medical staff survived. I have no idea how serious the injuries are. But I know some of them need attention."

"You need to get looked at yourself, Mar- er- Your Highness," Bryte said. "A couple of Sceritzene in the woods isn't enough to be sure you're okay."

"Later," I replied, trying not to chuckle at his near slip of my first name. I didn't know whether Colonel Gertrune was aware he was a Royal cousin, nor if she had any idea he and I had ever met before last night. Either way, I'd found his stumble amusing; Bryte had never been known for letting his tongue slip. But I didn't need his CO to know I was having a private giggle at his expense.

"At your leisure, ma'am," Gertrune said.

"Again, I thank you," I said. "And I will avail myself of your facilities and personnel in due time. But first," I said, letting my tone grow a bit firmer. "We need to see to the people down in — what did you call it — the Emergency Deck?"

"Yes, Your Highness," Gertrune answered. "It's all there is at ground level," she explained. "It can serve as egress and ingress in cases such as this — when we're compelled to send a team outside the mountain. But it's also our prime defense against intruders. Even if we were to lose power, anyone accessing our base from without will find themselves trapped in that room."

"I understand," I said back. But I was only sort of being honest. Trapping your enemy in a windowless room was an old Feirin war-fighting technique. The original Palace of Feirin City, which was still contained within the walls of the modern Palace, had been built with its true entrance hidden and an apparent doorway that led only to an empty room with no way to open the door again once inside.

I understood those kinds of places existed — as theories and as historical curiosities. But I didn't understand at all how this one worked, nor why the builders of this base felt the need to put it there.

"It's self-contained," Gertrune expounded. I wasn't sure why. "We have control over everything that goes on in there-up to and including the very atmosphere. In the event of enemy incursion, we can seal it off, fill it with a gas the Xylans can't breathe, then turn on the acid sprayers and wash away all traces of the intruders." She seemed proud of this situation — one I found remarkably creepy — but my guess was she was letting me know how tightly sequestered she intended to keep my crew.

"I understand," I said again. I didn't, not really. But I was here to garner cooperation and I wanted her to think I was with her. I did understand one thing, though. "The space my crewmates currently occupy is certainly the least-compromising place for them to be while we try and figure out what's to come next for everyone. And for the time being I won't insist they be billeted elsewhere aboard the base." I sat up straighter. "But I am going to have to insist they be provided with some proper furnish. These are all Alliance servicemembers," I reminded her, with a touch of added emphasis on the word 'Alliance'. I had no intention of letting her forget the right and proper authority to which she *should* be answerable. "They should be received as such to the utmost of this installation's ability."

I tilted my chin just so as I folded my hands in my lap. I hadn't been sure I remembered how to speak like a Royal Highness. But apparently, I'd been paying more attention to my mother than I'd realized. And what's more, Colonel Gertrune appeared agreeable.

That was good.

I didn't want to take command of this place. Honestly, I wanted absolutely nothing to do with this place. I'd much rather have forgotten the fact of its existence than spent another moment inside it. But since I was stuck here for the time being, I was going to see to it the Alliance personnel who were stuck with me were treated as well as was practicably possible.

They weren't a marauding enemy. They hadn't done a damn thing wrong. And I wouldn't have them treated like prisoners.

"Yes, Your Highness," Gertrune replied. But she fidgeted as she said it. Her fingers were tightly laced together, but twitched visibly against each other, and a slight sheen of sweat began to appear at her brow. She was nervous. That didn't bother me in the slightest, seeing as she was operating an illegal installation.

She'd just had the singular misfortune of having been discovered by the one member of the Royal family who was far more attached to the Alliance than to the Nation or the Crown. Seated before her in this moment was the one person on the face of the entire planet who had both the authority to see inside this place and an inclination to blow the whistle and bring the whole damn thing crashing down. If I was her, I'd be nervous, too.

Whether or not I would choose to tattle on her

remained to be seen. And if she wanted to think my long-term cooperation was contingent on the short-term treatment of my people, I was not about to disabuse her of that notion.

"Yes," she said again. "Of course. We will do our best to be as hospitable as we possibly can. But I do hope you'll understand …. Just by virtue of our mission, our location … logistics …." She wrung her hands as she stumbled over what she was trying to say.

I decided to let her off the hook. A little.

This whole ordeal would go far more smoothly with the Colonel inclined to help me.

"I don't expect palatial accommodations," I assured her. "Not for myself nor for any of my fellows. I won't even insist on proper quarters. But what I do expect, and will insist upon, is for this installation to provide for everyone's comfort to the best of your ability. That will need to include rations and water as well as access to proper shower and toileting facilities, which I believe to be unavailable on the Emergency Deck."

Gertrune was sweating harder. I didn't really care. This was a hill I was prepared to die on. A comfortable place for my crewmates to lay their heads and access to proper plumbing were absolutely not too much to ask.

"I will see what we can do," Gertrune said back.

That was enough for now. There was no telling how much longer I was going to be able to keep up the princess façade, and I wanted to get back down to the Emergency Deck to check in with everyone. Plus, knowing I was down there waiting would likely speed up the hospitality considerably.

I also had a lot to think about, and I wasn't going to get much thinking done sitting here.

"Colonel," I said, rising from my seat and setting my shoulders back in what was probably the best Queen Salian impression I'd ever pulled off. "We'll speak again."

I hadn't meant to make a move so abrupt as to leave both Bryte and the Colonel scrambling to get out of their seats before being accused (by each other; I surely didn't give a damn) of disrespect. But I'd done it. I donned my most patient expression as I waited for them to stand.

"Yes, of course, Your Highness," Colonel Gertrune said as she settled into a parade rest. She tensed her jaw as her gaze shifted to Bryte and back to me. "Allow me to make my second-in-command available to you for as long as you're with us," she said.

I looked over at Bryte and crinkled my nose enough to be sure he'd see it. My, how the tables had turned. When we were children, Bryte and Acca — the bigger kids, and pair of heirs to boot — liked to gang up and boss me around. Now he was being formally placed under my command. That was rich. I had half a mind to order him to source me a proper hot norby pie.

If I was going to have to have a minder, which was absolutely what was happening here, I might as well have a little fun with him.

"Thank you, Colonel," I said back to her. "I am sure Lieutenant General Sonneman will take fine care of me. I'm going to check on my people now. We'll talk later."

"Yes, Your Highness," she barely managed to say before my back was to her and I was headed for the door. Bryte had to dash ahead to have the door open as I approached. I almost sped up but decided against it. As amusing as the idea of messing with my old friend was, I didn't want to make him look bad in front of his CO. Until I was absolutely certain how I felt about this place, its mission, and its personnel, I wasn't going to do anything to sully anyone's professional reputation — least of all my childhood buddy.

I let Bryte catch up as we walked past Byron's tiny

desk and into the hallway beyond the Colonel's outer office. We reached the far door, and he held it open as I passed through. But he stopped me before I could turn back toward the lift.

"This way, Your Highness," Bryte said, gesturing to his left as he closed the door quietly behind him.

"But the lift …?"

"Trust me."

I wanted to say, "no," or, "fat chance," or "not on your life, treason-face." But I held my tongue.

He'd brought me into an illegal, underground spy base and there was absolutely nothing trustworthy about that. But friendly banter had no place in the work room of the Command Level. Same as I didn't want Bryte to look bad to his CO, I also didn't want to disparage him in front of those under his command. Until I decided otherwise, Bryte was my friend, and these people were my allies and there was no reason to sow discord here.

"Where are we going?" I asked.

Bryte shook his head and kept walking. He turned another corner to his left and pointed ahead to a standard lift portal built into the wall.

"I don't understand?"

"We're taking the mechanized lift," he said, a hint of incredulousness creeping into his voice.

"Sure," I said back. "That seems obvious. The thing I don't understand is why we didn't come up this way to begin with. I mean … why in the name of the Queen did you crank that damn handle all the way up here if you didn't have to?"

"Because I actually did have to," Bryte said plainly as he pulled the lever that would summon the mechanized lift to our position.

"Huh?"

"That manual lift is the only way to get to or from

the Emergency Deck," he explained. "It's a safety precaution. There's only one way to get further into the base from that entrance, and that way is both hard to find and real damn slow. If someone were to break in, manage to find the right panel and how to get behind it, and get themselves into the lift before we can stop them, they're not going to make it far before we cut the cable."

"Sure," I said, pretending he'd made more sense in my head than he had. Seeing as I wasn't sure whether I was rightly confused or due for another dose of Sceritzene, I figured I'd just go with it. "But if the hand-cranked lift is the only way to get where we're going, why are we getting into this one instead of that one?"

"Because this one will get us most of the way there without my needing to squeeze the brake the whole way down," he said. "And, possibly more important to you than to me, taking this lift as far as we can means staying out of the way of the medics and the people who'll be bringing down the rations."

"Right," I said. "Okay. This is fine."

CHAPTER SEVENTEEN

By the time we returned to the Emergency Deck, the
base's medical staff had arrived and were already hard
at work. In all my years around the Air Service and the
Diplomatic Corps, I'd never seen an installation
mobilize so quickly. I was tempted to ask Bryte whether
this was SOP or an impressive scramble on account of a
visiting princess but decided I didn't care.

What I did care about was Raline. I could ask my
operational questions later. For now, I wanted to see
she was being tended to.

I found her, alongside another burn patient,
propped up on several half-inflated cushions and being
seen to by no fewer than three members of the medical
staff, all of them dressed in mismatched surgical scrubs
and winter underthings. As much as I wanted to go sit

with her, hold her hand, and ask how she was doing, something in me knew better than to approach. There was a good chance the medical personnel would react to my proximity the same way the Command Level personnel had, and I didn't want the three of them to stop treating the injured in order to come to attention or fall to their knees.

Instead, I moved close enough to eavesdrop and continued to survey the goings on elsewhere in the room. My attention was grabbed promptly when a baby-faced corpsman dashed away from the burn victims and toward a pile of gear in the middle of the room. He was dressed in a sleeveless undershirt, too-large scrub pants, and sport slippers and was scrawling notes on a clipboard with such focus his shoulder bumped squarely into mine as he passed.

"Everything all right?" I asked.

He jumped around to face me before dropping to his knee and bowing his head.

"Yes, ma'am ... yes ... y ... Your Highness," he stammered. "My eternal apologies ..."

"Apology accepted," I said, cutting off what I suspected would be a protracted apology. "On your feet."

The young man nodded and rose slowly, but he still wouldn't look at me.

I sighed and shook my head before turning to look for Bryte. "Lieutenant General Sonneman!" I called, using his full title so I'd be sure to get his attention above the hubbub of conversation in the room.

"Yes, ma'am?" he replied as he jogged toward me.

"General," I said softly, stepping away from the contrite corpsman. "Is there any way ...?" I put my face in my hands and took a deep breath. "Bryte," I began again, choosing his first name so he'd know what part of me was asking him this. "Bryte, could you ... I don't know ... could you make an announcement, maybe? Put out a memo? Something to tell your people that I would prefer they not drop to their knees every time I approach?"

"I beg your pardon?" Bryte replied.

I wondered what part of what I'd said wasn't making sense. Understanding the problem might have been my concussion and not his comprehension, I took a deep breath and tried again.

"We have found ourselves in an utterly bizarre situation," I said, trying to find a good place to begin an explanation. "And I can only imagine the level of tension in this place even on a normal day. So if I'm trying to talk to one of your people, I'm probably trying to tell them something important. Or I'm trying to get them to tell me something important. It's operational, it's very likely time sensitive, and I don't have it in me to keep standing on ceremony," I explained. "Every moment spent on genuflecting and orders to rise is a moment wasted. It's a delay in the exchange of information. And it's ... it's a problem for me." I shrugged my shoulders and shook my head. "I absolutely and unequivocally acknowledge that every member of the permanent complement of this outpost is a loyal and reverent Feirin subject. But if there is any way, any way *at all* I could get them to just ... I don't know ... salute me as a Field Marshal of the realm instead of falling to their knees out of Royal adulation, I would really appreciate that."

"I don't know, Maran," he said, quietly enough I was sure no one overheard him calling me by my given name. "Some of these people are very religious. I'm not sure I could get them to stop kneeling even if I ordered them to."

"I need them to stop," I said plainly. "If that means we have to do some sort of formal ... thing. What's it called? The thing my mother does when she arrives in a place she's going to be for a while or where she needs to get actual work done ...." I knew I had the word for what I was asking about, but my concussed brain didn't want to give it up. "A ... the ceremony," I finally landed on, "that lets everyone pay that certain kind of respect and be done with it so we can all get past the formality and the reverence and let us all just function. Do you know what I'm talking about?"

"You're talking about a formal Veneration," he answered me.

"Yes." That was the term. Good thing someone's brain was firing on all cylinders, because mine was a mess.

"You know, Maran, that's not a bad idea. But I wouldn't have the first idea how to make one happen. I'm not even sure we're equipped for something like that."

"Who would have an idea?" I asked. "The Colonel?"

"Actually," he said, "we have a Protocol Officer. He's probably our best bet. If you're okay being stuck down here for a little while, I'll go have a chat with him and see what we can do."

A base in the middle of nowhere Xylanth — that didn't officially exist, had no legal authority to be here, and should never have had any contact with anyone — had a Protocol Officer on staff. Because this place was nothing if not fussing ridiculous. I decided not to say so out loud.

"Sure," was what I said to Bryte instead.

"You want me to go now?" he asked, looking around to assess the situation on the Emergency Deck.

"Yeah. Go. As quick as you can."

"You really hate it when people kneel."

"Kind of," I admitted. "If this were someplace normal, I'd find a way to put up with it. But being where we are, and with everything that's gone on and all the possible things that could happen as a result ..." I shook my head and shrugged my shoulders. "I really am afraid we're going to need to move quickly and that we're not going to be able to because people won't cut it out with the kneeling. I want to feel like I can ask a corpsman how one of my crewmates is doing, or where to find a Sceritzene without having to go through a whole ceremony before getting an answer. So, yeah: the sooner the better. But I also want you to hurry so you're in and out of that lift in case one of these medics discovers they need something they didn't already bring down."

"Okay," Bryte replied. "I get it. I see what you're getting at and, honestly, it makes sense. Especially the part about wanting me in and out of the lift in case medical needs it."

"And I don't want you in the way of whomever is bringing seats and blankets and rations, either."

"Yeah, okay," he agreed. "I'll be back with word from Protocol as soon as I have it. Until then, you're sure you're okay here?"

"Yes," I assured him. "I'm going to check in with Major Gowon — make sure everyone made it through the wilderness no worse for the wear."

"And you're going to take another Sceritzene," he said. "And maybe a Briasol before all the adrenaline wears off and the body aches set in to make you feel like — well, like you've just lived through an airship crash."

"Yeah. You're probably right. That's a good idea. I'll see you when you get back."

Bryte gave me a nod before he turned on his heel and dashed off toward the hidden lift behind the panel in the far wall.

I looked back at the corpsman who'd been the

impetus for the whole conversation. He was still standing where I'd left him and had gone back to writing on his notepad.

"Corpsman," I addressed him as softly and gently as I could while simultaneously being sure he'd hear me.

"Yes, Your Highness," he replied, this time only bowing his head as he addressed me.

"How are things down here?" I asked, taking a step in his direction. "How is my crew?"

"You'll want to talk to our Chief Medical Officer about that," he said back. "Lieutenant Colonel Tors is just over ..."

"But I asked you," I interrupted him. "I'll speak to Colonel Tors when the time comes. But I've found the officers tend to give one kind of report and enlisted persons another. And right now, I want your perspective. How are things? How are my people? The burn victims you were just looking at — how are they?"

"Um ..." the Corpsman started. He was fidgeting, tapping his fingers against the tin of his clipboard and shifting his weight from foot to foot.

"Whatever you say," I told him, "it's all right. Even if you were to say something that made me mad, I wouldn't be mad at *you*. See, that's the beauty of being the low-ranking guy. Literally nothing happening in this room is your fault. Although," I qualified, "if you've done any good, I'll see to it you get credit."

"Yes, ma'am. Things are all right," he answered. "Mostly these folks have just been knocked around. From what I've been able to overhear, the crash was pretty much a binary thing: if you were on some decks, you got a little banged up but got out okay, and if you were on some other decks, you didn't get out at all. The best I can tell, the folks with burns, I think didn't get out till later," he said, shaking his head. "And some of them I think inhaled a little smoke. A couple of the guys who went back in after, to try and get more people out, they have some burns, too. But there are only a few things the doctor thinks are serious. And the staff is tending to those people now."

I nodded my head. Raline was clearly among those whose wounds the doctor thought were serious. I would have guessed as much, but it was good to have official confirmation. It was even better to know she was being prioritized by the medical staff. If I'd had to use my Royal prerogative to see to it she got the best care possible, I'd have absolutely done that. It felt good to know I wouldn't have to.

"Thank you," I said. "That's all very good to know." It was. Mostly I was glad to hear that the serious injuries were few and that they were being ministered to presently. And hearing there were cases of smoke inhalation made me that much gladder for the men who'd gone back into the wreck to bring out survivors. Who knows how much longer those people would have lived if no one had come looking for them?

"Thank you, Your Highness," he said.

"Now," I said, "I have one more request and then I'll let you get back to your work."

"Yes, ma'am. Anything you need."

"I was on the bridge of the airship when it went down, and I seem to have hit my head on impact. I'm running late for my next dose of Sceritzene, and it's been suggested I ought to add a Briasol to that in case the rest of me starts to hurt in concert with this knot on my noggin. Now," I said extra firmly, "I do not want to take any of you away from the patients who need you. These people are under my command and their health and well-being are my utmost priority. So I am in no way asking for anyone to stop caring for serious injuries to tend to my royal bumps and bruises." I made sure to catch his gaze as I said that last bit. I wanted him to know I meant it. "But if you would, please, tell me whereabouts in these stacks and racks of supplies I might find a dose of each so I can go snag some before I start feeling less than wonderful."

The corpsman frowned. He fidgeted some more and began to shake his head. He opened his mouth to give the answer then shut it again. That happened twice before he looked pitifully up at me, still shaking his head.

"I'm really bad at describing things, Your Highness," he said, his voice suddenly edged with a tiny tremor. "I can try and tell you, but it would take all day and you probably still wouldn't find what you need. It would be much faster if you'd permit me to get the medicines for you. Please."

I nodded my head.

"All right," I agreed. I could tell he was being sincere. Seeing as the whole point of wanting to get my own medicines was to save time, I'd let him pull the doses for me if that was the faster way to get things done.

By the time he was back in front of me with a pair of Sceritzene tablets and a dose of Briasol in a sealed cannikin, I was sure the nameless corpsman had been right about his way being quicker. He'd gotten in and out of that medical crate faster than I'd have figured out the latch on its lid.

"If you need water," the corpsman said, "we brought down a rack of pre-filled field canteens." He pointed to the rows of gear racks I'd noticed when I first arrived. Of the two I could see clearly, one was filled with supply crates labeled as medicines, bandages, and sterile supplies and the other was hung from top to bottom with dark-olive field canteens.

"Thank you," I said. "May I ask your name?"

"I'm Corporal Els, ma'am," he replied, casting his

eyes to the floor again.

"Well, I thank you, Corporal Els, and I shan't forget your good treatment of me. Now please," I said, "carry on."

"Yes, Your Highness," he said. "Thank you, Your Highness."

I smiled before turning toward the rack of canteens. I could swallow two Sceritzene without water, and I didn't find the taste of the Briasol at all objectionable. But medicine or no medicine, I couldn't remember the last water I'd drunk, and adding dehydration to my list of ailments wasn't going to help the situation.

I popped the pills into my mouth as I reached for one of the hanging canteens, unscrewing the lid in time to wash the medicine down. I took another swallow of water, and another, before capping the bottle and proceeding to peel back the foil on the dosing cup far enough to let me knock back the liquid Briasol. It tasted worse than I remembered; maybe the military recipe had extra preservatives or skipped the usual flavoring agent.

I drank the rest of the water.

It took me a moment, but I was able to pick out Major Gowon sitting on the floor on the far side of another set of gear racks. Of everyone in the room, with the possible exception of Raline, he was the person I most wanted to talk to. There were a lot of things going on here that were way above my duty station — Royal bona fides notwithstanding — and he was the ranking Intelligence Officer.

He was also someone I both respected professionally and genuinely liked. If there was anyone on this whole planet I could talk to frankly about what was going on, it was Ayan Gowon. I made a beeline to where he was and plopped down to sit on the floor beside him.

He'd been having a conversation with a couple of

young officers also sitting on the ground with him, but all three stopped speaking as I came to join them.

"Your Highness," Major Gowon greeted. His words were formal, but his tone was personable, and he made no move to show any further august respects.

"Am I interrupting?" I asked, gesturing to the others who were seated with him. I though it only polite to acknowledge I'd butted in on whatever conversation they'd been having.

"No," Gowon answered readily, "not at all. We're just passing the time. I'm not sure you've met," he added, gesturing toward the others seated with us.

"I don't believe we have," I replied. I reached out my hand toward the nearer of the two. "Maran Lohengrin," I introduced myself with the most casual iteration of my proper name I could come up with.

"Swahna Swar," the young woman answered, extending her hand in turn. She was T'wesh, wore her hair short, and her newish-looking flight suit showed her rank to be Lieutenant Junior-Grade.

"It's a pleasure to meet you, Lt. Swar," I said, taking her hand and shaking it only once, as I understood to be the T'wesh custom.

"The pleasure is all mine, Field Marshal Lohengrin," she replied. I smiled back at her and nodded, appreciative of her choice to address me by rank and not by title.

"I'm Ginna Pon," the Mangan girl sitting beside Swar said. She clasped her hands in front of her face and briefly bowed her head — a traditional Mangan greeting of respect. I did the same.

"Pleased to meet you," I said, looking her briefly up and down for any indication of rank. But she was dressed still in her nightshirt, with boots and an overcoat hastily thrown on over top before she evacuated. She must have realized what I was looking for, because she spoke up almost as soon as I hesitated.

"Staff Sergeant," she said. "Ma'am."

"Pleased to meet you, Staff Sergeant Pon."

"Sergeant Pon and Lieutenant Swar were part of my detachment," Gowon told me. "I'm filling them in on what they didn't know about where we were going and why."

"Oh," I said, then turned my head to face the other two again. "It's a lot." I couldn't think of anything else to say. It *was* a lot. And not knowing how much they were privy to already, I suspected it might be even more than I figured.

"I was telling the Major," Pon replied, "that I suspected our mission might have something to do with the Xy — although I definitely had not guessed we'd be headed into Xyland itself."

"Really?" I asked, my curiosity piqued. "What was the hint? What gave it away?"

"My normal job is clerical," she said. "Mostly, I file things. Sometimes I get things out of files. Sometimes I even pull out whole files and take them places to be filed by other clerks. I'm really good at my job, but I don't imagine there's a lot of work for a file clerk on a long-distance airship mission. But I got to thinking .... I'm sort of an armchair expert on Xy culture and customs. I've always found it fascinating — I don't know why. But it's not like I make any secret of that. And even if I did, I work for the Intelligence Service, I'm pretty sure they know me better than my own mother. So when I first got the assignment, I thought it was weird for Major Gowon and a couple of diplomats to want a file clerk along. But then I wondered if maybe they might instead have use for someone who knows about Xy greeting customs or culinary mores."

"And indeed we did," I affirmed. "Or ... we probably would have."

"Yes, ma'am," Pon replied.

"How about you?" I asked, turning to Swar.

"I'm a cryptographer," she replied. "I've never done any sort of field operation before, either. But it seems to make sense to want someone aboard an expedition who's comfortable using and operating in codes. Unlike my colleague here, I had no suspicion at all we might be headed toward the Xy Federation."

"It's good to know we have a cryptographer here with us," I said. "We may need you in the next couple of days."

"You know something I don't?" Major Gowon asked me.

He had no idea.

"We'll talk," I replied. "Because ... yes. But what I meant by what I said to Lt. Swar is that I don't know what kind of comm gear this place has and I double don't know what they're going to let us use. So someone who can make do with whatever they offer to get out a message our side will understand and the Xy may wind up our most valuable player."

"You have a point there," Gowon allowed. He stood up and held his hand out to me. "If you two will excuse us," he said to Swar and Pon as I got to my feet. "I need to have a word with the Field Marshal."

"Yes, sir."

"Of course."

"It was nice meeting both of you," I told them in parting.

"You as well."

"Thank you, ma'am."

Major Gowon took me by the elbow and led us toward the lift, away from everyone else in the room.

"I feel like you've got something you want to tell me," he said quietly.

I bit my lip and sighed.

"What's your clearance?" I asked.

"All Words. All Codes."

"Yeah." I shook my head. That was the highest clearance level there was in the Alliance Service. But the secrets I'd just learned weren't Alliance secrets.

They were Feirin secrets.

The problem was, of course: there wasn't supposed to be such things as Feirin secrets — so what the hells was a Feirin secret if not also an Alliance secret?

I didn't even know anymore.

"I can't decide if I should tell you."

"But you want to."

"For me, I want to," I said. "Because I don't even know how to process what's going on here and I want someone to talk to. I don't like being the only person to know things — especially things this dire. But the fact is, if I tell you this …. Once you know this, you can't un-know it. And knowing it could turn out to be really bad for you. It might be better for everyone if I keep my mouth shut."

"With all due respect, Field Marshal Your Highness," he said, "I've been in Intelligence a lot longer than you've been in diplomacy. I know a lot of things — including a lot of things you don't know. I'm pretty sure nothing you could tell me right here is any bigger a secret than ten I already know about."

"They're wearing red uniforms," I said quietly.

Gowon frowned and leaned his head closer to mine.

"Come again?"

"Upstairs," I said, only slightly louder. "Everyone upstairs is wearing a red uniform."

"Holy damn," Gowon whispered.

I pursed my lips and nodded.

"Bryte tried to tell me," I said, "on the way here from the wreck site. He told me this was a Feirin base, and I kept telling him there's no such thing as a Feirin base —

that any base with a Feirin garrison was automatically an Alliance base and he kept calling it a Feirin base, but I wouldn't listen because I just couldn't imagine there even being such a thing, but ...."

"But the people upstairs are wearing red uniforms."

"Yeah." I swallowed hard, wishing there was still some water in the canteen I hadn't managed to put down yet. "All of them. Did you notice the medics are down here in scrubs and base layers?"

"Yeah," Gowon said. "But I've been in tight bases before. When an emergency happens, you've got to respond; it doesn't matter that it's not your shift. It doesn't matter if you're sound asleep. And since we've got a couple of folks out here walked off the wreck wearing nothing but their pajamas and a pair of boots, I didn't think anything of it."

"I had to talk the Commandant into sending them down here. Because of their uniforms. She only agreed when I came up with the idea to put them in scrubs."

"It was a good idea," he said. "Some of these folks really needed to be looked after."

I couldn't help myself but to turn my head and look at Raline. She was still propped on pillows, and the medics had moved to bandaging the burns on her arm and shoulder. Her eyes were closed, but there was a tension in her forehead that told me she was still in some pain.

"Thanks," I said. "I'm glad I thought of it. But ...." I looked back at Major Gowon and shook my head. "I don't know what we're going to do here. So far, the Commandant's listened to me, but I don't know how far I'll be able to push her. She accepts my Royal authority, but .... I don't think they recognize Alliance dominion."

"Damn."

"Yeah."

"You were right: this is big," he said. "And you were

right to hesitate in telling me. But you were also right to tell. I can see where you may have divided loyalties here, and ..."

"I don't," I said. And for the first time since I'd come upon the crimson-clad officers on the deck above, I knew how I felt about it. It took that presumption from a colleague to make me see for sure that my allegiance was now, and had always been, with the Alliance.

"You okay?" he asked then, leaning into me further and putting his hand back on my arm.

"My loyalties aren't divided," I said, shaking my head as I drew in a ragged breath. "I don't think I was sure until you accused me of it, but ...." I bit my lower lip, trying to fight off the hot tears welling up in my eyes. "This is an illegal base operating outside the lawful authority of the Alliance to which I have sworn an oath — an oath I intend to uphold, even in defiance of my mother's authority."

"All right," he said. "That's good. I can't imagine how you're feeling, but I'm glad to know we're on the same side."

I nodded.

My jaw was clenched, and I started to shake. Things were starting to click into place in my head: disturbing things, terrifying things. This was not okay. My stomach churned and it took everything I had not to retch where I stood. I grabbed Major Gowon's forearm, using him for support as my knees began to give.

"Oh, Queen Salian help us," I whispered, bending at the waist as my gut continued to twist. My head was spinning, and I was pretty sure it had nothing to do with my concussion.

"What ...?" Major Gowon asked. "Maran, are you okay? What's going on? Do you need ...?"

"I don't think we're safe," I whispered before he could finish asking me his question.

"What do you mean?"

I managed to stand back up and look him in the eye. Still thoroughly nauseated and with a hand on his arm, I stepped closer to where he stood.

"Ayan," I said, using his given name in hopes he'd understand further the gravity of what I was about to ask. "You've got to act like you don't know."

"Yeah, I figured that out," he replied.

"No," I challenged. "No. You don't know. The rest of it." My heart was racing, and my stomach churned. The pieces were all coming together in my head and the picture they revealed was blood curdling. "She told me," I said. "She said it right to my face. She told me what she planned to do, and ..."

"She told you what?" Gowon asked.

"Don't make a show of it," I replied. "But do you see the nozzles in the ceiling, do you see the spigots? The grates? The drains in the floor?"

"Yeah," he said back, taking a brief look around using only his eyes.

"She said it's for enemies," I whispered, shaking my head still. But then I looked back at him and tried to pull myself together. I needed to get these words out without falling apart. He needed to know what I knew. He needed to know how much danger he and the others were in. "They can pipe in gas," I told him. "And acid. She said .... Kill everyone in this room, dissolve the remains and wash it all away like no one was ever here."

"And you think ...?"

"I do," I answered plainly. I shook my head and wiped my eyes with the back of my sleeve. "I don't think she'll do it with me down here," I added. "That's a bonus of being the daughter of their principal God — I'm kind of ... half god ... or something. And I know a lot of these people are religious," I explained. "I know because Bryte's gone to talk to his protocol guy about putting together a proper royal veneration hootenanny so I can walk around without everyone flopping to their knees. I was sort of dreading it, but now …."

"What are you thinking?" Gowon asked.

"I'm thinking the more people who know I'm here the better. The more people who know, and the more religious those people are, the less likely the Commandant will be to try and get rid of me. So when Bryte gets back I'm going to see about putting a rush on that damn ceremony. And aside from that," I said. "I think the best thing I can do is to not leave this room. And the second-best thing will be to keep asking for accommodations. I don't think this base has much redundancy among its personnel; I don't think she'll try anything with her people down here, either."

"What if she wants to see you again?" he asked.

"I did say we'd talk," I replied. "But I'm not leaving this room alone again. If she won't come to me, I'll insist on bringing a retinue, at least one adjutant. I'll claim royal prerogative; even if she doesn't like the idea, she'll have to put up with it. The more of our people who would survive any attempt to erase us, the less likely I think she'll be to pull the trigger on mass murder."

"Yeah," Gowon said, "I think you're right."

I nodded my head. I felt like I sounded crazy: poison gas and acid sprays and murder plots sounded like something out of a cheap novel. But Major Gowon took my words seriously enough for me to know I was at least making some degree of sense.

"And I think in the meantime we need to come up with a plan to take care of ourselves," I said. "The top six or seven decks of *Dawn* looked to me to be mostly habitable, even accounting for the smoke damage there's likely to be usable gear. Can you get Lieutenant

Swar together with anyone we can find from Operations? Have her start thinking about what there might be on those six decks that she could use to cobble together a message to the Sluudi? I'd like to send her out first thing tomorrow if we can," I added. "I'd say we try overnight, but after hearing what the garrison had to say about being in the woods after dark, I'm not sure that's a good idea. Either way: the sooner we let Alliance people know what's happened and where we ended up, the better. Bryte said the alarm won't sound if the door is opened from inside, so I don't think sneaking people out will be too hard. It's got to be worth a try, right?"

"Yeah," Gowon answered, "I agree. Even if they turn on those spigots, if someone knows to come looking and we can tell them where to look, at least nobody's going to get away with murder."

"Agreed," I said. "I don't like feeling this paranoid," I added.

"In my experience," he said back to me, "paranoia can only be properly diagnosed in hindsight. So as long as there's a chance of what you think she might be planning actually being the thing she might be planning, you're not being paranoid — you're just being vigilant. And too much vigilance never killed anybody."

"True."

"Look," he said, taking me by my shoulders. "You're making sense, okay? You need someone to tell you that you don't sound crazy? Listen to me. You don't sound crazy. Having a room with acid sprayers in the ceiling and drainage grates in the floor? Now *that* sounds crazy, but you said somebody already admitted to you that's real. And we're standing in it right now. So every conclusion you've drawn is a logical conclusion based on the facts you were given — as crazy as those facts may be. You are not the one who introduced crazy into the equation. Okay?"

I let out a deep sigh and nodded. I'd needed that.

I was not the one who had introduced crazy into the equation. Colonel Gertrune had been the one to do that.

Now to keep her from adding murder to the mix.

CHAPTER EIGHTEEN

I could never have predicted I'd be so grateful for a concussion.

I'd always thought I had a pretty decent fooler face. I'd managed to keep my cool in many a daunting situation, and I'd certainly done my share of straight-faced lying to my caregivers and tutors as a child. But today, as I sat with the ever-growing suspicion that one of my mother's most loyal subjects was likely planning the mass murder of my colleagues and that my presence among them might be the only thing keeping them alive, I found myself lacking the capacity. My usual ability to put on a front and pretend everything was all right had escaped me entirely.

Hence my gratitude for the bump on my head.

Any outward appearance of dismay or upset could

be easily attributed to the trauma of having been on the bridge of the *Dawn*, losing the fight to keep her aloft, and my resulting concussion. It was a convenient lie and a believable one. And as much as I didn't enjoy having to lie to my crewmates, especially in light of the fact the thing I was covering up was the possibility they were all in unbelievable danger, I knew it was best to keep my suspicions to myself.

The less they knew about where they were the better.

As far as they understood, they were inside a top-secret Alliance installation. The general sense seemed to be that, as assignees to a secret mission, they'd been allowed to know of the existence of this place, but not about its inner workings. According to Major Gowon, the survivors were perfectly content to stay where they were and wait for the officers with higher-level clearances to figure out what was to come next.

I appreciated their patience, even as I wanted to scream at them to run for their lives.

I couldn't let myself dissolve into screams. I needed all my energy directed toward keeping the Emergency Deck from becoming a killing field. I sent Corporal Els up and down the hand-powered lift half a dozen times in search of blankets, pillows, crates sturdy enough to serve as stools, ration bars, and extra scrubs for the few survivors who had escaped the wreck in their nightclothes. I insisted on comfortable cots for Raline and the others who'd been badly wounded and made Corporal Els assure me they were being given adequate pain control on top of their treatment.

I also talked one of the Corpsmen who'd come down with Els and a load of gear into taking small groups of my crewmates to the nearest flushroom. It took some negotiating with the ranking Medical Officer for her to allow our personnel to see the base beyond this room, but I was adamant Colonel Gertrune had agreed showers and toilets were to be part of our accommodations.

I didn't know where, precisely, the flushrooms were located, but wherever they were I could only guess that place was safer than this one.

Bryte's return from his chat with Protocol prompted the assignment of a full-time Deck Officer: an older Commander named von Floran who had been sent to oversee the movement of base personnel and supplies into and around the Emergency Deck. He arrived wearing his white class-A blouse, a pair of what looked like khaki riding pants, patent leather jackboots, and a sour expression. I was glad we were being looked after, but mostly I was comforted by the assignment of a higher-ranking member of the base's complement to our midst.

The more of them were down here, the less likely catastrophe became.

Of course, there was still every chance I was wrong.

There was every chance I had jumped to the worst possible conclusion. Colonel Gertrune might very well be too honorable to resort to murder. Maybe we were in no danger at all.

But maybe not.

Paranoia, as Major Gowon said, could only be diagnosed in hindsight.

So I remained vigilant, and made it my mission not to leave this room again. Which became an issue when Bryte came to speak with me about putting together a formal veneration ceremony. He was adamant we do the honors on the base's Top Deck, which had been built to serve as a proper a prayer chamber. The garrison used it for regular religious observances, and the Protocol Officer thought it was the only appropriate place to hold such an auspicious event. I came back with the insistence that any religious Feirin among the crew of the *Dawn* should be welcome to attend the ceremony alongside the station personnel.

And, of course, Colonel Gertrune was not about to allow any of my people, even those who were Feirin subjects, to go any farther off the Emergency Deck than to the flushrooms they'd already visited. The Top Deck was far beyond the privilege any visitor without a Royal Feirin pedigree was about to be extended.

"So we do it down here," I insisted for the half-dozenth time.

"But we can't bring everyone down here," Bryte argued.

"Why not? Because they won't all fit? Because if they don't all fit down here, I can't imagine it's going to be any more comfortable in some room on the Top Deck."

"It's not that," he replied. "It's the same problem as with the medical and logistical staff. The problem is the uniforms."

"What about the uniforms?" I snapped back. So far, every member of the station's garrison who had come down here had managed to do so in some nondescript mishmash of underclothes, hazmat gear, BDUs, and pajamas. If there weren't enough of those garments to outfit the whole base, I had no intention of making that my problem. And I wasn't about to use such a flimsy excuse to leave my people alone and in danger while I ran off to be worshipped.

"You know what about them," Bryte said back.

"You mean the part where you don't want anyone down here to see them because there might be some *real* uncomfortable questions?"

"Maran," he said, but he hadn't any follow-up. I could tell he was frustrated, but I was frustrated, too. And, as the person who hadn't done a damn thing wrong and yet who was terrified for the safety of the people she'd arrived here with, I was not going to be the one to acquiesce.

"Bryte," I said, making sure my voice sounded just as exasperated as his. "What about Prayer Whites?" I asked. "Anyone who's particularly religious ought to have a set."

Prayer Whites were garments I'd long derided as an unnecessary display of privilege. My mother didn't give a sliver of a damn what a person wore to pray in their own homes. Large group gatherings for directed prayer more often than not took place outdoors and the appropriate clothing was whatever was suitable for the weather. But there were certain Temples — ancient places where Queens of old once held court at semi-regular cadence — that were considered particularly holy and particularly powerful within the Feirin faith. Those places required white robes not unlike the ones Ambassador Berholtz had worn on the day of our departure from Feirin City.

Prayer Whites were as bourgeoise a garment as could be found available for purchase. I'd never paid much attention to the specifics of the material and the construction, only to the fact my mother seemed to have a higher opinion of those who owned such vestments than she did of those who'd never invested in a suit. It had been mostly a guess that a set of Prayer Whites might be among the wardrobe of the personnel aboard this installation, but I could tell by the look on Bryte's face that I was on to something.

"Maybe," he allowed, tensing his jaw as his head nodded up and down slowly. "But your people won't have them. You don't think that will be a problem?"

"My people just survived an airship crash," I said back, frowning at him the way I had when he'd said something asinine back when we were kids playing together. "I don't think they're going to give a damn if the locals in the room put on fancy clothes."

"Yeah, all right," Bryte said. "Let me talk to Protocol. I think I may be able to work that angle."

"Good," I said. "Because the only way this thing is going to happen is if every Feirin subject is equally welcome."

"And what about the others?" he asked. "What about any of my people who don't have Prayer Whites? And what about the Mangan, the Gammran, and the T'wesh from your ship? What do you see them doing while we're having the ceremony?"

"Any of your complement who doesn't have prayer whites is welcome to attend in BDUs," I replied. "And as for the others: none of this is closed practice. We've allowed respectful outside observers for as far back as the records go. So I don't see any reason we can't welcome everyone to participate to whatever degree they choose. Everyone can just be here."

Bryte shook his head and ran his hand through the mess of dark hair I was sure he hadn't taken a moment to comb since finding me in the woods the day before.

"I think I may be able to make that work," he said. "Most of our people probably have Prayer Whites. I'm going to have to talk to Protocol about whether anyone who doesn't can wear BDUs, but I'll see what I can do."

"Good," I said. My tone was sharp and carried enough finality I was sure Bryte wouldn't dare re-open the topic. "You go and do that and meet me back here when you've got things all arranged."

"You could come with me," he said. "It might be easier to arrange things if I wasn't having to shuttle messages back and forth between the two of you."

"No thank you," I said. "I get plenty of protocol discussion back home. I'm perfectly content to sit this one out. You go up and handle the details while I go and find one of the escorts your CO sent to take me to the flushroom."

"We have flushrooms upstairs, you know," he said. "If you come with me ..."

"No," I stopped him before he could say any more. "I'm down here because I care how these people — who have been with me through airship hell this past week — are being treated. And you know as well as I do they wouldn't be getting this level of care if it weren't for the princess in their midst." I stole a glance at Raline again before turning back to look him in the eye.

"If it weren't for you being here," Bryte replied, "they'd still be sheltering under that fallen canopy out in the woods. You've already looked after them plenty, Maran. You're not doing anyone any disservice by choosing to use a nicer flushroom than the one in the garage."

"Bryte," I said flatly. "I'll be fine. Go talk to Protocol. I'm staying here."

"Fine," he said with a roll of his eyes so subtle I doubt most people would have caught it. "You sure you don't want me to take you to the flushroom first?"

"Lieutenant General Sonneman," I said, bringing forth all the sarcasm I could muster. "I do believe walking even a Royal guest to a flushroom is a bit beneath your station. There are plenty of folks down here who can be my escort. But only you can make the arrangements with your Protocol Officer. So go."

Bryte shook his head but did as I asked. I heard him muttering as he walked away, but he didn't talk back.

I wasn't sure what to do next. I'd never been good at waiting, but that was pretty much all I could do. Raline was still being looked after, and I knew my presence would be distracting at best. Major Gowon and the other members of the Intelligence staff would likely have an easier time making plans without me inserting myself into the conversation.

I wondered for a moment if I ought to check in with the Deck Officer, but quickly decided against it. He was standing just in front of the seam in the wall beside the lift, having a spirited discussion with Major Malli. My first inclination was to rescue him; the unsuspecting gentleman surely didn't deserve whatever it was Malli felt the need to dish out. But when I looked closely at the interplay between them, I could see they were laughing.

And as long as Major Malli was engaged in a pleasant conversation with the Deck Officer, he wasn't trying to assert undue authority over the rest of the crew. It was in everyone's best interest to leave that alone.

And anyway, I really did need that trip to the flushroom, as I'd downed that whole canteen of water. Entangling myself into Malli's conversation would have kept me from that necessary errand for more time than was reasonably prudent. I looked around the room and spotted a young woman who'd come down at the same time as von Floran, whose current task seemed to be more interruptible than most.

"I beg your pardon," I said as I approached her from behind. She'd been attending to one of the gear racks of hanging canteens — sorting full vessels from empty and tagging the ones in need of refilling. She turned immediately at the sound of my voice, and I was able to watch as her eyes grew wider with the realization of who had just spoken to her. "Lieutenant Frey," I addressed her by name as soon as I was able to read the tape on her BDU blouse. "I believe you might be able to show me to the flushroom? And please don't kneel," I added. "I'd rather not waste the time."

"Oh," she said, nearly dropping the empty canteen in her hands. "Yes. Of course, Your Highness." She set the canteen down carefully and gestured for me to follow. I fell into step just behind. The whole walk to the lift, she kept turning her head to see whether I was keeping up, as though there was some chance of my getting lost between one side of the room and the other.

The silence was awkward as we waited for the lift to come. It occurred to me it might have been smart of me to wait to send Bryte back up several levels until after I'd made use of the lift to see to my increasingly full bladder. I tried to maintain decorum and not fidget too much, but I didn't mind that Lt. Frey kept her attention on the indicator for the lift.

When the car finally arrived, she held the door for me.

"Thank you," I said as I passed.

"You're most welcome, Your Highness." She stepped aboard the lift and secured the door. "And you're sure you just want to go to the garage?"

"As quickly as possible," I replied, hoping to stress the growing urgency of the situation without being too indelicate.

"Oh, yes ma'am," she said, reaching out and beginning to crank the lift upward more quickly than Bryte had done earlier. Within seconds she was setting the brake and unpinning the door latch. "This way, Your Highness," she said, taking off at a lively clip down the hall to the left of the lift.

I followed in an equal hurry.

She stopped at the door to another lift and pulled the lever to summon it. Fortunately for my dignity, the door opened almost immediately and the two of us stepped aboard at the same time. Lt. Frey turned the dial to take us one floor down, which confused me to no end.

"That's only one floor," I said, gesturing to the dial's setting as the left began its descent. "Isn't that where we just came from?"

"Oh, no ma'am," Frey replied. "Your Highness."

"Ma'am is fine."

"Yes ma'am."

"So where are we going?"

"Oh, yes ma'am," she said again, obviously flustered. "The only way in or out of the Emergency Deck is the manual lift," she explained. "So all the other cars just skip it. Same with the stairs. We're going to the garage level, which is below the Emergency Deck, but since the lift doesn't acknowledge the space between the two stops, it looks like we're going right back to where we came from. But we're not."

I nodded my head. I supposed that made sense. And I wondered if there were people aboard this installation who didn't know what the Emergency Deck was — or even that it existed. That could be behind some of the trouble getting the Protocol Officer to agree to holding the ceremony there.

I was trying not to devise too many more upsetting theories as I followed Lt. Frey off the lift and into the garage where I'd been assured there would be functional, if not comfortable, facilities. Two things came clear to me immediately: why this was called the garage, and where the tread bikes and walkontainers had gone when we'd parted company outside.

Rows of neatly parked tread bikes, jet speeders, mechanical stilts, and walkontainers of varying sizes stood in racks at various points around the room. There were hand-cranked battery charging stations, and cans of motor oil, axle grease, industrial alcohol, and standard petrol set up as dividers adjacent to the vehicles they were most intended for. At the far end of the space from us was a chain-rolled slat door that drew sideways to allow for the entrance or exit of vehicles of varying widths.

Lt. Frey led me in the opposite direction from the

vehicles, toward a plain-looking swinging door not far from the lift.

"Just in there," she said.

"Thank you," I replied, speeding my steps in the direction she'd indicated. But when I turned to acknowledge her properly, I could see something in her eyes that gave me pause. "Everything all right, Lieutenant?" I asked. I hoped her answer would come swiftly. I didn't have a whole lot of patience left.

"Do you ..." She pursed her lips for a moment as her brow furrowed. "... mind?" she asked quietly.

It took me a second, but only a second, before I understood what she was asking.

"Oh, no," I insisted, "not at all." I reached for the door to the flushroom and pushed it open, shaking my head for emphasis. I knew how uncomfortable I'd felt being forced to wait for an escort down here and there was absolutely no way I was about to force another woman to escort me all the way back to the Emergency Deck and then get permission from a superior to return to relieve herself. I had no objection to shared facilities.

"Thank you," Frey said, taking the door from me and urging me into the room ahead of her.

I should have known better than to think she would let me hold the door for her.

The flushroom was a smallish one, with polished chrome walls that looked as though they got a proper rubdown every day whether they needed it or not. Even the knobs on the doors of all five latrine closets were gleaming with high-buff shine. That was a feat, considering how much traffic this flushroom had been getting for the past couple of hours.

Not that I was about to let that matter. If the Commandant felt the need to keep her flushrooms spit-and-polished, who was I to complain? I ducked quickly into the first closet and locked the door.

Once my bladder was empty, my whole body seemed less on edge. But when I went to wash my hands, I caught a glimpse of myself in the shining metal wall above the sink. Somehow I'd managed to forget I'd been through an airship crash and spent the night in the woods since the last time I'd seen a bar of soap or a hairbrush. My reflection was a harsh reminder.

I looked like all seven hells had come to nest.

There was little I could do about my rumpled flight suit or matted tresses, but I'd found myself in possession of a soap sheet and a hot water spigot. It was the least I could do to try and wash some of the dirt off my face and hands. I was in the process of rinsing the first volley of lather off my face when Lt. Frey emerged from the far latrine closet and came to join me at the wall of sinks.

"Oh, Your Highness," she said as she started at the foot pump to get the water flowing. "If you'd like to wash up, there are proper washrooms on the upper decks, I'm sure I could take you to ...."

"Really," I said back, working the remnants of the soap sheet between my fingers in preparation for one last go at my face, "it's fine."

"Are you sure?" she asked, soaping up her own hands. "because really, I could ...."

"I promise," I said back. I rinsed the soap off my face and reached for the towel hanging beside the sink. "This rank I wear may be honorary, but it isn't entirely ceremonial. I graduated from the Gammran Air Academy. I can handle washing my face in a flushroom sink."

"Oh," Frey said, then immediately clammed up. I looked up at her reflection and could once again see discomfort on her face.

"What is it?" I asked, meeting her reflection's gaze

with my own. She frowned and shook her head.

"I'm sorry, ma'am," she said, shrugging as she took her towel off its hook and started to dry her hands. "It's just that usually when someone says they went to the Air Academy, I answer them with a cheer and a derogatory remark about their slamball team."

"You went to Maritime," I surmised. The Gammran Air Academy and the Mangan Maritime Academy were old rivals, with sporting histories dating back to long before the Alliance was formalized. It had long been tradition for graduates of the two elite institutions to greet each other with chants and heckles.

"I did."

"Which campus?" I asked. Mostly my curiosity was piqued at the idea of an officer who had graduated from one of the Alliance's premiere military academies having chosen to come to work in this hive of bald-faced treason.

"I did my three standard years at Main and my Advanced Proficiencies and Leadership Accreditations at Feirin Offshore."

"That's really impressive," I said, not afraid to let my admiration of her achievements show in my voice. Maritime was at least as competitive as the Air Academy, and in some ways more difficult to graduate from. Over half the candidates who managed to get through the exacting admissions process to attend the Alliance Maritime Academy in Mangan washed out within their first year. Barely a tenth made it into APL, and maybe only half of those left with any Accreditations at all — much less two of them. "What's your Advanced Proficiency in?"

"Ballast Ships," she said, pride coming through loud and clear in her voice.

"Wow," I said. "So you can fly, too?"

Ballast ships were one of the most peculiar assets

found within the Alliance military; I had always found them to be uniquely fascinating. They were an extreme combination of sailing ship, airship, and submarine. Depending on the deployment of the dagger keels and which of its ballast bags were filled with water, these vessels could sail the oceans the same as any other ship of the line, rig their sailing canvas into gas bags and operate as an airship, or pack them up altogether and run submerged beneath the sea. Ballast ships were notoriously difficult to master, seeing as the operation of one demanded proficiency in three separate disciplines. I'd never met a qualified ballast ship captain before that I knew of.

"I could command the ship while it flew," Frey said. "Understand what was going on, know how to lift and lower, that sort of thing. But I wouldn't want to be the one doing the flying. I'd need an actual pilot for that."

"That makes sense," I allowed, as the two of us made our way out of the flushroom and back into the garage. "But can I tell you what doesn't make any sense to me?"

"What's that, Your Highness? Um … ma'am?"

"How is it," I began, deciding not to acknowledge her royal slip, "that someone who went to Maritime and graduated with Accreditations wound up here." I gestured vaguely around to the underground garage.

"You'd be surprised how many skills translate," Frey answered me. "Honestly, the closest thing to being stationed inside an enemy mountain is the submarine service. Constant vigilance, no way to step outside for fresh air, and if something breaks, you've got to fix it with what's on hand. And I mostly work on the power plant," she added, "the hydros are based on the emergency turbines they used to install in the big sail ships. Seafaring skills are surprisingly useful when living inside a mountain."

I smiled and nodded. She'd managed to thoroughly

answer the question I'd asked without even beginning to answer the question I *thought* I'd asked. Because that might have been on purpose, I decided not to turn around and ask her point blank how it was someone who had graduated from one of the Alliance's premier military academies found themselves recruited by, and agreeing to be posted to, an illegal outpost.

"That makes sense," I said, trying not to sound too exasperated by her non-answer answer.

"And from what I understand," she added, "people get promoted a lot faster here than in the more mainstream duty stations. So, what's nine years locked in a mountain while I'm young and single if that means a better career after I'm home again?"

My stomach dropped.

"Nine years?" I asked. I tried not to let it show in my voice how disturbing I found the idea of being stuck here for that long.

"Yes ma'am," Lt. Frey answered. If she'd noticed my dismay, she didn't mention it. "It's a nine-year tour. One third of the staff rotates out every three years."

The pit in my stomach got a little lighter. Three years was still a long time, but it wasn't as daunting as nine. I couldn't be sure of a single-purpose rescue mission coming for me and the other survivors. I'd gotten the idea into my head that our most likely means of escape would be to hitch a ride on the return trip the next time there was a scheduled crew rotation. Three years was certainly better than nine, but I still couldn't help but hope we'd gotten lucky, and the next transport would be due any day now.

"And how long have you been here?" I asked, both as a matter of friendly curiosity and in hopes of gauging where in the cycle we were.

"A little over a year," she said. "And I've already advanced from Lieutenant JG to First Lieutenant." The two of us stepped onto the waiting lift as I bit my lip. Two years. Better than three and much better than nine, but that was still longer than I wanted to be stuck inside a mountain in Xylanth.

I didn't say anything more while we made our way back up and down to the Emergency Deck. Maybe I should have congratulated her on her promotion. But I wasn't sure whether a rank earned while posted to an illegal installation with allegiance to only one of the Alliance's member states would even be recognized in the greater military. If Lt. Frey had cared to get into that, she'd have answered differently when I asked how she'd wound up here. And I wasn't in the mood to push her on the subject. It was a conversation better had with her superior officers anyway. So I kept quiet.

When my brain was less foggy, I could discuss those details with Bryte, or maybe even with Colonel Gertrune. And it sounded like I had the better part of two years to get around to having that conversation.

CHAPTER NINETEEN

Bryte was back on the Emergency Deck when I returned from the flushroom. He and Corporal Byron raced toward me the moment I emerged from the blind by the lift. My first guess was they were bearing urgent news from Protocol, and by the looks on their faces that news was unlikely to be good.

"What's up?" I asked, closing the gap between us.

"We may have a problem," Bryte said back.

I shook my head, suspicious. Just because something qualified as a problem to Bryte and his cohort didn't mean I was going to care to solve it.

"What?" I asked, trying not to let too much sarcasm into my tone. "The cook can't decide what to make for the post-ceremonial dinner?"

"Oh, no ma'am," Byron said. "They're already

soaking the nuts for an adasha pudding."

"Wow, okay," I said, hoping my smile appeared genuine rather than annoyed. Adasha pudding was an all-day affair, and I was a little surprised this place had the ingredients in stock. But that was hardly the first surprise of the day, and it certainly wasn't the biggest. It seemed a silly thing, but if that's what the cook wanted to make, I wasn't going to argue.

"We think the Xylanthians are headed this way," Bryte said, leaning in toward my ear as his volume dropped. "There's a proximity sensor that's tripped, and ..."

"Of course they're coming," I replied.

"What?"

"It only makes sense," I said. "If something as large as the *Dawn* crashed on the Feirin frontier, we'd have a team there to check it out within twelve hours. The Gammran or the Mangan would be there in eight. So the fact the Xylanthians are coming should not be a surprise."

"Yeah," Bryte said softly.

"But what does that mean for us?" I asked. "Do we need to change what we're doing? Is there some sort of silent running protocol we'll need to implement? What's the SOP for when the enemy is in the vicinity?"

"Honestly," he replied, "I don't know."

"You don't know?"

"It's never happened before."

"You've only been here for, what?" I asked, trying to remember the last time I'd heard of him attending an event in Feirin. "Four years or so? Maybe one of the officers who's been here longer ...."

"No, Maran," he interrupted me. "It's never happened before. Never. Not ever."

"Wait," I said then. "The alarm has never tripped before or the Xylanthians have never been in range before?"

"The latter."

"Do you mean to tell me there's been a goshdang secret base hidden in this mountain to watch the Xylanthians for almost *thirty years* and in this whole entire time you have never actually seen the Xylanthians?"

"Yeah." He looked contrite, at least.

"What the ..." I was starting to see red; between my fury and my concussion, I could barely form words. The very idea of this base was an affront to everything I believed in and the knowledge it had thus far proven itself to be absolutely useless was making the whole thing worse.

"We were put here to watch the coastline," he explained. "We're here to keep an eye on things and to sound the alarm if any Xy expeditionary force comes out to make war on Feirin. I'd say, all-in-all, it's a good thing that never happened."

My eyelid twitched when he said "Feirin." The fact he didn't even think to temper his comment to include the Alliance was nearly as infuriating as the fact they'd been standing watch uselessly for nearly three decades.

"You may have a point," I allowed. "But that's not exactly helpful right now." I shook my head and shrugged. "So what do the regs say? What's the theoretical plan for having Xylanthians in the neighborhood who aren't trying to mount an invasion?"

"Maran," Bryte said, "I'm trying to tell you there isn't one. There are no regs. This base was put here on the presumption that any approaching Xy assets should be presumed hostile and outbound with aggressive intent. But I think we can both agree that's not what's happening right now."

"Queen fussing Salian," I cursed, angrier still at the jollyhoppers who'd put in this base. How in all seven hells had they thought it was a reasonable thing to install a base into the side of a mountain in enemy territory with absolutely no rules of engagement other than 'sound the alarm if you think they're headed toward home'?

Bryte shoved his hands into the pockets of his coverall. Looking the most infuriating combination of sheepish and terrified I could imagine possible, he seemed to have nothing to say for himself. Byron, on the other hand, was clearly put-off by my colorful language. I almost laughed at his expression. I doubt I could have been farther from his expectation of a princess.

"How about a person, then; someone with an educated guess as to what the next move is?" I asked, still looking for some official, or even quasi-official guidance as to what to do as the enemy approached our hopefully well-hidden position. "Cultural expert, staff anthropologist, anyone who might be able to predict how the Xylanthians are going to react when they find a wrecked Alliance warship in the woods?"

Bryte shook his head.

"No."

"What the actual fuss, Bryte? This place — where no one should ever come — has a Protocol Officer to see to all conditions of etiquette, but not anyone who's any sort of expert on the enemy population that lives just outside the mountain."

"We were never supposed to deal with anybody outside the mountain."

I wanted to smack him upside his fussing face. To push him down into a puddle of mud and kick dirt on him like when we were children. But there was no mud on the Emergency Deck and, more than that, other than satisfying my momentary frustration, perpetrating some minor violence against Bryte wasn't going to accomplish anything.

The enemy was possibly headed toward the wreck of our ship, and we had absolutely no idea how they would react, or what to do next.

I was within a moment of screaming and stamping my foot when I realized the answer I needed was right across the room, sitting on the floor.

"Come with me," I said. I turned and went, heedless of whether Bryte and his companion were behind me. In fact, I only checked to make sure they'd followed after I'd come to a stop. They were coming, but they still needed to catch up. I waited until I was sure they were in earshot before I turned to the surprised-looking people I'd just approached. There were more of them now than when I'd come over originally — a bunch of young enlisted personnel who I guessed had been intimidated by the presence of Major Gowon and who'd come to join their fellows after he'd absented himself from the conversation.

I was mad as hell at what I was about to do, but I didn't have a whole lot of choice. It wasn't fair to lay this on a twenty-something file clerk. But here we were. "Sergeant Pon," I greeted.

"Field Marshal," she replied, scrambling to her feet and to some approximation of attention.

"General Sonneman," I said, turning to Bryte by way of introduction. "Corporal Byron, this is Sergeant Ginna Pon. Sergeant Pon, this is Lieutenant General Sonneman and Corporal Byron — the installation's XO and the CO's adjutant respectively. Gentlemen: Sergeant Pon is the closest thing it appears we have to an expert on the Xy. As far as I am aware, there is no one in this room, nay, in this mountain, who's better equipped to make an educated guess as to what happens next."

All the color drained out of Sergeant Pon's face.

"What's going on?" she asked quietly.

Bryte signaled for all of us to step away from the others. It probably wasn't a bad idea. These kids were likely to find all this out eventually, but panicking them right now when we had little to no idea what was going on wouldn't do anybody any good.

"Ginna," I said, taking her by the elbow and pulling her closer into our small circle. "There's a very high probability the Xylanthians are on their way to the wreck site right now. Seeing as an Alliance airship wreck isn't something the local garrison has ever dealt with, no one is sure how the Xylanthians are going to react to finding it nor has anyone the first clue as to what we should be doing. We'd like your best guess as to how they'll respond to the wreck, and to what they're likely to do next. That way we can be better poised to form a plan of our own."

"Oh." Pon's eyes got wide. She might have been about to faint.

"Anything you can tell us," I encouraged, shaking my head. This was so far above the expectations of her rank; we had no business laying this burden on a Staff Sergeant, but she was the only person here who may have insight.

"Um ..." Sgt. Pon shrugged, looking back and forth between the three of us as she shook her head and frowned. "The Xy are a pragmatic people," she said. "They're practical, unsentimental. I'm not a military expert," she qualified, "so I can't really speak to what the larger ramifications are going to be of their finding an Alliance ship crashed on their frontier. But as far as the people who find the ship itself ...?"

"That's mainly what we're concerned with," Bryte told her. "That other stuff — those *larger ramifications* — that's not in our sphere. We can leave that to the politicians. What we need to know in this moment is what's about to happen a couple of miles from here so we can know if there's anything we can do about it."

"Like I said," Sgt. Pon replied, "they're a very practical people. And the continent is so resource scarce. If they find the ship, the most likely thing I can think of is that they'll strip it for parts."

"They'll ...?" Byron seemed to have no concept of what she was saying. "What do you mean, exactly?"

"I mean ..." She shook her head and shrugged. "Have you ever seen a swarm of boggarwasp larvae on the corpse of a draedabird?"

"Haven't had the pleasure," Bryte replied, the look on his face a clear indication he was trying to imagine it.

"They'll probably pull the wiring first," Pon continued, this time without metaphor. "The conductive alloys used in Alliance warships are hard to come by anywhere — and *Dawn* was a pretty big ship, she's liable to have a lot of it aboard. And after they've done that, they're likely to go deck by deck, pulling off the metal for scrap and sorting out any components they think they can repurpose."

"Aren't there ... bodies on that ship?" Byron asked quietly. His face was ashen all of a sudden. If I had to guess I'd say he was a religious, and as such was thoroughly appalled at the idea of anyone trespassing on the dead. The Feirin edicts against disturbing the recently deceased were age-old and intractable.

"Yeah," I replied.

"What will they ... what will the Xylanthians do?" Byron couldn't finish his whole question, but what he'd managed to say was enough.

"The Xy spiritual tradition recognizes no connection between the physical body and the spirit, or the soul," Sgt. Pon told us. "As far as I'm aware they have no reverence at all for a person's mortal remains. I don't know what they'll do. But it's not going to be anything solemn or respectful."

I thought for a moment Corporal Byron was going to be sick. He stood still for a beat, his face taking on a series of increasingly upsetting expressions, before swallowing hard and snapping to attention.

"Field Marshal," he addressed me. I stood up straighter at that. The fact that a religious Feirin was addressing me by my Alliance rank said a lot.

"Yes, Corporal?"

"We need to know what else was on that ship," he said. "Were there weapons, machines, proprietary technology? Anything that, were the Xy to learn to make use of, would constitute a threat to Feir ... Alliance security going forward?"

I'm sure he knew I caught that slip. And I could only hope that Sgt. Pon hadn't. I wasn't yet ready to explain to the rest of my crew what we'd stumbled upon here in the enemy frontier.

"You know," I said, looking back and forth between Bryte and Byron, "I have no idea. I served aboard the *Dawn* in a diplomatic capacity. I did some work on the Mechanical Deck — helping to knock out a stabilizer that wouldn't cooperate. And I happened to be up on the bridge when we crashed. But I don't remember seeing anything that stuck out as new, or interesting, or .... And I certainly didn't see any weapons."

"Can you be sure there aren't any aboard?" Bryte asked.

I shook my head.

"I really can't," I replied. "Oh!" I exclaimed without having meant to. It was so obvious, and yet somehow I'd surprised myself by realizing it. "Major Malli would probably know," I told them. "That is, if anyone here would know, it would be him. He was Captain Taiko's second in command. If the *Dawn* were carrying any kind of special equipment or weapons, he'd have been told about them."

"I should speak with him," Byron said, sternly.

"He's still over talking to the Deck Officer," I told him.

"Thank you." He turned on his heel to go.

"Corporal," I called after him.

"Yes ma'am?" he replied, pausing his progress and turning his head to face me.

"Be sure to introduce yourself as Colonel Gertrune's adjutant."

"One of *those*, huh?" Byron asked.

I nodded. Men like Malli, who only respected rank and had seemingly no use for interpersonal communication outside the scope of operational necessity weren't hard to come by in the military. If I was sending Byron, who seemed nice enough, and had at least had the good sense to address me by rank, to speak with someone of that character, I wanted him to be prepared.

"Indeed," I replied.

Byron nodded, then went on his way.

"Thank you, Sergeant Pon," Bryte said. He turned toward her and gave a nod — a universal gesture of dismissal.

"I'm at your disposal, sir," Pon replied. She clicked her heels and nodded once before leaving us to return to the group she'd been chatting with before we came over.

Bryte was frowning. And I could see the wheels in his head were turning.

"What are you thinking?" I asked.

He frowned harder. "What do you mean?"

"Oh, come on, Sonneman," I ribbed. "You don't have any fooler face at all — never have. You're plotting something and I want to know what it is."

"You're not going to like it," he said quietly, closing the distance between us.

"Well, here's a bulletin, genius," I replied. "I don't like any of this. I can't imagine anything you're about to say making me more unhappy than I already am. So you're probably good on the angry princess front. Now spill it."

Bryte nodded and stepped even closer to me. Whatever he was about to say, he was going to say it quietly.

"The more I think about it," he said, "the more I think we need to beat the Xylanthians to the wreck site. And I think we need to blow it up."

"Well would you look at us on the same page?"

I could tell he was a little bit astonished I'd said that.

"You're serious?"

"As an airship crash," I replied. "Look: weapons or no weapons, I don't like the idea of the Xylanthians ransacking our ship. Just because I'm not religious doesn't mean I'm okay with them intruding on our dead crewmates. But more than that," I added, "their finding bits and pieces of *something* that crashed is going to be better for us in the long run. It could have been anybody, right? Gives the Alliance some breathing room and gives the Xylans plausible deniability about wanting us to talk with them. We need to blow it up," I concluded. "The less of *Dawn* that's left to find, the better."

"I'm glad we agree on this," Bryte said. "Now I just have to figure out how to make it happen."

"Do you have explosives?" I asked what was, in my mind, the only pressing question.

"Yeah," he replied. "We've got dynamite — construction charges left over from building this place. We've got hundreds of them. That's not the problem."

"Then what is?" I asked. With that much dynamite

there shouldn't be any issue with blowing the ship to splinters.

"Personnel," he replied. "We're about an hour away from the Veneration Ceremony, which we've already announced. Some folks are already dressing for it. There's no way any team I send out now will be back before it happens, and I don't think I'll get many volunteers who are willing to miss out."

I was sure the look on my face was that of complete exasperation. Of all the cockamamie reasons for not taking an assignment .... I was about to offer a private audience to anyone who volunteered for the mission to blow up the ship when a much better solution occurred to me.

"Send my people."

"What?" Bryte asked. "No."

"Why the hell not?" I challenged. "What are you worried about?"

"Well, base security, for one."

"Listen," I said, taking him by the arm. "They've already seen the garage. And the way to and from it — because that's where the flushroom is. Add to that my Mangan, Gammran, and T'wesh colleagues are unlikely to mind missing a Feirin religious ceremony. Plus," I added, "it's their ship. Some of them were part of restoring it from scrap. They know their way around and they probably know where to best place those charges to get the most ... you know ... bang for your bang."

"That's not a bad point."

"And," I added. "Bonus: if they run out of time and the Xylanthians show up before they're done, they won't have come upon a cadre of tidy Feirin in starched BDUs and shiny boots. All they'll find are a bunch of crash survivors with the singed flight suits to prove it."

"Dammit, Maran," he said. "I think you've got a

point."

"I know I've got a point," I replied. "Have you got somebody who knows how to use those explosives?"

"I'll go," Bryte said. "I'll probably take Byron, too. Between the two of us we should be able to give your people the quick and dirty version of how to set the charges."

"All right." I took a deep breath as I raked my nails across the crown of my head. It was an old T'wesh calming gesture that Raline had taught me one of the first times we'd found ourselves together in a social situation.

I didn't get any calmer.

"I'll get started on getting the charges moved to the garage and loaded on walkontainers," Bryte said. "Do you think you can round up a dozen or so of your people who'll know what they're doing and be up to the task?"

"Yeah," I said back. I was sure I'd require Gowon's and probably even Malli's help, but Bryte didn't need to know that. "I'll see what I can do."

CHAPTER TWENTY

I had never felt more spectacularly foolish in all my life.

The getup I was expected to wear for the Veneration was an unflattering approximation of Royal Vestments cobbled together by the station's Protocol Officer from Prayer Whites belonging to at least half a dozen crew members of various shapes and builds. Had he not had some degree of pride invested in what was happening, I was sure the fellow himself, a lanky Lieutenant Colonel named Walmfrus, would have found the costume as preposterous as I did.

But his reputation was on the line — far more than mine was, thankfully. I was suffering this indignity for the express purpose of sparing myself further frustration while I was stuck in this treasonous hellscape of a base. Well, that, and the tiny matter of making sure everyone here knew the *Dawn* survivors were aboard this base and thereby making mass murder that much less likely.

What was a ridiculous outfit compared to all that?

Still. As I looked at my reflection in the Emergency Deck's polished chrome wall, I wondered if Colonel Walmfrus would mind if I at least rolled up the sleeves.

But, then again, maybe the outfit wasn't the problem.

I couldn't help but resent this part of the process. Having a formal Veneration Ceremony was one thing, but spending all this time *preparing* for a formal Veneration Ceremony was something else altogether. Especially in light of the fact Bryte was, at this very moment, gathering a team to go out to the wreck.

Helping coordinate that effort would certainly have been a better use of my time.

Corporal Byron, however, had disagreed with that contention. When Walmfrus had appeared with a satchel of prayer books and a pile of vestments for me to try on, Byron had insisted I stop what I was doing and go with him.

Bryte had been quick to remind me the one thing I might hate worse than the Ceremony in theory would be the Ceremony in practice if I hadn't had a hand in the preparation. These things could be protracted and unpleasant under the best circumstances, and if I wanted to spare myself the longest and absolute most ostentatious iteration of this rite, my best bet was to be as involved in the planning as possible.

"We'll open with the traditional prayer of Invocation," Walmfrus declared, thumbing through the prayer book in his hand. We were less than an hour away from the start of the whole affair and he seemed to be vacillating between the energies of a focused professional and a nerve-addled mother-of-the-bride. He flitted about the room, sizing up the space (and me, probably) only occasionally stopping to write something in his prayer book.

"And you're going to do that, right?" I asked. "The prayer. That's not up to me?" I tugged at the waist of the overlarge tunic he'd put me in, hoping to maybe blouse it over the tied sashes in such a way that it at least stopped dragging the floor.

"Unless you'd like to, Your Highness," he replied.

"Oh no," I said. "No. That's your thing. You can handle the invocation."

"Yes, Your Highness." He jotted down another note. "And after that, we'll have the opening hymn. Do you have any favorites?"

I shook my head. I absolutely did not have any favorites.

"Not off the top of my head, no," I replied, as diplomatically as I could. "What about you, Declan, got a favorite hymn?"

I'd dragged Ensign Declan into this corner with me. My story to him was that I required an adjutant, but really, I hadn't wanted to be left alone with a religious Protocol Officer if I could help it. If I was forcing Declan to hang out where the planning and coiffing was being done, the least I could do was involve him in it. Plus, I couldn't think of any hymns.

"'How Majestic'," he answered quickly.

"Really?"

"It's catchy," he said. "I like it."

"Well then," I said to Walmfrus. "We'll open with 'How Majestic'."

"Yes, Your Highness," he replied. "And a closing hymn?"

"Declan?" I asked.

"Um," Declan fidgeted and bit his lip.

"You're all tapped out on hymn titles?" I surmised. Declan nodded.

"This one's on you, Colonel," I said.

"'Rise of the Ruler'," he replied as though there was never any question. "And I suppose I should ask you if there are any pieces of music you'd prefer not to hear. We've only the single tagelharpe player, and I don't know her full repertoire. But we'll have music during the Adoration and the Benediction as well as the hymns we sing, and I'd like to tell her to avoid anything you're not fond of."

I shrugged my shoulders. There was one I didn't like. But I'd be damned if I knew what it was called.

"I can't think of any," I lied. "Tell her she can play whatever suits her."

"'Glory and Wonder', then," Walmfrus said, scrawling another note into his book. "I've heard her practice that one, and it's certainly appropriate for an Adoration."

"Good," I said, trying to sound as upbeat and encouraging as I could. Not that I had any real preference for the hymns.

"Will you have time to teach me the words?"

I froze.

I knew that voice. Doing my best to steady my breathing, I turned my head slowly to see Raline standing just a few feet away. I did my best to smile, but I was sure I looked much more like a fool in pain than a person happy to see someone.

My face was hot and my palms were sweaty. So was my head; I could feel the curls forming against my follicles. The urge to go to her was so strong I forgot I'd been standing on a supply crate. I moved absently, tripping over my ill-fitting ceremonial robes as I attempted to take the first step. I landed hard, in a heap of white silk and colored sashes, but the feeling of embarrassment was far greater than the pain of having smashed my palms and kneecaps into the concrete.

"Your Highness!" Declan called, darting over from where he'd been observing.

"Are you all right?" Raline asked as she bent down to help me up.

"I should be asking you that," I replied. Her shoulder was bandaged, her arm hung in a proper sling. She looked better than the last time I'd seen her, and much, much better than she had out in the woods, but still I was far more concerned with her injuries than I was with my own bruised knee and wounded pride.

"But I'm not the one who just fell down," she said. Raline was smiling as she brushed a stray curl off my cheek. Suddenly I was glad I was already on the floor. My knees were weak beneath me, and the buzzybugs were back in my stomach.

I could handle all manner of international crises. I could abide royal expectation, entertain dignitaries, fly off into enemy lands, and stand my ground against high-ranking military officials — but I absolutely could not keep a hold of myself when Raline Khatri touched my face.

Damn.

I managed to get to my feet. Slowly, but without a further stumble, I rose. Gathering the too-long and too-voluminous garment in both hands, I turned back to Walmfrus.

"Can we have the room?" I asked. My tone was enough to tell him it wasn't a request.

"As you wish, Your Highness," he replied. Walmfrus signaled for Declan to follow, but he'd already started toward the exit. "I'll just go and check in with our musician."

I smiled and nodded. I couldn't have cared less

where Walmfrus was going, as long as he was leaving. As soon as I figured he and Declan were out of earshot, I turned my attention back to Raline.

"How's it going out there?" I asked.

"Do you want the truth?" she asked back. "Or should I sugarcoat?"

"The truth will do."

"Major Gowon is putting together a team to go back to *Dawn*," she told me. I knew that much, but I didn't want to interrupt her to say so. "And Major Malli insists on going along. Which is causing everybody difficulty, because he's demanding he be put in charge of the whole thing. But your friend Sonneman and the other fellow who's with him are saying no to that. Meanwhile, one of Gowon's people is trying to figure out whether she'll be able to send out a coded message from the wreck without any help from anyone because she doesn't think she can trust anyone to keep quiet about it, so she doesn't want anyone to know."

"But you know."

"Major Gowon thought I might know where there was com gear other than on the bridge," she told me. "Because Major Malli is being such a headache, there's a chance Lt. Swar won't be able to make an attempt with the bridge equipment. They were hoping my office had the means to send a coded message on its own."

"Did you ... have that equipment?" I asked.

"Sadly, no," Raline replied. "It was my understanding that we were strictly prohibited from sending coded messages for the duration of this mission."

"That makes sense."

"It does?"

I shook my head. Of course Raline didn't grok why it made sense to keep Berholtz and his staff from sending an encrypted message from the *Dawn*.

"Yeah," I replied. "This whole thing started with a coded message. One the Xylans sent on a channel they knew we'd compromised. So we know they have long distance communication capability. But what we don't know is what kind of long-distance *listening* capability they have. And we certainly don't know what kind of communication or decryption capability exists with the Xylanthians. Since we were headed to Xyland, I'm sure the Intelligence Service would have known any message sent from the ship would likely have been heard in Xylanth, and they'd have wanted to stop that from happening. So they'd have wanted to make sure only Captain Taiko had the ability to send a communique of any variety."

"All right," Raline conceded, "that does make sense."

"What doesn't make sense," I said back, "is that somehow Major Gowon didn't know that."

It was Raline's turn to shake her head. And she laughed a little, a sound that made my stomach all fluttery again.

"Oh," she said. "He did know that. What he didn't know was whether Ambassador Berholtz had been willing to follow the directive and funnel all his communication through the Captain. According to Major Gowon, the Ambassador arrived with rather a lot of luggage, including several crates into which he could have secreted all manner of communications apparatus."

My mind flashed back to the sight of Berholtz's cabin the day we'd come aboard *Dawn*. It had been packed nearly to the rafters with cases, crates, and duffels. I'd presumed him a particularly fussy egotist who insisted on proper attire for all occasions and refused to travel without all his favorite creature comforts and religious implements. But there was an argument to be made for his having snuck contraband equipment aboard.

"Not an unfounded suspicion," I conceded. "And Gowon thought you might know about it if he did?"

"Of all the survivors, I would be the most likely to know."

"Except you don't?"

"Except I don't. Berholtz only spoke to me the one time."

"He spoke to you?" I asked. This was the first I was hearing of Berholtz having spoken to anyone at all. I'd presumed he still hadn't emerged from his cabin when the ship went down.

"He did," she replied. "He came to find me just as the storm was getting bad. I think he thought I could do something about it ...? I don't know. But he certainly didn't let me in on any secrets he was carrying."

"Okay," I said, trying to sort my still-aching head out. "It might be worth it to give Lt. Swar good directions to Berholtz's cabin. If he did smuggle aboard any com gear, it's probably still in its case. But I think the better option may be for her to try and locate the ship's emergency radio beacon. Damn," I added, "I wish we had someone from mechanical with us. Eiji or Phamm would have ..." My voice caught in my throat as my eyes filled suddenly. I squeezed my eyes shut, but it was too late; a tear fell down my cheek even through my closed lashes.

I inhaled sharply and clenched my jaw. Now was not the time. Letting myself break down now would only make things harder. I could cry later. I could wail and scream and kick and throw things and hurl curses all I wanted to once we were safe. But right now, we were decidedly *not* safe, and I could not let myself succumb to grief and upset.

In the middle of a shaky exhale, I felt Raline's hand on my hair, combing her nails across my scalp in that same soothing way I'd tried to do myself earlier. Somehow it worked better when she did it. I turned my head toward her and smiled.

There was so much care on her face I couldn't even be nervous looking at her.

"Please tell me about the radio beacon," she asked softly.

I nodded and sniffed.

"Every aircraft has one," I explained. "Or at least they're supposed to. The older kind — the ones they used to put aboard airships — the kind *Dawn* would have been equipped with during the war — was nothing more than two halves of a circuit separated by a thin bit of glass. In the event of a hard landing, the glass would break, the circuit would complete, and it would transmit a mayday signal that anyone with a receiver could follow to attempt a rescue. Post-war, though, the new machines — especially the bi-wings — flew too hard for those beacons to survive maneuvers. There were a lot of false alarms there for a while, so the design got changed. Now most aircraft have a modified version of the naval beacon. It's a device suspended over a flagon of water by a gelatin seal. Those beacons start transmitting the moment they get wet — really useful for cases when the inside of a tall deck on a ship has water incursion. In the aircraft-modified version, the idea is that a crash would burst the beacon through the gelatin; it would land in the water and start squawking. I know when I learned to fly, it was also drilled into us that we should manually force the beacon into the water before ejecting to make sure it would transmit our position."

"And you think *Dawn* has one of these aboard?"

"I don't know," I replied with a shrug, taking another deep breath as I let myself revel in the feel of her nails against my scalp. "In theory it's supposed to.

But maybe not because ....”

“Yeah.”

“And if it’s the old style, I have no idea where they would have put it. Airships were already so antiquated when I went through the Academy; we didn’t learn much about them outside of history classes. But if it’s the new kind — the naval kind —it should definitely be someplace a person could manually activate it on their way to abandon ship.”

“Which means it might be near an exit?”

“Maybe. That would make sense, but so little on *Dawn* made any sense at all, so ....”

“True,” Raline conceded, “but that would be a good place to look?”

“It would.”

“And you think this radio beacon could be the best way to send a message?” She moved her hand from my hair to take my hand instead.

“I mean ...” I took another deep breath. I was calmer now, less likely to melt down, but I still didn’t have all my wits about me. I could only hope I was making sense. “There’s a chance it’s already squawking,” I said. “There’s a chance that’s what alerted the Xylanthians in the first place. And if it is, that’s all the better. Every minute it’s transmitting is a chance someone will hear and come looking for us.”

There were parts of this, of course, I couldn’t tell her.

I couldn’t tell her about how this base we’d come aboard wasn’t under the Alliance purview. I couldn’t tell her about the red uniforms. And I certainly couldn’t tell her about the fact there was a very real chance the commandant of this base had plans to gas us all to death and dissolve our mortal remains via the acid spigots built into the ceiling above our heads.

Which meant I couldn’t tell her how dire our

situation was, and therefore how critical it was for word to get to someone that we were here, and alive, and in need of help.

I squeezed her hand.

"The point is," I began again, "if it's been triggered already, then all the better. And if it hasn't, Swar should do what she can to find it and set it off. If it's the naval variety, pouring a canteen out over it should do the trick. Whatever it takes to get the message out. And the Xylanthians are coming either way, so it's not like she'd be tipping them off to our position."

"Yes," Raline agreed. "That makes sense. I will tell her to try and find that beacon. Maybe she will have a better idea where to find it."

"Maybe," I allowed. "And tell her, if she can, to set the thing off and stash it in her pack when she leaves. Then dump it in the woods on the way back here."

"You don't want her to try and bring it all the way?" she asked. "So the beacon would lead right to us?"

"No," I snapped, shaking my head hard enough that it left me a little nauseated. "I don't … I don't … she shouldn't." I paused for a moment to gather my thoughts. "It's just that I want it out of the blast radius if at all possible. You do know they're going out there to blow it up, right?"

"Yes, I did know that part."

"Those radio beacons are hardened. They're designed to survive a crash, but there's no way to know whether it'll survive the intentional destruction of a giant airship with more than half a tank of diesel onboard. And there's also no way to know what the people in command of a top-secret base would do if they found out a member of our crew brought a beacon into their mountain that was just as likely to summon our enemies as our allies."

I shuddered at the thought of what Colonel Gertrune

might do in that case.

"So the idea would be to leave it far enough afield that it won't get destroyed by the explosion, but could reasonably have been blown there instead of dropped? Close enough to where we are that we could still be rescued, but far enough that we don't get in trouble for summoning anyone to the secret installation?"

I couldn't help my smile. Raline got my point exactly. I moved my other hand to close over hers as I nodded.

"That's exactly it," I replied.

"I can do that." Raline leaned her head toward mine, resting her forehead against my temple for a moment before moving to stand. "I'll need to go now," she said. "The team is already being prepped, and I'm not moving so quickly. If I'm to get to Lt. Swar at all, much less in a manner that doesn't draw suspicion, I'm going to have to hurry."

"Okay," I said, rising to my feet. I wasn't ready to let go of her hand yet.

"And you will be okay here?" she asked. She wasn't trying to let go of my hand, either. I liked that, and I was pretty sure she could tell.

"For certain values of 'ok', yeah," I replied.

Raline giggled. Normally I'd have gotten defensive about that, but somehow, I could tell she was laughing *with* me.

"You know this isn't ...." Once again, I was stumbling over what I was trying to say.

And once again Raline seemed to understand without my having to say much at all.

"Major Gowon told me," she said. "And I think it's very smart."

I looked down at my ridiculous clothing and shook my head.

"I guess that's one word for it."

"You had to do something."

"I did, huh?" It was good to hear from someone else — someone who wasn't enthralled at the idea of a High Ceremony happening in their midst — to tell me I was doing a good thing.

"I can't imagine the frustration of trying to get a point across and having to interrupt my train of thought to tell a person to get up off their knees before we could have a conversation."

I squeezed Raline's hand. That was it exactly and I could not have been more grateful to know that someone else understood. The fact it was this specific someone else made things all the better.

"I'm glad you don't think I'm ...." I didn't even know what I was so afraid of her accusing me of being.

My sister, maybe?

"Maran," she said, stepping closer to me as she squeezed my hand. "I know you. Maybe not as well as I'd like," she added. "Maybe not as well as I hope to someday. But I do know you. And I know you're not ... whatever it is you're afraid of people thinking. But you are a Princess."

"Yeah." My face was hot. I bit my lip and squeezed her hand in return. What was that about wanting to know me better?

"You're using your position to do the best you can for the people you lead. It's like Major Gowon said on the way over here: that's very Royal of you." She leaned in and kissed my cheek.

I had absolutely no idea what to do next, and I didn't think I could blame my concussion. I knew my cheeks were flushed red and could only hope Raline would at least pretend not to notice.

"Thank you," I managed to say. "And thank you for talking to Lt. Swar," I added, hoping that talking about operational details might help return my heartrate to something closer to normal.

"You are welcome," Raline said back. She let go of my hand and smiled again. "And you look good in white."

I didn't have time to answer before she turned to go.

That was probably for the best.

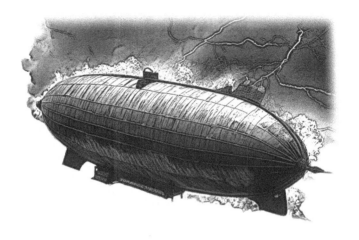

CHAPTER TWENTY-ONE

Glory and Wonder.

That was the hymn I hated. Leave it to me not to remember the name. The tagelharpe player sure did seem to like it, though. She had chosen the long version — the one with two extra lines at the end of every stanza, and I was struggling to maintain a serene expression as the Adorative Meditation was going on.

Not that anyone was supposed to be looking at me. Even Walmfrus had his eyes shut for this part.

The Adorative Meditation was the piece of the ceremony wherein all in attendance — save the Royal object of adoration — were to kneel in reverence, close their eyes, and concentrate on ... something. The details were still kind of sketchy in my head.

I suppose that was on me for a lifetime of not paying attention. I'd always tuned out royal rigamarole because I figured it would never apply to me. Some might call this my proper comeuppance.

But at least I knew better than to make silly faces. Or any faces.

Just in case anyone in this room was more like me than like Walmfrus, and opened their eyes when they weren't supposed to, I did my best not to appear anything less than regal. And owing to the fact there were Gammran, Mangan, and T'wesh personnel at the back of the assembly who might not know the expectations, my chances of getting caught in a frown were higher than usual.

So I stood still. Wearing my ill-fitting whites on the makeshift dais, I waited while the enthusiastic tagelharpe player went on with my least favorite hymn as the assembled complement of this base — around a hundred of them as best I could tell — knelt in silent contemplation.

A confluence of circumstances I was suddenly very grateful for when Bryte sprinted into the room from behind the blind masking the lift.

I definitely let my face go when I caught sight of him.

I also gestured like an angry draedabird for him to stop running before he tripped over his kneeling comrades. The overhead lights had been doused for the occasion, replaced by a series of amber emergency lanterns staged in rows along the front of, and extending parallel to, the raised dais. If the lift he'd just come from was as bright as it had been when I'd been aboard it, there was no way he could see his fellows properly.

I, on the other hand, was perfectly well-lit. As soon as I was sure Bryte was looking at me, I motioned to the cordoned-off area behind the dais where I'd been fitted for my ceremonial whites. He shook his head. I slammed my fists onto my hips and pointed again.

Bryte shook his head again but went in the direction I'd indicated.

I gathered the overlong skirts of my vestments into my hands and snuck off the dais. If I played this right, I could talk with Bryte in private, be back up in my place before the hymn was over, and maybe no one would be the wiser. We wouldn't have time for any sort of substantive conversation, but at least I could find out what the hells he was doing barging in like he did.

I scurried on tiptoes away from the dais and around the screen of canteen racks that made up the barrier to my ersatz-dressing room. Bryte was fidgeting, wringing his hands at his waist and dancing back and forth from one foot to the other as though his bladder might have been full.

"What's going on?" I asked.

Bryte shook his head and bit his lip for a moment.

"We were too late," he said after a moment.

"What do you mean, 'too late'?"

"I mean ..." he took a deep breath and ran both of his hands through his hair. "I mean the Xylanthians were already at the wreck site when we got there."

"Fuss."

"Yeah," he replied, still shaking his head. "And when they spotted us, Major Malli freaked out and started shooting."

"He *what?!*" The bitter taste of adrenaline was in my mouth, and my face grew hot.

"He just ... opened fire. He started shooting at them and so then they started shooting at us, and ...."

"Back up a second," I said. "What the fuss was Major Malli doing with a firearm to begin with? Who the hells thought it was a good idea to give that jackhole a gun?"

"Nobody!" Bryte insisted. "We didn't give him a gun. But my guys went out armed because it'll be dark soon and I don't know if you've ever seen the kinds of wylbears that live in this mountain range, but they're big and they're aggressive, and they're nocturnal, and their fur blends in with the dark foliage really fussing well so we don't let a detachment off the mountain unless a couple of them are armed."

"Okay," I conceded. "That part makes sense ... I guess. But how, might I ask, did Malli get his hands on someone else's sidearm?"

"I wish I knew!" Bryte squeezed his eyes shut and balled his hands into fists. "Best I can tell he just spotted the pistol on Corporal Byron's hip and started shooting."

"He took Byron's gun?"

"Yeah. And when Byron tried to get it back ...."

"Where is he now?" I asked, afraid of the answer but wanting the information, nonetheless.

"Dead."

"Byron?"

"Both of them." Bryte had tears in his eyes. "Malli was shooting before Brad had any idea ..."

"Brad?"

"Corporal Byron," Bryte said back. "His first name was Braderick. By the time he realized Malli had his weapon, he'd already opened fire. I don't know if he'd hit anyone, but he was shooting .... And Brad grabbed his arm, tried to stop him, tried to get the gun away from him. But then Malli shot him too ...." Bryte's voice broke, and he had to stop for a second.

My stomach dropped. This was bad. Really bad.

"Damn," I whispered as Bryte struggled to pull himself together enough to relay the rest of the story.

"And then the enemy returned fire," he said. "And that's when Malli went down. And a couple of my guys, too."

I could hear the key change signaling the hymn would soon be coming to a close. I needed to get back on that stage before anybody panicked. But there was a lot more I needed to know about this.

"Where is everybody else?" I asked him.

"In the garage, mostly," he replied. I've got a couple of my guys checking the proximity radar. I ... I think some of them followed us. Maran," he said, taking in a deep breath, "I think we may be under attack."

My stomach jumped into my throat, and I had to actively keep myself from throwing up on his boots. And here I'd thought things couldn't possibly get worse.

"Fuss," I cursed. I shook my head.

The music was about to end. I had to decide right then and there whether it would be best we continue this conversation and thereby let literally everyone on board this base know something was wrong, or to get my hindquarters back up on the dais and keep this information need-to-know for now.

I decided in favor of not inciting widespread panic.

"Wait here," I told Bryte. "I've got to get back up there or else everybody's going to know something's wrong, and I don't think we're ready for that yet. I'm going to send Ensign Declan back here. Tell him as much or as little as you want but make sure to tell him who you need from the audience. Tell him where they are in the crowd and let him pull them back here. I'll see to it everyone shuts their eyes again for long enough you can get your CO and whoever else you need out of the room without the rest of the crew seeing them leave."

"Yeah," Bryte said. "Good. Go."

I did.

I scurried to the spot beside the dais where Ensign Declan had stationed himself at the start of the ceremony, feeling oddly fortunate that he had enough religious background to know where the Royal

Honoree's adjutant was supposed to stand during such things. And also grateful for my earlier decision to deputize him as such. I tapped him lightly on the shoulder as I bent to whisper in his ear.

"Declan," I said as softly as I could possibly make my voice sound. "Nod your head once if you can understand the words I'm saying."

He did.

Good. That was good. The last thing I wanted was to raise my voice enough that the base's religious officials, standing far too close by for my comfort, might be able to overhear.

"I need you to head back behind those racks where we got dressed for this," I told him. "There's been a development. And it's going to be an emergency."

Declan opened his eyes and turned his head to look at me.

"Going to be?" he mouthed; if his voice sounded at all, I didn't hear it.

I nodded in reply and leaned toward him again.

"Go talk to Bryte," I whispered, gesturing toward the racks he was currently hidden behind. "He'll tell you what to do."

Declan nodded as he turned to dash off.

I took a deep breath as I scampered back onto the dais just in time for the tagelharpist to play the final phrase of the hymn. Nothing like cutting it close.

I did my best to get through the next movement of the ceremony. The prayers and declarations were as uninteresting as they were protracted, and I was suddenly thankful for the length of the robes I wore; they were doing a good job masking my nervous habit of tapping my toes.

When the third and final Declaration was finally complete, it was my turn to say something. I'd planned to make this part as brief as was royally possible, but the recent turn of events had me rethinking that strategy.

I would have to draw this out as best I could. But first …

"Subjects and guests," I called out, lifting my arms in a gesture of welcome I'd seen members of my family do dozens of times throughout my life. "Let us all now close our eyes so that we may experience this moment in the same piece of reality."

I'd never been so thankful for having been present for my sister's princessing lessons. This was one of those old Feirin things that was supposed to remove a person's individual perspective on a moment and make everyone's experience more uniform — which made it more whole … or something. Whatever the justification for it, I was glad to have remembered it existed as a mechanism of ritual. Because it was about to do us all a whole lot of good.

As soon as I could see that everyone in attendance had indeed shut their eyes, including the small party of officers beside me on the dais, I turned my head and made a 'go ahead' gesture to Ensign Declan, who I could only just see peeking out from behind the racks where Bryte was still hidden.

Declan nodded and took off at the quietest run I had ever witnessed a person execute.

First, he found Colonel Gertrune where she stood on the center aisle in the first row of votaries. He tapped her on the shoulder and whispered something in her ear in much the same way I'd first approached him. The Colonel looked angry at first, shaking her head as she opened her eyes. I could tell she was about to give Declan some kind of dressing down for interrupting her silent devotions.

Fortunately, she looked up at me before blowing her stack. I looked back and forth between Gertrune and

Declan, nodding my head and gesturing for her to remain quiet. She frowned a little but turned back to Declan. He whispered to her again before the two of them moved quietly into the aisle and past the dais toward where Bryte was waiting.

They were only out of sight for a moment before Declan appeared again, this time to fetch a member of the Colonel's staff I didn't recognize.

He repeated these actions, over and over again as I faked my way through the best possible re-enactment of my mother's usual pontifications — enough times that I'd lost count before he approached the dais from behind and tugged at the hem of my robe to let me know I could move on.

And thank the Queen for that favor. I wasn't sure how much longer I could have kept on rambling. I turned the program back over to Walmfrus for the benediction and tried not to be too obviously in a hurry as I headed off the dais when it was over.

I was already tearing off my ceremonial whites as I rounded the corner.

I counted ten people in the makeshift dressing area, including the two I'd already spoken with. To a person, they were dressed in Feirin Prayer Whites. Of course they were. Bryte and Colonel Gertrune had been calling the shots — there was no way they'd have invited any of my people to join this meeting.

But I wasn't about to stand for that.

"Declan," I called, "Please go and find Major Gowon and Sgt. Pon and bring them back here. Quickly."

Declan nodded and darted away. No longer needing to employ as much stealth as before, he moved with the kind of quickness only achievable by the young and fit.

"Maran, what are you doing?" Bryte asked me, charging through the group of his fellows to meet me where I stood.

"Mister Sonneman!" Colonel Gertrune yelled before I had a chance to answer. "How dare you address a daughter of the Queen in the familiar?!"

"Colonel," I answered so Bryte didn't have to. "It's really ..." I shook my head and frowned. "It's fine."

"It is most certainly not fine, Your Highness. I ..."

"Colonel!" I interrupted her before she could finish her thought. "First off, he's my cousin." I had gotten the vague impression she hadn't known that when I was up in her office. I could tell by the look on her face in this moment that I'd guessed correctly on that one. "And second," I went on, "didn't we just have a whole Royal hoop-de-doo about people not needing to be so damn deferential?"

I wasn't sure whether she was more stunned by my referring to a time-honored and very solemn religious ceremony as a 'hoop-de-doo' or the fact I'd followed that with a very non-princess-like swear word. But I could tell by the shift in her expression that she was, indeed, stunned.

I let her have a moment to gather her face before I went on.

"Now, I would propose that if, under the circumstances, Lieutenant General Sonneman — Bryte — to whom I am related and who I have known for approximately my entire life, has something he needs to say to me that he considers so urgent as to not have taken the time to remember to address me properly while in the presence of all of his very official, and in some cases very religious colleagues, I think the best course of action would be to let him say that. Don't you?"

Colonel Gertrune pursed her lips as she nodded her head. She adjusted her posture into what looked to me like the closest thing to Parade Rest her formal garb would allow as she took a deep breath and turned to

Bryte.

"By all means, General Sonneman," she said, her voice as cool and as calm as any I'd ever heard.

"Yes ma'am," Bryte replied. "I was merely about to remind Maran — Her Highness — that the nature of our operation doesn't allow for the inclusion of her comrades in matters as delicate as what we're currently dealing with."

I frowned, but I didn't roll my eyes again. That was certainly not what he was about to say. The gist might have been the same, but there was no way he'd have been so eloquent about it had Colonel Gertrune not interrupted. He was still every bit the dweeb he'd always been — doing his best to earn the title of Teacher's Pet.

I didn't envy him the moment he was about to have.

Because I was about to make him pick a side.

"My people have every right to be party to this conversation," I told them both. "It was a mission involving their ship that set this crisis in motion, and the XO of their mission was one of the first casualties. Not to mention the fact that the two people I've sent for were instrumental in the planning and coordination of the expedition, the fallout of which will be the entire substance of the upcoming discussion. And let us not forget that this installation, although present on the Xylanthian frontier for nearly three decades, lacks any expert in the local culture — a deficiency made up for only by the knowledge possessed by Sgt. Pon, who you are now trying to exclude from further conversation. And anyway," I added with more smirk than I probably should have let show. "It's too late."

Because at that moment, as if on cue, Ensign Declan rounded the corner with Major Gowon and Lt. Pon right behind him.

Bryte and the Colonel both looked sheepish. Good.

I was getting better at talking like the head princess in charge. Apparently. It was a skill I was likely to need in spades over the next several hours.

"What is it?" Major Gowon asked as he took stock of the group he'd been summoned to join. "What's going on?"

Sgt. Pon didn't say anything at all. She stood quietly behind the Major, looking as though she somehow hoped no one could see her there.

I did my best to fill him in as I stripped the remaining pieces of my ceremonial costume off from over my uniform. In this moment I felt like I needed both my Royal Signets and my Field Marshal's bars as visible signifiers of the fact I was going to make the Colonel listen to me whether she liked it or not.

I could tell Major Gowon was trying not to swear when I was finished.

"Yeah," I said, entirely in response to the look on his face.

"If that man wasn't already dead, I'd be about to kill him," he replied. I was sure he was referring to Major Malli and I was also sure I agreed with him.

"Too bad we can't explain to the Xylanthians what a pewtypot he was and tell them we're super sorry and exactly how mad we are at what he did and ask them very nicely to turn around and go home while we promise to do the same thing as soon as we're able." I crossed my arms over my chest and shrugged. It wasn't the worst idea I'd ever had ....

"Hells," Colonel Gertrune replied in a tone so casual it startled me, "if I thought for a second that might work, I'd tell you to give it a try."

I could see Sgt. Pon beginning to fidget. She likely had an opinion on the subject, and also a notion she ought not interrupt superior officers with it.

"Ginna," I called, extending my hand to wave her

into the circle of discussion. "I don't believe the two of you have met."

"No ..." she said quietly as she slowly moved toward us in response to my outstretched hand. "I ... I haven't met anybody."

Had she always been this timid? I didn't remember her being particularly shy when we'd first met. But, then again, I'd joined in a friendly conversation already in progress. This time she was being called upon by a Field Marshal who she now understood to be a venerable deity to join a discussion between angry strangers.

"Sergeant Pon," I said. "Meet Colonel Gertrune. Colonel Gertrune, meet Sergeant Pon."

Sergeant Pon saluted. Colonel Gertrune looked confused for a moment and then saluted in return.

"A pleasure to meet you, ma'am," Sgt. Pon said.

"Colonel Gertrune is the CO of this installation," I explained before turning back to the Colonel. "Colonel, Sgt. Pon is the closest thing to a Xy cultural expert you're going to find. She was assigned to the *Dawn* due to her knowledge and understanding of the Xy people, culture, and customs. I have a feeling you may have use for her expertise in the coming minutes and hours."

Colonel Gertrune was pissed.

I could see it. I doubted anyone else could — except maybe for Bryte, if he was paying close enough attention. There was a certain way the Feirin upper classes learned to mask their fury; from the time we were bitty children, we were taught how to clench our gut, flex our fingers, pull down on our shoulder blades, and perform several other deliberate acts of muscular diffusion so as to keep any appearance of rage from manifesting upon our countenance.

Colonel Gertrune was doing all of them.

"How very thoughtful, Your Highness," she said

after a moment.

Oh yeah — she was steamed.

And it didn't escape my notice that she still hadn't said so much as a single word to Sgt. Pon.

Good thing I was better at masking anger than she was. I made quick eye contact with Major Gowon, who gave me a subtle nod and a knowing look. He could tell Gertrune was mad the same as I could.

"We're at your service, Colonel," I said. It was the most magnanimous way I could think of to tell her that my crew and I shouldn't be excluded from consideration when it came to planning the response to what happened outside.

"Good," she said. But she didn't mean it. "Thank you, Your Highness."

"Of course."

I waited for her to say something else. It didn't take long for the silence to get awkward.

"So what's next?" I asked, because apparently somebody had to.

"I need to head upstairs," Gertrune answered. "To meet with my senior staff and get a look at what the maps and our seismometers say. I'll have a better idea after that."

Oh.

Well — that made sense then.

She wanted to go back up to the higher decks, put her treasonous legion back into their red greatcoats, and get on with business as usual, as though the rest of us weren't her concern.

There was absolutely no way I was going to let her do that. But checking maps and seismometers did sound like the next reasonable step. I put on my most royal of smiles — the one that said, "you have one chance to do this the easy way. Best not spoil it."

"By all means, Colonel," I said. "Lead the way."

CHAPTER TWENTY-TWO

I had to hand it to the Colonel; I was pretty sure no one else could tell she was mad. But she *was* mad. Whether her anger was directed solely at me or at the situation as a whole didn't matter much. Either way I was going to have to be wary.

Voicing my opinions, inserting myself into decision-making spaces, and generally making the case for what I thought to be the best course of action was one thing, but openly challenging her was another. I may have been royalty, but I was not a Majesty, and my position within the chain of command in this place was tenuous at most. And the people to whom I held the most loyalty had no position here at all.

Meanwhile, Colonel Gertrune was the Commandant of this base and had been for more than half a decade. I was sure she had the loyalty of every one of the hundred or so people who'd just been dismissed from the ceremony — my cousin and childhood friend included.

There was only so far I was going to be able to push her without her pushing back. And if she pushed back, she'd be doing so with the combined force of the base's full complement behind her. But I was going to push.

I made a point to be one of the first into the lift, and I brought Ensign Declan with me when I did. I would have liked to have Major Gowon along as well, but I knew better than to start by insisting I be accompanied by someone who was not a Feirin subject.

And besides, I needed him to handle things on the Emergency Deck while I was gone: responsibilities I did my best to explain during the mad dash to be the first on the lift.

"Get all our people in the lift," I told him. "Put as many of them as you can in the garage — the garage is where the flushrooms are — all our able-bodied people should go down there. Anyone who's been to the flushrooms can lead the way. As far as I know all our people who left on the away mission are already there; have all our healthy people join them. Then get Raline Khatri..." My voice broke as I caught myself using Raline's first name. I shut my eyes and shook my head for a moment; Major Gowon had probably already figured out what was going on in my head where Raline was concerned, but I didn't need to be pointing it out in the middle of a crisis. "Find Chief Khatri," I began again. "And get her to round up the injured survivors. There may be more. There may be wounded with the away team. I don't know. But everyone who's not healthy: put them in the hall upstairs — the one between the lift out of here and the one down to the garage."

"Are you sure?" he asked, "it's awfully crowded down here. You sure you want me jostling our wounded through all this?"

I frowned as I took a quick look around the room. Most of the base staff was still milling about, chatting casually about the dinner they'd been promised that only a few of us now knew they wouldn't be getting. I felt a little bad about how thoroughly their spirits were about to be dashed. But, then again, it wasn't my fault the Xylanthians had shown up at the wreck ahead of schedule. And it wasn't like I was going to eat an adasha pudding without them.

It wouldn't be long until word of what had gone on outside got around. Any minute now every one of these people could be called back to their posts to deal with the impending crisis.

And I intended to have my people off this deck by the time that happened.

I looked Major Gowon square in his eyes and nodded.

"Get all our people out of this room," I said, as slowly as my harried pace toward the lift would allow.

His mouth fell open for a moment. Then he nodded in reply. He understood.

If our people had been in danger on the Emergency Deck to begin with, they were in exponentially more danger now. Whatever chance might have existed of Gertrune and her abettors using the most terrifying features of this installation against us was magnified a thousandfold by the possibility of an enemy incursion. Were there to be so much as a credible claim of the Xylanthians breeching the base's defenses, that would give them all the cover they needed to wipe out the totality of the *Dawn* survivors with all the plausible deniability in the world were anyone to blow the whistle later.

The Princess and her companions were killed by the Xylanthians in the ensuing fracas.

Not if I could help it.

Fortunately for all of us, Major Gowon was as perceptive as he was smart. I could tell by his reaction that he understood exactly what I was worried about, and I was sure he'd know precisely how to use the ensuing chaos to get our people out of murder's way without raising too many concerns among the hoi polloi.

It felt good knowing I had someone I could count on. Major Gowon could handle keeping our people safe.

I was going to go deal with the enemy — both within and without.

After the impossible and ridiculous things I had already encountered aboard this base, I might have judged myself ready for anything. But the Top Deck was something else altogether. Part observation command, part ceremonial aerie, the circular chamber was quite possibly the least practical room I had ever encountered outside the Royal Palace. When I thought about what it must have taken to build such a place, I couldn't decide whether to be more impressed or annoyed. It was the most distilled example I'd seen so far of the architectural wonders contained within this installation.

I could see why Walmfrus had wanted to hold the Adoration here. Much like the Emergency Deck, the Top Deck was a massive, mostly empty, glistening example of Feirin architecture at its most pretentious.

Bryte had told me they used this space for religious observances on the regular, but from the looks of the place, I'd have guessed no one ever came in here except to clean it. Then again, I'd had a similar impression of the flushrooms off the garage. Maybe there wasn't much to do around here save for spit-and-polish.

Everything in this room shone. Instruments gleamed in flawless copper, brass, and chrome. The natural stone of the mountain had been carved into buffed and waxed perfection — silky smooth marble from the slick gray floor to the coffered white ceiling. Even the black rubber handles of periscopes and dials were reflective.

This room made me extremely uncomfortable.

A few of the people who had been in the lift seemed to know what they were doing in here; a fact that did nothing to quell my discomfort. Still in their Prayer Whites, they went to work powering on what appeared to be surveillance stations at points all around the deck's perimeter.

"Tell me there's a game plan," I said to Bryte and Gertrune. I was pretty sure there wasn't one, and I suspected getting them to say so out loud might have been a step toward making one.

"General Sonneman tells me there was an exchange of fire," the Colonel said.

"Indeed," Bryte affirmed. "Casualties on both sides."

"Corporal Byron," Gertrune replied.

"And Specialist Meybrun," Bryte said. "Along with three of the crash survivors."

Those words hit me like a brick. Three. Three of the less than thirty people who had made it out of the wreck of the *Dawn*. Three of the less than twenty who had made it out of the wreck well enough to walk away without requiring medical attention. Three of the twelve who had volunteered to return to what was left of the airship they had boarded to an unknown destination in order to try and keep it from falling into the hands of the enemy. Three of them were gone now.

I had known about Major Malli, but I wondered who the other two had been. I wondered if I'd met them, knew their names, would remember their faces. I wondered what I would say to their families back home if I ever had the chance.

But getting lost in grief and questions wasn't going to do any of us any good right now.

"How many of them were there?" I asked.

"How many?" Bryte sounded confused.

"Xylanthians, Bryte," I snapped, my patience suddenly far thinner than I might have guessed. "How many Xylanthians were there?"

"Fifty?" he answered, his head shaking and his voice unsure. "Eighty? Too many. There were more of them than there were of us."

"But not more than the full complement of the base?" Gertrune asked him.

Bryte shrugged.

"Not that I could see," he answered her. "But the whole thing happened really fast, and we got the hell out of there before enough of them saw enough of us to decide we might be worth following."

"So you're sure you weren't followed?" Colonel Gertrune asked.

"I think so," Bryte replied. I could tell he wasn't sure. What I couldn't tell was whether his CO was convinced.

"*Think so* isn't good enough, Lieutenant General," she said. "You're sure they spotted you and there's a chance you could have been followed."

"Colonel," he replied, sounding as defensive as I had ever heard anyone sound. "It all happened so fast. There's no way to know. My priority was to get everyone out of there as quickly as possible. I honestly didn't stop and turn around to check whether or not they were following us."

"So you have no idea as to whether or not you've given away the location of our base?"

Of course that was her priority. She wasn't asking

about injuries, or about whether the team had even managed to get aboard the wreck. She wasn't asking about the location of her explosives. And she wasn't asking what had become of our fallen comrades.

It wasn't like I didn't care about security, but there were human factors to consider here. Perhaps that was the difference between a princess and a commandant.

"No, ma'am," Bryte answered officially.

"Fifty or eighty, you said?"

"Yes ma'am, maybe more."

"General Sonneman, I need you to put together an armed expeditionary force."

"Expedition, ma'am?"

"I need you to liquidate them," the Colonel replied. Her voice sent a chill down my spine. I had never in my life heard anyone speak of killing with such cool indifference. If I'd ever held any doubt of her ability to order the murders of all the *Dawn* survivors, the last of it evaporated in that moment.

"Do you really think that's necessary, Colonel?" I asked. I don't know what possessed me to insert myself in that moment. Maybe it was the fact I still didn't know if there were bodies of people I'd spoken to just a couple of hours ago lying out there in the woods. Maybe it was the look on Bryte's face in response to her order. Or maybe it was just my lifelong belief that armed conflict ought to be avoided if at all possible.

"Your Highness?" she said in a tone that expressed very clearly just how unaccustomed she was to being challenged.

Probably almost as unaccustomed as I was to keeping my opinions to myself.

"This place is a fortress," I reminded her. "And there's no way to know whether the Xylanthians tracked the team back to the base. There is every chance they didn't. And even if they did ..." I gestured wildly to the stone walls surrounding us. "They can't get in. So what if they suspect you're in here?" I went on. "So what if they try to lay siege? You weren't expecting anybody to come or go for the next — what was it ...? Two years?" I couldn't help but throw my hands up in frustration. "What the hells does it matter if the enemy is coming this way?"

"What matters," she replied, harshly, "is that if they so much as suspect a base is here ...."

"And why would they suspect that?" I interrupted her. "If you recall, the team we sent was specifically chosen to look like all of them survived the crash. So it stands to reason for the enemy to presume they got scared off in the firefight, ran into the woods, and will be written off as wylbear food by morning."

"Or they could have seen some of our people disappear into the mountain and already be calling for reinforcements."

"And those reinforcements finding a battle already in progress would be better for this installation than their arriving to find their fellows staring in confusion at a sheer rock mountainside?"

"Your Highness ...."

"Are you even prepared for overt warfare?" I asked, pivoting my argument since my first tack didn't seem to be working. "Do you have trained infantry? Sharpshooters? How about equipment? It's my understanding that the resupply rate of this place is pretty scant, and I can't imagine a giant cache of modern weapons taking up valuable space on the transports that could be used for your garrison's food, medical, and religious needs. So unless some special trip was made, and very recently, I might add, there's every chance whatever weapons you might have on hand — no matter how well-maintained I'm sure they are — could be grossly outdated in comparison to whatever the enemy is bringing."

"We have weapons, Maran," Bryte insisted, inserting himself back into the conversation — apparently on the side of his CO. "And we have people who know how to use them. Overwhelming force may be called for here."

"What kind of weapons, Bryte?" I asked, not caring that I was referring to him by his given name instead of his rank. "And what do the Xylanthians have? You gonna bring a dart gun to a tank fight?"

"We have a little better than dart guns, Maran ..."

"Again I ask: what do the Xylanthians have?" I looked at him pointedly. "And what kind of air cover? And how fast can they travel? And how fast can they get a message back?"

"I'm not sure," Bryte answered softly, in a tone of voice that told me he wasn't used to being asked questions he didn't know the answers to.

"Then how about you *at least*," I implored, looking back and forth between Bryte and Gertrune with as stern an expression as I could allow myself without looking downright angry, "let me bring Sgt. Pon and Major Gowon up here?"

"No," answered Bryte.

"Absolutely not," said Gertrune at almost the same time.

"And why?" I challenged them both. "You're so afraid the enemy might have an idea of the existence of this base that you're ready to head into the woods half-cocked with the intention of killing every Xylanthian in the time zone. But you're not willing to make use of a cultural expert and an Alliance intelligence officer who are already inside your mountain to at least give you a better idea what you're up against? Never mind the fact that either or both of them may know something that could help inform the decision as to whether to leave this mountain in the first place."

"No," Colonel Gertrune said again. "I will not hear of it. General Sonneman," she said, "prepare an assault force."

"Yes, ma'am," Bryte replied, turning to go before I had a chance to say anything more. The Colonel turned to me once he was gone. "You are here as a courtesy, Your Highness," she said. "But my orders, and the standing operational conditions of this installation, come from Her Majesty the Queen. Make no mistake: it is your Royal authority only that grants you this access. The rank you wear holds no meaning in this place as it belongs to an entity my command does not recognize. This is a Feirin base, Your Highness," she declared. "And we shall meet the enemy with a Feirin response."

Wow.

Okay.

She'd just said the quiet part out loud.

I had no idea how to reply to that. The Colonel had admitted her treason in plain language. Did she think I would understand — be on her side? I doubted that sincerely. It was much more likely she was of the opinion one or both of us wouldn't be alive to tell the tale or face the consequences.

That person wasn't going to be me.

Nor would it be Ensign Declan.

He was standing at parade rest just behind me — the perfect example of the invisible adjutant. I surely hadn't foreseen such a dire turn of events when I'd dragooned him into the position, and I couldn't help but be impressed with how he'd risen to the occasion. I'd be awarding him a field promotion as soon as we had a moment to take a breath.

I shook my head a little when I realized he was trembling.

"You heard all of that, didn't you?" I asked.

Declan nodded.

"Yes, ma'am."

"Do you have any questions?" I asked next. I was going to need him, and I was going to need him focused. If there were doubts or uncertainties, I wanted to do my best to quell those now.

"No ma'am."

"Are you sure?" I stepped closer to him and lowered my voice. The din in the room from the clamoring of voices and clatter of boots on the polished stone floor seemed enough to keep us from being overheard, but in a place like this at a time like this, I figured there was no such thing as being too careful.

"I think I heard everything I need to," he answered quietly. "I'm not sure I fully understand what we've walked into here, but I understand enough. If I have questions, I'll bring them to you, ma'am," he added. "But for the time being I think I would rather focus on getting through the immediate crisis."

"You're a good egg, Declan," I said.

"Thank you, ma'am."

I looked around the room. Another load of personnel had come up on the lift, and the duty stations around the perimeter were nearly all filled. The stations themselves seemed to be of three alternating varieties, staffed by two, three, or four persons depending on their configuration — save for one.

Colonel Gertrune had taken a seat at what I could only presume was the room's command post, watching intently as messengers from each of the other stations dashed to and from her position, updating the readouts on a large display table in front of her. With Ensign Declan by my side, I stood behind Gertrune long enough to figure out what most of it meant.

She was aggregating data from all sides on troop numbers, vehicle types, varieties of weapons, and the weather — and there was space available for information from our side, too. From here she could observe and coordinate whatever was going on outside in the vicinity of the mountain.

I was close enough to be able to overhear her expressed frustration at the difficulty they were having getting information from ground level. This place had been built to monitor for an outbound invasion force; they'd been set up to watch the airspace and the coastline. Trying to get a read on the ground directly outside and immediately beneath their mountain redoubt had been, at best, an afterthought when the observation equipment had been set up. It was almost funny, how little care had been taken to make this secret mountain redoubt defensible. But under the circumstances, I could find very little humor in anything.

I shook my head. This was going to be a mess.

And possibly a bloodbath.

"You understanding all this?" I asked Declan quietly.

"Yes ma'am."

"Good," I replied. "Stay here. If anyone tries to move you more than three feet in any direction, tell them you're here on my orders — that you're my eyes and ears until I get back — and that if they try and interfere again, they had best say their prayers because Her Highness will be greatly displeased."

Declan cracked a hint of a smile as he nodded. He'd gotten to know me well enough by now to know how little store I set by all things holy; I'm glad he was willing to be in on this with me.

"I can do that ma'am," he replied. "And if they ask where you've gone?"

"Tell them that's none of their business," I said. "Most likely, they'll guess I'm in the flushroom. Which is exactly what I want them to think."

"But that's not where you're going?"

"Sort of," I replied. "The flushroom we've been given access to is off the garage. I told Gowon to move our people down there for reasons I promise I'll explain later. And I'm guessing that's where Bryte will be staging the defense force out of. I'm going *to* the flushroom," I explained, "just not inside it."

"Yes ma'am," Declan said, taking the position of formal parade rest as he looked down to check the condition of the borrowed set of Prayer Whites he still wore. He was trying to look like he belonged there, and I appreciated that.

I smiled as I turned to go and told him,

"I'll be back as soon as I can."

CHAPTER TWENTY-THREE

I had never been the kind of person to grossly underestimate my circumstances, but my guess as to how bad things were downstairs would qualify as having done just that.

Getting to the garage had been easy enough, as it was connected to the Top Deck by a proper mechanical lift. The pandemonium I found when I arrived made me want to turn right back around and leave.

Troops were running to and fro: unlocking ammunition boxes and lowering giant metal crates from where they'd been stowed on ceiling-mounted rails. Soldiers were scrambling with field kit they looked to have no idea how to don, while support personnel doled out camouflage tunics, trousers, and combat boots to half-dressed troops struggling to get out of their ceremonial robes. Walmfrus went behind them, adding the soldiers' hastily shed Prayer Whites to the ever-growing pile in his arms lest they accidentally touch the ground and become forever sullied.

What a fussing nightmare.

Bryte was barking orders I was sure no one was trying to follow. Everyone appeared to know their job, and waiting for orders seemed to be the last thing any of them was about to do.

Each of the task teams must have drilled for this, but the teams had never bothered to do so simultaneously. I'd learned in my days at the Air Academy: it was one thing to drill in a vacuum, when everything was clear and your job was the only one that needed doing, but it was an altogether different experience to have to get a job done in the presence of a bunch of other people also trying to get *their* jobs done. Add to that the stress of this being the first real-world engagement this base had ever seen, and it was no wonder the place was a madhouse.

At least the chaos meant nobody appeared to give a damn about the foreigners in their midst. Major Gowon had stationed all our people in an alcove between the flushrooms and the generator closet.

I tried to count heads as I approached. Were all of our people who'd gone back to the wreck accounted for? How many had there been again? Minus the wounded — who I really should go check on — minus Major Malli, and the other two .... Trying to do the figures in my head was enough to remind me I still had a concussion.

"Everybody here?" I asked Major Gowon as I approached. He would have a level head, and the information I was looking for.

"Field Marshal," he greeted me, reaching out a hand to bring me closer. "We're all accounted for. A few of our people volunteered to go back out." He pointed to three Mangan women and a Gammran man having a spirited discussion with a Feirin officer holding a case of repeating pistols.

"I don't think they need my permission," I said. "But if they ask me, they'll have it."

"You support this, then?" Gowon asked.

"No," I replied curtly. "In fact, I think it's a terrible idea. And I told the Colonel as much. I see absolutely no need to send a squad out from her amply supplied, hermetically sealed, impenetrable mountain to face off against an enemy we know almost nothing about, on the off chance they have an inkling this place might actually exist. All she's doing is further exposing her base and her people. But she was quick to remind me it isn't my call. It's her base, her people. My authority here is dubious at best. She's sending out a strike force and there's nothing I can do about it. But what I can do is bless the choices of the people who recognize my authority. If they would rather go out and fight than stay here and hide, I'm not going to stop them."

"You're a hell of a leader, Princess," Gowon said. "And I'm honored to serve beneath you."

"You serve *alongside me*, sir," I corrected. "But thank you. I appreciate that."

"The rest of us are just trying to stay out of the way," he said, pulling the conversation back on topic.

"Probably a good idea," I said. "Lay low. Let them forget we're here. Except those four," I added, gesturing back to the troops in conference with the local officer. "Those four we make sure they remember."

Gowon nodded. He got it; I could tell. Every one of their people who fought alongside one of our people was one more person who'd be tempted to blow the whistle were Colonel Gertrune to pull the trigger on exterminating us later. And every member of our complement who was out on maneuvers was someone who wasn't liable to be on the Emergency Deck if the spigots got turned on 'by accident' 'in the heat of battle' or some other nonsense.

"Yes ma'am," he said.

"I want to go check on our wounded," I told him.

"Yeah, all right," he said. "Chief Khatri should have them all up in the hallway by now. From what I gather, a couple of their guys came back hurt, so the medical staff left for sickbay to look after them. I don't think any of our folks are bad off enough for that to matter."

"Me either," I agreed, thankful he hadn't chosen to needle me on what I was sure had been a visible flush in my cheeks at the mention of Raline. "Although I worry what's going to happen if one of our people comes back injured next time."

"Don't think they haven't thought of it," Gowon assured me. "Those are trained Alliance service members. They know what they're signing up for."

"I don't doubt that," I assured the Major. "But I do doubt this installation's capacity to take care of them were something to go poorly out there. I'm not going to stop them. And I believe they're as prepared as possible — likely far more prepared than the local troops, to tell the truth. But I want us to be prepared as well. If they come back wounded, I want someone ready and equipped to look after them. Our medic ..." I said, grasping at my memory for the name of the woman who I'd seen with Raline in the forest the night of the crash.

"Lt. Mieko," Gowon replied. "She's up in the hall with Chief Khatri."

"There were still some medical supplies on the Emergency Deck," I said, "Maybe I should sneak down there — snag some things, bring them to her."

"I don't think that's a bad idea. Get in, get the stuff, and get out while things are still so chaotic nobody's gonna notice."

"Yeah," I said, nodding my head as the plan crystallized. "I'll get the supplies, check in with Raline, then I'll come back and talk to you before heading back up to the command center."

Gowon nodded and I turned to go.

When I'd made the initial decision to go back to the Emergency Deck before checking in with Raline and Lt. Mieko I had somehow forgotten I was going to need to walk right through the lot of them on the way. It was only when the lift from the garage deposited me in the hallway where they'd quartered themselves that it dawned on me.

I wanted to blame my concussion for that. But maybe I just wasn't thinking straight.

The corridor was as crowded as the palace garden on a festival day; a fact that made sense when I took a moment to think about it. The troops would want to get off the Emergency Deck as quickly as possible, and the fastest way for them — individually and as a whole — to do so was to use the manual lift only as far as the next available floor, then transfer to one of the properly mechanized lifts to make the rest of the trip to wherever they might be headed.

This hallway, being the nearest available stop for the mechanical lift, had thus become the clearing house for personnel heading to all points in the station. Voices hollered from inside the lift cars on either end, calling out which levels they were destined for so that any of their fellows headed the same way wouldn't waste time waiting on a lift. Others gathered in clumps based on duty station to wait their turn for a car to take them up to work.

It was loud and frantic and too bright, and if I

thought I'd had a headache before ....

"Maran!" I heard Raline before I saw her, and the sound of her voice saying my given name boosted my mood more than I'd guessed possible. Even my headache calmed a bit.

I could see her hand waving above the heads and shoulders of the crowd as they milled and gathered, and I did my best to get to her as quickly as I could.

"Raline," I greeted her, oddly breathless, as I took her by her elbows. I steered her into a gap in the crowd, against the wall opposite the lifts.

"It's okay I used your first name?" she asked. "I thought if I yelled 'Your Highness' everyone would look. And since we're not supposed to be up here, I figured it was best not to call attention."

"Yes," I said back, stumbling over my words as I gathered myself. "It was good. That was good thinking." I smiled at her and shook my head, knowing full and well my concussion was not the cause for my sudden bout of tongue-tie. "You can always call me Maran," I added quietly as a flush I couldn't help came to my cheeks.

"I like that," she said. The way she was looking at me made me want nothing in the world so much as I wanted to kiss her. But this was absolutely not the time or the place.

I had to satisfy myself with squeezing her elbows where I already had hold of her.

"Has it been like this the whole time?" I asked, hating the fact I needed to move the conversation back to the crisis at hand, but knowing I didn't have a choice.

"Yes," she replied. "Major Gowon had us in the lift up here before the base personnel started to come. I guess it took a while for one of their officers to tell them the dinner was off."

"Oh." I had to work not to laugh out loud at the thought of the base's entire complement milling around in their Prayer Whites waiting for the adasha pudding and roast vyshr, all the while their CO and her staff were upstairs planning a ground assault.

"It worked out in our favor," Raline told me. "No one has seemed to notice us. They're all terribly self-involved."

That time I did chuckle. She had no idea.

"Have you seen Lt. Mieko?" I asked.

Raline nodded.

"She's sitting with Ensign Osei and Yeoman Asare down on the far end, past the lifts."

"Are they stable?" Osei and Asare were two of the volunteers who'd gone back with Bryte to blow up the wreck. I kicked myself for not checking in on the rest of the wounded earlier.

"They're okay," she replied. "It's minor ... flesh wounds. Lt. Meiko said bandages and pain management. They'll be fine."

"I was going to head back down to bring up more medical supplies," I told her. "But with how crowded the lifts seem, I'm not sure I could get down there."

"There's no need," Raline said. "Lt. Mieko thought ahead. She told us what to bring; we have cases of the stuff."

I let myself sigh in relief. The *Dawn* was a pewty of a ship, but her crew had proven themselves capable time and again.

"Okay, good," I said. "Stay here. Hopefully everyone will continue not to notice you. If anyone asks, you're here on my orders and you refuse to move without an overriding order from me personally. You can call me the Field Marshal or Her Highness or whatever works — I don't care. I just want you and the rest of our people to be safe until this is over."

"But I thought since they're back ...." she said. "I thought, for the most part, it was over."

I shook my head.

"No." I lowered my voice even further in case anyone in the room who didn't need to know might overhear. "There was an exchange of fire," I told her. "And the team retreated back to the base. I thought it would be over, too. But the Colonel is afraid the enemy might have deduced the location — or at least the existence — of her fancy treason hole here. So she's sending out a strike team."

"Oh."

"My sentiments exactly."

"And our people?"

"Some of them have volunteered to go back out," I shared. "The others I have quartered down in the garage. I don't have time to explain it, but they're safer down there. And you're safer up here," I added, shifting my tone to sound as stern as I could whilst talking to Raline. "I need you to make sure that none of our people go back to that room we just left, okay?"

"Okay," she replied. "Can I know why?"

"Later," I answered. And I meant it. I would have loved to tell her everything — to tell her everything I knew and everything I feared and everything I suspected. I would have loved to have given her a full and thorough warning as to what I had guessed might happen to anyone who dared go back into that chamber of horrors from which we'd escaped. But even if I'd had the time to say the words, I wouldn't have the time to process how I felt about them, and I knew there was no way I could tell these things to Raline without having feelings.

And I had no time for feelings.

"Later then," she said.

"I promise."

"Okay."

"Until then just know it's not safe for anyone from the *Dawn* who isn't a Princess of Feirin to be on the Emergency Deck."

"But it's safe for you?" She looked genuinely concerned and once again I was fearfully tempted to kiss her.

"Safe is a relative term," I said back. "Suffice to say saf*er*. I'm far safer than any of you. Just … lay low and stay here. I'm going back up to the Top Deck to check in with Ensign Declan and see what the Colonel's gotten us into. I'll be back when I can."

"All right," Raline said. She reached up with her good hand and pressed her fingertips against my cheek; it was a gesture of affection in parting I'd often seen T'wesh couples share.

I returned the gesture, and the look on Raline's face made my knees go weak again.

Just then I heard a voice from the nearby lift call out that he was headed to the Top Deck.

"That's my ride," I said.

Raline nodded.

"Go," she said. "Be safe. I'll see you soon."

I dashed into the nearby lift, wedging myself into the crowd of clamoring soldiers who could not possibly all be headed to the Top Deck. Not that there wouldn't have been room for all of them up there; the chamber was enormous and could easily have accommodated the base's entire complement and then some — hence the reason it had been the original choice for a Veneration Ceremony. But there were only so many duty stations up there, and I couldn't imagine this many extra people doing anything more than getting in each other's way.

For damn sure they were in mine.

When the lift came to a stop, we were not on the Top

Deck. We were instead on the Command Deck, the place where Bryte had brought me to meet the Colonel when we'd first arrived. Nearly two-thirds of the elevator's occupants debarked, leaving only two others aboard with me when the doors closed again.

That made more sense. Two floors, all the higher ranks, one lift car.

But now it wasn't crowded anymore. And the silence felt awkward. But what the hells was I supposed to say? Not twenty minutes ago these two men had been on their knees before me offering loyalty and adoration and now here I stood in a lift with them wearing the uniform of the Alliance to which they may bear no loyalty. Meanwhile, they were still in their Prayer Whites.

The only thing I could imagine more awkward than the silence would have been me trying to say something. I'd never been particularly skilled in royal eloquence. Adding a day-old concussion to the mix was enough to convince me to keep my trap shut for the interminable minutes until the lift doors opened again at the Top Deck.

When they finally did, I suddenly missed the awkward silence of the lift car.

A klaxon was sounding. Piercing, strident, more unpleasant even than the scramble drill sirens along the runways at the Air Academy, it was the loudest thing I have ever heard in my life. Perhaps these sirens were the same model as those scramble alarms, only amplified by the stone-domed ceiling of the Top Deck. Whatever they were, they were horrible. I could barely hear myself think.

The two men who'd been in the lift with me dashed off as soon as the doors were out of their way. Apparently they understood what was going on well enough to know where to head — and in a hurry. I, on the other hand, had not a single clue.

I looked around for Ensign Declan.

He was standing almost exactly where I'd left him, just behind the throne-like chair where Colonel Gertrune had been the last time I'd seen her. She was no longer in that chair. As I headed toward Ensign Declan, I could see her crossing back and forth between the big map table and a nearby crewed position I wasn't sure the purpose of.

I walked a little faster.

Everyone else in here was either glued to a seat or moving at a flat run. Whatever had this alarm going off had lit a proverbial fire under the normally deliberate and methodical servicepersons in this room. And if they thought it prudent to move fast, I had every intention of following their lead.

"Ensign, report!" I called as I closed the final few feet between Declan and myself. I could tell I'd startled him — he jumped as he came to attention. I was pretty sure he'd only come to attention to try and mask the fact he'd been startled, but I honestly didn't care. "As you were," I instructed. "And then please tell me what the hell is going on."

Declan was shaky, but he let himself stand at ease.

"Is it all right that I honestly don't know?" he replied.

I frowned. It wasn't all right. But the fault wasn't with Declan here.

"Tell me what you do know?" I asked.

"Someone said they were about to open the door," he told me. "And then the alarm started going off."

Of course it did.

Had I been given to belief in the supernatural, I might have convinced myself this wasn't the real world — that I hadn't survived the crash of the *Dawn* and that this place was one of the seven hells. But I didn't believe in that. Hells were a poppycock notion cooked up by royalty to keep the peasants in line. This was really happening, and I was going to have to figure my way through it.

How does a person make sense of a military base that has an alarm to tell everyone the door is open, but no procedure for when the enemy is approaching? It was ridiculous. And the din was making my concussion more miserable by the minute.

I thanked Declan and told him he was welcome to cover his ears. I stood up straighter and approached the Colonel where she stood.

"Can I get a Sit Rep?" I asked, as formally as I could whilst my head was being assaulted by the echoing klaxon.

"This alarm means the doors are open," she replied coolly. I tried not to frown too hard. No surprise she would presume that was my principal question. It's not like she could have overheard my conversation with Declan over the wailing.

"When they close the doors behind them, will it stop?" I asked.

Before she could say another word, I had my answer.

The alarm didn't so much stop as *change*. It got softer, although not by much, and its tone modulated to more of a whistle than a siren.

"Is that ...?" I began to ask, but the look on the Colonel's face told me more than I figured she'd be willing to say out loud.

She was just as clueless as I was. That was bad.

Worse still was the sound of the explosion that echoed through the coffered dome. The room shook — the whole mountain shook. Bits of dust and chips of marble fell from the ceiling, dinging and cracking the polished floor beneath.

Cries of surprise and upset sounded from all sides. The Colonel lost her balance as the floor beneath her trembled. She stumbled toward the display table, trying her best to stay on her feet. Looking over my shoulder I could see Ensign Declan had grabbed hold of the Colonel's chair to keep from falling himself. I had no idea why I hadn't fallen but chalked it up to a combination of luck and having already been braced for whatever the next strange thing this base was about to throw at me.

I wanted to scream but found myself utterly speechless. I reached out to the Colonel, either to steady her or to get her attention; I honestly wasn't sure which. But in doing so, I accomplished both.

She was shaking — possibly from having been tossed about the floor by the force of whatever just happened. But when I looked her in the face, I got the distinct feeling that wasn't the reason. Her pallor was ashen, her eyes glistening with unshed tears.

If I'd thought to ask her what we'd been through, I thought better of it now.

"Heavy artillery!" a man's voice called out from the far side of the room.

I turned my head to see him running toward us. Still in his Prayer Whites and bare feet, he sprinted across the dusty and cluttered floor with one arm above his head, holding up a bright orange flag with a pin at the end. The young man blew past us, leaving bloody prints on the stone from a cut on his foot as he approached the Colonel's map table.

Once he was closer, I could see he'd brought not one, but three orange flags. He planted each on the map table, in a semi-circular formation that I surmised was to indicate the relative positions of the heavy artillery he'd reported.

"Aerial bombardment!" another fellow called just

before the room shook again.

More bits of marble rained down on our heads as I held onto the Colonel, trying to keep us both steady.

A woman dressed half in Feirin red and half hospital scrubs ran into view, carrying with her at least a dozen bright blue pins which she attached with trembling hands to the area of the map table that stood for our position inside the mountain.

Colonel Gertrune didn't seem to even see them. She was stock-still. Frozen. Catatonic.

I couldn't stand still any longer.

It was one thing to watch a simulated battle play out on map tables and over intercoms, but it was another thing altogether to be standing inside a mountain under heavy bombardment. Watching the map fill with icons of the enemy's position wasn't at all what I wanted to be doing. I turned to take stock of the room and spotted Ensign Declan, still standing beside the Colonel's chair.

"Ensign," I called, "get down to the garage. Check in with Major Gowon — and General Sonneman if you can find him. Find out what's going on down there. I'm going to spend a minute getting a handle on things up here and I'll be down soon."

"Yes ma'am, Field Marshal." He snapped to for a moment before turning to go. Yeah. He was getting a promotion out of this. And a permanent job as my adjutant if I could talk him into it.

That was, of course, presuming we survived whatever the hells was going on right now. That was my next puzzle to solve. I needed to know what was happening outside.

I ran to the nearest periscope.

The operator's support person saw me coming in time to shoo him out of the seat and offer it to me. I slid into position and began scanning the sky for whatever it was those blue pins were standing for.

And there they were: a full dozen Xylanthian light bombers. They weren't what I remembered a Xy Federation aircraft looking like, but neither could they possibly have been mistaken for anything else.

These were new. They were sleek and streamlined with none of the sharp angles I remembered from the wartime Xy aircraft I'd studied. But the sweep of the wings and the taper of the fuselage were distinctly Xylanthian.

I wanted to scream.

The Xy had been re-arming.

Maybe it was just the Xylanthians. Maybe that was the problem that had put this whole mess in motion to begin with. Maybe the Xylanthians had wanted to re-arm and the Xylans hadn't and that had put the Xylans in fear of being the object of Alliance retaliation — or of an act of aggression from their sometime ally in the ever-looming struggle for resources on their shared continent.

Not that any of those things mattered. The politics of the situation were decidedly unimportant. The only thing that mattered in the here and now was the squadron of enemy aircraft overflying our position and dropping ordnance on our heads.

I turned the periscope to its maximum range in both directions, and in doing so began to understand the layout of this room. With the mountain itself in the way, each of these stations was only able to surveil a small slice of the airspace, and very little of the ground below. If I wanted to see what Bryte and the others were doing, I would need to find a station on the other side of the room.

With a quick glance back at the stock-still and unresponsive Colonel, I slid from the periscope stool and ran to the far side of the room, trying my best to triangulate where in this vast rotunda would give me the best vantage point to the forest just outside the garage. Using the relative position of the two lifts, I was able to hazard a reasonable guess and headed as quickly as I could in the direction of the station I'd chosen — thankful in that instant for having been summoned from my bed to the Mechanical Deck on the eve of the *Dawn*'s destruction and also for my personal aversion to all things religious. This situation was bad enough in my flight suit and tanker boots. I couldn't imagine having to go through it in pajamas or bare feet.

"Specialist," I addressed the lone woman at the periscope by the rank displayed on her red wool coat. Her support person had made a run toward the map table with another handful of colored pins, so at least I knew the battle was visible from here.

She looked confused at first when she turned her head toward me. Likely she'd been expecting only a familiar voice to address her — or maybe no one at all. The fact of my presence probably startled her.

"Y ... Your Highness," she stammered, eyes wide in recognition.

"May I?" I asked her, gesturing to the periscope she'd just turned away from.

"By all means," she answered. "Yes, Your Highness." She slid from the stool and took up the position of the operator's support person.

I slid into the seat, overwhelmingly grateful for having suffered through a formal Veneration — this exchange would have taken at least three times as long had the Specialist felt the need to stand on formalities. A combat headquarters is no place to make folks genuflect.

I'd chosen my periscope station well. I could see a second squadron of fighter/bombers approaching in the distance, and thick smoke rising from whatever munitions were being fired on the forest floor below. Turning the lens downward was, frustratingly, albeit predictably, less than useful. This place had been set up to watch the coast for an outbound invasion, not to keep an eye on things at the base of their own mountain.

"Damn," I cursed softly.

The mountain served as a reasonably good sound-dampening insulator, but my Academy-trained ears could clearly make out the sound of the aircraft I'd seen through the other periscope coming in for another run. This whole thing was only going to get worse.

"Your Highness?" the young Specialist beside me said.

I shook my head. I wasn't in the mood to explain things.

"Those bombers are coming back around," I said, as curtly as possible in hopes my tone would dissuade her from asking more questions.

"I'll go update the table," she said.

"No!" I called, reaching out a hand to stop her.

"Your Highness?"

"I'll go," I said, hopping off the stool and steering her back toward it. "You retake your post."

"Yes, ma'am," she replied, moving to do just that.

I took off at a sprint in the direction of the Colonel, who I could see still hadn't moved. There was a flurry of activity at the map table: personnel from all over clamoring for space alongside it so they could reach the places they needed to keep the pins and flags accurate to the moment.

It wasn't worth fighting the crowd to turn those blue pins.

"The air force is coming in for another run!" I said, right in the Colonel's ear so there'd be no question as to whether or not she heard me. But still, she didn't seem to. "Does this base have any surface-to-air capability?" I asked. "Or anything at all that flies?" I shouldn't have been surprised that my first inclination when the bombs started falling was to get into an aircraft and blow something out of the sky.

But I was.

A lifetime of princess-hood and a decade at a diplomatic desk hadn't tamed me. Apparently.

The Colonel shook her head and turned to look at me. She appeared confused, addled ... as though she somehow had absolutely no idea what was happening all around her. This was going nowhere.

I took her by the shoulders and looked her squarely in her vacant eyes.

"SAMs!" I yelled, "or fighters?"

Suddenly it was like the light came back into her eyes.

"Fighters," she said softly.

For a moment, I let relief wash over me. Whatever kind of pewtypot, illegal, treasonous circle of hell this base was, if it had a secret cache of fighter planes — even horribly out of date ones — I was about to be very happy to hear that.

"We're all fighters," she said. "We will fight to the death to defend Feirin, the Queen, and our ...."

I didn't wait to hear the last part.

"What? No!" I exclaimed. "I was asking about planes. Or anything you have to shoot down planes."

But she hadn't heard me.

She stood up straighter and took a step toward the map table. Gertrune reached beneath the table and drew forth an oversized microphone on a telescoping gooseneck. She pulled it up level with her mouth and flipped a little switch on the side. "Attention all personnel," she said, her voice still shaky to my ears, but not in a way that the public address system could convey. "Prepare for ground assault. All personnel on decks five through nine should immediately commence major combat operations."

Ground assault? Major combat operations?

"Colonel," I said, closing the distance between us.

When she turned to face me, she looked like a woman possessed.

"We have to defeat them," she said.

"You're not going to defeat an air force with a ground assault!" I reminded her. But I could tell I was getting nowhere. She wasn't listening.

I had to decide what to do next, and I had to decide quickly. I could formally relieve her of command — maybe. My Royal authority may or may not be enough to sway the loyalty of the whole base; this probably wasn't a good time to test that.

The better thing, I figured, was to get back down to the garage and try to head off any troop deployment at the door. I'd be safer from the aerial assault in the lower levels anyway. I shook my head at the Colonel again and took off for the lift, silently wishing the next bombardment might knock out the Top Deck's public address capabilities. Colonel Gertrune could do far less harm if she couldn't give any orders.

The lights flickered as I stepped aboard the lift car. Across the room I could see sparks cascading from the area of the map table — had I just gotten my wish? But I hadn't time to stand around and hope for the best out of a series of falling bombs. I pulled the lift door closed, turned the dial to the garage level and willed the thing to move. If those bombs had taken out the lift motors, I wasn't sure what I would do.

My toes twitched in my boots as I waited for the car to start downward. It was taking too long. How the hell was I going to get there if the lifts weren't working? Was there even a way? I tried call up what mental map

I'd been able to construct over the course of my time here. Did I remember someone mentioning stairs? But my concussion didn't want to let me concentrate.

At the very least, I was going to have to find some way onto the Command Level. If all else failed, as long as I could get there, I could use the manual lift to take me almost to the garage.

To the level above.

To Raline.

Somehow she was all I could think about as I fidgeted under myself. What were things like down where she was? Had the chaos died down? Was she all right? Was the pain in her shoulder returning with the same force as the pain in my head?

I needed to see her, to go to her.

I caught myself reaching to dial the lift to take me to the level above the garage. I spun it before I could think too hard.

The car began to move.

The motor sounded off somehow — grinding, grumbling — and the lights continued to flicker as though the bulbs had been shaken loose from their sockets. It was eerie and I hated it. With my palms pressed against the metal grate of the lift car's inner door, I held my breath until the damn thing stopped.

I wasn't sure whether the lift itself was shaking or if it was just me, but either way I was glad to have arrived someplace. I waited what felt like forever for the door clamps to align and then threw the lever to open them with all my might.

I don't know how I'd gotten it in my mind that the lift might not open, but I was more relieved than I'd have been able to articulate when the door slid out of my way like there was nothing wrong at all.

The hallway beyond was pitch black. I couldn't know whether the bombardment had knocked the electricity out, whether power had been diverted from down here to the Top Deck, or something else. I had no idea what this level's usual function even was, so there was no way to even begin trying to figure that out.

I stood in the open doorway of the lift car, hoping the little light coming from inside of it would get someone's attention. It started to flicker a little brighter as I scanned the distance for anything familiar it might have spilled onto.

"Chief Khatri?" I called out, my voice sounding softer than I'd intended it.

My stomach lurched when no answer came.

"Raline!" I shouted, not even caring who heard. Still nothing.

I couldn't remember the last time I'd been so terrified. Not on the bridge of the *Dawn* as it crashed nor in the woods as strangers approached had I felt this afraid. The tears I'd been fighting for — how long had it even been? — sprang from my eyes suddenly, very much out of my control.

I slid the lift car door closed again and leaned against it, letting myself have these feelings for exactly as long as it took to turn the dial and let it carry me down to the garage. I don't know how long I was standing there weeping into my forearm before I realized I hadn't started moving, but the fabric of my flight suit was soaked clean through.

The motors sounded wrong again — the earlier grinding noises replaced now by a droning hum. Thinking back to the mechanical lessons I'd taken at the Air Academy, I could pretty easily diagnose a slipped or broken belt. The motor was turning, but the gears weren't getting power.

This lift wasn't going anywhere.

I took a deep breath as I shoved the car door open again. There was a bright side to this. Whatever massive ground force Colonel Gertrune thought she might send out to face the incoming enemy would now be relegated to a single mechanized lift along with the manual — provided both of those were still on their tracks.

Which gave me a brilliant, terrible idea.

Using what little light spilled from the flickering bulbs in the car that had brought me here, I managed to triangulate my way to the second mechanized lift and throw the lever to summon it to me. I could only hope that the troops were still being readied and wouldn't be on their way down yet.

But even if they were, these lifts didn't have overrides — at least not that I'd been able to spot. If a cadre of armed soldiers was on its way to the garage level, their lift would stop here to pick me up. They had no way to keep that from happening. Some of the lifts in the more sensitive areas of the Palace, and the Air Academy for that matter, had key-and-tumbler mechanisms installed to force a car into point-to-point only operation; it was a feature installed to facilitate rapid and secure movement of high-ranking personnel. But it was also expensive, difficult to manage, and required a keeper of keys to be always available lest they be needed.

It had been my impression all along that this base's priorities were unwise and jumbled, but in this case, I was thankful they'd never put in such a protocol.

The second lift arrived in moments. And it was completely empty when it did. I had been right to presume no one from the upper levels was yet ready to deploy. Good.

I dashed aboard, spun the dial to take it to the garage and tried not to think too hard about what had become of Raline and the others.

CHAPTER TWENTY-FOUR

If I thought I saw pandemonium in the garage when I'd been there last, I didn't have words for what I walked in on this time.

For one thing, there was an active firefight happening at the partially open door. Half a dozen uniformed men were trying to get the bent and damaged metal sheet to close, but I could see from where I stood it was off its track and there would be no sliding it back into place without major mechanical repairs — the kind that were not going to be possible whilst taking enemy fire.

The Feirin forces had set up a barricade of sorts, piles of crates and heavy walkontainers all shoved together as a bulwark against incoming munitions. I could only hope those who'd cobbled this thing into being had thought to check for live ordnance. The last thing we needed right now was an incoming grenade setting the whole thing off and blowing us all to oblivion.

But, then again, if we were all going to die here anyway ....

No.

I shook my head and shoved all thoughts of death and defeat down my gullet. It might be hopeless, but it might not. The opening to the outside was barely two men wide, and it was manned by five Feirin sharpshooters who were holding the line with machine rifles and something that looked like an antiquated grenade launcher. I recognized Bryte as one of them.

Putting my back to the wall so as to be as far out of the line of fire as possible, I started in his direction. But then I stopped myself. There was something I needed to do first.

When I turned around, Ensign Declan and Major Gowon were right behind me. I smiled in spite of myself.

"What happened?" I asked.

"Best I can tell the enemy caught sight of them leaving," Gowon answered me. "I'm not sure the whole team had cleared the door before they called for a retreat, but it was already too late. They lost a couple of troops out there," he added, "but I couldn't tell you how many or who they were. The guys inside were already trying to close the door but it got hit and you see what happened."

"Yeah," I replied. "And the Xylanthians have air cover, too."

"Ensign Declan was just telling me about that."

"There are more," I said. "Incoming. I stole a look through a couple of the periscopes. It's bad."

"Real bad," Declan affirmed. "I have it on good

authority this base has no surface to air capabilities at all. I was hoping for maybe something handheld in a crate down here, but … I talked with the ordnance master and … no."

"Of course not," I spat, suddenly furious again at the fussed-up priorities that had gone into this place. "Watch for enemy assets, but whatever you do don't shoot them down. Of all the messed up …"

"I hear you," Major Gowon interrupted me. Probably for the best. The words I had on the tip of my tongue were decidedly un-princesslike and that was not the image I wanted to be projecting. Not that I gave too much of a damn about my image in general — but if I was going to dissuade an entire garrison from heading out into a battle that was tantamount to suicide, I would need to do so as Her Highness.

"I should let you know I brought our wounded down here," Declan said.

"You …" I couldn't even finish that sentence, the sense of relief was so powerful. "Are they all okay?"

"Yes ma'am," Declan replied. "On my way down, the power flickered — badly. I thought it would be better to have everyone together, and I wasn't sure we'd be able to move anyone if we lost power entirely. So, I …"

"No need to explain yourself," I said. "That was good thinking. You did the right thing. You keep doing the right thing. We get through all this, and I promise to take time to properly express my gratitude."

"No need for that, Your Highness," he replied.

He was right, of course. Not about his not deserving the acknowledgement, that he most definitely did — but the middle of a firefight was absolutely not the time to be discussing such matters.

"Did you hear the announcement?" I asked both of them.

"Yeah," Declan replied.

"I don't think any of them did," Gowon added, indicating the folks in the midst of exchanging fire. "But they do need the reinforcements."

"I can see that," I replied. "But that doesn't make it a good idea for Colonel Gertrune to march every last person this base has aboard it through that tiny hole in the door straight into overwhelming enemy fire."

"Yeah," Gowon replied. "I agree with you there."

"Good," I said. "Because the other lift is busted. The one I came in is the only one that's working. And as long as it's stuck down here, no one above can get on it."

"What are you saying ... exactly?" Declan asked. I smiled when I looked back over at him. That boy didn't have a devious bone in his body, but he was about to learn a thing or three about Royal machinations — starting with my plan to keep armed troops from getting down here to be slaughtered.

"I'm saying we're going to keep that lift car down here," I said plainly. "Put somebody on it," I ordered. "Better yet, put our wounded on it — all of them. There's plenty of room. The extra layers of steel between them and the flying bullets won't hurt, and they'll have a door they can close if the enemy breaks through the line. But don't let them close the door yet," I added, my voice growing frantic as I could tell he was ready to move on my order. "As long as the door stays open, the car won't move. And as long as it can't move, no one else can use it."

"You're sure?" Major Gowon asked.

"I'm sure," I replied. "It's the same old Feirin design as every pre-war lift back home. Locking the door into place is what engages the gears — lets the pulleys work against the counterweights. With the door open, all that gets turned is air."

"All right," Declan said. "I'll move everyone."

"Good." I was shaking again.

"Should I say something to Chief Khatri?" he asked.

I closed my eyes as I shook my head in reply. What the hell could I possibly have to say? *Tell her I think I'm madly in love with her* probably wouldn't be too well received under the circumstances.

And since there was every chance I was about to go and get myself blown to pieces, I figured maybe that wasn't the best impression to leave her with.

"Tell her I said I'll see her later," I said back softly. Maybe that was a lie, but it felt like the right thing to say.

"Yes ma'am," Declan said as I turned to head into the fight.

"Where are you going?" Gowon asked, stopping me with a hand on my arm.

"I've got to talk to Bryte ... er ... General Sonneman."

Major Gowon shook his head. His hand still on my arm, he turned away from me. When he turned back, he had a repeating pistol in his hand.

"I don't like the idea of you heading over there, Field Marshal Your Highness," he said, putting equal emphasis on both my ranks. "But if you're going to insist — which I can tell you are —I'd prefer you take this. As a graduate of the Gammran Academy, I can only presume you know how to use it."

"Yes sir," I took the pistol and slid it into the loop on my flight suit I knew was there to hold a sidearm; I'd never had one before, but I knew the theory.

I was running along the wall, trying not to imagine the worst — grenades or poison gas or heavy mortars flying through the door to devastate all of us — when a scream so loud and so strident as to carry over the noise of battle pierced my eardrums. I looked ahead and saw Bryte crumpling to the deck in front of the open door.

I ran faster.

One of the men on the machine gun dropped to the floor to pull Bryte out of the line of fire, leaning him against the wall beside the sniper positions before returning to his place. I couldn't even pay attention to the firefight after that; all I could manage to focus on was my old friend, pained and bleeding, lying against the wall ahead of me. I dove to the ground beside him as soon as I thought I might be in range.

"They didn't know," he said when he saw me.

I shook my head.

"What?"

"They were scouting. Charting. They didn't know we were here. Some of them had walked right past us. They wouldn't have found us," he said. "They wouldn't have found us."

"I know," I said, more as an affirmation than an *I told you so*. Although I had told him so. "But you had your orders," I reminded him.

"More troops," he said. His voice was getting weaker. "She's sending more troops."

"Yeah, well," I replied, "Those troops are going to find they'll have a real hard time getting down here."

"Maran," he whispered. He reached up and touched my face as his eyes rolled back up into his head.

"I'm right here, Bryte," I said, looking around for something — anything — I might be able to use to put pressure on his wound. The bullet had gotten him just above his right hip; it was bleeding heavily, but other than that I had no idea how bad it was. There was every chance it had gotten only flesh and fascia, that it was a minor thing and he'd recover easily provided we could get the bleeding under control. But what rudimentary knowledge of field medicine had left the Academy with me told me there was an equal chance the bullet had ripped through his bowel and was already spreading infection that would kill him no matter our intervention.

Whichever it was, we needed to get him the hells off the floor and out of the line of fire. I looked over my shoulder; the wounded from the *Dawn* were being loaded aboard the lift. That was my answer. Our Lt. Mieko might not have a full sickbay, but what she had would be better than nothing. And, on top of that, she'd know what to do.

"I'll be right back," I told Bryte.

"Maran ...."

"Bryte, I'm not leaving. If you can open your eyes, you'll see I have people - people just a few meters away. I'm going to get them," I assured him. "I'm going to get help."

I couldn't wait for him to acknowledge what I'd said. I put my back to the wall and moved as quickly as I could to where Major Gowon was still standing.

"Field Marshal," he greeted me.

"We've got to get General Sonneman back here," I said.

"He got shot," Gowon said, glancing over my shoulder at Bryte where he lay.

"Yeah."

"Is it bad?"

"Can't tell."

"Yeah, all right," he said. He looked quickly back and forth between the lift and the fire line.

I followed suit. Everyone seemed occupied. Ensign Declan was working with Lt. Mieko to get our people aboard the lift — including, I realized for the first time, Lt. Swar who must have gotten injured on the initial sortie to the wreck. Everyone else had found a weapon and taken up a position against the enemy.

"Come on, then," Gowon said, "it's me and you."

"Yeah," I agreed as I took off after him.

I wanted to shout at him to watch himself, to be careful of the incoming fire, not to get himself shot in the process of going into rescue someone who'd already been shot. But the last thing I wanted to do was to cause him to turn his head; losing focus now would make him more likely to wind up injured — not less. So I kept my concern to myself and followed his lead along the wall toward the door.

"I've got his arms," Gowon said when we got to where we were going. "You get his legs."

I nodded and did as I was told, scooping up Bryte's ankles and tucking one under each arm in a posture I somehow remembered from the emergency training I'd taken at the Academy. Bryte groaned as Major Gowon got him up by his underarms. Good. He was still conscious.

"Go!" Major Gowon ordered.

I took off running — backwards — somehow remembering only then that I'd also been taught how to do this carry facing away from the patient. Moving as fast as I could in a backwards run with a pounding concussion, I swore to myself I wouldn't forget there was a forward-facing option if I ever found myself in this situation again. I trusted Major Gowon to warn me if I was about to run into or trip over anything — so I made a point to concentrate on his face as we went. There were still bullets flying, some of them terrifyingly close to us, and I was pretty sure letting them pull my focus would have caused problems for all of us.

Fortunately for all involved, the path was clear, and in the space of only a few seconds, we were behind a barricade and headed into the lift car with the rest of the wounded folks. Major Gowon set Bryte down gingerly, just on the inside of the door to the lift. I was lowering his legs to the floor when Raline called out to me.

"Maran!" she shouted.

I turned to see her stumbling toward me, taking what care she could not to step on or trip over any of her comrades as they sat or reclined on the floor of the lift. There were local garrison wounded here, too — just a handful of them, shellshocked and dirty, with bandaged limbs, one sporting a makeshift eye patch. Looking around briefly, it was clear Bryte was the worst off among them, although a young Gammran man I didn't know by name had a bullet wound in his forearm that Lt. Mieko was still working to bandage.

I dropped Bryte's legs — probably far less gently than I should have.

"Raline!" I gasped. I couldn't help myself. As soon as she was in range, I grabbed hold of her, taking her in my arms and burying my face in her neck, careful not to aggravate the painful place on her shoulder, but needing to be close to her so badly I couldn't stand it.

She took hold of me as well, squeezing my side with the hand in a sling, and wrapping her good arm around my back as tightly as anybody ever had. She held me — for what might have been a minute or more — letting me draw whatever comfort I could from her nearness and care.

"The General," she said after a moment, stepping away as she brought her hand to my cheek. "Your friend: what happened?"

"He was at the door," I said back, taking her hand in mine as I turned back to Bryte. Lt. Mieko had come over with one of the medics I'd seen on the Emergency Deck before. I didn't know her name, and there was no name tape on the scrub top she wore. But it was obvious she knew what she was doing — tearing away the fabric of Bryte's BDUs so she could get a better look at the wound.

"He got shot," Raline surmised.

I nodded.

"How bad is it?" I asked the medics as I took Raline's hand and crouched down to check on Bryte.

"Can't tell yet," Lt. Mieko replied. She and the other medic were working frantically; I decided not to interrupt them again.

I squeezed my eyes shut. These tears were going to fall whether I wanted them to or not.

"They have to shut the door, Maran," he said, opening his eyes and locking his gaze on mine. "They're going to keep coming. We have to get that door ...." His voice trailed off.

"He's going into shock," the Feirin medic announced, reaching into her kit for an ampoule of something.

I grabbed hold of Bryte's hand and squeezed.

"You've got to stay with me, buddy," I said. There were tears in my voice as well as on my face and I couldn't be bothered to give a damn.

"The door," he said again, softly.

"They can't close the door," I told him. "It's broken. It's off the track. And the track is broken. Bryte, we can't close it. It won't close."

"They'll keep coming."

"I know," I said back, squeezing his hand even tighter. "That's why we've got to get out of here." I couldn't believe I'd said that out loud. I'd been thinking it since the moment a bomb fell on my head up on the Top Deck, but I hadn't managed to articulate it until now.

"Can't," Bryte told me. "Enemy is everywhere. They'll keep coming."

"There's got to be a way," I said. But no one answered. I shook my head again. It was getting harder and harder to gather my thoughts into coherence. "You got a Sceritzene in there?" I asked the medic.

"I think so," she answered. "Yes. But ...." She shook her head, looking utterly helpless; her hands were covered in her XO's blood, from a wound she was still assessing.

"Raline," I said. "Could you look in the medkit for a Sceritzene for me?"

"Of course," she said back, squeezing my hand before moving to reach the kit.

"Bryte," I said, my voice suddenly harsh. My anger and upset were getting the best of me, and I didn't have it in me to talk like a diplomat anymore. "You cannot be telling me I have seen every way in and out of this place. I grew up in the Palace — I know better. This is a Feirin base," I reminded him, giving not one tenth of a damn for the possible reaction of the *Dawn* survivors around me. "Which means it would have been built to Feirin spec. So how do we evacuate?"

"Can't," Bryte answered.

"Pewtyshoes!" I snapped. "Bryte Sonneman, you listen to me. I am speaking as your friend, as your kinfolk, and as the daughter of the Sovereign, second in line to the throne and I will not be lied to."

"Maran ...."

"No," I stopped him before he could say any more. "You will tell me the truth," I insisted. "Because not only am I certain this super-secret mountain of yours does not handle its personnel changes in the broad damn daylight, I also happen to know the way Feirin designers put together important buildings. There's always a secret way out. Always. It's there in case of a ... a groundquake, or a fire. Or a ... plague of insects ... or whatever. I know there's a way because there is always a way. We don't build a place like this without a way. So I am asking you again: how do we evacuate?"

"Can't."

"For Queen's sake, Bryte!"

"What about the little ship?" a tiny voice called out.

I snapped my head around so fast my eyes wouldn't focus right away. Raline crouched back down beside me, pushing a pair of Sceritzene pills into my hand. I kissed her cheek without thinking before popping the pills into my mouth and standing up to get a better read on where that voice had come from.

"There's a ship," the voice said again. It was the girl with the gauze patch on her eye. She was a tiny thing, smaller than me in every dimension, with blood caked in the fringe of her golden hair and her BDUs covered in mud.

"A ship?" I asked.

"What good is a ship going to do?" Major Gowon asked. "There's no way we'll make it to the coast!"

"No, it's here," the young woman replied.

"Here?"

"Yes, Your Highness."

"In this base?" I quizzed.

"Yes, Your Highness," she repeated.

"What's your name, soldier?" I asked her.

"I'm Private Margeaux, Your Highness," she replied.

"Call me 'ma'am,' Private Margeaux," I told her. "And then tell me about this ship."

"I think it's been here since the base was built," she said. "it's parked in the under level — where the troop transfer and supply ships come in. We keep extra rations there. And medicines. Below the water line it's like cold storage. I'm in there to pull out stock every couple of months."

My eyes got wider as I tried to make sense of what I was hearing. Had she just said ...?

"This base has access to water?" I asked. "We can get to the ocean? Under the mountain?"

"I think so?" Margeaux answered.

"And there's a ship? Just ... just sitting there?

Parked?"

"Yes, ma'am."

"Can't," Bryte said again.

"And why the hell not?" I asked, looking down at him but not bending over again.

"We just use it for storage," he said. "It's an old ballast ship. Here since construction. Even if ... even ...."

"Even *what*, Bryte?" I shouted. "Tell me!"

"Even if we could get it running, it's got to be four miles through tight underwater passages. No one here would even know how to drive it."

"An old ... ballast ship ...?" My mouth fell open as the pieces fell into place in my head.

"Maran?" Raline asked, putting her good arm around me. I must have looked a fright; her face was pure concern.

"Do you know Lt. Frey?" I asked, ostensibly addressing Pvt. Margeaux, but making sure I was heard by everyone in the lift. "Do any of you know where she might be right now?"

"She works in the power plant," the Feirin medic answered me.

The power plant. This couldn't be more perfect.

"And where is that?"

"It's three decks up from here," the medic answered me.

"Where are the stairs?" I asked. I was sure now that someone had, at some point, told me this place had a staircase, and with the one lift broken and the other occupied, it was the only way possible for me to get up three decks.

"Out and to the left at the end of the hall," Margeaux answered me.

I turned and kissed Raline's cheek again.

"Why are you going to get this Lieutenant from the

power plant?" she asked me.

"Because she's going to get us out of here," I replied, squeezing Raline's hand before letting go of it to head out of the lift.

"What?" Raline wasn't the only person asking me that, but she was the one I chose to answer.

"She went to Maritime!" I called back, already out the door and headed toward the staircase. "Got an advanced proficiency in ballast ships!" I was saying it, I knew it was happening, and yet it still felt too good to be true. "Ayan!" I called back, "Yvan!"

"Yes, ma'am?" Major Gowon and Ensign Declan answered in concert.

"Gather what supplies you can then move this lift to the under level. Have anyone who's able get aboard that old ship and start making as much room as possible — we're going to try and get every soul aboard this base onto that thing and if it's being used for storage there's no telling how much gear we'll have to jettison to make that happen. I'll be back with Lt. Frey as quickly as I can, and we'll figure out our next moves from there."

"Yes ma'am," Major Gowon said, moving from where he'd been standing near Bryte's head toward the stacks of crates beyond the door to the lift.

"Aye-aye, Field Marshal," was Declan's reply.

I looked back at them. I had never meant to be in charge of this base, or this mission, but if I had to take charge, I was glad to have the two of them behind me.

I saluted before turning to run for the stairs.

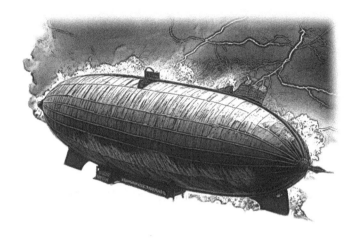

CHAPTER TWENTY-FIVE

I had always considered myself to be a person who kept herself in reasonably good physical condition. Even after the rigorous PT requirements of the Academy were no longer a daily fact of my life, I had made a point to stay in what I thought was pretty decent shape.

But the three flights of stairs between the garage and the power plant had me convinced otherwise.

It was only after I'd arrived at the level in question that it occurred to me I hadn't bothered to ask for further directions. This base was large, and my experience of it so far — with the exception of the Top Deck and the Emergency Deck — had been tight hallways and winding passages.

That was a Feirin thing, too; places called decks were wide open and cavernous while places called levels were labyrinthine, tight and confusing. It was an outdated idea of war fighting — to either leave the enemy entirely exposed or confused and indecisive. Apparently, it worked on princesses just as well as it did enemy agents. I found myself thoroughly flummoxed by the network of halls and passages on the level to which I'd been directed.

Feirin.

Power plant.

Think, Maran!

Those Sceritzene couldn't start to work fast enough. I'd have had a hard enough time figuring this place out without a concussion.

I might have stopped and screamed had I not thought it would further upset my throbbing head. But it would have. Also, there were lives on the line — mine included — so taking a moment to vent my frustration seemed a poor use of my time.

The enemy was at the door. Literally. And the door couldn't be properly shut. Finding the power plant, and with it, Lt. Frey, was the only hope we had.

"Power plant," I whispered to myself, running my fingers across my scalp at a clip Raline would probably say was too hurried to induce relaxation. "Feirin. Power plant." I knew these things. I knew these things same as I knew the difference between a deck and a level.

The power plant: what had Lt. Frey told me about it? Something about 'in common with a submarine ....' No. No, that was the mountain as a whole. The power plant on a submarine was an isolated thing in the aft of the ship that could be sealed off and jettisoned at the surface in case of an emergency.

No.

The power plant in a Feirin installation would be shielded. Central. Someplace with easy access to water — that would explain why it was only these few decks up and not halfway between the top and the bottom. It should be in the middle.

All the way in the middle.

I paused for a moment to get my bearings. I would need to move toward the center of this level. Somewhere along the way I'd find the door I needed.

I wound my way left and right and left again, doubling back and looping around on myself, passing doors labeled "Electrical Supplies," "Fuses," and "Maintenance." Some of those signs might even be accurate. But if my knowledge of Feirin military architecture and strategy bore out, they were probably decoys — designed to confuse and waylay an enemy, to get them to pass by the actual operational locations in favor of easily-accessible places they could wreak havoc upon with little consequence.

It was bogus, but at least it was predictable.

And it also meant I was getting closer.

Experience told me not to follow the signs, but instead continue to follow my gut.

Eventually I found it: a pair of nondescript double doors near what my internal compass told me was the front-to-back and side-to-side center of this level of the base. They were trick doors, I was sure of it. The left-hand door had a silver handle near the center line, and the one on the right was featureless as though it could only be opened from the inside, or by a switch in the space between. But these were Feirin doors, in a Feirin base, built by Feirin loyalists in the wake of a war.

There was no more chance of these doors working the normal way than there was of our getting our hands on tonight's adasha pudding. Damn — I had looked forward to that pudding. How long had it been since I'd eaten anything, anyway?

I slipped my fingers into the crevice between the right-hand door and the jamb. Finding the tiny toggle right where I expected it, I pressed the switch and jiggled my finger until it gave. When I heard the whirring of the servos, I knew I'd done the right thing — and also that I had to be in the right place, as I was deep enough in the mountain not to be hearing the booms and bangs of the firefight from either above or below.

The door panel popped out of the jamb, springing gently away and seating itself into the track hidden on the far side of the frame. I started through it as soon as it began sliding away, never mind that I had to turn sideways and squeeze my way through. Waiting for the door to clear so I could walk through it normally felt like a waste of seconds we might not have.

At least I was sure I was in the right room.

The base's power plant appeared to be a strange hybrid. Hydroelectric generators similar to the ones in the power plant at the Royal Palace in Feirin City operated side-by-side with solid fuel boilers like those I'd seen dormant in the engine room of the *Dawn*. Both sets of machinery seemed to be running at full capacity as a good dozen or so personnel, some of them still in partial Prayer Whites, tinkered and monitored.

If anyone noticed me, they didn't acknowledge it.

I looked around for Lt. Frey. Would I even recognize her in Prayer Whites or her normal uniform? Even in the best of times my memory had always been contextual. I could recognize the Third Secretary for Agriculture's new mail room intern anywhere in the building once we'd been introduced, but not the Third Secretary himself were I to run into him in any *other* building. Change a person's clothes, their hair, or take them out of the place I expect to see them, and I was far more likely than not to have no idea we'd ever met.

Fortunately for me, Lt. Frey hadn't changed her hair. Although now dressed for duty in service grays and epaulets, she looked enough the same from the neck up that I had no trouble picking her out of the crowd. It was adequately noisy in here — with the rumbling of turbines and the rattling of belts — that I thought it best not to try and call out to her. She probably wouldn't hear me, and it would surely make my headache worse.

She was constantly dashing back and forth between one of the hydroelectric turbines and what I figured was a gauge of its output. Or maybe it was a monitor of the base's overall power situation. I was basically clueless about electricity, and it wasn't like I needed to know the exact specifics of what Lt. Frey was doing.

What I did need to know, and what I was easily able to discern, was where and how I ought to intercept her. I strode intently to a spot near the gauges that should have put me directly in her path, but she diverted as she approached, taking the few steps necessary to avoid running into me.

Maybe her facial recall was as conditional as mine was. Or maybe she was so focused she didn't even bother to see who was in her way. I was able to turn and snag her by the elbow within a step or two of where she passed by and turn her around to face me.

"Lt. Frey," I said.

Her mouth had come open and I could tell she was about to unload some very strong feelings on whoever had interrupted her flow of tasks. But she stopped before any sound escaped her lips.

"Yo ... Your Highness," she said, her voice trembling with fear and contrition. I could only hope she remembered she wasn't supposed to kneel. "Wha ... what ...."

I didn't have time to wait for her to form a coherent question.

"We need you," I said plainly.

"You do? Why? How? I mean …."

"How much do you know about what's going on right now?" I asked.

Lt. Frey shook her head.

"Not a lot," she admitted. "I know the Top Deck is in use," she elaborated. "And not just the lights, but the periscopes and the gauges. That's never happened before — at least not in the time I've been here. Actually, not in the time any of us who are up here now have been here. I don't think it's a drill because we've had drills before, and we didn't have to power the periscopes for longer than it took to prove they were able to turn on. And then the Colonel made that announcement about a ground assault and major combat operations and so …." She shook her head and shrugged. "I just have to keep the lights on."

I was pretty sure she meant that to be the end of the conversation.

I guess it was fair she thought I was asking if she knew what was going on because I wanted her to tell me what was going on. I probably should have phrased things better.

"I've been up on the Top Deck," I told her, "and down in the garage. And it's bad."

"It's bad?"

"Really bad.

I gave her as complete a rundown as I could in the little time I had to give it. I told her about the proximity alarm, the sortie to the wreck of the *Dawn*, the Xylanthians untimely arrival and ensuing shootout, the Colonel's decision to try and cover the evidence, and the battle that was raging outside.

"Name of the Queen!" she swore. "They're dropping bombs on us?"

"And that's not the worst part."

"Do I want to hear the worst part?" she asked. "And

also, should you maybe tell me why you came looking for me to tell me all this?"

"No, and yes," I answered back, realizing that the Sceritzene had started to kick in and my head was beginning to feel clearer.

"What?" Lt. Frey shook her head again. She was obviously befuddled; maybe my head was cloudier than I knew. "I mean ... Your Highness ..."

"Even without hearing the worst part I think you will agree this is bad."

"Yes ma'am."

"We need to get out of here," I said. "And it seems you're the one person qualified to actually do that."

"Me?"

"Yes."

"How? I mean ..."

"Did you know there's a ballast ship in this installation?" I asked.

The look on her face was all the answer I needed.

"There's a ...?"

"Yeah," I said back. "You might have seen it when you first deployed."

"There was another ship," she recalled — with some effort if I was assessing things correctly. "It was tiny: an old hulk of a thing, and it's dark down there. I didn't really get a look at it. You're telling me that's a ballast ship?"

"That's what a supply officer named Margeaux just told me. Says it's used for cold storage — that she's on and off it all the time."

"And you want me ...?"

I could see the dots connecting in her head.

"Yes, I do."

Lt. Frey's eyes got wide, and she started to nod slowly. The movement of her head got quicker and before I knew it, she was practically bouncing.

"Okay," she said, somehow managing to nod with her whole body. "Yes. Okay." She reached out and took me by my upper arms.

"Okay," I affirmed.

"Wait here," she instructed before turning around and dashing off.

"What!?" I called after her. "Where are you going? We don't have time!"

"I'll be right back!" she shouted over her shoulder.

What the ...?

Not that I had much of a choice, but I did as she said and waited for her to come back. True to her word, she was back before I had a chance to get too impatient.

"Had to turn the lights on," she told me as the two of us took off toward the still-open door. She took off in what I figured to be the direction of the small lift. I snagged her by the elbow and shook my head.

"Stairs," I insisted. "That lift's broken and the other won't work."

I think my words confused her, but she started running toward the staircase anyway.

As it turns out, running down four levels of stairs isn't a whole lot easier than running up three. But as we went, Lt. Frey was able to explain to me how the base had protocol for the routing of power in an emergency and how fully activating the Command Level and the Top Deck meant shutting off the power to the parts of the station that weren't necessary for the duration of the drill — or the *not a drill* as were. The only way we were going to have lights where we were going, was for her to go and throw a switch.

I didn't ask her what that meant for the power supply on the Command Level or the Top Deck, mostly because I didn't care. Hells, if she'd just made things harder for Colonel Gertrune and her irrepressible need to make as many deaths happen as possible, I was all in favor. I preferred to save as many of these people's lives as I could.

I had no idea how quickly the personnel who'd been ordered out for a ground assault could be readied and deployed, and I was pretty sure I didn't want to find out. Armed personnel had probably already started down the stairs to the garage with only the orders to charge ahead at all costs, and the ranking person down there who might be able to talk them into pausing was lying in a stalled lift on the under level with a bullet wound in his middle.

We had to work fast — faster than the Colonel's agenda could be worked.

If the Top Deck had been too big, too tall, too fancy, and too much in every way, the under level qualified as its polar and exact opposite. Rather than a polished marble floor and coffered, domed ceiling, this place was uneven natural rock as far as the eye could see, save for a few areas decked over with rough-hewn planks strung between rusting pipe scaffolding.

I'd never been in a more incongruous space in my life. Every other inch of this base had been cleaned and waxed to Palace spec and then some. In all the places I'd been since arriving here, I hadn't seen so much as a fingerprint on a brass knob. The leather covers over periscopes and signal flags were oiled and polished as well as any piece of cavalry parade tack back home. Even the flushrooms in the garage were buffed like the palace keep. And yet here I stood in a chamber within the same damn mountain administered by the same damn people that looked as though it hadn't been cleaned or maintained in the entire thirty years of its occupation.

The lights Lt. Frey had dashed to turn on looked to be nothing more than a bunch of re-purposed signal lamps mounted on easels or tied onto nets bolt-fastened to the walls. The walls themselves, same as the ceiling and most of the floor, were the unimproved natural features of this cave.

It didn't make sense. But then, when had anything about this installation made sense?

The one thing that did make sense, once I had seen the place with my own eyes, was the fact Lt. Frey had an Advanced Proficiency in ballast ships and yet had somehow failed to notice one moored in the chamber into which she'd first debarked to begin her tour of duty. According to her, when new personnel arrived, their transport pulled up alongside the temporary quay built up alongside the water's edge. There, a gangplank was deployed, over which the crew came to land, their path to the lift lit only by the tiniest possible subset of the old lights. It was highly unlikely anyone could have caught sight of a vessel moored thirty feet away in the dark.

Hells — we could barely see the thing and we'd come there looking for it.

The ship was low in the water, in what Lt. Frey described as a "surfaced sub" condition — a thing she said made sense if they were using it for cold storage — and which I did not even pretend to understand. I sent her to check out the ship while I dashed off toward the open lift at the far end of the cavern.

Major Gowon was fighting with the car's door when I arrived. The landing cut on this level was an uneven mess of iron and rubble. I wasn't sure whether it was due to lack of care during construction or whether some of the loose detritus from the bombings shaken its way down the shaft and landed here at the bottom. Either way the car was askew. It sat so cockeyed in the compartment gravity was trying to pull the door closed.

"Ensign Declan, hand me that case," I said, pointing

at a supply crate sitting by Bryte's feet.

Declan did as he was asked, shoving the mostly empty metal crate toward me. I hastily pulled the lid off. Then, with Major Gowon's help, wedged it into the groove of the car door, bending and twisting it enough to make sure it was well and truly stuck. It might have been the simplest problem I'd encountered in days, but at least it was one I could solve — and that felt pretty good.

Once I was sure the door wasn't going to slip, I ducked back into the lift to check on Bryte. Lt. Mieko was still with him, and I couldn't tell whether he was still conscious.

"How is he?" I asked.

"It's hard to tell," she replied. "I've managed to slow the bleeding," she said. "But there's only so much field medicine can accomplish. Without a proper exam room and an operating theater, it's mostly a wait and see. I've given him what little antibiotic we've found in these crates, but if the bullet got his bowel, it's probably not enough. If he spikes a fever ...."

"Yeah," I cut her off. "I get it."

So Bryte was either going to die or he wasn't. And there was no way to know without proper medical facilities. I was sure the sickbay aboard this base was probably a whole lot better for Bryte and the others than the floor of a lift car. But I both had no idea what level their medical facility was on and absolutely no idea how a person might find the place once they got there. I didn't necessarily trust the wounded base personnel to give a Mangan medic directions — even if it did mean the life of their XO — nor did I trust the lift to carry them anywhere and back without being stopped by some detachment hoping to make it to the garage.

Getting them all onto the ship seemed like a much

better proposition.

And hadn't Margeaux mentioned there were medicines stored on that old hulk? I looked over at her. Bandaged eye notwithstanding, she seemed all right. She was sitting up mostly straight, her back against the wall of the lift, and looking mostly like she was concerned about the well-being of everyone else.

"Margeaux," I called to her.

Apparently, I'd said her name in a very particular tone of voice, because she scrambled to her feet and snapped to attention as though I'd sounded a bugle call. I hadn't meant for her to do that, but at least her change in posture told me what I needed to know about her overall condition.

"Yes ma'am," she replied, her boot heels clicking in a way I didn't know jump boots were capable of.

"There are medicines on that ballast ship?" I asked.

"Yes ma'am," she replied.

"And you know where to find them?"

"Yes ma'am."

For a moment I thought to ask her if she knew if there was anything on board that might be helpful for Bryte: like stronger antibiotics or something to help with the bleeding. But I barely knew enough to ask an educated question. Meanwhile I had a medic ten inches to my right who would know exactly what she needed.

"Could you take Lt. Mieko aboard and show her where those things are?" I asked.

Margeaux's eye grew wide. I didn't know how much she had been told about the Mangan, Gammran, and T'wesh members of my crew, but her body language said she wasn't sure how much of the base she was at liberty to share. She cast her gaze down at Bryte — just for a moment — and looked back at me.

"Yes, Your Highness," she answered. Margeaux began making her way carefully toward the door just behind me.

"Lt. Mieko," I said, "Follow Pvt. Margeaux. Have a look at the medical supplies. If there's something you need for Bryte ... er ... General Sonneman that isn't there, we can have a conversation about trying to go up and filch things from sickbay. But if there's any way to avoid that ...."

"Yes, ma'am," Lt. Mieko replied, standing up and moving to follow Pvt. Margeaux out of the lift. I knew I ought to go with them. If I was going to have to decide whether to send a team up to the base's sickbay, I wanted to know that as soon as possible.

"Raline," I called. She'd smiled at me as I first came aboard the lift car from a place all the way at the back passing a canteen around to a few of the more badly injured survivors from the *Dawn*.

"What do you need?" she asked. "What can I do?"

The answers to that were many and varied. But I had to focus on the task I had in mind for the immediate term.

"Do what you can to get these people off the lift." I tried to make that sound more like a request than an order, but I was pretty sure as soon as the words left my mouth I'd failed at that. "We may need it to get more medicine, or we may just need it to get people aboard the evac ship, but either way we should start getting the wounded off the lift.

"Okay," she replied, moving to screw the lid back onto the canteen as she stood back up.

I wanted to run to her, to grab her and hold her and kiss her and forget where the hells we were and everything that had happened for the past however long we'd been inside this treasonous mountain. But I knew if I did that, I would never be able to let go. And there were a lot of people counting on me.

"Major Gowon," I said, trying not to think too hard

about Raline. "Ensign Declan: please do what you can to help Chief Khatri clear the wounded from the lift. Not everyone's going to be ambulatory, and she's wounded herself. Her shoulder ...."

"Your Highness," Ensign Declan said, a tension in his voice I wasn't sure I'd ever heard before.

"Yes, Declan?"

"I am happy to help Chief Khatri and Major Gowon with the wounded," he said. "But I think I may be of better use elsewhere."

"I beg your pardon?"

"You ..." he began. "I don't guess you know this, but my MOS aboard the *Dawn* was airship electronics. And if we're talking about a ballast ship ... trying to get one up and running after it's been sitting for way too many years ... ma'am ...."

"You're saying you want to go help Lt. Frey get that vessel going?" I asked.

"Yes, Field Marshal."

"Yes," I replied swiftly. "Go. Quickly. I'm right behind you."

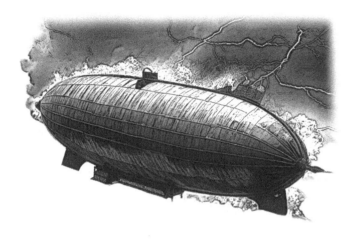

CHAPTER TWENTY-SIX

Chipping paint on the side of the old ballast ship gave her name as *Glimmer*, a misnomer almost as egregious as *Dawn*. And the first thing I noticed when I stepped aboard was the smell. The moment I was through the boarding hatch, I was hit with a foul mixture of must, rust, mildew, and engine oil that only got stronger as I descended the stairs in the boarding tower. I tried not to think too hard about the fact our best-case scenario had us traveling for days aboard this thing.

When I reached the bottom of the boarding stairs, I found the cabin below so dark I could barely see. And I was the last one in. I had no idea where Lt. Frey, Lt. Mieko, and Pvt. Margeaux had gotten to. Even Ensign Declan, who had come down just ahead of me, was nowhere to be seen, although it was dark enough, he could have been ten feet away and I might not have seen him.

I'd only come down here to assess logistics — to see the size and shape of the thing and start to puzzle out how we were going to get so many people aboard. Even in the dark I could tell the answer was: with great difficulty. If this was the kind of ship that came and went every three years, I could see why they only ever swapped out a third of the personnel. With supplies stacked floor-to-ceiling in almost every available space, I wasn't sure we'd even get that many aboard.

I reached out for the nearest crate and lifted it off the top of its stack. Not too heavy, but not easily moved about, either. And there was no telling how many of these were in here. This ship may have been our only hope, but it was little hope to be had if we couldn't get everybody aboard.

One thing at a time, though. There wasn't any hope at all if Lt. Frey couldn't get the old bucket up and running. I wasn't even sure the damn thing was seaworthy. Maybe it was sitting this low in the water by design — in order to better insulate the perishable supplies. Or was it sitting this low in the water because it had begun the process of sinking and happened to run aground?

I needed to find Lt. Frey and Ensign Declan and see if either one of them had any clue about the operational condition of this vessel. I had to admit to myself that when Pvt. Margeaux had first mentioned a ballast ship afloat in the under level, I'd pictured a larger boat, and one in markedly better condition. I was beginning to understand why Bryte had so quickly dismissed our ability to use it for escape.

Then again, the reason he'd cited for its disutility was the difficulty in navigating the sole passage through the underwater rivers; he hadn't mentioned anything wrong with the ship itself. My trying to guess as to its ability to get us out from under this mountain, much less all the way back to Alliance waters, was only wasting time.

"Declan!" I shouted.

No answer.

Damn.

I had no idea what to do with myself. Part of me thought maybe it was the right idea to run up to the Top Deck, grab hold of that public address microphone, and rescind the order for the ground assault. I could order everyone who wasn't actively holding off the enemy into the stairwell and down here to begin offloading supplies to make room for passengers.

But then what? We empty everything out only to find out this rotting scow wasn't going anywhere, meanwhile we've given up what little we had by way of a defensible position? That was no good.

Besides, I had no idea how many levels there were in this base; what if I couldn't get all the way to the Top Deck before collapsing from exhaustion? Three levels had been more than enough, and I knew that wasn't even half the distance between here and the top.

I needed more information, and I didn't have a whole lot of time.

The ship rattled. It rumbled and shook. There was a chugging noise, and then another. Lights flickered on and the smell of diesel fumes joined the olfactory assault.

I had no idea what was happening, but at least the lights were on.

The good news was the piles of crates didn't go on for nearly as far as I'd feared. There were more — lots more — but they were stacked in pallets with space between, likely sorted by category, and not all of them floor-to-ceiling like the first few I'd encountered. Some of them could stay, be used for seating and, depending on their contents, maybe help us weather the trip back into Alliance waters.

The ship shuddered, quaking harder than I found comfortable — physically or psychologically. And then I felt it move. I wasn't sure how or why, and I could only hope it was the work of Lt. Frey and not some accident of physics.

"Declan!" I called again.

Again, I got no answer.

But merely a moment later I could distinctly hear screaming. Or was it squealing? It was a very loud sound out of which I could not parse any known language. But then a word emerged. Two words. Two words I understood.

"Your Highness!" It was Lt. Frey. From somewhere in the bowels of the ship, carried on the metal plates and pipes up a stairwell a few feet in front of me, which I could see now that the lights were on. Lt. Frey was calling to me. "Your Highness! Your Highness!!" she called again.

"I'm up here," I yelled back.

"Your Highness," Frey said again after a minute, poking her head far enough up the stairs to be able to look me in the eye. Her face was damp at the hairline and tiny curls had begun to erupt from her bun at her temples. But she was grinning — beaming, if I had to describe it.

"Tell me."

"She can make it," Frey replied. Her eyes were glistening as she shook her head in thrilled disbelief.

"You're sure?"

"Yeah," she said. "I'm sure. Took me a minute to crank enough juice into the starter to get her to turn over, but I got her to start. And now that she's running all the gauges check out fine. Oil pressure was a little low, but there was a fresh can, so I topped it off and now it reads just right. Also, I had to refill the fuel from emergency jerricans, but we're good there now, too. And I checked the dagger boards, and I keeled up the ballast tanks. She's not running great," she added, "a bit of a rough idle, wants to stall out at low RPMs if I put the choke in too soon, but she'll run."

"And you can steer us through the underwater rivers?" I asked. No use in getting the ship up and running — roughly or otherwise — if there was no way to control it.

"Oh, yes ma'am," she replied. "I'll need someone else with some engine knowledge to keep an eye on things as we run deep, but I can drive this old girl no problem."

"Back to Alliance waters?"

"I don't think we have that kind of fuel," she replied. "But that's why I checked the air bladders and the dagger boards. Even if the canvas is shot," she explained, "and it's probably not — it's probably just moldy — but even if it's in rotten shape we can sail at least part of the way. And every mile we sail is a gallon of fuel we don't have to use."

"So you're saying we 'run deep' just far enough to get out from under the mountain and then we ... sail the rest of the way home?"

"Sort of," she replied. "We run deep until we've cleared the mountain. Then we ascend to periscope depth and make sure we've also cleared the Xylanthian air force. And then once we're sure it's safe to surface, yes. We keel up to full freeboard, pop in the dagger boards, step the masts, hoist the canvas, and we let the wind carry us home."

"And that can really work?"

"Oh yes, ma'am."

There was a quiet pride in the way she said that. It

was the same way I might have told a superior officer I could fly a twin-prop. It wasn't an overconfidence, and it wasn't a boast. She'd been full of excitement and surprise at the revelation the ship was in running trim. But when asked about her credentials Lt. Frey was all calm assurance. She was letting me know in no uncertain terms she had the skills to do the thing I needed her to do.

I trusted that energy.

And I trusted Lt. Frey.

"Good." I hoped my tone echoed her quiet confidence with my own. "How are we on space?" I asked, highlighting the most pressing concern I had left. The ship could get out of here, but could it get *all of us* out of here?

"It's going to be tight," Lt. Frey answered. "To be perfectly honest, Your Highness, it's likely to be miserable."

"But we'll all fit?"

"Fit is a strong word," she replied. "But this is a ballast ship. And since we have no plans to try and lift her out of the water, she won't have any problems with weight. She'll be a little harder to steer under water, but she'll dive easier. Maybe she'll sit low while we're sailing. I may have to tell able bodied people where they can and can't sit to keep us on an even keel. And if folks start getting seasick, well ...."

"Yeah," I interrupted her, preferring not to hear the natural conclusion to that possibility. "I get that this is going to be terrible," I said. "I just want to know that it's survivable."

"Yes ma'am. It absolutely is."

I had to believe her. I didn't have any other choice.

"Should we offload some of these crates?" I asked.

"I'm afraid that decision outranks me, ma'am," she answered.

"I'm asking for your opinion, Lieutenant."

"Just based on the situation you described to me up in the power plant," she replied. "I don't think the space we'd save would be worth the time we'd lose. Once we're out at sea, we can take a good look, figure out what we don't need to get us the rest of the way home, and dump stuff overboard if it makes sense. But trying to move crates out now, much less to make decisions about what to keep and what to toss, is going to take longer than it sounds to me like we have."

"Yeah," I said back. "Okay. Good. Have you seen Lt. Mieko and Pvt. Margeaux?" I wanted to check in with them before I moved on to figuring out how to get people down here. If we were going to need to send someone for medical supplies, that would have to happen fast.

"They're down here," she replied.

I nodded and headed toward the stairs into the lower level.

It was only once I reached the bottom that I got a reasonable picture of the actual size of this ship. It was larger than it looked on the surface. The middle deck of the vessel had an uncomfortably low overhead but was otherwise much roomier than the upper deck had been — extending out for dozens of yards fore and aft and with a beam at least half again as wide as the upper deck. It still wasn't going to be a comfortable ride, but at least now I could imagine getting everyone aboard. Not that I hadn't trusted Lt. Frey when she had told me it was possible — just that I hadn't been able to picture it.

I could picture it now.

"Which way?" I asked.

"Aft," she replied. "Up front is all machinery and equipment. The only place there's room for stowage is in the stern,"

"Thanks," I replied, turning to head astern.

Lt. Frey stood there looking at me. She wanted orders. Probably. But, between us, she was the one who had more of an idea as to what needed to come next. I didn't feel qualified to be the one giving the orders in this scenario, but I was the higher-ranking person and if she needed me to tell her to go about the rest of this operation under her own authority, I could do that.

"What do you need from me?" I asked. "Or from the rest of us, to get this operation underway? Because as far as I'm concerned you are the skipper of this vessel and it's up to you when and how and under what conditions we cast off."

"I'm going to let the engine warm up," she said. "And then I'm going to shut it down. If I can have another person from the power plant down here to help, I can be at the helm without worrying about anything going wrong that I'm not there to react to."

"Would Ensign Declan be able to do that?" I asked. I honestly had no idea as to the extent of his credentials, nor of the specifics of the job she wanted done in the engine room, but a person who was currently present beat one we had to wrangle from several decks up. "Or would we be better served by sending him up to one of your coworkers from the power plant?"

"Neither?" she replied, audibly hesitant.

"Neither?"

"He's an electrical guy," Lt. Frey replied. "Right now, I've got him checking all of *Glimmer*'s connections and watching the alternator in hopes we get enough charge in the starter that I won't have to crank-start her next time. I don't want to take his focus off his area of expertise if we don't have to — especially considering we've got diesel experts better than me just a few decks up."

"All right," I agreed. That made sense. I, too, didn't

want to pull Ensign Declan off a duty he was uniquely qualified for that was also a necessary component of the evacuation's success. "I'll send someone. You let me know if there's anything else you need. But I want you to understand you're empowered to make any decision you think is right without checking in with me. You need neither my direction nor my permission to operate this vessel however you see fit."

"Yes ma'am."

"And that goes for all the brass," I said. I had a flash there for a moment of Colonel Gertrune getting a hornet in her helmet and deciding she was in charge even though there was every chance she had no idea how to sail, much less to operate a vessel with as many quirks and foibles as a wartime-surplus ballast ship that had been sitting neglected for three decades.

"Ma'am?"

"I mean that, from this moment forward, while aboard this vessel you have no superior officer. You understand? You and I are *peers* for the duration and in that sense we both outrank everybody. This is your ship, Lieutenant. I'll work with you, I promise. But there may be officers brought aboard here in a few minutes who don't like that. I'll enforce your authority, and hopefully that will be enough to shut them up. But in case it isn't, I want to make it perfectly clear that their authority over you is suspended until we're safely moored somewhere in friendly waters."

I was careful not to say, "Alliance territory". I wanted to. But I wasn't sure how much of a sticky wicket the Alliance versus Feirin authority situation was going to be. Now was not the time to start poking at allegiances. Borrowing trouble from later on when we had plenty of it right this minute seemed like a bad plan.

"Yes ma'am," she replied.

I could tell she was trying to contain a smile, so I smiled at her first. She gave a nod and turned to head forward as I proceeded aft.

I found Mieko and Margeaux three compartments back, in a room that looked as though it had once been a reasonable medical bay. Currently, every available surface appeared to be occupied with cases or crates of bandages, desiccants, and hygiene supplies. The smell of soap and industrial alcohol almost completely supplanted the other smells in this room and, although I wouldn't say it was *pleasant*, it was a welcome change from the odors elsewhere on the ship.

Lt. Mieko let me know she was satisfied with the antibiotic, coagulant, and antipyretic medicines she'd found aboard. She hoped to find more pain killers but promised me she could make do between what was there and the crates back in the lift with Bryte and the others.

Her plan was to make room for Bryte and the worst of the other injured personnel to lie down in here. After that she hoped to set up an area for the rest of the wounded — those who needed occasional checks, passive monitoring, or a periodic dose of medication — nearby so that she and any of the garrison's medical staff could keep an eye on everyone.

I could tell by the way she said things she was beginning to understand what was going on. I wasn't sure whether it was Pvt. Margeaux's red uniform jacket, something she might have overheard over the course of the day, or just having paid close attention to the attendees at the Veneration Ceremony, but she was definitely at least clued in to the fact things were not altogether copasetic inside this mountain. She reassured me more than once she would tend to the injured *Dawn* personnel — in a tone that belied suspicion the base's medics might not.

That was good.

When I told them Lt. Frey's plans and the shape of the next little while as best I understood it, Pvt. Margeaux volunteered to go and fetch personnel from the power plant. She was very clearly on board with the idea of this evacuation. Seeing as she was a supply officer and I'd passed boxes of fuses on my way down here, I had to presume she knew her way to the power plant better than I did. Even after I reminded her she'd need to take the stairs to get there, she seemed happy to go.

I followed her out of the little med bay, leaving Lt. Mieko to set things up as she saw fit. She didn't seem to want my help and I knew she didn't require my supervision. Anyway, I had other matters to tend to: like figuring out how to talk a base full of people hells bent on keeping their secret and perfectly willing to die trying to come with us.

Not that I wasn't willing to leave without them. Because I absolutely was. I'd realized sometime between assuring Lt. Frey her authority wouldn't be challenged and hearing Lt. Mieko's intimation that *Dawn* survivors would be cared for even if she had to fight for the right to see it happen that I didn't give a damn whether the Colonel authorized an evacuation or not. Nor did I care in the slightest whether the personnel under her command decided to come along. I was getting my people, and Bryte, and the other wounded, and anyone else who cared to save their skins, the hells out of this mountain and off this continent.

Anyone who wanted to stay behind was fussing welcome to.

Maybe that wasn't the most Royal attitude to take. Maybe it wasn't the Noblesse Oblige Major Gowon had accused me of back in the woods on the way here. But it was my truth.

I hated this base and all it stood for. It was tangible, documentable proof that my mother, Her Royal Majesty Queen Salian Siobhan Feirin Lohengrin, had been suborning treason for some years longer than I'd been alive. If the people aboard it wanted to go down in flames along with their traitorous installation rather than safely return to the Alliance and face whatever justice they had coming, I wasn't going to drag them home kicking and screaming.

But, at the same time, if any of the junior personnel, like Lt. Frey or Private Margeaux, wanted out of here, I wasn't about to leave them behind. My best guess was that these young officers had taken this assignment with a less-than-thorough understanding of what they were signing up for, only the promise of fast-tracking their Alliance military careers. Whether any of them were culpable in this treason remained to be seen, but it wasn't for me to lay blame at their feet.

As I headed up the second set of stairs and back onto the exterior deck of the ship, I was subject to the most peculiar sensation — I was going up and down at the same time. It seemed Lt. Frey had chosen that moment to re-fill the ballast to the surfaced sub level. It made sense when I thought about it: having the ship in that trim put the outside deck at approximately the same level as the pier to which the vessel was tied, making boarding a large number of people a far easier prospect than it would have been using a steep gangplank.

Major Gowon stood just beyond the pier, taking stock of the ship as she sank lower and lower. I could tell by the look on his face he was as dubious as I had been as to the vessel's ability to get us home.

"Remind you of anything?" I asked, waiting at the rail for the deck to be low enough to easily step off.

"A coffin," he said back.

I had forgotten about the Gammran superstitions around being under the water. I was glad that moment reminded me; I would need to be extra sensitive to the Gammran among my people. They were going to hate this more than most. I made a mental note to ask Lt. Mieko if she had access to any Tonwara or other anxiety-reducing medications when I got back on board. Panicking crew had not been factored into the plans for our escape.

"We'll only be under the water for little while," I assured him. I waited until the deck was nearly even with the ground before stepping off the ship and onto the land where he stood. "Lt. Frey wants to surface as soon as we're sure we're clear of the Xylanthian forces, shut off the engine to conserve fuel, and sail the rest of the way back."

"Sail?" he asked. "This thing can sail?"

"Listen," I said, placing my hand on his arm. "Before today, I'd never so much as seen a ballast ship in person. And as much as I went to the Air Academy and we like to rib them about literally everything from slamball to the food in the mess, I know they don't fool around at Maritime. Lt. Frey down there earned not only her bars, but an Advanced Proficiency in these beasts and if she says she can sail us home I'm going to believe she can sail us home. And since it's that or stay here and deal with the Xylanthians ...."

"Allow me to pull up the anchor myself," he replied.

I couldn't help but chuckle — a momentary respite from the madness all around.

"The ship is moored," I informed him, still chuckling, "not anchored. We just untie a few ropes and we're off."

"Whatever it takes," he said back.

"Go below," I told him. "Talk to Lt. Mieko. Help her

get her room set up. As soon as she says she's ready, let's start getting our injured aboard."

I turned, heading toward the lift the wounded personnel had recently vacated.

"Where are you going?" he asked as I walked away.

"Colonel Gertrune may be willing to die defending this place," I answered him. "But I mean to make sure everyone else here has the choice not to."

CHAPTER TWENTY-SEVEN

After an all-too-brief check in with Raline, I un-jammed the metal lid from the door to the lift and stepped inside, sliding the door shut and pulling down on the locking lever all in one motion as though I'd been doing it all my life. I turned the dial for the Top Deck and held my breath as the car began to move.

I had no idea how much time had passed since I was up there last. I had no idea how long it should take for a squad to kit up and be ready to deploy. And I could only hope that, if adequate time had passed, and this car was currently being summoned by a mob of soldiers eager to go and shoot at something, I would be able to be Royal and authoritative enough to keep them out of the lift until I was done with it.

I also had to hope the other lift was still inoperable.

Although the broken lift was barely a quarter of the size of the one I was in, if it was working there was a chance potential combatants would be using it to get to the garage. And that was without considering the perfectly operable manual lift leading to the Emergency Deck — from which I was certain all manner of assaults could be mounted.

I wasn't going to run out into the woods and spread the word an evacuation was taking place. Not only had I no interest in getting myself shot and killed, I wasn't about to let on that we were even capable of evacuating this mountain in possible earshot of the enemy; that could foul our plans significantly.

But I wanted to give as many people as possible the opportunity to come with us. Which meant hoping time was on my side.

I was fidgeting as the thing moved upward, but thankful when the lift finally stopped and I found myself back on the Top Deck when I opened the door. The relief, however, only lasted a moment.

Things up here had deteriorated since I'd been here last. Badly.

The dust and pebbles that had fallen from the ceiling earlier had been joined on the floor by chunks of marble the size of zaftiballs and dinner plates; at least one of them was as big as my mother's throne. On the far side from the lift, a piece of the wall had collapsed into the room. I could only hope the people who'd been working there had gotten out from under it in time. A glance at the other lift saw the doors pried open and a crew of three braced on a ladder, trying to work on the pulley and motor system. I wondered how they'd figured out that one was broken while the other was just interrupted, but not enough to go and ask them.

I didn't have the time to indulge those kinds of curiosities.

The bombs seemed to have stopped falling. It could very well be that the second wave had finished their run and a third was incoming any second. There was no way this room was going to survive another bombardment. In fact, there was no guarantee the place wasn't about to collapse from the damage it had already taken.

I ran toward the map table; it was the only place I was sure had a public address microphone. My fingers were crossed it was still working. Colonel Gertrune had returned to sitting in her elevated chair. She was staring straight ahead with a white-knuckled grip on the arm rests as I approached.

"Colonel!" I shouted. I didn't think she heard me. It was loud in here, but not that loud. I was pretty sure my volume wasn't the problem. "Colonel!" I yelled again.

Still no response — not a turn of her head or a twitch of her lip. I followed her eye line to the map table. It was covered in flags: orange, green, and blue — but none in red. Either the troops from the base hadn't yet deployed or the people at the periscopes couldn't see them. From where I stood, either of those scenarios were equally possible, and as much as I wanted to know which was true, it didn't change what I was here to do.

"Where are they?!" the Colonel shouted, her voice ringing out and echoing eerily across what was left of the stone dome. "Where are my troops? Where are our defenses?"

She let go of the arm rests only to pound her fists against them.

"They're waiting to deploy, Colonel," an anonymous voice called from somewhere near the map table.

"What's the hold up?" she yelled. "Open the door and get them out there!"

I saw red.

I was furious.

She had no idea of the situation in the rest of the base, only a myopic determination to kill or be killed — to defend her treasonous redoubt with the lives of everyone in her line of sight.

"The door is open, you feckless traitor!" I screamed. I couldn't remember the last time I'd lost my temper like that, but my temper was well and truly lost. "When your last team went out, they got ambushed. The Xylanthians blew the door off its track. So now your people are pinned down in the garage with no way to shut it again, your XO's been shot in the belly and is in very real danger of bleeding to death — being tended to, by the way, by a Mangan medical officer you'd just as soon have left out in the woods to die!"

She looked at me but didn't say anything.

Not that I blamed her. I'm not sure how I would feel if I'd just been dressed down by a minor deity. Good thing I didn't believe in such things.

And good thing I didn't give a sliver of a damn how she felt, either. I didn't need a response. I wasn't here for her.

I was still seething as I made my way to the map table. I reached underneath and took hold of the microphone where I'd seen Colonel Gertrune stash it after calling for the ill-considered ground assault.

I brought the microphone to my mouth and took a deep breath — realizing I had absolutely no idea what the hells a person was supposed to say at a time like this. But I didn't have time to think too hard about it. I was just going to have to wing it.

I flipped the switch to turn it on.

"Attention all personnel," I started. "Attention all personnel. This is Her Royal Highness Princess Maran Merteuil von Feirin Lohengrin, daughter of Queen Salian Siobhan Feirin Lohengrin, to whom you have just paid homage, addressing you now. The installation is compromised. The enemy is aware of our position and will soon breach the garage level. Further attempts to defend our position will be in vain. Fall back!"

"What are you doing?!" Colonel Gertrune screamed in my ear as she grabbed my arm in an attempt to rend the microphone from my grasp. Somehow, she'd snuck up on me while I was talking.

I snatched my arm, and the microphone, away from her. The toggle was still engaged; I had no idea how directional this apparatus was nor how sensitive, but I figured whatever bits of this exchange it happened to pick up wouldn't hurt my case any.

"I am saving these people!" I said, dodging her next attempt to come at me.

"You are destroying my base!"

"No," I snapped back. "You've done a fine enough job of that yourself. All I am doing is giving a chance to anyone who doesn't want to be destroyed along with it!"

"We have to!" she bellowed, swinging her fist at my head. "Protect the base!"

I managed to get my head out of the way of her fist, but only just. The punch landed instead on my shoulder, squarely in the center of a bruise I'd sustained in the lead-up to the crash.

That hurt.

I did not want to hit her back. I had never been any good at hand-to-hand combat and losing a fistfight against the base's commandant would probably do nothing for my perceived authority. But I also couldn't stand here and let her wail on me and keep me from telling these people how to get out of here with their lives.

I stepped in closer and flung my leg out, striking her just below the knee with the heel of my boot and knocking her to the ground. I must have caught her more off guard than I'd have guessed. She fell flat sideways, slamming into the marble floor shoulder first, her head hitting the stone with a loud crack a moment later.

This was my chance.

I turned back to the microphone and spoke again.

"There is a ship preparing to evacuate," I said. "To evacuate us all. Everyone not currently engaged on the garage level should immediately proceed via the stairwell to the under level to await further instructions. The stairwell!" I repeated. "The lifts have been compromised by structural damage and are currently inoperable."

It was a lie, but a white lie. I was going to need that one working lift, and not for selfish reasons. I held the microphone closer to my face.

"May the grace and protection of Her Majesty be with us," I added before toggling the switch off and turning to leave. I didn't believe in my mother's divinity, but there was something comforting about those words anyway.

Colonel Gertrune was still on the ground when I went to leave. Out cold. Apparently, she'd hit her head harder than I'd realized. Part of me was tempted to leave her there. She'd been willing to let dozens of young officers under her command die to defend the secret of a place that ought never to have existed. It would be some kind of justice to leave her here to die in it alone.

But what I wanted for her was *actual* justice. I wanted to see her stand trial for what she'd done in this place. I wanted to see her stand at the bar beside my mother and anyone else in the Feirin aristocracy who had blessed the construction and operation of a place outside the auspices of Alliance authority.

I bent down briefly and checked her pulse. Yes. She was alive and breathing. And I would be damned if I didn't see her live to face a judge.

The others from the Top Deck had already abandoned their positions and were heading quickly toward what my educated guess told me was the door to the stairs. It seemed they needed no further encouragement to evacuate. I could only hope those on the lower decks were as easily persuaded.

I stood up quickly and ran into the crowd, grabbing the first fit-looking young man I could by his forearm.

"Your Highness?" he said, looking at me with a combination of terror and confusion so palpable it made my mouth go dry.

"I need your help," I said. "The Colonel ...." I pointed to where she was lying on the floor by the map table. "Could you ...?"

"Consider it done, Your Highness," he said with a nod, his face changing from upset to resolve. He snagged the arm of another passer-by and the two of them headed to fetch her.

Good.

That was handled.

At a flat run, I headed back to the lift, slamming the door shut and sending it back to the garage as soon as I was there. I don't know whether it was the adrenaline or the concussion or a loose cable in the mechanism, but the lift seemed to fall faster this time than usual. I threw the door open the moment it stopped.

Things down here hadn't changed much since I'd last departed. I made my way, sprinting and ducking, from barricade to barricade until I was reasonably sure the troops at the open door could hear me.

They'd made themselves an additional barricade there; five feet of piled walkontainers now concealed the men who had been trying to budge the door in addition to those who had been firing from that position to begin with.

"You wait two more minutes!" I called to them. "Two minutes and then you fall back."

"Yes ma'am," one of them called back.

"You fall back," I ordered. "And then you hold that position. You hold it for another two, five if you can, but no longer. Do you understand me?"

"Yes ma'am," he answered again.

"Then all of you — every single body in this room — you get aboard that lift and head down to the under level."

"The lift is out of service, ma'am," the man said, squeezing off another round at some unseen enemy in the distance.

"No, it's not," I countered. "That's a lie I told to make sure it would be available for you. The stairs are going to be crowded. Trying to get through the door and into the crowd is only going to be trouble. The lift is for you," I assured him. "We won't leave without you."

And with that, I left again, dodging and juking my way to the rear of the garage, past the lift, and into the crowded stairwell.

This was it.

Sometime in the next five to ten minutes, we were getting out of here.

CHAPTER TWENTY-EIGHT

I had been right to presume the stairs would be crowded.

Too crowded. But it was as orderly a mad rush as I could have possibly imagined. Everyone was hurrying, but no one was moving too fast. No one was being dangerous, reckless, or visibly selfish.

I had to wonder if some of these people thought this was a drill.

It would have made sense: for the Princess to show up and demand all sorts of unusual exercises to test the base or the Colonel or ... something.

Honestly, I didn't care. Everyone was proceeding in a speedy but orderly fashion, and it didn't matter a hill of tubers to me whether or not they understood what was happening. I moved through the crowd with barely contained frenzy and dashed straight to where Major Gowon was standing on the pier alongside the ship.

He let me know the wounded were aboard and being seen to, and that Pvt. Margeaux had returned from the power plant with three others who were below decks and getting to work.

I told him about what had happened on the Top Deck, and that Colonel Gertrune would likely be joining our little boarding party whilst unconscious. I got the tiniest bit of personal satisfaction telling him she should be immediately slapped in irons — or the closest thing we could cobble together — whether or not she'd regained consciousness by the time she got down to us.

The rush of people pouring out of the stairwell had slowed to a trickle by the time the lift opened to reveal the dozen and a half or so armed soldiers from the garage.

Several of them had cuts and scrapes and other minor wounds. A few were worse off than that, but no one seemed badly hurt. I could send a medic to have a look at them once we were away from the dock.

The new arrivals joined the crowd standing anxiously in the space between the stairs and the water. If I had to guess based on the attendance at the Veneration Ceremony, everyone left alive was here. It was going to be a tight squeeze aboard that old ship, and I had no idea how to organize the boarding.

I started with the obvious. Calling out across the assembled personnel, I ordered anyone with an injury to get aboard as quickly as possible, adding to my order that anyone still carrying a weapon was to leave it behind. Most of the wounded were soldiers fresh from the garage, but the group also included the fellow who still had Colonel Gertrune slung over his shoulder as well as several others from the top deck with cuts and bruises from falling marble.

It was only as I was informing them of the location of Lt. Mieko and her med bay that I realized this was the first time I'd shared we'd be evacuating aboard the storage scow. Oops. I probably should have mentioned that earlier.

There were grumbles of discontent, but nobody seemed to be changing their mind about leaving. When given the choice between certain death in a compromised base and the possibility of escape, most people would choose the possibility — even if it was aboard a rickety old ship. A few of the others with minor injuries helped get Colonel Gertrune aboard, and I watched as they cleared the quay.

I called for anyone who'd been to Maritime to board next and head straight to the dive bridge to speak with Lt. Frey. And then anyone with naval experience or a private boat at home. Every skilled and knowledgeable seafarer we could put to work during the voyage would raise our odds of getting home. I was pleased to see nearly half a dozen fit-looking men and women coming forward at this request.

Next up, I asked for any other trained medical personnel. Probably should have gotten to them before the casualties and the sailors, but in my mind, Lt. Mieko had all the medical needs seen to and that was that. I asked the medics to board as soon as my concussed brain realized they existed. I recognized Corporal Els and Colonel Tors from earlier, and I counted four more officers with them. Maybe one of them was a trauma surgeon and would know what to do for Bryte; he could use all the help he could get.

Group by group, category by category, two, five, twelve at a time we got the rest on board — cramming the healthiest-but-least-likely-to-be-useful members into the last crevices of available space as two of the trained sailors untied the old craft from the pier then hurried below to seal the hatch to the boarding tower.

By the time I made it to the dive bridge, the engine was running. It sounded better than it had earlier, too. Smart move on Lt. Frey's part, bringing in help from the power plant; they had clearly made some difference already.

Situated just forward of midship on the center deck, the dive bridge was a cramped compartment with scarcely enough room for the people who were expected to staff it. Nearly every inch of the place, ceiling included, was covered with some gauge, wheel, knob, or switch necessary to operating the vessel underwater. The sonar display was the most prominent, taking up the majority of the space on the forward bulkhead. It hung in the same place, and served the same purpose, as would a windscreen were we running someplace where light might reach our eyes.

I hadn't thought about that: about the pitch damn darkness and the need to navigate by instruments alone. But I was sure Lt. Frey must have. I once again had to make the decision to trust she knew what she was doing.

The large screen was flanked on both sides by a pair of stations for the sonar operators. Two sonar units working in tandem were, I supposed, better than one. It appeared, however, there was only one officer aboard able to operate this old sonar, so it looked like we were going to have to make do. A position for a periscope operator stood in the forward starboard corner, but there was no one sitting there. I presumed it was going to be a while until we had any reason to try and put up a periscope, and with space at such a premium, I took that seat myself.

Just behind and to the left of my seat was the place for the helmsperson, with a platform and wheel that looked too much like the ones on the *Dawn* for my comfort. In fact, a lot about this ship reminded me of the *Dawn*. Poetic, in a way, for this cursed adventure to be bookended by voyages of the damned on ships with perky-sounding names that were as likely to come apart and kill us all as they were to carry us safely to our destination.

Lt. Frey took her place at the helm and looked around.

"Sonar?" she called.

"Engaged," the young man seated at the port sonar station called back. He threw a switch, and I watched as dark areas of terrain came into relief on the screen in front of us.

"Hatches?" she said next.

"Aye, ma'am!"

"Aye!"

Lt. Frey looked down at a set of gauges just to the left of the steering column.

"Engine temperature is good," she said softly. "Oil pressure within range. Alternator's charging. Fuel level's the best we can do." She looked up, making eye contact with me for split second before turning her attention back to the screen and saying to everyone, "Let's get out of here."

She turned the wheel hard over, shifted the propeller into forward gear, then eased the throttle lever ahead. The ship's hull groaned as we started to move. But the motion was smooth, slow and steady. Lt. Frey eased us off the dock slowly, then turned us around to face the cave we'd need to dive through in order to get out to sea.

I'd tried not to look too closely at its entrance, but for a moment while we were getting folks aboard, I hadn't been able to help myself. The opening was scarcely two meters off the water and didn't look nearly wide enough for this ship to fit through. I just had to trust that the features of this mountain hadn't changed for the worse in the years since the builders of this base had navigated the caverns in this exact ship.

If it had made it in through that cave, it could make it back out again.

Lt. Frey eased off the throttle and shifted the propeller back into neutral.

"What ...?" I asked. "Why are we stopping?"

She didn't seem to have heard me. Either that or she wasn't willing to disrupt her concentration enough to reply.

"Sonar," she said, "I'm going to need you actively pinging. I shift us back into forward before we're deep enough to clear, then this whole thing is for naught."

Oh.

That's why we'd stopped.

"Preparing to ballast down," she said. When no one said anything back, Lt. Frey nodded once and reached for a handle that appeared to once have been painted red. "Diving," she said as she pulled the handle slowly upward. The dull roar of rushing water filled the tiny chamber, and I could feel the ship sinking. I shivered at the thought of going underwater, even though I knew that was madness; the upper deck had been level with the waterline — I'd been underwater since I'd reached the bottom of the stairs.

Still, it felt disconcerting and claustrophobic all of a sudden. I closed my eyes and took a deep breath. It was this or the Xylanthians.

I looked back up at Lt. Frey. Her face was determined, focused, but without visible worry. While that was mildly reassuring, the creaks and groans from the hull were still terrifying. When the handle was as far out of its shaft as it would come, Lt. Frey let go. She fixed her gaze on the screen in front of us and waited for it to refresh three times in a row with no changes before moving again.

"We're down," she announced to everyone as soon as she was satisfied.

I blew out a tense breath as I watched her engage the forward gear again. I found it less stressful to watch her steering than to try and make out the way forward by the blips and contrasts on the sonar screen.

She was a master. They didn't call it Advanced Proficiency for nothing.

We were moving slowly, but surely forward, navigating what I imagined was a very narrow channel. Lt. Frey piloted the ship deftly, precisely. Using the red handle and the ship's wheel, she moved us left and right, up and down, steering, raising, and lowering the vessel to keep us off the rocks.

I was honestly beginning to relax when the screaming started.

First it was a single, startled wail, the kind I might imagine a person would make if they suddenly discovered a fledderbug in their bed. There easily could have been an insect. It wasn't hard to imagine some sort of pernicious whatever that feeds on mold, lives in the dark, and had made itself at home aboard a mostly unused ship with cases of foodstuffs aboard.

But the second scream, and the third, told me it was something more upsetting than that.

"Water!" someone yelled.

What?!?

I jumped from my seat and darted across the room, careful to duck as I crossed Lt. Frey's line of sight. The only thing that might be worse than what I was pretty sure was going on already was blocking the view in such a way that could lead to her dashing this bucket on the rocks. I ran aft, through three crowded compartments, toward the source of the yelling. The people I passed seemed to be on the verge of panic, but they'd been told in very firm language that they were not to move about the cabin while we were underwater — any shift in the weight of the passengers or cargo could rock the ship in a way that could doom us all.

Technically that edict was supposed to have applied to me as well, but what was one diminutive princess running fore-to-aft directly along the center line in comparison to our possibly taking on water?

I needed to find out what the hell was up and tell Lt. Frey. If I was in command of a ship in an emergency, I would want to know about that emergency as soon as possible. If we were taking on water, I had no idea what a solution could be — as we could neither surface here nor turn around — but I still figured she'd want all the available information.

As I was passing the stairs to the upper deck, I could hear the screaming was coming from up there. Following the sounds of distress, I grabbed the metal handrail and spun myself around. I swung my feet up onto the bottom step and dashed up the steps, through the open hatch, and onto the deck above.

My hair was wet by the time I got there. What I saw when I arrived was panic inducing. I absolutely did not blame any one of these people for their screaming. Water was seeping ... no ... water was *spraying* into the compartment from several places all along the seam between the deck and the hull. It was coming in fast and loud, and there was absolutely no way I could see to stop it.

"Fuss," I said, out loud, not caring what the amassed crowd was going to think about their princess cursing.

This was bad.

This was worst-case-scenario bad.

I spotted an intercom on the back side of boarding stairs — one of the few places on this level that seemed mostly sheltered from the shower the rest of the room was getting. I tiptoed over terrified people and squeezed myself between stacks of crates to get to where I could reach it. The thing looked like it might have worked, but so had the unit in my quarters aboard the *Dawn*. It was worth a try.

A panel with six colored buttons and a microphone mounted to it stood beside a speaker box with an earphone jack on the side. The painted labels beside the buttons had long since chipped away, so I made my best guess as to which jumble of paint chips was meant to say "dive bridge" and punched the button.

"Lt. Frey," I called into the mic. "This is ..." Who the hell was I in this situation? "This is Field Marshal von Feirin Lohengrin." I decided on—a hybrid of my Royal and Alliance ranks. "I'm in the upper compartment and we are taking on water. I repeat: we are taking on water!"

There was no reply. Not a squeak or a crackle. No indication at all the thing was working. It seemed the intercom was as dead as the lot of us were about to be if we couldn't figure out what to do about the water incursion. I was going to have to go back to the dive bridge and tell the skipper about this in person.

I was halfway through wedging myself back out from between the stacks of crates when I heard static over the sound of rushing water.

"Your Highness," a voice called. It was a man's voice. Whoever I'd called, it hadn't been the dive bridge.

I lunged for the intercom anyway.

"Yes!" I called, pushing the same button as before — at least I knew that one had gotten me through to someone. "Yes, I'm here."

"Your Highness," the voice on the other end said back almost as soon as I released the button. "This is

Sergeant Rakunas. Lt. Frey doesn't have a free hand, but she can hear you. Please repeat your status report."

"Yes, Sergeant," I replied. "Yes. I repeat: we are taking on water. I am in the uppermost compartment. Near the boarding stairs. We are being showered on all sides from a number of leaks."

"How much?" Sgt. Rakunas asked. The engine rumble changed. If we were getting water in the fuel or in the mechanics ....

"It's spraying from all over! At least a dozen places."

"Running like a faucet, or spraying like a sprinkler?" This time it was Lt. Frey's voice. She sounded muffled, distant; she was probably shouting at the mic from quite a ways away.

"Sprinkler!" I answered. "Like a bunch of really angry sprinklers."

"Has the water pooled on the sole?" she asked.

I looked down and shook my head.

"Pool? No," I replied. "It's not like a puddle, it's more like a sheen. Everything up here is wet, but there's no standing water yet — at least not that I can see."

"And is it running down the stairs to the lower deck?"

I had no idea. Without pushing the button again, I yelled out to the crowd in the room.

"Can anyone see whether there's water running down the stairs?" I called.

"No, Your Highness," a young woman's voice answered me from somewhere I couldn't see. "Not down the stairs. Just into the corners. I think the floor is sloped? It's running out through the grates."

I pressed the button again.

"I don't think so," I told the intercom. "I can't see but people are saying it's heading down a sloped bit of the sole and through some grates in the corners." I very much needed to hear those weren't access for electrical or steering apparatus.

"Okay, good." Lt. Frey said back.

Good?

"I ... please repeat?"

I'm pretty sure I heard Lt. Frey chuckle.

"I said that's good," she said back.

"It is?" I did not understand.

"That sole is sloped on purpose," she replied. "Those grates are scuppers. They're designed for sailing — spray can get in up there, even through the double hatch, when crew have to go in and out. Those scuppers lead to the ballast tanks where the water will either get used for the dive or pumped back out. As long as they're able to handle the spray, we should be all right."

I wanted to believe her. How very desperately I wanted to believe her. And had the water been spray or overtopping that splashed its way into the vessel while under sail, I probably would have. But we were deep under water, even deeper under a mountain range, with no telling how many miles to go until we could come up for air, and we'd just discovered the vessel we're aboard to be something less than watertight.

I felt like this was a bigger deal than she was making it out to be.

But her assurance would have to be enough. I squeezed my way back through the piled crates and looked around the room, hoping to identify the smallest of the waterlogged personnel, my eyes finally landing on a slight lad with shaggy hair and a terrified look on his face.

"You," I called to him.

"Yes, Your Highness," he replied scrambling to his feet.

"I want you to stay by that intercom," I told him. I could tell he had no idea why he was being tapped for comms duty, but he'd figure it out soon enough when he saw how narrow the path through the cargo was. "Any water starts to pool on the floor or run down the stairs, you call the dive bridge, you hear me?"

"Yes, Your Highness," he said again before clicking his heels together and heading to the station I'd just assigned him.

"Everybody," I yelled, hoping to be heard clearly over the sound of the water. "Watch the floor. Watch the corners. If this water starts to pool on the floor, or run down the stairs, tell ..." I realized I never caught the name of the kid I'd sent to the intercom. "Tell your comm officer if you see either of those things. And if that means you have to get up and move," I added, "you have my permission."

I figured personnel moving about was less of a danger than not letting the skipper know if the scuppers weren't handling the water incursion. A chorus of nods and a few sounds of "yes ma'am," were enough to tell me the crowd had heard well enough. I took off running back toward the dive bridge.

Lt. Frey and Sgt. Rakunas were back at work, focused on the screen where the sonar showed a passage so tight, I wished I hadn't looked. I had so many questions. Mostly I wanted to know how it was possible for a less-than-watertight ship to make a passage through an underground river system to the sea without sinking to the bottom and drowning us all. But the crew had enough on their plate without a nosy, panicking princess demanding to be informed.

So I returned to my seat and did my best to hold myself together — taking slow, deep breaths, and combing my fingers over the crown of my head.

"There was no way we could have checked the seals," Lt. Frey said.

I looked up at her. Her gaze was still fixed on the

sonar display, but I was still sure she was talking to me.

"I guess ..." I said back, unsure of how to respond.

"I knew there was a chance they'd be bad," she said. "There's always a chance when rubber gets old and hasn't been properly conditioned. But the only way to know for sure is to dive the ship and see. I tested the pumps," she assured me, turning the wheel sharply, but not far, to starboard. "You were here. I pulled the ship up to full freeboard and then put it back to surface run. The pumps are working fine. And as long as I can keep pumping the water out faster than it's coming in, the worst it's going to get is uncomfortable." She pressed down on the pump handle again.

That use of the pumps had been to raise the ship — I could tell. I turned to face forward, unable to keep looking away from the terrifying sonar display for long. I had rudimentary understanding of sonar, and it was enough to tell me we were navigating through some very tight passages.

"I sped us up a little," Lt. Frey said. "I'm getting the hang of her, and these ships are more maneuverable with some speed. The sooner we're out of here, the sooner we can surface, and all those hatch seals and deck seams will stop spraying water into the cabin."

"As long as you're sure," I said.

"I'm sure ... Fuss!" Lt. Frey's eyes got wide, and she jerked the gear shift back so roughly I was afraid the thing might break. If I was reading things correctly, she'd put us in reverse — a direction in which we had no way of looking; these ships weren't equipped with rear-facing sonar.

I was pretty well convinced the swear word was unconnected from the assurance she was trying to offer.

"What?" I asked. "What is it?"

"Sgt. Rakunas, get me a sweep from the other side!"

She wasn't talking to me anymore. This was serious.

I watched as Sgt. Rakunas darted between the two sonar positions, flipping switches and turning knobs on the starboard station similar to how he'd been on port, only with a degree of frenzy I hadn't before seen.

"How, in all the hells ...?" Lt. Frey whispered.

I was sure that wasn't meant for my ears, and I was fully sure I wasn't about to ask her about it.

"Want me to keep alternating?" Sgt. Rakunas asked.

"Yes," Frey answered, pushing down on the pump handle. She was diving us deeper — much deeper by the looks of things.

Rakunas finished a sonar pass on starboard, then immediately went back to port. He went back and forth between sides maybe half a dozen times while I sat stock still, my toes twitching in my boots, waiting to find out what was happening.

When I looked back at the display, I was able to figure it out. In front of us was solid rock. There was no way to keep going. Surely that's what had caused Lt. Frey's outburst, and her need to slam the system into reverse so abruptly.

Lt. Frey put the engine gear back into neutral as she continued to gently dive the ship, her attention firmly fixed on the display. Either this cave was going to open up or we were going to die here.

"Am I ..." I couldn't help myself. "Am I just very bad at sonar or does that display say there's no way out of here?"

"There has to be," Lt Frey said, turning the wheel hard to starboard. "Two years ago, I traveled here aboard a Vultyx class. This is a Cyretz class. The Vultyx class is bigger in every dimension. If that boat could get in, we can get out."

I bit my tongue. I had a million challenges to that notion. What if we'd missed a turn — a corner we should have rounded way back? What if the obvious exit wasn't an actual exit and we should have left the under level via some passage that wasn't visible from the surface? Or what about ground quakes? What If there was something nature, or the recent aerial bombardment, had done to partially collapse the cave?

I couldn't decide whether to run screaming out of the dive bridge, find Raline wherever she was aboard this bucket, and confess every last feeling I had to her; or to stay here, frozen in terror, staring at the display as though by some means I could force it to show us a way forward.

The indecision itself was enough to keep me there. I sat forward in the seat, my whole body trembling, silently begging the mountain to give way.

Lt. Frey turned the ship slowly, letting each side of the sonar scan the terrain ahead resulting in a confusing offset overlay of data on the display screen. Confusing to me, anyway. She was trained for this. She could probably read it as clearly as I could read an artificial horizon and an airspeed/groundspeed indicator.

"There!" she shouted, taking one hand off the wheel to point at something on the screen that made no sense to me whatsoever. She adjusted the ship's trim again, pumping out a little ballast water while shifting the engine gear back into forward. "Get me a good picture!"

Rakunas did as she asked; darting repeatedly back and forth between the two sonar stations several times before turning to look at me.

"Your Highness," he said. "I need your help."

"Anything," I replied. "Whatever you need."

"See the lever there?" he said pointing out a metal rod with a black rubber grip.

"Yes."

"When I say so, I need you to pull it. Watch me," he

instructed. "Try to do it at the same speed as I'm moving this one."

"Yeah, okay," I replied, moving from my seat to the starboard sonar position and waiting for his order to move.

"All right," he said. "Now."

He moved his lever from left to right slowly and smoothly, and I did my best to move mine from right to left in perfect tandem.

"Is this ..." Either my concussion symptoms were coming back with a vengeance, or my adrenaline was taking over completely. Either way, I had some bone-level, insatiable need to understand what was going on. "Are we trying to get the two sonar units to overlap a certain way?"

"Yes, ma'am," he answered.

"Usually," Lt. Frey chimed in, easing the throttle forward, "in a dual-sonar situation, we'd have two operators and an OIC. The OIC would give the orders, and everything would happen all at the same time. I've been managing okay with the single view, but ...." She gave the wheel a tiny correction to starboard. "Yes!"

"Yes?" I asked.

"There it is," she replied. "Right there."

I didn't see it.

"Back the other way, Your Highness," Rakunas said. I looked at him and nodded, then followed his lead as he drew his lever back to starboard. "One more time," he told me. I mirrored his actions again as he pulled the lever on his side toward the vessel's center line.

Lt. Frey throttled up again and I looked back at the display.

And there it was. Had it not been for Lt. Frey's earlier assertion I would have chalked what I was seeing up to wishful thinking. But if she was seeing what I was seeing then it had to be real. There, in the distance, maybe half a fathom deeper, was an area of nothing — an area the sound wasn't coming back from ... at all.

An opening.

I looked over to try and catch Sgt. Rakunas's eye. Was he seeing it too?

He wasn't looking back at me. But someone else was.

I didn't know how long Raline had been standing in the hatchway leading from the dive bridge to the forward stores, but she was there now and that was all I could think about. I jumped out of my seat, blew past Rakunas, and ran into the walkway, grabbing her around her waist tighter than my bruised body was really happy with.

Before I could so much as think, she was kissing me.

She was kissing me, and I was kissing her, and it was everything I had ever wanted. And I didn't want it to end. But it did end. She looked up at me with tears in her eyes but made no move to let me go.

"I heard we were taking on water," she said.

"Skipper says the ship can handle it."

"And then were we having trouble navigating?"

"Looked like it," I said, not even bothering to wipe the tears from my cheeks. "But we found the way out. Just now. It's on the screen if you want to see."

"No," she said. "I don't need to see it. If you say it's there, I trust you."

"It's there," I assured her.

Raline held my hand as Lt. Frey sped us up even further, steering us through the ever-growing open space on the display. It felt fast, almost too fast, but I'd trusted her this far; I just had to trust her a little while longer.

I much preferred to keep my attention on Raline anyway.

So I was surprised when Lt. Frey pushed in the plunger on the ballast control and moved away from the helm.

"What ...?"

She stepped to the starboard fore of the dive bridge and onto the little periscope platform I'd just left. I watched her closely as she spun the wheel to ratchet the periscope into place and pulled the viewer to her eyes. I held my breath and squeezed Raline's hand as we watched Lt. Frey turn the periscope slowly 360 degrees, ending up with it right where it started.

Lt. Frey was smiling as she stepped down from the periscope platform and went back to her place at the helm. But instead of taking the wheel again, she pushed the ballast control back into its seat and signaled to Sgt. Rakunas.

"You're with me," she said as he stood and followed her past Raline and me.

"Wait!" I called after her. "Where are you going?"

"The sail bridge," she replied, her smile unmistakable even though there was still tension in her voice.

"You think it's safe to surface?" I asked.

"See for yourself," she offered, turning again to go.

A moment later Raline and I were alone on the dive bridge.

We exchanged a glance and I decided to take the Lieutenant up on her offer. We walked together to the periscope platform. I climbed up and leaned my face into the glass of the viewer.

Ahead of us lay nothing but open sea, and a calm sea at that. It was the kind of water that would make a hobby sailor run for their little sloop. I turned the periscope slowly, searching the sea and the sky for any sign of Xylanthian forces — anything that might make me think twice about wanting to bring this craft above the surface.

But there was nothing.

Nothing above, nothing alongside, and nothing behind us save a still-smoldering mountain in the distance.

"What do you see?" Raline asked.

I looked away from the periscope and back at her. Shaking my head, I reached for both her hands as I stepped down from the viewing platform.

"We got away," I said.

"We got away?" she repeated. Her voice sounded unsure, but hopeful.

"Yeah," I replied, leaning my forehead against hers. "We did."

"We did." This time her tone was without question.

"I think we're going to be all right," I said.

And for the first time since arriving at the airfield in Feirin City, I believed it.

THE END

About the Author

Amanda Cherry is a Seattle-area queer, disabled nerd who still can't believe people pay her to write stories. In addition to her novels, she's the author of TTRPGs, screenplays, and short fiction, and a cast member in the Dungeon Scrawlers GREYMANTLE game on Twitch. Her nonfiction writing has been featured on  ToscheStation.net, ElevenThirtyEight.com, and StarTrek.com.

Amanda is a member of SAG-AFTRA, SFWA, & Broad Universe.

Follow Amanda's geekery on Twitter & TikTok @MandaTheGinger or visit www.thegingervillain.com

Special Thanks

Writing acknowledgements for a book that's been thirteen years in the making is perhaps more daunting than any other step in this process. Beginning at home, I have to thank my husband, Andrew, who has been here for all of it, and our kiddo, Mac, who has been here for most. Thanks to the Seattle NaNoWriMo community for going on twenty years of friendship and community and especially to all y'all who were around in 2008 when the first version of this book happened.

Thanks to my amazing friends for years of support and encouragement, especially during the months and months I spent actively looking for a home for this book. Seanan McGuire, Laura Anne Gilman, Elsa Sjunneson, Jennifer Brozek, and Erik Scott de Bie, y'all are the best people in the whole wide world and I would quite literally not be here if it weren't for you.

Shout out to my writing and gaming groups for being incredible company and dynamite inspiration. Wit & Word, Cobalt City Writing Church,We Blend, Greymantle, and the rest of the Dungeon Scrawlers, Brewery Patio Writers, and the Lake Wine bunch: y'all are top tier ib every way and I am forever grateful to spend time and energy with you.

Thanks to Dawn Vogel, Jeremy Zimmerman, Nathan Crowder, and Rosemary Jones for letting me sit at the cool kids table. Thanks to all my con friends and Star Wars friends for making my life richer and sweeter and more interesting.

Thanks to Claire Draper for telling me to "put them together". You were right.

Thanks to Karen and Benjamin and everyone at Not A Pipe for the support and the enthusiasm.

I'm sure I'm missing people, because thirteen years is a long time and for most of those I never thought I'd see this book in print. I'm overwhelmed with gratitude and so, so excited....

.

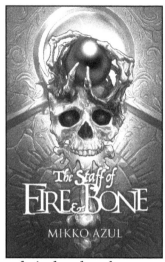

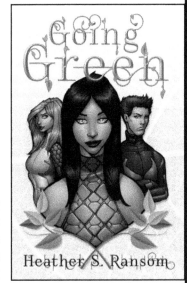

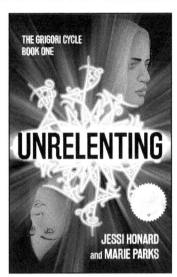